AFTER MARY

Isabel Stanhope, daughter of one of King James I's favoured courtiers, is expected to marry Francis Bourne, a distant cousin. But for Isabel the prospect of a life spent childbearing and plying the needle is an intolerable denial of the Catholic faith inherited from her mother.

Since birth, Isabel has led a double life, outwardly an obedient daughter, actually part of the turbulent and persecuted Catholic underworld. In the great country houses where she is educated, priests flit in and out under cover of darkness, mass is said secretly in attic rooms and a plot is hatched to murder the king.

And this is the life Isabel chooses. She rebels against her father by following an outlawed order of women established by the charismatic Mary Ward, and finds herself pulled fast and deep into a world of subterfuge where the attractions of those who live dangerously are very powerful indeed.

But other people have plans for Isabel. Francis Bourne will not easily let her go. The Catholic church has its own ideas on how women should behave, and Isabel's quest for the ideal life leads her to Rome and back as she becomes enmeshed in the treacherous politics of seventeenth-century Europe.

'I recognised her immediately, the woman with the face and the smile that could change a young woman's life. This is a story of passion, power – and dashed hopes. A tale to conjure with, down to its final twist.'

LAVINIA BYRNE, author and broadcaster

Also by Katharine McMahon

A WAY THROUGH THE WOODS
FOOTSTEPS
CONFINEMENT

After Mary

Katharine McMahon

Flamingo
An Imprint of HarperCollins*Publishers*

Flamingo
An Imprint of HarperCollins*Publishers*
77–85 Fulham Palace Road,
Hammersmith, London W6 8JB

www.**fire**and**water**.com

Flamingo is a registered trademark of HarperCollins Publishers Limited

Published by Flamingo 2000

1 3 5 7 9 8 6 4 2

A catalogue record for this book
is available from the British Library

Photograph of Katharine McMahon © Caroline Forbes

Endpaper shows a detail from an early seventeenth-century embroidered
textile. Courtesy of the Trustees of the V&A/Photographer: Richard Davis

ISBN 0 00 225843 9

Set in Meridien by
Rowland Phototypesetting Ltd,
Bury St Edmunds, Suffolk

Printed and bound in Great Britain by
Clays Ltd, St Ives plc

ACKNOWLEDGEMENTS

Thanks to Ania Pateli and Barbara Paech who introduced me to Munich and Augsburg, to Jackie and Michael Batchelor who showed me the Bodensee and to Philippe and Patricia Etienne in Brussels. Also thanks to Morag Jordan and Gillian Rowlands, and especially to Charonne Boulton who braved Rome with me through three days of torrential rain.

Also thanks to the Catholic Central Library which proved an excellent source of material; to Henriette Peters for her comprehensive biography, *Mary Ward: A World in Contemplation*; and to Gillian Orchard for her book *Till God Will: Mary Ward Through Her Writings*. Also to Antonia Fraser for her book *The Gunpowder Plot: Terror and Faith in 1605*, which provides a superb background to the situation of Catholics in the early seventeenth century.

For Margaret

ONE

Powder

1605

Chapter 1

At the top of the house was a windowless passage with unwaxed floorboards. After a few visits people knew which would creak so only the feet of strangers made a noise.

Isabel Stanhope, resident at Oakshott for six months, walked soundlessly to Compline. Ahead rustled the ample skirts of cousin Susannah and behind came their tutor, Nicholas Turner. Isabel didn't like to think of his eyes on her back. He smelt of dirty hair and his flesh was slack inside his clothes.

At the far end of the passage was a low door and a small flight of steps. Oakshott had been extended over several generations and you could never stay on one level for long. Isabel loved the door at the end of the passage. The household filed in and out of it five times a day and to her it was the boundary between complication and simplicity, darkness and light. Inside, people faced the same way and spoke the same words. She assumed they all had the same thoughts, even Susannah and Nicholas Turner who claimed he wanted to be a priest some day.

The only person not entirely engrossed by prayer, Isabel supposed, was herself.

In chapel the silence was deeper than any other at Oakshott, a house where everyone always moved softly. People shuffled in felt slippers to their given places. Isabel's was by a wall under the sloping roof, next to Susannah. Despite the crush they managed not to touch. At the front knelt Anne Winshawe, their grandmother, in a black veil and mourning hood. To her right was Susannah's mother, Teresa Thewing, who sometimes swung round to stare fiercely at the rest of the congregation. On Anne's other side huddled Martha Canton.

Anne led Compline and all prayers unless there was a priest in the house. Isabel's lips followed the responses though she twitched with irritation every time Susannah said an 's'. 'Ssspiritusss Sssanctussss.' Isabel longed to shake Susannah out of her head, in fact out of Oakshott. Every step she took was dogged by Susannah. The pair of them slept in the same bed, washed in the same water, studied from the same books and ate at the same table.

But after quarter of an hour even Susannah faded. Compline marked the end of the evening's work. It was midsummer and the chapel under the rafters was warmed by dusty light pouring through tiny dormer windows. There was a smell of grassy dusk and candle smoke. Anne Winshawe, the person Isabel wished most to please, was feet away.

'*Tu, puer, propheta Alitissimi vocaberis.*'

Thanks to Master Turner and her wish to outstrip him, Isabel could now translate Latin easily as breathing. 'Thou, child, shalt be called the Prophet of the Highest.' Is it me? she wondered. Shall I? Am I? The dormer window was at waist level. She dipped her hand in and out of the sunlight that fell slant-wise through it and by stooping could just see the glimmering greens of Aunt Teresa's herb garden far below.

Anne Winshawe's voice was high pitched and passionate as if to make the point that she was holier than everyone else.

'*Alleluia, alleluia,*' murmured the household, Isabel's voice quick and precise, Susannah's slow and musical, each trying to better the other.

The sunlight trailed over Isabel's grey skirt. She bowed her head and prayed that one day she might manage an entire hour in the chapel without once finding fault with anyone except herself.

A sudden movement in the garden caught her eye. She ducked to get a better view.

It was impossible to walk in a straight line from the gate because of the maze of little hedges which bordered the herb

4

beds. However, a thin figure in dark clothes had emerged from the shadow of the wall and was crossing the garden in a series of leaps and strides, ignoring the paths. This was an extraordinary sight, especially from the third floor, for the man moved like an acrobat, swinging his bag in one hand. Isabel twisted her neck to watch him out of sight.

At Oakshott time was chopped into neat parcels. Pray, eat, pray, work, pray, sleep. Children, adults and servants moved quietly from one activity to the next, stepping aside in the passageways to let each other pass. Nobody shouted or jostled. But when a priest came he caused a stir. A gust of fresh air blew through the low rooms.

Isabel straightened her back. I am special, she thought. Only I know he's here.

Later in the silent refectory she took her place at the end of a long table. The new priest was at Anne Winshawe's right hand and said grace in a voice which clipped each word off from the next. Nothing in the crowded room moved except steam from a pan. It seemed to Isabel that all her life had been leading here. God's hand drifted over the bread and the spoons.

Priests came quite regularly, usually in pairs. This one was different because he was alone and because he was beautiful.

Isabel couldn't resist the occasional peep to where he sat at the far end, eating very fast and apparently with all his attention. He had a high forehead and long cheeks. His nose was very fine but slightly hooked and his eyes were large beneath straight brows. Usually people at Oakshott made the most of their food because there was never enough but this man treated his meal as if it was a necessity to be got through quickly. Isabel, who was always hungry, felt guilty about her usual greedy interest in each mouthful.

Perhaps he knew she was watching for he turned to her suddenly and his whole face changed. He became smiling and tender like a father or a brother – well, not her brother. Isabel smiled back at him, ablaze with happiness because for once someone at Oakshott had noticed her. Then she looked abruptly away because you shouldn't stare at anyone, let alone a priest.

She tried to think only of scooping her spoon through soup but it seemed as if there was an invisible ribbon tied between herself and the priest. She daren't glance at him again in case he thought she was drawing attention to herself. Instead she looked sideways at Susannah who loved food but pretended not to. There was usually a battle between them to see who could finish last. This time Isabel gave up the contest and ate quickly.

'Will you be making the pilgrimage this summer?' The priest's voice broke the rule of silence into a thousand spinning pieces.

Isabel's hand faltered and her eyes flicked fearfully towards her grandmother. Anne Winshawe never seemed to eat anything but sat in her black bodice and veil, hands folded on her lap, observing everybody else. Yet she was plump and soft-fleshed with papery fine skin. Where all her bulk came from was one of the many mysteries of Oakshott.

Nobody was allowed to say a word at mealtimes.

'To St Winifred's shrine?' asked Anne, as if in the middle of an ordinary conversation.

'There's going to be quite a gathering. You could bring one of the children if you came.'

'I'll bear it in mind.'

Soup spattered Isabel's chin. She risked another peek at her grandmother. This new Anne was almost playful and her eyes were bright. Other people at table, usually so solemn, wore shy smiles which said: We're not really listening but we all understand this evening is a sort of festival. Only disgusting Nicholas Turner kept on sucking up soup through his wet lips and seemed not to notice anything strange had happened.

Isabel said a hasty prayer. Dear God, if grandmother goes on pilgrimage, please let her take me.

Selfish prayers were never answered so she added unwillingly: And Susannah or the boys.

'I'm always glad of a chance to visit Wales,' said the priest.

'I wouldn't be so keen on a pilgrimage to a Scottish shrine.'

His eyes were smiling over his spoon and a ripple of laughter ran uneasily round the table. A near joke about the untrustworthy Scots during supper. What next?

At the end of the meal the household stood for the final litany. The candlelight flickering across the priest's smooth forehead made the moment sacred. His long hands were clasped tightly together and he put all his energy into talking to God.

Isabel followed him into his prayer. *'Quid retribuam Domino pro omnibus quae retribuit mihi?'*

She knew for sure that God was listening and repeated in her head: 'What shall I render to the Lord for all the things that He hath rendered to me?' But she was frightened for the priest. If he gave everything to prayer like this how could part of him keep watch? He was a hunted man. Susannah said that in York priests received no mercy but were executed horribly at Knavesmire outside the city walls. Could he be trusted to take care of himself?

Afterwards the household filed out past Anne and the priest. First Teresa Thewing who seized his hand and gave it a smacking kiss. Next Martha Canton, then the Thewing children, two boys and Susannah, and finally Isabel. Each paused to bow or curtsey.

Anne's large blue eyes fixed on Isabel. As usual it was impossible to tell whether she was pleased or annoyed when she said: 'Wait, Isabel.'

Oh, the glory or the disgrace of being tucked behind Anne's shoulder while everyone else crept away. Isabel was so close to the priest that she could smell his difference; a faint whiff of the wide sky, dripping woods and places far from Oakshott. Meanwhile someone else had been singled out for attention, a dimply maid who had been heard singing a folk song while making the beds. 'I don't mind the singing, Alice, I mind the sentiment. I want your heart and mind to be pure. Do you understand? An hour's silent prayer in the chapel now and no breakfast tomorrow.'

When there was only the priest and Isabel left, Anne went back to her chair. Wine and two goblets were still on the table. Anne, suddenly cosy and grandmotherly, held Isabel close. 'This is Thomasina's daughter, Isabel. I told you she'd been sent here.'

Close up the priest seemed not much older than Isabel's brother Robin who was twenty-one. 'So, Isabel. I know your mother very well and your brother. We've said mass together often.' His voice was gentle as if he was taking great care of her.

Isabel longed to say something brilliant but nothing came out so instead she bent her knee in a bobbing curtsey. Anne's short arm drew her closer. For months at Oakshott there had been no physical contact, except unavoidably with Susannah, and now here was Isabel crushed so hard that Anne's stiff bodice bruised her ribs and she could smell the must of old fabric. Solid layers of wool and linen covered grandmother's thigh and when Isabel blinked her eyelashes flicked across the edge of starched ruff which supported Anne's several chins.

'Yes, my little Isabel is not unlike Thomasina in looks,' murmured Anne. 'It's the hair, I think. And I'm delighted because as a daughter Thomasina has always been a great joy to me. Despite her marriage. But Isabel's been sent here because she needs calming down. You're rather a wild little thing, aren't you, my dear one? You love to be the centre of attention and we can't always allow that.' Grandmother stroked the back of her hair.

The blood burnt in Isabel's face and she fought back tears. Here was a double blow, mention of her much missed mother and a swipe at her own less than perfect nature. Grandmother was still smiling down at her fondly. Could she read minds, then? Surely, surely Isabel hadn't done much wrong at Oakshott except think wicked thoughts.

'And then there's the question of her future,' continued Anne, 'which we must all pray about. Her father has in mind an early marriage to solve complications with his estates. To a distant cousin, a heretic. But I'm not sure marriage, even to a devout Catholic, would be the right vocation for my darling. So I watch her all the time. You love it here, don't you, Isabel? You're very well suited to our type of life.'

8

This was almost praise. 'I hope so, grandmother.'

'Off you go then, my precious,' and grandmother kissed her forehead.

The passage outside was empty but a single candle burned on a highly polished chest. Its flame flickered and ducked in the draught that blew from the kitchen passage. Isabel was doubled up suddenly with home-sickness because life at Oak-shott was so confusing, worse than home. She thought of her mother, Lady Thomasina Stanhope, who though aloof and sometimes cutting was at least constant in her love for Isabel. Here you could be floating in a bubble of piety one moment only to have it burst by a cold-eyed glance or wounding reprimand the next.

Isabel picked up the candle and went upstairs. The house, though very quiet, must be full of secret movement as people got ready for bed. She saw herself in the light of the trembling candle, small, plainly dressed and full of anguish, a martyr in fact. No Isabel, you have to earn martyrdom. Think of grandmother, eighteen years a widow, twelve times a prisoner in York for sheltering priests or refusing to attend Anglican services and still unwavering in her faith. She had made the Spiritual Exercises with Edmund Campion and then been named by him when his nails were torn out one by one to make him betray his friends. And Anne Winshawe was one of the women who had converted Margaret Clitherow and been present at her execution. Proof of this was the dreadful relic kept by Anne in a locked chest near her bed, Margaret's right hand cut off by her friends after death. The brownish little hand with its thin, dried-out fingers sat in Isabel's memory as a reminder both of Protestant evil and of the importance of Anne Winshawe in the Catholic scheme of things.

The staircase and passages on the first floor were unlit. Tonight the starkness of the house and her isolation within it seemed pitiless to Isabel. Sometimes, when the oval face of one of her ancestors loomed out of a portrait she glanced up with a half smile for fear of being impolite. Guided by a thin rail she tiptoed up another flight of steps and came at last to the room she shared with cousin Susannah.

This Susannah, like her mother and brothers, was a permanent fixture at Oakshott. She was thirteen, over two years older than Isabel, a big girl with dark skin and protruding eyes. Daily contact with Susannah who never looked in a mirror and kept her eyes shut when dressing had convinced Isabel that good looks were a disadvantage. And Susannah also had the upper hand when it came to family background. Her parents were such loyal Catholics that the penalties imposed had made them destitute and her father had died of grief. Isabel's father, on the other hand, paid the occasional fine on behalf of his recusant wife but still managed to be a very important figure at court where his genius with figures had made him famous. And although Isabel's brother Robin had spent a couple of years at school abroad there was no question of the priesthood for him. He was too fond of the sword.

Susannah was of course at prayer. She would never stoop to ask why Isabel had been kept back, though the downward tilt of her head suggested that she was more than usually angry.

After they were both in bed and Susannah had snuffed out her candle the room went absolutely black for a moment. Then one or two stars glittered behind the lattice. A breeze was rushing in the trees beyond the lawns but no sound came from inside the house.

'Susannah. Susannah.' She couldn't possibly be asleep already. 'Susannah.'

'What?' Susannah pretended to be startled.

'Grandmother wanted to tell the priest who I was. That's why she asked me to stay behind.'

'Did you stay behind? I never noticed.'

'Have you seen him before?'

'Who?' At its most exasperating, Susannah's voice became silky smooth.

'The priest.'

Susannah turned her fat backside to Isabel, shoving her to the edge of the mattress. 'Can't this wait till morning? I'm so tired.'

'He seems different to the others.'

'He is. Of course.' A long pause. 'He's a Jesuit.' She gave a deep sigh and thereby closed the discussion.

Isabel lay on her back with her arms crossed on her chest. She should have known straight away. He had the look of one who as Christ's foot-soldier had travelled from far countries, read a thousand books and spent night after night in meditation. Of all priests, the Jesuits were hounded the most.

Was Oakshott safe enough for him? In imagination she paced its uneven passages, crooked staircases and warren of servants' quarters and attic rooms. According to Susannah, Nicholas Owen, a genius at carpentry, had visited the house and burrowed his way into ceilings and floors to create hiding places for priests and other Catholics on the run from pursuivants. Somewhere a false brick floor covered a secret ladder and behind a certain panel was a tiny room. The authorities had turned the house over so often that they thought every cavity had been found, but they were wrong.

Maybe even now the Jesuit was gliding upwards behind the wall or worming his way along this very ceiling. Isabel hated to think of him so undignified. She remembered his long legs clearing Aunt Teresa's rosemary and couldn't help smiling again.

Actually of course he would still be downstairs with grandmother in the hallowed circle of their intimacy. Later she would bring him upstairs to one of the empty rooms on this second floor. He could sleep safely at Oakshott, guarded night and day by servants who had grown old in Anne's service.

In the morning the household was summoned one after another to confession in the chapel. Edmund Thewing was absent from the schoolroom only ten minutes but his brother Alan took longer than half an hour and came back with an unusual flush in his pallid cheeks and a refusal to meet Edmund's mocking eye. Isabel's turn came after Susannah who was gone for ages. Not that she could have committed many sins, of course. She probably had minute scruples of conscience to discuss.

Alone, Isabel crept upstairs to the chapel. The door at the end seemed more charmed than ever for behind it was the priest. She waited, very still, breathing the warm scent of resin from the eaves.

Be ready, Isabel, she told herself. This is your moment.

Susannah opened the door with exaggerated care and slid out, hair combed sleekly under a white cap, heavy eyelids downcast, a faint smile on her lips.

She's trying to look like a nun already, thought Isabel, dropping a little curtsey. But her time with him is over and mine is to come, so for once I'm best off.

Inside the chapel, cool morning light flowed across the little folding crucifix on the altar. The priest was seated on a bench, hunched over himself. Isabel felt a stab of envy because she was the merest dab of a girl in a tight bodice and stiff skirts while the priest in his plain robes was all clean lines, significance and knowledge.

She knelt beside him and murmured: '*In nomine Patris, et Filii, et Spiritus . . .*' Her nervous voice died. Never had she felt so full of silly ideas. This man had been called to change the world and here was Isabel Stanhope bothering him with a list of dull failings.

'I had an unkind thought in Vespers . . .

'I'm envious of my cousin for being more pious than me . . .'

There was no reaction from the priest though she was so close to him she could see the light brown curling hairs on his wrist. His hands were very fine but roughened and probably strong. She hated to think of them performing stealthy acts; dropping a latch in the dead of night or clearing a pathway through dense undergrowth. He should be in a proper church standing before a thousand people. Last night when he gave the blessing he had flung his arms wide like Christ on the cross.

A little catch was released in her mind. Say more, Isabel, speak the truth. Her voice sank lower. 'I was angry with my grandmother for criticizing me yesterday evening. But I think she's right. I want to be good but I can't keep hold of my thoughts. Inside my head I mock everyone. I can't seem to help myself, even though I know I'm the most sinful of all.' He was still bent over, his face covered by his hand. How terrible to waste his time like this, she thought, shaking.

'Whom do you despise?' he asked.

'Oh, the other children in the schoolroom because I know that if I was allowed to I could work much faster than them. The boys are really slow, especially at French, but of course the lessons are meant for them so we go at their pace. I gallop ahead and then spend the extra time jeering at them inside myself. And then there's Susannah. I'm always finding fault with her.'

When he looked up at last his smiling eyes were less than a yard from her own. 'You're Isabel, aren't you, daughter of Thomasina?'

Was he wondering how Thomasina could have produced such a flawed child? 'Yes, I am.'

'Well, Isabel, which are my weak spots?'

'Oh, not you. I don't criticize you.' What had happened to confession? Normally an uninterested little priest gabbled absolution and glanced impatiently at the door. 'I really mean it, Father. I hate myself. I wish I could shut down my thoughts or tear them out. Why can't I make my mind do what I want it to? I'd much rather not question everything I'm taught all the time. I want to be peaceful and perfect.'

There was a long pause. She held her breath under his steady gaze. 'Give me your hand, Isabel. Listen to what I have to say. You should pray to be like Christ and of course you should attend more to your own failings than those of others. But never pray not to have a good mind. Your intellect is precious. Remember, all of you is needed for God's service, body, mind and soul. He wants hard-thinking, strong people to do His work. He needs girls like you in His church, Isabel.'

'My tutor says I'm too sharp.'

'I'm not your tutor, Isabel. I'm telling you that your gifts are God-given.'

'What must I do?'

'He has marked you out. You, Isabel.' She saw herself through his eyes, little Isabel with the white forehead and

13

fair hair hooked back under a clean cap. Isabel the chosen. 'I think He wants you, Isabel, and Oakshott is your testing ground. You have also the gifts of good birth, wealth and physical beauty. Some girls would throw these qualities away on marriage. But not perhaps Isabel.'

She was ready to take flight into his grey eyes but her head remembered to hold back one moment more. 'I am to marry, though. My husband will be Francis Bourne, a distant cousin. My father has always wished it.'

'Your father is one authority. God is another. A priest can only speak for God.'

Now Isabel saw herself dressed in black garments, stepping forward into the single ray of light shining in a dark cell. 'You mean I must be a nun.'

'You sound disappointed.' He let go her hand and her fingers felt lonely. 'Women in religion can do great things. Have you heard about St Teresa of Avila? What a witness to God's word, a mystic, an intellectual and a reformer. She never forgot that we must be poor and rejected before we can come to Christ. She gave up everything, even her reputation.'

'I would rather be you, travelling about, ministering to people.' Really, Isabel, you push him too far. Don't you want him to take you seriously?

'You'd rather be me. Little girl, I'm not worthy of such a wish.'

'I mean it.' She was trying to pull him back from the cold, distant place he now saw. She could almost hear the abrupt closing of screens around his hidden self. Straightening up he held his hand stiffly for the penance and absolution which he intoned without feeling. Then he sank his head back in his hand and she knew she should leave.

Heavily she moved away. The chapel had become a pit of disappointment. She had ruined it all by saying the wrong thing.

But he called after her: 'Find a few favours to do your cousin that will make her happier. And come back here a moment.' He enclosed her wrist with his fingers. Warmth seeped from his flesh to hers. 'Go in peace. *Benedicat vos omnipotens Deus, Pater . . .*' His blessing fell like rain and his

14

gaze followed her hand as she touched her forehead, breast, left and right shoulders.

Anne's steward was waiting outside the chapel. Isabel smiled tenderly and floated away, her skirts brushing the wainscotting. Behind, in a long train, came all the responsibilities the priest had given her.

When she reached the schoolroom she thought her face must be shining like a statue of the Virgin Mary. She sat opposite Susannah, deaf to Master Turner's instruction. Her hands felt gentle on the edge of the table and she was distracted by the problem of how to make Susannah happy. He could not have set a more difficult task.

At midday Isabel passed her own bread to her cousin. Of course Susannah nudged it back. A tussle of wills followed which Isabel finally allowed her cousin to win. She ate the bread.

In the end she had to resort to the most difficult prayer of all.

If grandmother does decide to go on pilgrimage, let her take Susannah and not me.

When a priest was staying at Oakshott there were two masses a day and, after confessions had been heard, communion. Everyone attended except a couple of manservants who kept guard. From a secret place deep in the house Anne Winshawe, accompanied by the steward, Oswald Fairbrother, unlocked the chalice, an ancient cup studded with three emeralds that had belonged to the Winshawes for two hundred years, the embossed plate called the paten for the host, the silk burse, the chalice veil and the linen altar cloths. These things held a powerful magic because they were kept hidden most of the time and were priceless. Nobody touched them but Anne, Oswald and occasionally Martha who was allowed to do the polishing, starching and pressing.

During mass Oswald served on the altar and he appeared first from behind the screen, grey beard trimmed very neat. Next came the priest. It was like the sudden appearance of a rainbow for he wore a floating chasuble striped in silks of crimson, green, cream, black and violet. 'Typical Jesuit trick,' sniffed Nicholas Turner later. 'Sheer affectation. It's supposed to be a vestment for all occasions, feasts, funerals and ordinary days.' But Isabel thought the cloak beautiful, a shimmer of brilliant colour in a house of dark corners.

The saying of mass was forbidden by law and priests often hurried through it in case they were caught in the act but this man took his time. Every gesture he made was weighted with meaning. Isabel felt so bound to him that the movements of his body and the sound of his voice hurt her, as if they had been wrung from her own. And the familiarity of the ritual drew her like a diver into a deep pool. Each word he spoke, though she had heard it a hundred times, was new and lovely.

At communion she knelt at his feet. He stooped over her and she closed her eyes. His finger brushed her lower lip and the host was a whisper on her tongue.

Isabel lay awake that night, not tortured by guilt for once but in a fever of hope. Her conscience had been cleared not just of petty sins but of frustration. The priest had given her a future.

She turned away from Susannah and travelled back to yesterday. The sight of him springing through the sunlit herb garden was as vivid as ever. His pleasure in movement and disregard for rules lay at the heart of his difference.

'So, Isabel,' he had said. He had given her name a singing quality.

'*Isabel.*'

There was someone else in the room. The night sky on the other side of the lattice was blotted out by a heavy figure standing over the bed. A voice hissed: 'Isabel. Wake up.'

Anne Winshawe carried no candle and her hand pressed on Isabel's mouth. 'I need you.' Isabel's breath moistened her grandmother's plump fingers. She slid obediently from the bed thinking that certainly life was no longer dull. What next?

Grandmother whispered something to Susannah who fumbled for Isabel's pillow and tucked it under her own. This action was disturbing for it was designed to suggest Susannah slept alone.

Anne muttered into Isabel's hair: 'Follow me. They're coming for Father Peter. You must help save him.'

From far away there was a muffled shout and beyond it the thudding fall of hooves on grass.

'Don't be afraid. We can look after him. But you must sleep in his bed. If they find warm empty sheets they'll rip the house apart.'

They were hurrying down the black passageway, Isabel shot through with fright. We'll all be hung, she thought, glancing into doorways as if a pursuivant might jump from any one of them. Once she missed her footing on a sudden step and seemed to fall through space, as in a nightmare.

There was a hammering in the entrance porch below and a loud cry. Isabel fell back against the wall but Anne seized her upper arm and pulled her onwards. They had reached the far end of the passage where there was a last door and, opposite at right-angles, stairs leading to another wing.

Anne's calm voice said: 'This is his room. I must go back to bed. Peter knows what to do. He'll be out in a minute. Isabel, we are all relying on you. Tell them you always sleep here. And stay alert, even when they've left. They often try to trick us by pretending to give up and then rushing back.' She squeezed Isabel's arm and was gone.

Isabel was alone, pressed to the stone frame of a small window. Downstairs there was a fumbling of bolts and the gruff voice of Oswald who could be awesome when roused. A further scuffle followed and then men's feet on the staircase.

The door opened and the priest slipped from his room. By grey starlight Isabel saw that he carried a small bag and was dressed in dark clothes. She huddled against the window to get out of his way and he sprang towards the shadows opposite. Then he paused and asked: 'Isabel. Is that you?'

You must go, she thought, please go.

He stood over her and with his free hand turned her face to the pale light. 'I wish we could have talked more. I'm praying for you. Remember that. Listen and read. If you ever get the chance, do the Spiritual Exercises. Remember.'

Doors were wrenched open further down the passage, male footsteps came nearer and nearer. 'Please hurry,' she whispered.

Still he held her chin and put his face so close to hers that she shared his breath. 'Trust me, Isabel.' And he was gone at last.

She fled into the more profound darkness of his room and closed the door, at first unable to get her bearings. Her shin hit a chest at the foot of the bed and she fumbled for the edge of the mattress. The quilt had been flung off and was indeed warm. Isabel dragged up the sheet and spread herself out, thrashing with her legs to wipe away his shape. She punched at the pillow and curled into a tight knot.

A nearby door was thrown open.

She could smell the priest, masculine, sweaty and foreign. Surely they would too. He lingered in the room with her.

When the door opened she shot upright, her plait of fair hair tumbled over the sheet. A lantern glared.

She burst into tears.

'All right, miss.' But the man, who had down-tilted eyes sunken in the upward glow of the lantern, was not at all moved by her distress. He lifted his light high and swung it about, catching the corners of the room in its beam. Isabel mopped her tears with the edge of the sheet. Had any clue been left? Surely the priest was too experienced to slip up but supposing he'd forgotten a book or garment?

Suddenly there was a great bustle in the passage and Anne Winshawe appeared swathed in a vast brocade gown. Her voice was the peevish wail of an elderly widow. 'What is this? Why have you woken my granddaughter? I won't have my house invaded time after time.'

The man held a long staff. He lunged forward and first swept it under the bed then tapped with its round top on the panelling. It was obvious that he expected to find something. He was like a rat-catcher who has heard the scrabbling of little claws.

18

'Where do you keep your clothes?' he asked Isabel.

'In the chest of course,' said Anne. 'She's a tidy child.'

He knocked up the latches of the oak chest and jabbed viciously among its soft contents. Anne exclaimed with exasperation. Isabel cried more.

The man backed away. His black eyes took in Isabel huddled damply among the dishevelled sheets and the grandmother in her rich robe, arms crossed on bosom, lips tight with disapproval. There was violent rage in him because he knew he'd been cheated. The room wasn't quite right though he could find no actual fault.

'Do you have a comb?' he spat at Isabel.

She stared at him with little sobs wrenching her throat and then was washed by calm. 'I share with my cousin. We share most things.'

'What about the clothes you wore today?'

'You mean yesterday,' cut in Anne. 'It's past midnight.'

'I've been very sick,' murmured Isabel, shame-faced.

'Do you wish to see the soiled clothes?' demanded Anne. 'Come with me and leave the poor child alone.'

The man looked uncertain but at last went out, followed by Anne. Isabel was left in darkness.

She drew the priest's sheets round her shoulders and sank down, rather pleased with her performance. Anyway she had avoided absolute lies. How the man interpreted what she said was up to him.

The warmth of the bed relaxed her. In the distance the search went on but she was sure they would find nothing. The servants would have disguised the chapel under piles of old furniture. Wherever the priest was, he was safe.

Grandmother had called him Peter. Perhaps he had flown down some hidden staircase and was already in a distant wood, leaping off into the dawn.

Isabel lay burning with excitement as she heard the men retreat at last, defeated.

If only all nights could be like this, she thought, tumbling to the edge of sleep through the warm solitude of the priest's bed. If only all my life could be this significant.

19

Chapter 2

Alice, the maid guilty of singing profane verses, left Oakshott on the morning after the pursuivants came hunting the Jesuit. Otherwise the usual round of work and prayer resumed exactly as before.

Day after day Isabel prayed that the suggested pilgrimage might actually happen and at the end of August Anne Winshawe announced that she would indeed be making the journey to Holywell and that her chosen companions were Martha Canton, three male servants and her two granddaughters, Susannah Thewing and Isabel Stanhope.

On 31 August 1605 the household ranked itself in the courtyard to say goodbye. Despite a fine drizzle Teresa Thewing prowled the rows of servants but her sons hung back, Alan reserved, Edmund derisive. Beside the carriage stood the tutor Nicholas Turner whose damp hand slid through Isabel's. 'Pray for me, my dearest child.' She gave him a dazzling smile and stepped inside. She could even like Master Turner that morning.

Susannah plumped down next, her padded sleeves crushed against Isabel's shoulder, then timid Martha Canton. Twenty years ago when she was fifteen, Martha, the orphaned daughter of unwavering recusants, had been taken in by Anne Winshawe. It was said that since that time she had never ventured beyond York, eight miles away. Anne got in last, still issuing instructions to Oswald Fairbrother.

The first day's drive was a long haul west on bad roads. It rained all morning and there was little to be seen through the high windows but drenched moorland merged with soaking skies. Within ten minutes Isabel's elation was dulled by travel-sickness. Hour after hour she fought nausea.

Nobody noticed. Worries about those left behind preoccupied Anne. Martha listened to her monologue sympathetically but said little. And though physically far from Oakshott they brought its daily pattern of prayer with them. The four females were packed so tight in the carriage that their skirts mingled and the effort of reading tiny, jiggling print was excruciating. Martha murmured the responses in her gentle voice and Susannah over-enunciated as usual while Isabel, who had started the day determined to love everyone, had soon compiled a mental catalogue of all their faults from Martha's untidy frizz of hair to Susannah's moist upper lip.

When the rain stopped the fug inside the carriage was thickened by a hot, low sun shining on the roof.

'We'll walk, Susannah,' announced Anne abruptly, 'just you and I.'

After they'd gone Isabel put her feet up on the narrow bench and pretended to rest but she was furious. From behind the carriage came a mutter of voices. What on earth was grandmother saying to dull Susannah? And why did she always pick people out for special attention? Surely not to hurt deliberately the ones left behind.

Martha soon fell asleep and Isabel was further tormented by her irregular snores. She stared fiercely at the woman's undersized chin and furrowed brow. Thirty-five years old and more than half dead. With teeth like that Martha should never allow her mouth to drop open.

Enticing glimpses of deep blue sky and the rounded summit of a hill appeared through the window. Isabel's cramped muscles ached and she craved fresh air. In horrified fascination she saw a dribble of saliva trickle down Martha's chin.

Suddenly she reached forward, unhooked the latch and flung back the door. The carriage was much higher off the ground than she'd expected and she hung on for a moment then sprang out, landing on all fours. A huge cogged wheel lumbered over the edge of her petticoats and her hands slid through a ridge of wet mud.

Martha's white face appeared. 'Isabel. Whatever happened?'

'I'm all right. I'll walk for a while,' cried Isabel, waving to the astonished coachman perched up behind the carriage. She breathed heathery air and marched on with her soggy skirts flapping against her heels. Grandmother and Susannah were by now far behind, followed by a footman at a discreet distance. Anne wore a tall hat and Susannah's face was hidden by a deep brimmed hood tied under the chin. Neither of them gave any sign they had noticed Isabel's clumsy leap. With clasped hands and bent heads they seemed too deep in godly talk to be aware of their surroundings. Isabel, telling herself they looked stout and gnomish, tried to be glad of her solitude.

Occasionally she trotted to keep up with the carriage and maintain a distance between herself and the others. They were passing through a valley between soft high hills and the setting sun fell on her neck. She imagined running up and up the valley side while the unwieldy carriage and the tiny puppets, Susannah, grandmother and the footman, moved on for ever without her.

The mellow clop of hoof-beat and the clunking sway of the carriage were oddly satisfying; full-blooded, masculine noises that soothed her jangling nerves.

Isabel Stanhope, little pilgrim. The priest was relying on her. And God was watching, happy to see her in the sunshine.

By late evening they had reached a Catholic house near Bradford. Anne was greeted like a dear friend and bustled into the great dining chamber with Martha scurrying in her wake. Isabel glimpsed a laden table and perhaps ten people interrupted in the midst of eating.

A woman looked round, saw Martha and sprang forward to hug her. Then her gaze met Isabel's. One side of her face was in deep shadow but three nearby candles lit the perfect curve of her arched brow. For a moment she studied Isabel gravely. Then she smiled.

The doors were shut abruptly on this affectionate scene. A maid took the two girls to a dim parlour and gave them supper.

During her long walk behind the carriage Isabel had vowed to make peace with Susannah. Hostility was exhausting. 'I felt sick most of the way,' she confided. 'Did you?'

'No. Not at all.'

'Did you and grandmother have a nice walk?'

Susannah swept bread round her plate and took a dainty mouthful. She lowered her eyes and put her finger to her lips.

Isabel ate in silence and wished she was old enough to sit at the candlelit dinner table and speak to the lady with the sudden smile.

Elizabeth, the youngest daughter of the house, appeared, a flat-faced girl with pale hair. 'Two of us can share my bed and there's a couch by the door,' she said. Susannah at once offered to sleep with Elizabeth. Isabel was amazed by such unexpected generosity but when they lay down the reason for it became obvious. The other two started whispering and occasionally Isabel thought she heard the hiss of her own name. 'Isssabel.'

Though her body was battered by the long ride she couldn't sleep. This narrow bed was a painful reminder of her own at home in Cuddington. Most nights her mother had come up to say a last prayer. When Lady Thomasina tucked in the sheet it was as if she fastened Isabel under the wing of her love.

Now Isabel didn't know where she was. The horses had trotted on and on until they came to this strange house somewhere in the north. Home was surely so far away she would never find it again.

The party from Oakshott made a diversion south to Shrewsbury in order to meet up with the pilgrimage there.

At noon on the sixth day they arrived outside the Bear Tavern in a street called Plough Shut. The girls and Martha were left in the carriage while Anne went up to announce their arrival.

Isabel closed her eyes. The bright flame of hope and excitement had been dimmed by the long journey but at last they had arrived and in a minute she would meet her priest again. She vowed that from henceforth she would be a good pilgrim and concentrate always on her own weaknesses.

Irregular buildings over-shadowed the carriage which was barged about by the noise and bustle of the city. The door opened but Isabel felt a moment's reluctance to leave this safe enclosure. They were handed out one by one on to a cobbled street, through a low entrance and up a flight of stairs to a crowded room.

They had exchanged the stuffy carriage for the lively smell of hot food and the muted babble of half a dozen different conversations. Grandmother was nowhere to be seen. Martha melted into a corner and Susannah stood at a distance with blank eyes as if to cut herself off.

Isabel's view of the room cleared. This was not a random mass of people but a series of little groups which often broke up and mixed again as people embraced solemnly. Old women dressed like Anne Winshawe drew each other apart to talk in low voices. Some of the men wore badly-fitting doublets and kept glancing at the door. Priests, probably, maybe Jesuits. Isabel wondered how so many of them dared gather in one room. What a haul for the pursuivants.

There was no sign of her own priest, the one called Peter.

Anne detached herself from a little cluster and beckoned to the girls. 'Here are some of my dearest friends for you to meet. Lucy Morton is your father's cousin, Susannah. And this is another Anne I've known for decades, Anne Vaux. Anne, these are my two granddaughters. Isabel is Thomasina's child. You see the likeness?'

Anne Vaux was a legend, the bravest of all women. She had given her life to the protection of Jesuit priests, particularly their superior, Father Garnet. Each time the authorities caught up with her she emerged again somewhere else, more devoted than ever. And here she was in the Bear Tavern, middle-aged and unremarkable-looking. Yet Isabel felt a crackle of fear. If Anne Vaux was here so must be Father Garnet, one of the most wanted men in England. Heaven help them all.

Meanwhile grandmother had tucked her hand through Isabel's and kissed her cheek. Ah, so she chose to play the doting old lady to her friends.

Lucy Morton's face had been formed by kindness. 'You girls are very fortunate. My guess is you will remember this adventure to the end of your days.' There was a marked contrast between grandmother and her friends. Anne Winshawe was usually secretive and dour, the others were all openness and smiles.

Then the crowd rearranged itself again leaving a clear path to one of the grimy windows. A male voice called. 'Izzie, there's my Izzie,' and a familiar figure, her brother Robin of all people, sprang towards Isabel and swept her into his arms. She was so surprised that she clung to him for a moment and held on to his hand after he had set her down.

He studied her with a pleased grin as if to say: Yes, you'll do, you look handsome enough to be my sister. Robin was ten years older than Isabel; in between their mother had endured a number of still-births. He was always a fleeting visitor, for ever in a rush and full of important business. When he burst in on Thomasina at home in Cuddington her lips would tighten and her face close up though she loved him passionately. They always argued behind the closed door of her parlour and then there'd be a long session of prayer led by Robin in which the triumph of Catholicism was the main theme. After that he'd race out on to the lawn with his tutor and the glint of their swords would scissor back and forth, clash, clang, shout, jarring the women's nerves.

But for all his faults, Robin was at least part of home. 'Have you seen mother?' Isabel asked.

'Of course. She's well. Sends her love.' Thomasina swished through the hall at Cuddington in her blue velvet over-skirt with an exquisite lace ruff frothing at her cool throat, on her way to comfort a bereaved servant or the sick on the estate. She called over her shoulder: 'If you see Isabel, don't forget to tell her I'm thinking of her.' And then she had flickered out of sight leaving a breath of her fragrance behind like a wafting ghost of herself.

Robin had much more important things to do than waste time on Isabel. He had already lifted Susannah's hand to his lips. Isabel recognized the old trick of winning admiration with a boyish grin and an impish narrowing of the eyes. Poor Susannah went dumb and heavy, overcome by the fierce blaze of his attention. But before she could recover he had moved away and given his arm to a lame man: 'Nicholas, a word . . .' For those he'd left it was as if the sun had passed behind a cloud.

'I'm amazed that Robin Stanhope should spend his time on pilgrimage to Holywell,' said Anne Vaux. 'Why do you suppose he's here?'

'He finds the company irresistible, I presume,' but the women were uneasy. Isabel realized that a serving woman was stationed as look-out at the window and the innkeeper hovered near the door. Fear was catching. This upstairs room with its single exit could well be a trap. At any moment they might be violently attacked and every priest and recusant arrested.

But nothing happened except that they were gently organized into parties of four or five and one after another each group slipped from the room.

Isabel had a great deal to pray for on the final stage of the journey, not least the state of her feet. It was traditional for women to walk bare-footed for the last two days and the pain was very bad. The girls had no time for exercise at Oakshott and weren't used to being in the open so their legs ached, their faces were burnt by sun and wind and the soft soles of their feet had blistered. The older women, of course, seemed to feel no discomfort but trod with complete assurance, as if on a soft lawn.

By the last morning Isabel had such a painful sore on her heel that she could barely put pressure on her right foot. She fell behind the others, sank down on a flat rock and buried her toes in the turf.

They were two hours from Holywell and Isabel's rock, jutting from the side of a hill, gave her a sweeping view west into Wales and north to the Dee estuary. She watched the other pilgrims side-step down the steep slope and toil up the other side, a straggling, untidy bunch, their complicated shapes and ugly clothes a sad contrast to the innocent blue sky and glittering water. But they were no longer an anonymous crowd. Isabel could now give each a name.

Near the front and sheltered by a cluster of deferential women was Father Henry Garnet, head of all Jesuits in England. Only his rapid little strides marked him out. Despite his importance and all he must know, he seemed to Isabel a very ordinary type of priest. Some of the others jostled for his attention, either to impress or to glean pearls of wisdom from his lips, but Isabel could think of only one thing to ask him. 'Excuse me, Father, do you know where the priest called Peter might be? When he stayed the night at Oakshott in June he said he would be coming on this pilgrimage.'

Garnet's melancholy eyes had fixed on her face. 'I know of no priest called Father Peter, Isabel.'

A little apart from the others but quite nimble despite a pronounced limp was Nicholas Owen, the ingenious architect to whom many on this pilgrimage, including Anne Winshawe, owed their lives. He'd once been imprisoned and tortured, said Lucy Morton, hung up by his wrists in a dungeon. But he'd revealed nothing even though he knew practically every hiding place for priests in the country because he'd built most of them. The thought of this reserved little man in such agony was awe-inspiring. It created a barrier between him and the other pilgrims, as if he had far outstripped the rest of them in experience and should not be bothered with mundane things. His usual companion was Father Gerard, so renowned among Catholics that Isabel could hardly bring herself to talk to him for he had actually escaped from the Tower, the worst prison of all.

'Master Owen, Father Gerard,' Isabel had murmured, 'do you know of a Jesuit priest called Peter?'

Father Gerard's eyes could be snapping and abstracted or warm, as when he replied to Isabel: 'My dear child, there isn't a priest in the country who hasn't used the name Peter at some time or another.'

Nicholas Owen as usual said nothing. He knew the danger of words and kept his secrets close. Knowledge was a curse that could be wrenched out of the bravest victim by the tearing of ligaments or the breaking of bones.

And there behind all the rest was Robin, dogged by Susannah and in company with his great friends, Sir Everard and Lady Mary Digby whom Isabel had met before on their occasional visits to Cuddington. The Digbys made unlikely pilgrims for even their plainest clothes were of the best fabrics and beautifully stitched. Martha Canton, a tireless needle-woman, loved to run the edge of Lady Mary's cloak through her fingers. 'The softness of the cloth. Never in my life have I made stitches as fine as this.' Lady Mary was an heiress and though just twenty-three had been married ten years. Her conversation was usually of the two small boys they had left at home, and she had been the only one to make a special fuss of Isabel on her birthday, the 8th of September.

'Lady Digby, I met a Jesuit priest at Oakshott once who called himself Peter. He was quite young and tall. Do you know him?'

'I know most of the Jesuits. Can't you tell me anything else about him?'

'He had a beard, a deep voice and grey eyes. Large eyes. He said he would be coming on this pilgrimage.'

'Then he may yet. But if it's the priest I'm thinking of he has many fish to fry and is probably busy elsewhere. Ask Everard. Everard knows them all.' But Sir Digby was always out of Isabel's reach, sought after by everyone but given also to long periods of meditation. How Robin must bask in the friendship of Sir Everard Digby, thought Isabel. Digby was rich, popular and a darling at court despite his recent conversion to Catholicism.

She now knew most of these pilgrims well enough to love them. They had shared meals, prayed together at dawn and by moonlight, and slept close, first in a friendly barn then in the grand chambers of a great house. She knew how Garnet woke with bloodshot eyes and carefully combed his neat beard and how Nicholas Owen stood apart from the group when they prayed, his head turned to one side as if he dare not look God in the eye. She liked to watch Lucy Morton with her grandmother and the other Anne. They would wag their heads like three gossipy market women, their talk a net into which were knotted all their friends and relations living and dead, linked by inter-connecting strands of marriage and blood. A name would be batted between them, fixed in time, given a history and joined with another.

But though Isabel's fellow pilgrims were unfailingly kind, they excluded her. There were too many secrets. Conversations would stop abruptly whenever she came within earshot. A name would be mentioned and then hushed. 'Catesby . . . Rookwood . . . Grant.' Robin was the worst culprit, for ever darting up and down the line; a word with Father Gerard, another with Digby, a brief exchange with Garnet: 'Salisbury . . . Wright . . . Catesby.' Then Digby would step aside for a while with Father Gerard and Anne Vaux would take Lady Mary's arm, their two veiled heads held very close together, pilgrims' skirts joined.

Robin noticed that Isabel had fallen behind and leapt back towards her, shouting her name. She presumed this sudden concern was because he had so many admiring witnesses who would think him an excellent brother. Susannah was dithering about whether or not to follow. To see her cousin, normally so reserved, at the mercy of a man as unreliable and self-seeking as brother Robin almost moved Isabel to pity.

Robin towered over her, breathless and laughing. 'You're letting the family name down, Izzie. Come on. Here, I'll give you a piggy-back.'

Piggy-backs with Robin had been a wonderful childhood treat, round and round the hot lawns at Cuddington until she was dizzy and sick with laughter.

'I think not,' she said.

He offered his arm. 'My lady?'

'My lord.' He dragged her up and she leaned heavily on him. The sore heel was worse than ever. 'I notice you men don't go bare-foot.'

'Winifred isn't our saint. We don't have women's problems to pray about.'

'Then why have you come? People think it odd that you have a devotion to Winifred.'

'I need time to reflect. And these are my closest friends.'

'Why are the Digbys here and Nicholas Owen? Robin, tell me what people are whispering about all the time. Why is Catesby mentioned so often? I keep hearing his name. Wasn't he at Gloucester Hall with you? They're always talking about him. What's going to happen?'

He loved her curiosity. It was delicious for him to know the answers but not give them. She could sense excitement buzzing under his skin. 'Little sister, don't ask questions, only pray for us.'

'What shall I pray?'

'Pray for the deliverance of all Catholics from persecution. Pray for the reconversion of England.'

'I'm always praying for that.'

'Yes but now, now especially, Isabel, you must beg Winifred to intercede for us. The church in England needs her prayers, believe me.'

'I thought you said Winifred was only a woman's saint. These seem very grand prayers for her to answer.'

He was sulky because she was laughing at him. 'I had stupidly supposed that you were serious, Isabel, and wanted to be of some use. I shan't bother again.'

'If you told me exactly what to pray for it would be easier to help.'

'Pray for what you like. We are only interested in those who commit themselves to our faith, body and soul.'

They were like magnets repelling each other. She wouldn't give him the adoration he wanted and he upset her by his reminder that she was just a powerless girl. Dropping his arm she forced herself to walk alone without limping. Inside she was cold as ice. Only a few minutes ago she had been full of joy, loving this journey through unknown country with people she thought were her friends. He had ruined all that.

*

30

The chapel at Holywell had a flat roof, crenellated walls and glittering lancet windows. Isabel had convinced herself that her priest would come hurrying out to meet them but there was no sign of him. All her hopes seemed very foolish and wasteful.

The authorities were afraid to close a shrine held in great reverence by hostile local people and preferred to turn a blind eye, so Holywell had survived the desecrations of Henry VIII's reign more or less intact. Once inside, Isabel, who was used to makeshift chapels in country houses, was intimidated by exuberant detail. Every spare inch was ornamented, wooden faces leered, a beaver coiled round the base of a pillar and an angel guarded himself with a bright shield.

The men were beckoned to a small doorway leading down to the well. When they'd gone the women felt suddenly unprotected and moved close together, listening to the occasional lap and splash of water below.

Isabel gazed up at the sanctuary candle and tried to pray. She had resolved to ask Winifred to strengthen her vocation but now she felt a frightening coldness and didn't know what she was doing here. The priest had abandoned her and everyone else kept her in the dark.

Panic-stricken she prayed for a whole-hearted union with Winifred through the holy waters. She didn't want the moment to pass her by.

After an hour the women filed down to the crypt, a soaring cavern open on one side so that cool air circulated the slender pillars reaching from the vaulted roof to the star-shaped well-pool. Stone Saint Winifred presided from a niche with a horizontal line round her neck to mark where a wicked suitor had cut off her head when she refused his advances. Fortunately the local saint had re-attached it to her body and the wound had healed instantly. Winifred had lived, but with the scar as a constant reminder of her martyrdom.

Slowly the women undressed, helping each other with laces and buckles. Isabel thought it terrible to see her grandmother stripped to her shift, her old woman's body released from its bodice suddenly just a bulging heap of flesh. Where was the stately Anne Winshawe now, and all her authority?

First into the water went the two Annes and Lucy Morton, hand in hand. They staggered, gasped and ducked under the surface, sinking down and down until their hair floated up in thin strands as if they were drowning. But when they emerged their faces were full of joy. Twice more they plunged then sank under a stone arch and out into the open stream beyond.

Isabel and Susannah were last. Susannah's thick flesh was greyish in the dim light. She was shivering as she inched down the steps and flung herself under, rising from the pool with a gasp, cheeks flushed and shift afloat. Isabel imagined her cousin's desire for Robin staining the crystal depths.

She was alone at the top of the steps. The pool was a fathomless cauldron for prayers. Its waters were potent but her mind was blank. Whatever I ask, I shall be given, she thought. I know it. What shall I say? What do I need more than anything else?

She inched her way little by little into the pool. As soon as they hit the water her feet ached. With a supreme effort of will she took another step down, and another. For a moment her shift billowed then fell against her flesh, winding like an icy shroud round her feet. She sank her head and water gushed into her mouth, ears and nose. Her neck arched backwards but she had time to cry inside her head: 'Winifred, can you hear me?'

She came up gasping for air. The water was so soft that it seemed to coat her skin. Submerging her head again she plunged forward, this time opening her eyes so that the water sank into her face and trickled against her eardrums.

'Winifred, please. I don't want a future like other women's.'

A third time she went down and saw her white fingers move like fronds through the water. 'I want change. I want to be made different.'

And then she was sucked up into the light. Ahead of her Susannah's shift had gone nearly transparent and clung to her pink buttocks. Martha Canton held out a cloak but Isabel waved it aside and flew out of the water with her hair streaming down to her hips and her wet limbs shining.

That night in the hostel it seemed as though more had happened than a simple spiritual cleansing. The group behaved as if it was at the end of a journey far longer than three days' walk from Shrewsbury to Holywell. People gazed lovingly at their friends and sometimes caught tight hold of each other's hands. More than ever the women tried to cosset the priests though Garnet was unapproachable. He chose to spend the night alone in the chapel. Robin sat for an hour in grave conversation with Nicholas Owen.

The next day they began the long journey home. There was no buoyancy now, just a dogged return to Shrewsbury. The holiday was over. They talked in low voices and glanced often over their shoulders. A small cluster of people always surrounded Father Garnet. Robin had arranged for horses to meet him at Chester and was the first to leave the group. He kissed everyone, squeezed Isabel tightly to his chest and told her he would take a good report of her conduct home to their mother. Susannah he tweaked playfully under the chin. The two girls stood side by side and watched until he was a tiny speck in the distance.

In Shrewsbury there were more tears and embraces. The last sight Isabel had of the pilgrims was from the dark stairs of the inn when she turned and saw through the doorway of the upper room Garnet's distracted face.

All the way back in the carriage, through days of swaying journey, Isabel nursed her memories. Again and again she dived through the miraculous water and tasted its peaty softness on her tongue.

The others were also very quiet but much more friendly than when they had first left Oakshott. Susannah even managed the odd smile and Martha stitched peacefully at a tapestry seat cover.

Only on the last day was their calm interrupted by a strained gasp as grandmother sank forward and buried her head in her hands. Isabel's startled eyes met Martha's. From deep in Anne's throat came dry, violent sobs. The others sat in horrified silence.

After a few minutes Anne sat up and shut her eyes as if exhausted. Then at four o'clock she opened her Missal and read Vespers, white-faced and with her hair unusually messy under her blackwork cap. Isabel was terrified by the way Anne wouldn't explain anything but had locked all her sorrow away again, as if nothing had happened.

An hour later the gates of Oakshott were swung back to allow their carriage through. By the time they reached the house most of the servants had already gathered in the courtyard. Aunt Teresa waved energetically from the doorway and her two boys lolled on the steps. Nicholas Turner stood exactly where they had left him, spongy hand raised in greeting.

Chapter 3

The schoolroom was in the oldest part of Oakshott, the wing into which the priest had vanished on the night of the search. To reach it the door of Master Turner's bed-chamber had to be passed. Isabel had peeped in once but never again. The thought of those tousled sheets had stayed with her all morning; Turner's dirty hair on the pillow, Turner's unhealthy flesh bunching the linen.

Next door was the schoolroom. Turner was always there before his pupils, waiting behind the door. Click, he closed it with exaggerated care. The room had three high windows and Isabel's chair faced away from them all. At the head sat Turner, on either side of him the two Thewing boys. Isabel was near the bottom of the table despite being the brightest. Master Turner thought his talents were wasted on girls and allowed them in the room only because ordered to by Anne Winshawe. At first Isabel had chipped in all the time, waiting for him to realize how much she knew, but as he never gave her a word of praise she instead concentrated her energies on finding fault with him.

On the day after the pilgrimage the girls went to their lessons as usual and Isabel smelt the sour atmosphere in the schoolroom. How could she endure Nicholas Turner's pettiness after the adventure of Holywell? Yesterday morning she had stepped through air sharp with wood smoke to begin a new day's journey. Now the monotony of Oakshott fell on her like a dragging cloak. She knew exactly what the next hour would bring, and the next.

She tried to brace herself. You must study. You were sent

to Oakshott to work. Remember what your priest said: read and learn.

I don't care about the priest. He let me down.

You wanted him to be there far too much so of course he wasn't. But the pilgrimage was an adventure all the same. You made something of it on your own. You don't need him or anyone else.

Two books lay open on the table. A week before the pilgrimage they had started on Horace. In the girls' absence the first book of Odes had been read and they were now working on the second. For Alan Thewing and Susannah, the least advanced, there was a Latin grammar to share. Poor Alan, at fourteen, should have been admitted to St Peter's School in York by now but he found Latin too much of a struggle. Since Father Peter's visit, however, there had been a marked change in him. Instead of tugging at his lank hair and yawning through lessons he laboriously followed every word, pausing only to sniff for he had a perpetual nasal blockage. His brother Edmund, who had no desire to learn, was as lazy as ever. When Turner asked him a question he would lift an eyebrow and leer with handsome, half-open lips, so he was usually left alone. In another few months he was leaving for London where Anne Winshawe still had influential friends. To Edmund, the oldest Thewing boy, fell the unenviable task of recovering the family fortune.

On the morning after the girls' return from Holywell Turner was particularly snide, probably because he had a full class again. It can't have been much fun ploughing through Horace with just the deadly Thewing boys and no Isabel to bully. Isabel shielded herself from his pungent smell of wet hair and cooked vegetables; the flush of his unhealthy skin and his gluey lips.

Discipline, Isabel. If you are to be a nun, you must be self-disciplined.

Tomorrow I will begin. Today I am too miserable. And these are my inferiors. I respect Nicholas Owen, Father Garnet and Lucy Morton. Not Turner or my cousins.

Susannah wasn't doing much work either. She had covered her face and was breathing loudly. From time to time a fat tear fell on the waxy surface of the table.

The book was handed to Isabel who read a paragraph in a clipped voice, translated a sentence and paused to phrase the next. It was the tiniest hesitation but Turner was on to her. 'Mistress Isabel, I can see you've made no effort to keep up your studies during the pilgrimage. I'm surprised considering you had all those brilliant Jesuits to teach you. I suppose I'll have to guide you word by word. Change places with me, Master Thewing.'

Turner's shoulder brushed Isabel's and his breath was biscuity as his forefinger with its bitten nail tapped down on the page. He had made dirt a virtue, calling it absence of vanity. She looked away from his caked ear and translated flawlessly, soothed by the familiar patterns of the language and her own competence.

'The clouds let fall a flood of rain; fields are churned mud . . .'

He pounced. 'You said "a flood". I think "a deluge" would be more appropriate.'

She said not a word.

'My translation is more accurate, please repeat the sentence,' he persisted.

The longer she said nothing, the more she regretted it. How could she haul herself out of this pit.

The room went deathly quiet. Turner's face was close to hers. Again Isabel thought of the men she had known on pilgrimage; Digby with his careless, flashing smile, Nicholas Owen, crippled and fearless, scholarly Garnet. She remembered her clear-eyed priest with his delicate hands.

'I assume silence means you agree with me.' She could feel Turner's gaze on her mouth. His own lips made a voiceless echo of her reply.

'If you like,' she said.

'If I like.' He was breathing more and more rapidly. 'I see those Jesuits haven't taught you manners.'

'Why do you keep saying "Jesuits" like that? Does my grandmother know what you think about Jesuits?'

He gave a private smile that tucked in his upper lip and

pushed air through his nose. The puce flush came and went for he was frightened of Anne Winshawe. 'I feel nothing but admiration for Jesuit priests, indeed for all our priests. As you know I hope soon to join their ranks.' His hairline was beaded with sweat and Isabel felt that she had won a cheap victory.

Winifred, she prayed, make me into a better person.

'Forgive me, I'm still very tired after my long journey.' She read the line exactly as Turner wished, much to the disappointment of Edmund Thewing. Throughout this exchange Susannah had wept more silent tears and Alan folded his hands and closed his sallow eyelids. So only Edmund had enjoyed it, softly drumming his manicured fingertips and smiling sleek encouragement on Isabel.

The girls spent the afternoons with their grandmother and Martha. Susannah's mother, Teresa, had no patience for needlecraft and never joined these quiet sessions but worked in the garden making violent assaults on weeds and stony ground. Martha helped the girls embroider their names on tiny squares of linen using ten different stitches. '*Isabel Stanhope. 12 years old. Ad Deum qui laetificat juventutem meam.*' To God, the joy of my youth. Less tiresome to the eyes but a strain on the nerves was an expedition to the village. Before her encounter with the priest, Isabel had stood furiously in foul doorways while her grandmother and Susannah crept inside with potions and salves. She should love these dirty people but could not. Now, as she was destined to be a nun, she jostled with Susannah for a place at grandmother's side, peering through the gloom at some child quivering with fever in its mother's arms. She made herself hold its stiff little body and rub ointment on its lips but knew she couldn't do it as well as Susannah who had a gift, according to Anne Winshawe.

Despite this display of normality there was a definite change in life at Oakshott. From the schoolroom to the dairy the house was on tiptoe. Approaching hoof-beats set nerves on edge and if someone was clumsy or forgetful they received a fierce scolding from Anne. Isabel found herself shrinking away from the walls as she trod the passages. She was haunted by the memory of lame Nicholas Owen and his habit of looking always away. Suppose she stumbled by chance on one of his creations, a loose panel opening on to a pitch black hiding place? What a terrible weight of knowledge. The fragile patchwork of her innocence would be ripped apart by such a find.

Without explanation all physical signs of religious observance were rubbed from the house and a week after the pilgrims' return it was announced that the chapel would be cleared the following day and henceforth prayers said in the refectory.

The next evening at bedtime Isabel crept up to the room in the roof although the children had been warned not to go there. She wanted to say goodbye to the place where she had met the priest called Peter. Perhaps there would be something of him left.

When she pushed back the door the smell of raw wood and incense was at once replaced by a rush of autumn air. The windows were open and Isabel had to guard the flame of her candle. She took another step and her shin caught on the corner of a heavy chest. The attic was crammed with household flotsam that might have gathered over a century, not a few hours. And a fruity smell climbed from the floor, apples, row upon row of the first windfalls in long trays.

She whispered his name into the perfumed air. Peter. Then she blew out her candle and stood shivering in the dark.

Dear Jesus, look after my priest wherever he is. Keep him safe.

Susannah was at the bedroom window downstairs. By way of invitation she stepped aside to let Isabel stand next to her. A little procession was skirting the edge of the lawn, at its head the mistress of outdoors, Teresa Thewing, brandishing a spade. More sedately came the black-cloaked figures of Anne, Martha and two men carrying a large box. Last of all trotted Oswald Fairbrother with his arms full of garden tools.

In less than a minute they had all disappeared among the rose-beds.

'Susannah. What's happening?'

There was the usual sucking pause before Susannah deigned to answer. 'They'll be burying the altar vessels. The sacred relics have already been sent away.'

'Why?'

'Because they don't want anyone to find them.' She separated each word as if speaking to a half-deaf idiot.

So in the box were all the precious things that Isabel loved to see at mass. Gold, emeralds, crystal; ciborium, monstrance, chalice. Even their names were holy. Surely their divine function was so powerful that they would shine through the deepest covering of earth. Why bury them now and what terrible danger had made grandmother surrender the hand of Margaret Clitherow?

Isabel whispered: 'Susannah, don't you wish it was still the end of summer and we were walking to Holywell?'

Already on her way to the bed Susannah said harshly: 'I never waste time wishing.'

'We could pray to go back there next summer.'

'Good things never happen twice.'

Be a saint, Isabel, try one more time. 'Susannah. Are you all right?'

No reply.

'I was wondering, you know, if you had been missing people since the pilgrimage. I have. I even miss Robin though heaven knows why, he's a useless brother.'

It was like lying next to a bag of sand.

'I suppose some people would call him handsome but I'm not so sure. What do you think?'

'Be quiet. Be quiet.'

That autumn it rained so much that all the greens in the gardens turned brown and sodden early. Day after day the girls were stuck inside and the house was like an over-strung instrument. At any moment, with a dreadful crack, something would break.

In the schoolroom Nicholas Turner was a clawless cat waiting to pounce. Alan Thewing, now intense and pious, was easy game and Susannah was unreachable in her swamp of misery so as usual Isabel was the most promising target.

One morning she stumbled twice in one sentence. Eagerness bloomed in Turner like a red snapdragon.

'Right,' he said when she faltered again. 'Right. Let's go back to the very beginning. Take the grammar and do the first exercise. You obviously can't manage our sophisticated studies.'

'There is nothing wrong with my work,' said Isabel. 'I'm not quite myself this morning.'

He stood so close behind her chair that his trunk-hose pressed her upper back. 'Perhaps you have women's troubles,' came his sly voice. The word 'women's' slithered on his tongue as if he could see, in his mind's eye, the hidden workings of her body. 'What else could account for such awkward translation?'

She sat with her arms crossed tight on her chest, eyes fixed.

'You give the impression, Mistress Isabel, that we are all beneath you. How wrong can you be? Have you any idea of the risks I take, day after day, to guide you in your studies?'

'We all take risks.'

'But none so great as I. A year's imprisonment if I'm caught teaching the Catechism. And for what? An ungrateful little girl who has no respect. Well, back to the beginning. I'm afraid it's the parsing of simple sentences for you.'

She pushed back her chair and tried to get up.

'Don't leave the room,' he shouted. 'I forbid it.'

'Then please don't make me work from that grammar, which is for babies.'

He is not worth a breath of your body, she told herself. He wants to fight you. Don't rise to the bait.

'I see. Latin, the language of the saints, has suddenly become pap for babies according to Mistress Isabel Stanhope.' He was talking very fast, scrabbling through the floppy pages of the old grammar. A clot of hair slipped across his forehead. 'Well, let me tell you, Mistress Isabel, that your opinion is worth less than nothing. We keep you girls occupied up here in the schoolroom but who cares if your heads are full of Latin or cross-stitch?'

She was beyond anger.

'Well, have you nothing to say to me?' he demanded, now so close that to avoid contact her ribs were bruised by the table edge. His hot breath was on her ear and when he took hold of her upper arm his fingertips brushed the side of her bodice. 'Mistress Isabel?'

She tried to side-step him. 'Get out of my way. You are disgusting. You make my flesh crawl.' The others sat paralysed. Turner's lips were thick and moist. 'I hate you. I hate you. Nobody would want you for their priest. You're evil. You're worse than a Protestant.'

Susannah got up. 'I'll take her to grandmother. She's beside herself.' Isabel, whose face and throat were sore from so much rage, felt her hand seized and she was tugged swiftly from the room.

'Wait for me. Wait. Oh, yes, I'll have something to say to Mistress Winshawe too,' screeched Turner as he came pounding after them.

Anne and Martha sat side by side in the window. The light was so poor they had to hold their work at chest level. Martha specialized in needle-point and was stitching at a frame but it was unimaginable that Anne would do anything merely decorative like embroidery, even if its ultimate purpose was a priest's sacred vestment or an altar cloth. She had been writing. There was a long list on her lap and a quill in her hand.

Grandmother's eyes were her source of power. They could be crinkly, old lady's eyes one moment, the next pale blue and staring as if on consideration she found nothing to love. Although she rarely touched anyone it was her habit to invite her charges close and thereby fix them within her space. For a long time she did nothing but look at Isabel. Somewhere behind, in the shadows, was Susannah. Turner had been heard and sent away.

'You will pack your bag and go home, Isabel.'

It was like diving through Winifred's Well again with voices swooshing from a great distance. 'Why, grandmother?'

'Because I will not have a member of my household speak to another as you have spoken to Master Turner.'

'I lost my temper. I'm sorry.'

'Isabel, I believe that uncontrolled anger is a revelation of a person's innermost self. So now I know what is in your soul. Well, Isabel?'

Isabel stared at her grandmother's left eyebrow. 'I don't think so.'

In the following silence Isabel thought she heard Martha's needle pass through fabric.

'Nobody knows what's in my soul, grandmother.' She didn't recognize herself. It was as if her body was a hot shell, empty except for a calm, tight kernel. All the rest of Isabel was gone.

Anne stared. Martha's needle stabbed faster and faster.

'Will you tell my mother why I am being sent home?' asked the unemotional voice belonging to Isabel Stanhope.

'Of course.'

'I shall be sorry to leave this house.' Isabel darted forward to kiss her grandmother's hand but Anne's fingers lay like dead things. At the door, where Susannah was, Isabel said: 'I think you should keep your eye on Master Turner, grandmother.'

As her slippered feet padded up to the bedroom her body filled itself in again and back came Isabel, shaking with dismay and disgrace. She tumbled face down on the bed.

Dear Jesus, I'm sorry, I'm sorry.

A weight carefully arranged itself close by. Isabel opened her eyes and there was Susannah, plump cheek flattened and one big eye out of shape because of being pressed to the mattress. She said: 'Whatever I do, grandmother can't send me home. I have no home to go to.'

The cousins were locked in a wide open stare.

To her guilty satisfaction Isabel had recently heard it whispered that far from being a martyr Susannah's father had actually squandered the Thewing money on law-suits. There was no hope of his wife, Teresa, rescuing her family's reputation for she had never made a sensible plan in her life. Instead she was given to barging against chair backs and sweeping cutlery to the floor with a random twitch of her elbow. If she came across her sons or daughter she would either look straight through them or grasp their heads and cover their hair with kisses. Isabel wondered how it was possible for Teresa to be the sister of her own mother, Thomasina, who was so beautiful and restrained. Teresa's mind seemed full of scrappy bits and pieces, like dry leaves blown along a path.

'Of course I want to go home, Susannah, but not in disgrace because of Nicholas Turner. Don't you think grandmother is very unfair?' she pleaded.

At first there was no reply, then Susannah said: 'Will your brother be at home?'

'It doesn't make any difference if he's there or not. He never bothers with me.'

'If I write him a letter, will you give it to him? Just a prayer really.'

Isabel went on gazing into those loveless eyes. First there was the black pupil that shrank and expanded even as she watched, then a thick, nut-brown ring, then an outer, thinner circle, fawnish in colour. 'If I see Robin, of course I'll give him your letter.'

Isabel returned home to Cuddington Hall in Warwickshire on the drowsy afternoon of 17 October 1605. A low sun poured down the long drive between beech trees and already, though it was barely three o'clock, the shadows had lengthened. Behind lacy iron gates the house was burnished the colour of toast.

Although Isabel had little luggage and her only companions were Martha Canton and a young maid, an astonishing number of horses, ten in all, had been sent from Oakshott to pull the carriage. Their hooves made a great scrabbling on the gravel in the courtyard behind the house. A servant appeared in the kitchen door and there were other faces at windows. Stable boys came out to unharness and the carriage door was opened by Mary Bonniface, Thomasina's maid since childhood, a dear, familiar figure, heavy-jowled and freckled. She hugged Isabel fiercely, then marched her through the kitchens and across the inner courtyard. 'I didn't think you'd last too long with Madam Winshawe up there. What did you do? Give her a bit of cheek? Have one of your turns?'

'Both, I suppose.'

'In my opinion you're best out of it. I never found the atmosphere in that house healthy. You know where to find your mother.'

Suddenly Isabel's life which had seemed knotty with unexpected emotion was simply full of longing. She took off across the low hallway and Cuddington flew past, a blur of warmth and rich colour, of liquid sunshine through clean windows and softness underfoot.

Thomasina was in her bedroom. She had adapted the next door dressing-room as her chapel and if her husband, Sir William Stanhope, was absent, a day at Cuddington echoed the regime of Oakshott. She must have heard her daughter's running feet for she was already half way across the room to greet her. Even so, Isabel propelled herself with such force into her mother's arms that Thomasina staggered backwards and folded down on the bed with Isabel buried in the billow of her rose-red skirts.

Her light voice said: 'You'll have to ask Mistress Canton to excuse me, Mary. I'll be down in an hour or so.'

The bedroom door closed softly. Thomasina lay back on heaped pillows and drew her daughter's head on to her shoulder. Her calm hand stroked Isabel's hair from neck to waist.

'I'm so sorry for being sent home from Oakshott,' said Isabel, nuzzling the soft fabric of her mother's chemise. There was no other perfume like Thomasina's, a milky, busy essence.

Isabel could never predict how Thomasina would react to things. Instead of her small mouth being pinched with disapproval she seemed quite amused and all she said was: Don't take it too much to heart. I was missing you so it's a blessing in disguise. And remember, Isabel, you are one apparently insignificant detail in the huge picture which is all of us. You can't see the many connecting threads that have brought you home.'

For a few more minutes Isabel lay in the safe tent of her mother's bed, loved and forgiven. The pain of rejection faded as her body was lapped by the rise and fall of Thomasina's breast.

The canopy above the bed had been embroidered by great-grandmother Wilhelmina whose portrait hung five along from Thomasina's in the great hall. Isabel loved Wilhelmina's embroidery because it was full of surprises. In one corner a spider span a delicate web while a fat bee prepared to land on a leaf and a ladybird clung to a petal nearby. Isabel stared up hungrily and found all her old insect friends. 'Martha Canton does embroidery all the time that she's not at prayer,' she said.

Thomasina tucked her thin arms cosily round Isabel's waist. It was miraculous to have her so still and attentive. 'Martha Canton has embroidered all her life. Every stitch she makes is a prayer. Her needle must have travelled a thousand miles, even further than you, Isabel, on your pilgrimage.'

'You had my letter then, mother.'

'Oh, I heard about your journey from many quarters and that you were a brave and stalwart little pilgrim.'

'Mother, while I was at Oakshott, I decided what I would do with my life.'

'And what was that, my lamb?'

Her voice quavered. 'I want to be a nun.' She was testing the words for the first time aloud and her mother was a cruel critic of ill-thought-out ideas.

Of all things, Thomasina laughed. 'Isabel, you'd make a hopeless nun.'

'I wouldn't. I've changed. I love to be quiet now and spend time in chapel. That's why you sent me to Oakshott, surely.'

'I sent you there because I wanted you to be rock solid in your faith. I thought with your grandmother and your Aunt Teresa you would discover what it was to live in a truly Catholic household. But you can't be a nun. It would kill your father. Your betrothal to Francis Bourne has been arranged almost from the second you were born. Heaven help us all if he finds out you've even thought about being a nun.'

'You must have known I'd become more religious with grandmother. I couldn't help it in her house.'

'I wanted you to learn discipline and how to pray, yes. But I promised your father you'd come to no harm and that you'd simply have a good education there. Besides, he wanted you safely out of the way.'

'Out of the way of what?'

'Oh, of Robin's influence, I suppose. And of himself. He's after promotion, Isabel. The last thing he wants is undutiful offspring underfoot, especially one given to rages and rash ideas.'

'But, mother, surely you at least would be glad if I was a nun.'

'I ought to be glad. It ought to be my one aim, to see my children enter the religious life. Perhaps if I'd had half a dozen. But God granted me only two, Isabel.'

'Mother, while I was at Oakshott I met a priest called Father Peter. He heard my confession and when he told me I had a vocation for the church I knew he was right. He talked about you.'

Her mother's arms had lost their affectionate grip. 'I know any number of priests who have called themselves Peter at one time or another.'

'But it was his real name. I'm sure.'

'Peter. Yes. I know a priest whose real name is sometimes Peter. He's got to you, has he? I see. The man is a wizard. He crawls under the toughest skin.' Moment by moment Thomasina was slipping into her more usual self, distracted, even unkind.

47

'Tell me about the Spiritual Exercises. He said I should do them.'

'They're a type of prayer practised by the Jesuits. They can be powerful, Isabel, and do great harm if undertaken lightly or with a bad director. You are far too young in any case.' Suddenly Isabel was pushed aside. 'Whatever you do, don't mention this to your father. Off you go now, lamb. I must speak with Martha.'

Isabel slept once more in her old bed but found it very cold without Susannah's body heat and though she kept herself awake for an hour, Thomasina did not come up to say goodnight. Her nerves were set on edge by this sudden change in her prospects. So, nobody was going to encourage her to be a nun after all, in fact they'd probably all laugh at her. And how would tomorrow and all other tomorrows be with no lessons in the schoolroom, no wordless battles of will with Susannah?

Suddenly she sat bolt upright. Her room was on the first floor almost above the porch and although there had been no sound something had happened. It was as if Cuddington had settled deeper into the earth because several weighty newcomers had come into the house. She could feel the message sent by their footfall from floorboard to floorboard. Then, from the hall below, came the unmistakable bark of her brother's laugh, not a warm or infectious sound but one that instantly reminded her of the pilgrimage; the heady, summery smell of outdoors, the tension of longing for her priest's company and the constant sense of being on the very edge of violent secrets.

Susannah's letter provided an excellent excuse for Isabel to creep out of bed. Robin might be gone by morning so surely she ought to give it to him straight away.

Important gatherings at Cuddington took place in Sir William's library. Isabel had never seen her father open a book but he had a fair collection and loved to catalogue his neat shelves. When she was alone in the house Thomasina spent most of her time there, for the library had south-facing windows and bright tapestries. Perhaps she was now seated in her usual low chair, close to her beloved son.

Through the closed door came the occasional murmur of men's voices, low and urgent. Isabel counted four or five different speakers and hastily revised her plan of taking the impulsive little sister's privilege and bursting in on Robin. Instead she would go back to bed and listen for the others to leave.

But then she heard something that brought her ear hard up to the door. Yes, there it was again.

The priest.

One roof sheltered them both. One oak door separated them. Isabel rubbed her cheek along the smooth grain and her body melted into the wood. In a few seconds she might kneel at his feet.

She forgave him at once the long months of waiting.

An argument was developing inside the library though she could make out few phrases. '. . . foolish to trust the Spanish . . .' someone said and her priest replied sharply, 'You cannot . . .' but his voice died and she heard only the well-remembered cadences of his voice. The blood pumped cold in her veins. Don't let my priest be angry, dear Jesus. Let him see me, please, and be glad I'm here. Find me a way to reach him. She retreated to the bottom of the staircase and huddled down. Level with her head were the feet and calves of the first Sir William, Wilhelmina's husband, builder of Cuddington, whose portrait hung above the entrance hall. Isabel dared not look into his ambitious eyes. What would he say to the presence of a Jesuit in his beautiful house funded by monies paid by a grateful Protestant monarch?

When at long last the door opened she bolted up to the half-landing. A group of men emerged in a bunch and she could see just the tops of their heads, neatly parted and combed hair, plain collars and dark clothes. They carried their hats and cloaks bundled up in their arms and at first all but Robin seemed to be strangers. But no, surely that was Digby; she recognized his fair hair and the cut of his green doublet.

Robin broke away from the rest to open the entrance door and others followed as a gust of earthy night air blew up the stairs. But two men must have stayed behind in the library because a voice said: 'Your blessing. Please.'

There was a long silence. Then Isabel distinctly heard her priest. *'Benedicat vos omnipotens . . .'* His words were like a pendulum struck in her heart. Had he not said the very same to her, in just that tone of calm reassurance?

The other man in the library was still not satisfied. 'You give your unequivocal blessing?'

A pause. 'Your audacity is breathtaking. I had expected nothing so extreme or violent. Something inherently wrong doesn't become right just because a priest has blessed it.'

'But this, for this cause, Father Carisbroke, you give your blessing.'

Another long pause. 'For this, I give my blessing.'

Robin called urgently, 'Catesby,' and a figure moved swiftly across the hall and snuffed the lamp. The latch on the entrance door clicked smoothly behind him. Isabel ran down the stairs and into the library. 'Father Peter, Father Peter, it is I, Isabel Stanhope. I'm here.'

She found darkness. A fire burnt low in the hearth and the smell of wine hovered warm above the embers. 'Father Peter.' Her voice hung petrified. She had heard his voice and he had not left with Catesby, yet he was gone. A moment ago she had been convinced of his presence but her certainty drained like water through her fingers.

Using the shelves as her guide she edged from one bookcase to the next. The safe floor of her life had sprung a dozen trap doors. Her brother and his friends had come and gone in the night like ghosts. The priest, whom her mother had spoken of as someone in the far distance, had been in this very room but was now invisible. Round and round she went looking for him.

'Father Peter. Father Peter.' At the far end of the room was the door leading to the servants' stairs, up to the first floor, down to the kitchens. Surely she would have heard him if he'd left this way? She was sick with the knowledge that it was because he had heard her voice that he had fled and he would never allow himself to be found by her.

When she came back to the hearth she stood very still, turning Susannah's letter over in her hand.

She was entirely alone. There wasn't a soul in the world, it seemed, who would tell her the truth. Behind every denial there was a possible yes. Behind every explanation was another, hidden.

On silent, bare feet she skimmed back up the main staircase to bed where she lay down and folded her hands on her chest. She listened. What had happened to Cuddington? Had it too been penetrated by the hands of Nicholas Owen? Had he hollowed out hiding places under the very nose of respectable Sir William Stanhope?

Dear Jesus, what is happening now?

Despite everything she had one piece of information that she'd been missing before. His name, Carisbroke. Father Peter Carisbroke.

The next morning very early Isabel was dragged out of bed to say goodbye to Martha Canton who was dressed in her narrow brown travelling gown and seemed flustered.

A modest pair of horses was harnessed to Anne Winshawe's carriage, their breath smoky in the cold air. 'Where are all the rest of grandmother's horses?' asked Isabel.

'Oh, I believe they're needed here,' said Martha vaguely. 'Your grandmother has no use for such a large number.'

'I'm so sorry to have put you to the trouble of coming all this way with me, Mistress Canton,' cried Isabel, realizing suddenly that Martha was her last link with the precious pilgrimage to Holywell.

'My dear child, it has been no trouble. I'll miss you, though, and shall watch your career with great interest. Believe me.'

Chapter 4

On 6 November Isabel and her mother rode out of
Cuddington into a freezing morning. A groom
trotted behind at a respectful distance and a pinched
stable boy ran ahead to unfasten the gates and swing them
soundlessly open. The horses were the only warm, solid
things on the landscape. Nothing else stirred except an old
leaf twisting down from a bare branch.

A clammy mist rolled across the flat fields, muffling colour
and sound. Yesterday Robin had passed this way with Anne
Winshawe's horses strung out behind him. Isabel had
watched him leave at dawn from her window above the
main entrance. That was the kind of thing that happened at
Cuddington these days. A brother visited at night, alone or
with companions, and left in the small hours with too many
horses.

Isabel, tucked up high on the saddle in her red habit, was
a crisp little bundle of resentment. This morning shortly after
five she had been prodded awake by Mary Bonniface who
had an ungentle touch at the best of times. 'Your mother's
taking you riding. Hurry up.'

Thomasina had inherited Anne Winshawe's monastic dis-
dain for fires in bedrooms so Isabel had to dress in stale,
freezing air which became trapped in layers of clothing.
Mary's impatient fingers were ice cold on the lace of her
stays.

'Where am I going?' asked Isabel between chattering teeth.

'That's for me to know and you to find out.'

'Do you know, though, Mary? I don't suppose you really
do.'

Mary, who was in a foul mood, abandoned Isabel's ribbons and headed for the door. 'You'll just have to manage by yourself if you're going to talk to me like that.'

Isabel petulantly refused breakfast. Thomasina whirled into the dining parlour, hatted, gloved, booted, white-faced and sharp-nosed with cold and haste. 'Ready, Isabel.' She carried a letter as if she didn't know how to put it down. Finally she pushed it awkwardly into a pocket within her cloak.

Isabel wouldn't ask her mother where they were going and Thomasina at first didn't volunteer the information. They just plodded on and on through the damp lanes. Isabel saw herself as a nugget of isolation, like a conker; untouched, untouchable, unloved, unlovable. She made a list of all the wrongs that had been done her in the last couple of weeks.

On the day after Robin's first visit, for instance, she had said: 'Mother, last night I heard voices. I thought it was Robin and the priest called Peter I told you about.'

Thomasina's eyes, though greener than Anne Winshawe's, could still be repellent enough to turn Isabel's heart to stone. She had made no reply.

So, thought Isabel, I ask questions and am ignored. I hear voices but see no faces. I have a brain, eyes and ears but nobody cares what I think. I am left to my own devices day after day with no one to teach me, pray with me, or laugh with me. Was this really what it was like before I was sent to Oakshott? Of course not. Mother used to be available for prayers and recreation. Mary Bonniface taught me needlework, though not very well. There were always visitors.

If this was disgrace, for how long was it to go on?

'I received a letter from your father,' said Thomasina suddenly. 'He is coming home as soon as he can.' Her voice was frail and her breath huffed back into her face.

Isabel was too far sunk in her black mood to reply immediately.

'As you know, I did not expect him before Christmas but he says he's particularly eager to see you and Robin.'

Thomasina was always precise and ended each phrase with an upward inflection for emphasis. Isabel's mind travelled quickly along this last remark. 'I wonder why,' she said.

'I suspect he's concerned for your safety. Perhaps he's heard something to trouble him.' It was as if Thomasina had lifted the lid on a previously sealed box and allowed a strand of information to escape before shutting it fast again.

'You mean about me being sent home from grand-mother's.'

Thomasina gave a bark of laughter, a rash explosion in the still air. 'Your father, as you well know, is hardly likely to mind too much that you have left Oakshott.' The distance between mother and daughter closed a little. 'We're going to Coughton Court to hear an All Souls' mass, Isabel. The Throckmortons are away and the Digbys have taken the house for the hunting season. I think you may meet some old friends.'

A flicker of hope warmed Isabel. 'Who?'

'I don't know exactly. It was just something a servant said.' Suddenly Thomasina pricked her sharp spurs into the sides of her chestnut mare who kicked up dainty hooves and gal-loped off into the morning. Isabel tightened her reins and followed. Through floating ribbons of mist they flew until Isabel's cheeks burned and all the hurt had been strummed from her heart. Thomasina allowed her to catch up and they rode side by side for a moment with joined hands. I love her, I love her, thought Isabel and longed to tell her mother so but they soon parted again and Isabel ducked her head as they raced under low trees.

Coughton Court, lowering out of the mist like a phantom house, at first seemed deserted but the door in the gatehouse was immediately flung wide by a steward who showed them upstairs to an over-neat parlour. Despite three storeys of mullioned window at either end and a small fire it was as if cloud had seeped in from outside. After a few minutes Lady Mary Digby appeared, breathless and far from calm. She embraced Thomasina and kissed Isabel but made no com-ment about the pilgrimage.

'How are your boys?' Thomasina asked. 'Kenelm must be two now, surely.'

'They are well. Yes.'

'I was surprised to hear you were at Coughton. You would surely rather be home with the children.'

'My husband had a whim to hunt here.'

'Is Sir Everard in the house? May I speak with him?'

'No, no, he isn't here yet. I expect him tomorrow.'

Mary Digby was in a sorry state. Her voice was high-pitched and she clasped her hands too tightly on her lap.

Thomasina leaned forward. 'Mary, I will be frank with you. I think my son is in danger. I have come for information. My husband has written . . .'

Mary turned her face away.

Isabel sat between the two women and saw that their eyes were full of dread. Her own excitement was gone.

Lady Digby stood up. 'Follow me.'

Isabel had visited Coughton before and knew it well. The Throckmortons, its usual owners, were family friends and it was odd to be in the house without them. She knew the intricacies of its passageways, its old furniture and sad portraits. But today they walked up a spiral staircase previously unknown to her and entered an upper room over the gatehouse.

Kneeling figures in a bare space. Three priests, each with a book. A low table with a single candle burning clear and steady through the gloom of the morning and a small crucifix which could be snapped in two and folded away in a deep pocket. It was like being in the chapel at Oakshott again or on the journey to Holywell when friends had prayed together in a shady barn; all the festivals of Isabel's childhood; the beginning, middle and end of each day, celebration, reflection, confession, communion. Here, surely, where so many of the dearest people in the world to her were gathered, there could be nothing to fear.

The Stanhopes' arrival did not disturb the Sequence, a prayer said each day within the Octave of All Souls'. There was a slight shuffling up to give them space and Lady Mary returned to her place. Isabel breathed deeply.

Dear Jesus thank you. Thank you. Thank you.

They were all here; Anne Vaux at the front of the small gathering, the whole of her sturdy frame intent on prayer, and beside her the shorter, softer figure of Lucy Morton. Nearby Nicholas Owen knelt awkwardly with his face turned to the window. Isabel felt a twitch of fear at the sight of him. He was always at the corner of her mind these days, his hammer and chisel breaking through the safe, familiar places of her life and filling them with secrets.

Leading the prayers was Father Garnet, dapper and well-fed, altogether more polished than on pilgrimage. He was flanked by two other priests, one a stranger to Isabel, the other . . .

At first she wouldn't peep again in case her first, fleeting glance had been mistaken but then she risked another careful look. He was not quite as she remembered. Today he wore a brown jerkin and long, loose green breeches, fashionably cut. His beard was trim and his hair neat. Priests were obviously well cared for at Coughton. His face seemed different too, the skin very pale and sunken under polished cheekbones. He was taller than in Isabel's imagination. She took a long sip at this new image of him before dropping her eyes.

'Dies irae, dies illa, Solvet saeclum in favilla: Teste David cum sibylla.'

Isabel was too preoccupied to translate swiftly but the words dripped coldly into her head like water on hot ashes. 'Day of wrath! Oh, day of mourning, See fulfilled the prophets' warning.' She became alert again to tension in the room. Only her priest seemed entirely steady and kept his gaze on his black Missal. Isabel covered her face with her hands to press this moment deeper into her memory and smelt the leathery tang left by her riding gloves.

'Mors stupebit et natura, Cum resurget creatura, Judicanti responsura . . .'

Garnet's voice faltered. Nobody moved. A horseman had come galloping across the bridge over the moat. Did the sound of our horses have this effect on everybody when we rode up? Isabel wondered. They heard his feet hit stone as he dismounted, a door open, a silence, then hurried footsteps on the stairs. Anne Vaux climbed heavily to her feet and with a regal movement of her hand caused a pathway to open between herself and the door. Isabel's gaze again flashed to her priest. Still his eyes were downcast and his hands steady. Still he seemed to be absorbed in prayer.

First came the steward in his Throckmorton livery, then another servant with exhausted eyes and boots covered in mud. Isabel was close enough to smell sweat and horseflesh. The rider made an unsteady bow, entered the space created by Anne Vaux and bent his knee to Garnet and the crucifix. He carried a letter.

'He's come from Catesby and Sir Everard, Father,' said the steward.

Isabel, being a mere girl, was pushed to the edge of things. There was an unknown world somewhere of which she knew snatches: a king and a parliament to whom she was connected by a father who did important work for them concerned with money, and a lot of anger among Catholics because the king had promised they could worship freely and then gone back on his word. Names like Catesby, Percy, Rookwood and Wright which whirled about and refused to make a pattern.

Garnet, with Anne Vaux at his right shoulder, was reading the letter. The others had moved into silent clusters but Isabel's priest stood side on to everyone else, one elbow resting on the wall above his head, forehead pressed to wrist. Isabel tipped from kneeling position to cross-legged.

Garnet turned his back so that he, Anne and his two priests formed a cluster but he made no effort to lower his voice. 'They would have blown up the Parliament House,' he said, 'and were discovered and we are all utterly undone.'

More silence. The letter was passed dumbly from hand to hand but for a moment nobody seemed to connect with anyone else until Anne said: 'Then we must all go from here. At once.'

Thomasina took Isabel by the arm, thin fingers cruel in their clawed grip and pulled her from the upper room. All the way downstairs they were followed by the sound of Mary Digby's hoarse sobs. When they came to the parlour where they had sat earlier that morning Isabel was pushed inside.

'I will find our cloaks. We'll go home at once. Wait here.'

'Don't leave me, mother.' It seemed quite possible that Thomasina could disappear for ever among the ample furnishings of Coughton. After all, courageous Lady Digby had just crumpled like wet linen, her slightly spoilt features dissolved in a howl of anguish.

Thomasina hesitated.

'What did Father Garnet mean?' persisted Isabel.

'I can't tell you. I don't know.'

'You do. You do.'

'I won't tell you. I can scarcely take it in myself. We expected a peaceful uprising. That's why Robin took the horses.'

'So what happened instead?'

'Don't ask me. Any crumb of knowledge, anyone you can identify, all the memories you have of these people are a danger to you now. And us. Dear God, I should never have brought you here.'

'Then why did you?'

'I came to Coughton because I couldn't stay at home waiting for news. I brought you because I couldn't bear to leave you. It was very wrong of me to come, especially as your father told me specifically to stay home.'

'But, mother, I am here. I have seen everything. It's too late.'

Thomasina flashed about the room with her butterfly-blue brocade skirts swirling and little wisps of fine hair afloat. She threw Isabel a wild, terrible glance and took her hand again. 'There was a plot to kill the king, his family and his peers, by using gunpowder. If the plan had succeeded they would have taken the Princess Elizabeth from Combe Abbey and made her queen, but it has failed. I think probably it was bound to fail. Your father's letter, which came this morning, seemed to be warning me that I shouldn't come near these people. If he knew, then so would others in the government. The conspirators are riding here to the Midlands because they still want to raise a Catholic rebellion. They won't succeed. Nobody will trust them. Nobody will dare.'

There was no mother and no daughter, no comforter and comforted, scolder and scolded, only Thomasina and Isabel who shook so violently that her lips would scarcely form words. 'Why not dare?'

'Isabel. It's treason to plot to kill the king. The conspirators and anyone who helped them will be imprisoned, tortured and executed. Priests, especially Jesuits, who are hated by the government, will be hunted down ruthlessly if they had even the remotest link with the conspirators. And all the rest of us, if we've heard mass or talked with anyone who knew of the plot, are also at risk.'

'But of course we know them. Is Sir Everard Digby in danger? Will he die? Did he want to murder the king? Is he a friend of Catesby?'

The room was filled with the blinding light of under-standing.

'And Robin? Did he know about the gunpowder?'

No reply.

'And Nicholas Owen?'

No reply.

'Father Garnet?'

'I don't know.'

'The priest, Father Peter?'

A pause. 'I think so.'

A black wave broke in Isabel's head. Thomasina spoke again. 'I'll send for the horses.'

Everyone was on the move. From all sides came the sound of hurried footsteps, doors opening and closing, commands given in low voices. Isabel stumbled after her mother down another flight of stairs where she was told to wait in the passage. A maid ran across one end, tripped on the uneven boards, corrected herself, rushed on. Through an open door nearby Isabel saw the criss-cross of a small window and beyond it a heavy grey sky, fold on fold of cloud.

Father Peter was there, quiet as a shadow with his old bag and dark cloak.

Isabel blundered across two fantastic birds of prey, beak to beak in the rug. When she was close enough she put out her hand and clasped his sleeve.

His grey eyes focused on hers at last. 'So, Isabel.'

'Did you hear me on the night you came to Cuddington?' she asked in a hot, tight voice.

At first his eyes were blank then he said: 'I heard a child, yes.'

'You must have known it was me.'

The shock was still in his face and he made no reply.

'I called out to you. Is that why you ran away?'

It was the first time she'd seen anyone smile that morning. 'Isabel, all I cared about was that I shouldn't be seen, especially by you.'

'Why?'

His face closed up and he twisted his sleeve out of her grip. He was breathing too fast. 'Forget me, Isabel. Forget you ever saw me, then or today.'

She remembered the blessing he had given the men at Cuddington. So he had known for sure what Catesby, Digby and maybe her brother Robin had wanted to do to the king and had given it his blessing as a priest.

'I can't forget. Why should I forget? You sound like Robin. I hate these secrets. I hate the way you all make promises and then break them.'

He touched a fingertip to his temple and looked down at her, his attention properly caught at last. 'I made you no promise.'

It was as if she was spinning backwards until she was a speck of dust. She had spent hours in expectation and suffering because he had mentioned the pilgrimage to Holywell while he, it was now obvious, hadn't given it a second thought.

He was looking to the window again and suddenly made a slight movement of his head and a lift of his hand. When he turned back he seemed surprised that she was there at all.

'Are you going now?' she asked hopelessly.

He tightened the lace of his cloak and threw his bag over his shoulder.

'Father Carisbroke.' Familiar blue skirts brushed past. Thomasina gripped the priest's shoulders and kissed him on each cheek, easy kisses, as between brother and sister. For a moment Thomasina seemed the stronger figure. Then she swept away. 'Isabel. Come.'

A few minutes ago Isabel had hated him for not giving the simple answers she wanted. Now she took a step towards him and tried to reach out her arms as her mother had done to give him a calm hug but her limbs felt stiff and useless and her eyes wouldn't soften.

He placed his hand on the top of her head and then was gone. His feet made no sound and the air was scarcely stirred by his rapid movement. She ran back to the window but saw no sign of him or anyone else in the garden.

When Isabel and Thomasina rode home the countryside was as empty as before with only faint rustlings in the hedgerow and, after half an hour or so, a light fall of rain. Soon heavier and faster drops whispered on dead leaves. The straw-coloured mane of her horse darkened and clotted but Isabel lifted her chin and kept her eyes on her mother's straight back

The gates of Cuddington were flung wide open and there were many horsemen, some facing inwards towards the house, others watching the drive.

Thomasina's pace did not slacken. Over her shoulder she called: 'Whatever happens, never forget to pray.'

Chapter 5

Sir Richard Whitfield, the justice from Alcester who had come with warrants to search Cuddington and arrest Lady Thomasina Stanhope, was quite well-known to Isabel because he had hunted with her father. He was a tallish man with a complicated face and flaky scalp. Isabel had always thought someone should tidy him up, brush down his doublet and get his hair in order.

He met them in a parlour next to the library, brandishing his documents. Though bristling with self-importance he was also very nervous.

Thomasina, by contrast, went deathly quiet, her face carved in ivory.

'Well now, young Isabel,' he exclaimed, pretending astonishment, 'I wasn't expecting to see you. I thought you were away in Yorkshire.' His voice was a mess too, the wrong words emphasized and too much spluttering.

Isabel curtseyed. She felt a deadly lack of interest in Sir Richard Whitfield. His smell of damp wool and the fact that he always clenched a wad of tobacco between his back teeth set her nerves on edge.

'So how long have you been home?' he asked.

'A little more than two weeks.'

'And what brought you back?'

I don't see that it's any of your business, she thought.

'You must tell Sir Richard the truth.' Thomasina's voice had a dangerous edge like the flat of Robin's sword when he practised in the garden. Cut. Cut. Stab.

'I came back because I couldn't get on with my tutor.'

'I see.' He blinked too much. Isabel stared at his face and

tried to sort its component parts. The nose wasn't too bad, quite thin and long but ending in a nasty straggling moustache. 'And what did you get up to while you were with your grandmother?'

'Get up to?'

'I expect you heard mass quite often.'

'Is it right to intimidate a child?' interrupted Thomasina.

'Oh, hardly intimidation, surely?'

'Then ask her questions directly. Did she hear mass? Yes, she did. Did she confess to a priest? Yes, she did. Has she seen her brother recently? No. Robin went abroad, as you well know, Sir Richard, to study.'

'So when did you last hear mass, Isabel?'

She thought of the gathering a few hours ago in the gatehouse at Coughton and her priest with his old Missal held between long hands. Her voice quivered. 'I just can't remember.'

'Then try to remember. Lady Stanhope, I expect you'll need to pack. I've arranged for you to be escorted to your room.'

'I won't leave the child alone with you.'

He raised his hands and laughed, kind old Sir Richard. 'You can trust me, Lady Stanhope.'

'Have you considered how my husband will deal with someone who arrests his wife, bullies his child and ransacks his house?'

Sir Richard blinked twice, the right eye more vigorously than the left. 'I am acting within the law. Fetch your things, Lady Stanhope. My wife will of course be happy to lend you anything you need but she's a big lady.' Ever the gentleman, he held open the door for Thomasina. Outside stood a nervous henchman who fell into step behind her.

Isabel sat on a low chair and folded her hands. Luckily Sir Richard didn't understand the power of silence. He put each question once and without waiting for her reply asked it again in simpler language, thereby leaving her time to pray for guidance. She pushed to the foremost part of her brain the information it was all right to give, the rest she tucked away. And in the meantime she was conscious of floorboards

63

being wrenched up elsewhere in the house. Had they gone to her mother's dressing-room yet and found the collection of prayer books and the Latin Bible? What about Thomasina's jewelled crucifix or the tiny statue of the Virgin Mary?

'Now, just tell me, Isabel, where you've been this morning. I mean, quite simply what did you do once you left the house? Your horses are very muddy and the servants say you went out at dawn. Where were you?'

Thou hast saved us, O Lord, from them that afflict us. 'This morning my mother and I went riding. There was no one about. We had the lanes all to ourselves.'

'Did you meet with your brother?'

. . . and hast put them to shame that hate us. 'Sir Richard. My mother told you Robin is abroad. He never writes to me. I wish he did.'

'Have you ever met any of your brother's friends? Robert Catesby. You must know him. What about Sir Everard Digby? Thomas Percy.'

She shook her head. 'I don't know a Thomas Percy.'

'Tell me about when you went to mass, Isabel. You're a good Christian child, I'm sure, and won't lie to me.'

In God shall we glory all the day long. 'Mass was said in my grandmother's house, yes. I don't know who the priest was.'

'Describe him to me.'

. . . and in Thy name we will give praise for ever. 'I've already told you. I don't know his name. I can't remember much about him. Short, I think. Quite plump maybe.'

'You see, Isabel, there's no need to protect your brother. We already have him. He was taken a few hours ago, near Alcester.'

After a long silence Isabel said: 'I wonder you never bothered to tell me that before, Sir Richard.'

He grunted, huffed and puffed, stood up, sat down. 'So, if you and your mother lie about him, how can we trust you? Your poor mother is already accused of harbouring priests. She's likely to suffer badly, very badly, if we think she's been up to anything else.'

He dared to meet her eye and Isabel knew exactly what he threatened. Under torture the martyr Father Edmund

Campion had been forced to name many of his friends. It was said he had been racked so often he couldn't write.

Thomasina in her butterfly-blue dress with her hair loose and her slender wrists and ankles bound with rough brown rope. The grind of a ratchet.

Sir Richard came so close that his sticky yellow saliva spat on Isabel's skin. 'You would help your family if you told the truth.'

'Have I ever told anything except the truth?'

'No, no, I'm sure you're a good girl. And you want to do right. So tell me, Isabel, have priests come to this house? Is there one here now, perhaps?'

'Of course there's no priest here.'

Thomasina marched out of Isabel's frantic imaginings dressed for riding as before, breathless and burning with rage so that her churning skirts filled the room. They mustn't make her be still, Isabel thought. They mustn't touch her. She hasn't eaten all morning so how will she stand the cold? When they hugged, Thomasina seemed to have shrunk, her bones become sharper. They had already boxed her in.

'Pray for me,' she said, resting her cool lips on Isabel's forehead. 'And pray for Sir Richard. I wouldn't be in his shoes when your father finds out what has happened here.'

Isabel and Mary Bonniface slept together in Thomasina's room, Isabel in the bed, Mary on a couch near the door. They did not speak for there were listeners in the passage outside. Thick shadows cast by three candles hid the embroidered insects on the canopy. Isabel lay on her back with crossed arms, as taught by her mother, and tried to find them among the stems and petals and to imagine a summer meadow full of flowers but could see only her great-grandmother's weary fingers trailing a crimson thread. Rain blew against the lattice and downstairs in the library the search went on; the thud of books dropped in haphazard piles, the splintering of wood. Cuddington had cracked open easily as an egg. Already Thomasina's little dressing-room had been taken apart, its panelling carved up and its cupboards emptied. They were looking for priest holes, hoping to find a Jesuit crouched like a full-term chick in its shell.

Nicholas Owen, I hope you did your work well at Cuddington, thought Isabel and prayed for her mother, Digby, Garnet, her priest and all the others on the run.

For Robin she had only anger. Thomasina had built her life of prayer year by year, a single-minded woman in a great house showering money, prayers and food on the sick and starving, grieving over an heretical England and kneeling through the small hours to build a ladder to God. Her weakness was Robin whom she idolized, even though anyone could see he was a self-obsessed bully champing at the bit for glory and action. And because of him her life at Cuddington had been blown apart.

Great-grandmother with her sternly parted hair took a black thread and began on the dots of the ladybird. Dot, dot, black on red. Lazy daisy. Up through the creamy fabric comes the sharp point of the needle, one twist, one thrust and the silk is knotted.

Isabel's father, Sir William Stanhope, was terribly vain. He was said to be one of the best-looking men at court and his daughter preferred to be told that she favoured him in looks rather than the pointy-nosed Thomasina, for he had level eyes, regular features and thick, fair hair. He never emerged in public unless perfectly dressed, gorgeous in his favourite crimson or azure, sleeves slashed under padded shoulder wings to emphasize the extreme narrowness of his waist. His well-shaped calves were encased in flawless stockings and he had an astonishing collection of ruffs and cuffs, once a source of great delight to Isabel who when tiny had been allowed to skim the tip of her index finger under the froth of a scalloped edge and study the complication of its gossamer netting.

In the past she had been afraid of her father because she never knew what he was thinking but on Saturday 16 November when he finally returned home to Cuddington it was easy enough to judge his mood. An hour after his arrival she was called to the library where he was seated in his low chair beside the oak mantel, the perfect line of polished buttons down the front of his doublet an awful contrast to the surrounding chaos.

The library had suffered very badly in the search. Sir William's books lay about in untidy heaps. The pursuivants had flicked through each volume in case it contained Catholic writing and some of the bindings were ripped. The shelves had been hammered and wrenched to check their solidity and a gimlet driven through every other panel in the wall and at intervals in the ceiling to test for cavities. Isabel, who had spent many anguished days wondering when they would find the hiding place Father Peter had used when he visited Cuddington, was as puzzled as Whitfield's men.

She and her father were strangers. As a career courtier he left domestic matters, including the upbringing of his daughter, to his wife. Although Thomasina was decorative, he rarely brought her to London where her unfortunate Catholic sympathies might lead her into trouble. He could turn a blind eye to what went on at Cuddington provided all seemed innocent on the rare occasions he was home. So he had appeared at intervals to look Isabel over, as he checked his French tapestries for signs of fading and his Turkish rugs for wear and tear. The library on these brief visits had been a scented shrine, enriched by Sir William's jewel-like presence. When Isabel, decked out in farthingale and ruff, had been presented to him his face relaxed into a proprietorial smile and her prettiness was rewarded by the present of a book or a coin and a kiss on the cheek.

But this time the full force of his attention was on her. The shock of recent events had crumpled his face, dissolved the firmness etched into vertical lines beside his mouth and made his eyes bloodshot and swimmy. One toe was kicked up as if to be warmed at the non-existent fire.

'So, Isabel. I come home to find my wife under house arrest in Alcester, my son in prison charged with treason and my house ransacked.' He had a way of dabbing his fingertips together that Isabel found very trying. She would have preferred him to do something fierce and definite. 'Can you shed any light on all this?'

She looked into his eyes which were now pretending to be crinkly and trustworthy. 'No, father.'

He knew of course that his wife had been a practising Catholic all these years. It was a fate he shared with the highest in the land and probably did him no harm for the king himself was married to Catholic Anne who heard mass in the privacy of her chambers.

'I have been at fault,' said Sir William. 'I trusted her not to involve my children.'

You gave up on Robin long ago and you've never been at all interested in me except as a bride for Francis Bourne, thought Isabel. It's hardly mother's fault.

She was struck by her father's coldness. Why was he not eaten up with worry about his wife and son? His fingers went bounce, bounce, bounce soundlessly against each other. 'When you last saw Robin did he talk about his friends?'

She looked him in the eye. 'Are you trying to catch me out, father?'

He shifted in his chair and the rhythm of his fingers changed, one tap of the middle, three with the index. 'Whatever can you mean, Isabel?'

'I'm sure you know that I told Sir Richard Whitfield I hadn't seen Robin.'

'Yes, I believe that's what you told Sir Richard.'

'Well then.'

'You wouldn't lie to your father, Isabel.'

Now, here was a problem. She shouldn't lie at all, indeed had managed to tell few direct lies, but the Jesuits taught that in certain circumstances, under interrogation for instance, a Catholic could say something which had a double meaning, one for the hearer, one for the speaker. This process had a special name, equivocation.

'My first duty is to God,' she said, sounding like cousin Susannah.

'They would have butchered the king, his family and

68

countless innocent peers and courtiers. They would have incited bloodshed and insurrection throughout the country. And all for a religion which feeds countless riches to a fat pontiff in Rome and worships the bones of discredited saints. Isabel, you shouldn't protect these murderers. A lot of people think Jesuit priests were behind the plot. So much for being men of God, eh? So much for staying out of politics. The ends justify the means, that's what they think. Garnet. Have you heard of him? He's at the bottom of it all. I might have been there, Isabel, very likely your own father would have been blown apart. You do realize I have a place in the Lords.'

For a moment Isabel wondered what she'd have felt had her father been exploded and decided she would not have missed him. But in any case what had happened during the summer could never have ended in something so dreadful. She remembered her priest in the attic chapel at Oakshott raising high the host, his face transfigured by the miracle. And Father Garnet walking in the sunshiny hills. 'You knew about the plot anyway,' she said. 'You wrote about it to mother. How could you be in danger when you'd been warned about it in advance?'

He stopped tapping. His lips were very pale and he was breathing more quickly than before. 'There will be no more of it, Isabel. No more masses. No more visits to your grandmother. No more pilgrimage. No more priests. You will ride with me to London next week and tomorrow we will go to church in the village.'

'But I thought you were at least sympathetic to Catholicism, father.'

'I am a Christian and a loyal subject to my king. I find after all I care nothing for a faith that can sanction the slaughter of innocent men and women.' He drew her so close that she could smell the headachy sweetness of the oil he used on his hair and see every loop and stitch in the lace on his ruff. 'Isabel. My darling. I have been a very bad father. I find you motherless and bewildered. Let me look after you now and be your guide.' He was silent for a moment, then murmured: 'If I ever find you with a rosary, speaking Latin, reading from a Catholic prayer book or talking to a Catholic without my permission, I shall beat you raw. Do you understand?'

'But it's what I believe, father. I have to be a Catholic for the sake of my soul. I haven't chosen it. It's what I am.'

He still had hold of her hand. Across the room was a large mirror, too high up for Isabel to see more than her eyes and the top of her head. He dragged up a stool and made her stand on it so that their heads were level, Sir William and his young daughter Isabel, he heavy shouldered, neatly bearded and smiling, she white-faced and black-eyed with misery.

'Look, Isabel, this is what you are. My beautiful daughter. You have a wonderful life before you.' He put his finger and thumb under her little ruff so that she felt his touch on the bare skin of her upper back. 'You are my precious child. I'm going to take you to town and show you off to my friends. I'm going to teach you a new, bright faith that does not rely on fake miracles or Latin gabble. You can still worship the same God, my Isabel, still believe in the same Christ. But you don't have to slaughter for the Anglican faith. We must be kind and gentle in what we believe.'

'They kill us often enough. What about Margaret Clitherow?'

'Treason, Isabel. She was a traitor. And don't use the word "us" when talking about Roman Catholics.'

Into the mirror she said: 'Will they take mother to London?'

'Yes. I think so.'

'Will I see her?'

He put his arms round her waist and tried to hold her but she wouldn't bend against him. His perfume was too cloying and his hair too smooth. 'Then I'd better go and pack,' she said and stepped neatly down from the stool. But she was horrified by her own ability to stay calm; it made her so much alone.

The next morning brought a new trial in the shape of Mistress Margaret Westward, a distant relative summoned from Warwick by Sir William to be Isabel's companion. Margaret, who had been living for years with an impoverished female cousin, tripped up and down the ranks of family portraits in the great hall popping with excitement. 'Oh, the quality of these paintings. What a family. The jewels, the texture, the nobility of the faces.' Margaret was a fragment of a woman with dark skin and hair, a voice small and neat to match her person, a careful smile and capable hands.

Her first task was to help with Isabel's packing although it was almost done. The outraged Mary Bonniface was sent from the room, the trunk emptied and every item of clothing unfolded. From between layers of petticoats fell Thomasina's little prayer book and tiny wooden cross. Margaret's dainty fingers scooped them off the bed. 'Oh, you won't want these in town, dear, let me put them away for you.'

'They are my mother's.'

'Then Sir William shall have them. Don't worry. We'll look after them.'

Isabel folded herself on to a chair by the window and refused to say another word.

'Of course, of course, you rest. You must be very tired.' Margaret ran about, eager as a little mouse. Patter, patter, tongue, hands and feet all busy. 'What a lucky girl you are. Lovely clothes. Velvet shoes. Where were they made? London, I expect. You may have noticed my shoes, similar shape. For church I think, the blue cloak, and for the journey?'

Beneath this window Robin and his fencing master had spent hours fighting, Robin's sword a sliver of flame in the sunlight, his white shirt blown loose. Despite his father's influence nobody would employ Robin because he was so blatant and outspoken a Catholic. So his sword had clashed pointlessly in the gardens at Cuddington until the last couple of years when he had suddenly become mysterious, self-important and hard to pin down. Well, they had put a stop to that. Into the black box of a prison cell for Robin.

*

71

The church of St Matthew, Cuddington, was barely half a mile from the gates of the house but Isabel had never set foot in it before. Later that morning, seated between her father and Margaret Westward, she witnessed an Anglican service for the first time.

Her attendance in this heretical church was a denial of the miracle of Christ's presence in the Host. Mary and some of the other servants had resisted by pleading ill-health but how could Isabel refuse when defiance might make things worse for her mother? She wanted Sir William in the best mood possible. It's only a matter of appearing in the church, she thought, just as priests pretend to be scholars or travellers. I don't have to mean anything.

St Matthew's was crowded with local people padded out in thick layers of clothing and shifting their cold feet and arms. Isabel lifted her chin and stared back haughtily into inquisitive eyes. They must all know what had happened at Cuddington and probably some were gleeful about it. Sir William was not popular because on his occasional visits he evicted or fined anyone who couldn't pay their rent and as a local justice hanged poachers and thieves. Even Lady Thomasina with her persuasive Catholic tongue had been a dubious friend to the needy.

Isabel was glad to be disliked. Make me suffer for this, she thought. At least let me take no pleasure at all in being here.

Stripped of ornament, its walls white-washed, its stained glass replaced with plain and its altar furniture stolen away, the church was a barren house for God who surely deserved all the beautiful things men could produce for Him. And the English words of the service sounded crude and irreverent, reducing God to somebody's uncle. When Isabel's priest had said mass his prayers had floated up and up to heaven.

In her head she recited the Latin Creed. '*Credo in unum Deum, Patrem omnipotentem . . .*'

Beside her Margaret Westward took one of Isabel's soft kid gloves and gave it an admiring stroke. She seemed to like animal skins. Against her chest she wore a cord with a rabbit's foot for luck, she said, and she carried a muff made from a thick fox pelt. Her neat feet were tucked precisely

under her gown and by the lift of her chin she pronounced:
Look at me, a true friend in need, I'll keep motherless Mistress Isabel safely in line.

Throughout the journey to London Isabel maintained an attitude of icy hostility to Margaret Westward, partly to cover her grief and fear. They had left Cuddington sealed up, most of the servants dismissed, and stony-eyed Mary Bonniface in charge of the few remaining. Isabel made a mental recital of every prayer she knew though more out of spite than piety. Margaret, apparently unaware of any animosity, sewed a lace collar and, as they neared the city, gasped at each new sight.

The carriage slowed though the wheels ran more smoothly on paving stones. Daylight was blotted out by the press of other traffic and the overhanging bays of houses three or four storeys high. Suddenly the door was flung open and Sir William's face appeared. 'We'll walk, Isabel. I want you to see the Palace of Westminster where I sometimes work.'

'You've taken me there before.'

'We'll go again.'

She got out stiffly and allowed him to take her arm. Her cramped legs were shaky and her eyes dazzled by a burst of sunshine though the stones underfoot were slimy after recent rain. For a moment she was gladdened by the rush of a breeze and the burst of sound and movement. Sir William led her to Old Palace Yard facing Westminster Palace, such a muddle of buttresses, crenellations and cupolas that Isabel couldn't make sense of it. There seemed to be an endlessly moving throng of people in tall hats, creased capes, muddy skirts, limp ruffs and beards, the stink of onion and alcohol and no sky suddenly, just towering walls. She thought it all too ornate, crowded and enclosed. Cuddington slipped into the back of her memory, a tranquil ship floating on hazy lawns.

'Look up,' ordered her father. 'Look up.'

She looked up. She saw a lancet arch, slender turrets,

smoking chimneys, the rushing blue and white sky, two long wooden poles capped by . . .

'Look up, Isabel. Look up.'

Men's heads. From ragged skin waved hair and beards, in place of lips were gaping grins and tatty lumps of flesh dangled from severed necks. People stared up, fascinated.

'Friends of your brother,' whispered Sir William into Isabel's hair. 'On the left, Catesby. On the right, Percy. Traitors. Murderers. Friends of your brother killed in a squalid shoot-out.'

Catesby. His breathing body, the top of his living head had been yards away from her when she'd crouched on the staircase at Cuddington. *Requiem aeternam dona eis, Domine; et lux perpetua luceat eis* . . . She looked again at the head on the pole and thought of the sharp stake piercing soft tissue inside the throat. She saw her priest's clear eyes and sloping forehead. Her own neck ached and her knees shook beneath the hoop of her skirts.

'They would have killed dozens in cold blood,' said Sir William. 'I wanted you to see them. Your Catholic heroes. Catesby.' The name was a curse. 'And these were the cowardly ones, these heroes, gunned down where they stood, thereby avoiding trial and a traitor's death. Some heroes. In case you're wondering, by the way, they boil the heads in salt and cumin to preserve them and discourage the seagulls.'

She said not a word but made herself gaze on and on at the heads, dizzily trying to flesh them out with eyes that blinked and mouths that spoke, until in the end her father had to pull her away.

The Stanhope town-house was in the airy suburb of Hoxton. Though much smaller than Cuddington it had many floors linked by staircases which groaned when servants ran up and down. The rooms were low-ceilinged but very stylishly furnished. All was clean, warm and fragrant.

Sir William insisted that Isabel should dine with him so Margaret laced her into a bodice so pointed that the flesh of her upper thighs was bruised whenever she sat down. In the glass was reflected a girl with a white neck and glittering eyes, hair flowing in gold ribbons down her shoulders.

The evening felt wavery and disordered because there were no prayers. Nobody here thought about God or pleaded with the saints waiting in patient ranks to intercede for suffering mortals.

At table she sat on her father's right, stared at a breast of partridge and saw discoloured flesh hanging from a dead man's cheek. Catesby. Sir William had no such qualms but ate a substantial dinner and afterwards sank into a deeply cushioned chair, his long-lipped face very handsome in the firelight. 'Goodnight, my dearest child.'

Isabel curtseyed over his fingers. 'Might I visit my mother tomorrow?' she asked.

Sir William's smile grew more fixed. 'Ah, now. I very much doubt if your mother will be receiving visitors just at present.'

'What about Robin? Where is he?'

'Do you know I'm not sure, Isabel. I'll tell you as soon as I find out.'

'Father, what else has happened? Did they find any of the other men they were looking for?'

'Were there others, Isabel? Whom do you mean exactly?'

She made for the door.

'Isabel. I hope you will be very happy in London. We must be everything to each other, you and I. All my hopes now rest with you. Don't you disappoint me.'

Chapter 6

Isabel was kept under close guard but hers was a prison of too much occupation and luxury rather than too little. Sumptuous meals were served, especially on fast days, she shared a downy bed with Margaret Westward and was dressed in elaborate gowns. Time was filled with meaningless activity; walks down the brick paths in the walled garden or the dull main street of Hoxton, embroidery, painting, harpsichord playing, poetry reading and French speaking. She was never alone.

Her warden, pernickety Margaret Westward, was rarely still or silent. Even while reading she kept up a running commentary and some of her affectations irritated her charge's nerves like the scrape of a fingernail on rough wood. One day Isabel cried: 'Margaret, how can you stand being cooped up with me night and day? Don't you get tired of it? Wouldn't you love to be alone?'

Margaret's lips curled up into a perfect semi-circle and her brows arched higher. 'I have never been happier.'

The shock of change overwhelmed Isabel. There was no one to comfort her or bring news. The servants had been ordered not to gossip, Margaret pleaded ignorance and Sir William, who was in any case scarcely home, never let slip a word of what had become of his wife or son.

Isabel wrote to her grandmother and even Susannah begging for news but there was no reply and she suspected her letters were opened and destroyed. She searched every face in Hoxton for a sign. Surely grandmother wouldn't desert her.

At first despair made her passive. Hour after hour tears

seeped between her eyelids and on to her needlework. When Margaret patted her hand she snatched it away. She refused to eat in the hope that someone would take pity on her and tell her what she wanted to know, but instead had to endure Margaret's unwelcome advice that the Hoxton water must have affected her stomach and she should eat no food at all until it had settled. Isabel's next ploy was to stay awake at night pacing up and down but Margaret lay with her little mouth half open, every exhalation a miniature snore, oblivious unless her charge tried to leave the room. Finally Isabel grew so weak from lack of sleep and food that the floors seemed to ripple. Angry, unanswered prayers pounded inside her skull.

In mid-December Margaret brought her a white silk bodice to embroider, the design already pricked out on the delicate fabric with a pin. Chains of gold thread were to be intertwined along the point of the deep V and crimson roses worked under the breast.

Out of pique at being given such a finicky task Isabel stabbed her finger and smeared blood on the crisp silk. Close to the fire Margaret sat at a tapestry frame, her little fingers flying across the canvas. She was sewing a cushion for Sir William inspired by the fleury cross on the Stanhope crest. At the end of a set of stitches she paused, gave the work an approving stroke and murmured: 'It's taking shape, yes it's taking shape don't you think, Isabel?'

There was an illusion of calm in the room and of a feminine, rustling warmth.

In the garden outside shrubs were petrified under a light frost. Beyond the high wall Isabel could see fields peppered with windmills and in the distance a random punctuation of church towers above the smoky mass of the city. Four turrets of the White Tower marked the river embankment. Margaret, who had spent quarter of an hour recounting the symptoms of a slight chill, for the moment had fallen blessedly silent. A log on the fire shifted and collapsed.

Isabel relaxed the tight grip of her fingers on the creased fabric. Gold thread glinted across her palm and in her lap the bodice unfolded to reveal a skein of red silk. Suddenly she was reminded of the spring flowers on the canopy above her mother's bed at Cuddington and of Martha Canton's careful needle-work in the panelled parlour at Oakshott.

She took a deep breath, then another. A life-line had been dangling within reach all the time, the fine, strong cord binding her to Thomasina, Martha Canton, Lucy Morton and all the other women who had spent years sewing in quiet rooms. In their hearts and in snatched hours between domestic duty they had lived quite different lives, subversive, devoted and passionate.

Isabel looked up and saw the White Tower again and the churches. The interiors may have been destroyed by greedy Protestant hands but the soaring spires still stood as memorials to a Catholic past. Within the walls of the Tower a host of Catholics had been interrogated and condemned, among them Edmund Campion and brave Father Gerard who had managed to escape by lowering himself from a high window and swinging along a rope, despite the pain in his tortured arms. Meanwhile in the jumble of London streets to the west a small army of Catholics was in hiding. It was said that Father Garnet rented several safe houses in London for his priests. Was it likely they had all stopped working and praying just because of yet another failed plot to kill the king? Would Anne Winshawe or Anne Vaux have sat weeping all these weeks while their friends suffered? Certainly not.

Isabel's stitches became ever longer and more slap-dash. It wasn't too late. First she would befriend Margaret. Easy enough to win favour with her surely, just by entering into discussion about health, fashion or poetry. And there was nothing to be gained by infuriating her father with sulks and rages. If she became a loving and dutiful daughter he in turn might soften and allow a visit to her mother.

That night Isabel began the second phase of this new campaign. When she was sure Margaret was asleep she eased herself out of bed and knelt on the bare boards. Using the knots of lace in the cuff of her night-gown as a make-shift rosary she began a long night of devotion. The occasional rumble of a cart outside, the shifting of timbers and Margaret's noisy breathing were blotted out. It was like climbing back into the womb, for these prayers had been part of her life since conception and were her passwords to another world. She could be quite sure that in their cells in the Tower, in cramped priest holes or secluded rooms in country houses her friends would also be at worship.

When she at last returned to bed the earliest birds were whistling their long winter calls and the lane outside was shaken by heavy traffic bound for London markets.

Even Susannah would have been impressed by my prayers tonight, was Isabel's last reflection, and she was too tired to reproach herself for the unworthy thought.

Isabel soon realized that there was a heavy price to pay for her sullen behaviour. The servants she had slighted or ignored during the past weeks were not easily won over. After days of kindness and coaxing, however, they became more forthcoming and as it turned out were only too glad to find a sympathetic ear. Sir William was mean with money, especially since his wife's involvement in the Powder Plot. At court people were treating him warily, his career had suffered a setback and he hated to be overlooked. Meanwhile, murmured Isabel's maid, he must endure the humiliation of having his son fester in the Clink. 'Oh – didn't you know he was in the Clink, Mistress Isabel? Perhaps I shouldn't have told you. It's the prison in Southwark. Terrible, terrible place.'

Margaret was a woman who could keep a secret only while no one else had let it slip. Once it was out she had to prove herself the holder of privileged information. 'Oh yes, your poor brother Robin's been in the Clink from the first. He's not considered a high-risk prisoner, you see, like Guido Fawkes or Everard Digby who's in the Tower. Dreadful business. What upsets me is that Sir Digby was such a favourite with the king, yet would happily have murdered him in cold blood.'

'Which others are in the Tower?' They were embroidering again. In the wintry light Isabel could scarcely see to re-thread the needle and across Spital Fields the four cupolas on the White Tower were only faintly visible.

'Oh, all those dreadful men. Rookwood, Winter, Grant. All those.'

'No priests?'

She was shot an unexpectedly sharp glance. 'Which priests are you thinking of?'

There was a long pause while Isabel diligently worked a row of chain stitch. 'At least my poor mother's not in the Tower then?'

'Oh, good Lord, no. They wouldn't put Lady Stanhope in a prison.' Here Margaret pressed her lips together and put her finger to them as if to say naughty Margaret for letting slip so much.

When they first came to London Sir William had tried to buy Isabel's goodwill with gifts of coins for lace, song-sheets or gloves. She at least had the sense to keep the money. One morning in January she tied on her thick riding cloak, pushed her feet into cork over-shoes and announced to Margaret that she planned an expedition to town. Margaret, who disliked the outdoors, protested at length and spent nearly twenty minutes getting ready. Her hair had to be loosened, combed and tucked under a silk hood, the hem of her gown must be looped up and tiny leather gloves fastened, thirty-six buttons in all. Meanwhile Isabel sat at the window, watched low billows of cloud roll across the city and tried to quieten the pounding of her heart.

If it is your will, my dearest Lord, let me see my brother today.

'Sir William would not want me to take you beyond Hoxton. He said Hoxton only. It's not at all like you, Isabel, to go rushing off into the city. You say you want ribbons. Well what colour? I have a box of ribbons, very pretty ones. It's a risk, you see. Neither of us knows London at all. I thought we might have read Sir Philip Sidney today.'

Isabel fixed a calm smile on her lips and crossed to the

door so Margaret had no choice but to follow. The pair clopped down the polished staircase and out into the morning.

A male servant went with them each time they left the house. Today it was the turn of Michael Latham who had been in Sir William's service for years and known Isabel since babyhood. His desire to please her was painful. Poor Michael, I'm afraid you have become my pawn today, she thought. Please forgive me.

Hoxton had few shops and Isabel's wish to stray a little way along the flat, mucky road across Spital Fields was quite understandable. Frost had hardened the mud underfoot but a cruel wind blew from the east. Isabel, conscious of Margaret's extreme reluctance, gripped the edges of her cloak and prayed.

The conflict between obedience to her father and duty to her faith was acute. And how could she be sure that she acted not from a rash craving for adventure but out of a high-minded desire to further the Catholic cause? She was determined to see Robin because it was the only thing left for her to do. He must be her link to the old life, the summer friends who had all been snuffed into darkness by the Powder Plot. Perhaps by taking Robin's hand she would leap across the void between the glossy surface life in Hoxton and the murky underbelly of Catholic sedition.

But she felt precarious and utterly alone. Her usual guides, the Virgin Mary and St Winifred, were not much help. It was hard to imagine scarred Winifred shouldering her way through a London crowd, stepping aside to avoid dogs and chickens or fingering lengths of lace to keep up the pretence of a shopping expedition.

Isabel had not been among crowds for several weeks. Hoxton was a gentrified village where nobody hurried much but beyond Spital Fields on the other side of Bishops Gate was an urban world where a multitude of feet churned the path and bodies barged past clad in bunched skirts and torn breeches, with mud-caked legs and matted hair. There was a potent mix of smells and noises: new wood from a building site, poultry, bread, rotting vegetables, excrement; the soft

thud of hooves and the rattle of a carriage, the sudden reek
and heat of a pair of sweating horses; a hundred voices,
dogs barking, the rhythmic thump of a hammer. The hem
of Isabel's cloak snagged in the mud and she jolted it up. Her
feet ached in the rigid over-shoes which gave her a stilted
gait and strained the muscles at the base of her spine.

'Haven't we gone far enough?' wailed Margaret. 'Surely
you can buy anything you want here.'

'No, a little further.'

Michael Latham walked with the dogged stamina of a
Londoner, elbowing a path along the driest portion of the
cobbles, ducking under props and rafters or peering with
vague curiosity into a dark interior. 'What exactly are you
looking for?' he asked Isabel.

She stood in the shelter of a doorway and straightened her
back. Above her head was the crazy overhang of the house
above. If she reached up her hand she would touch somebody's floor. 'I'm looking for the Clink. I'm going to visit my
brother.'

Ignoring Margaret's horrified gasp she looked Michael in
the eye. He was square-jawed and had far-seeing eyes, more
like a sailor or farmer than a London servant. She was sorry
for him because his eagerness was instantly replaced by anxious obstinacy. 'Oh, I can't take you there, Mistress Isabel.
Not without permission from your father. Besides, it's much
too far.'

'If you don't take me I shall go by myself.'

'We'll ask your father tonight. How about that?'

They were in somebody's way so she moved along the
street a little. From a yard nearby came the chink of metal
and the blaze of a blacksmith's fire. Isabel wished she could
curl up close to its brightness and watch the sparks fly.

'My father will never let me visit Robin so I'm afraid I
must go today.'

She made herself into a tight little nut of determination,
strong enough to withstand the coming argument. Don't
think ahead to the problem of gaining access to the prison
or what your father will say when he finds out, she told
herself. Don't consider the pain you are causing this good

man, Michael Latham. Think about Robin and what you need to learn from him.

There followed a tense argument between troubled Michael and spoilt Mistress Isabel. By the time it was over Margaret was weeping. 'You can't possibly . . . Oh, if I'd known . . . I'll be sent home.' Then they were walking towards London Bridge, led by the unhappy Michael whose thin hair blew wispily out from under his hat. Short of carrying headstrong Mistress Isabel home under his arm or abandoning her, what could a loyal servant do but stay close? Next Isabel, brisk and light-footed despite her sore back. Margaret brought up the rear, whimpering and holding on to her skirts.

Last night Isabel had crept down to Sir William's parlour and traced the route to London Bridge on a plan of the city that hung over the mantel. It had seemed straightforward enough but now was endless. There were so many carts and stalls blocking their way, so many side-passages and sharp twists. Down Bishops Gate Street they went and by Leadenhall Market. Margaret tried a new ploy of loitering and browsing in the hope that Isabel would lose heart. 'Oh, Isabel, why don't we just take a look in here? Aren't you tempted?' But Isabel had not spent six months with her grandmother for nothing. She stood with folded hands and a polite smile waiting until her little party was ready to move on.

In Gracechurch Street even Margaret picked up speed past heaps of rotting fish and then at last they came to the arch of a church called St Magnus the Martyr which had been clearly marked on Sir William's etching close to the Thames.

St Magnus, pray for me.

Beyond the churchyard there was the damp stink of filthy water and seagulls screeched overhead, reminding Isabel suddenly of Holywell and that shining glimpse of the estuary. Then they were up on to the bridge, plunging under archways into a rank passage between overhanging house-fronts, briefly out into the open and a snatch of the river where hundreds of little boats jostled, into darkness again and a sudden, sickening smell from the south gateway where poles topped with gaping heads spurted from the roof at crazy angles. 'Oh no, no no, I can't bear it, I can't take any more of this,' moaned Margaret.

Isabel, in no mood for sentiment, walked by with scarcely a glance. Anyway, they're unlikely to be Catholics, she thought, just ordinary criminals.

The Clink lay west of St Mary Overy's church which was a soaring swan among the dirty little lanes of Southwark. Once through the graveyard they had to shuffle along between tumbling shacks where dirt oozed over cobbles and doorways were crowded with blank-eyed women. Isabel became conscious for the first time of her expensive cloak and gown. It was beginning to dawn on her how little she knew about anything.

Here was Mistress Isabel with shoes so dainty they couldn't be allowed to touch the ground, while these other women stood about in bare feet or gaping boots. Mistress Isabel might well be broken-hearted by the imprisonment of her mother but here surely death and violence must happen regularly. Who cared for the souls of all these?

By now Margaret was so overcome that she could barely manage the odd, feeble sigh.

Winchester House might once have been a great palace but its high walls were intimidating rather than grand. The Clink, set deep under their overhang, was hemmed in on all sides by timber and brick. There was an arched entrance with heavy oak doors and on one side at foot level a barred, unglazed window. A listless crowd had gathered as if out of habit. Little interest was shown in Isabel who marched straight up and hammered on the door.

Latham set her firmly aside when the warden came. 'Give me your purse. Mistress Isabel Stanhope,' he announced, 'come to see her brother.'

Anything, it seemed, could be bought here. Margaret could be sat by a fire in the warden's lodgings while Isabel, for a larger fee, could be taken to see her brother though a letter from someone in authority would normally have been expected. Yes, she would even be allowed to talk with him in private. The whole negotiation cost five shillings.

The calm voice in Isabel's head that had directed the expedition thus far spoke words of reassurance. Nothing can touch you here, Isabel. In an hour you will walk free.

She remembered, as she penetrated deeper into the Clink behind the warden's upheld lantern, her bedroom in Hoxton with its bright fire, cleanish water in a white jug, crisp sheets and perfumed air. Much of what she had expected was here; the dark and cold, the flat, miserable voices and even the occasional dragging of a metal chain. What she was not prepared for was the terrible smell of enclosure, the stillness of some of the prisoners, the bitterness of others. The darkness was full of eyes and underfoot were dreadful softnesses that might have been bundles of clothes, bandaged limbs or worse. She had expected dirt but not the filth of decaying bodies and air breathed in and out, in and out by the same hopeless human flesh. Some of these people would never see the sun again.

Sir Robin Stanhope was housed above ground in a room with glass in the tiny barred window and a small fire. It was relatively clean and sweet smelling though the floor was bare and the room below could be glimpsed through cracks in the boards. There was even a view across the narrow street to a warehouse which blotted out the river. But when Isabel embraced him his body smelt wrong, tired and unwashed, very different to the outdoor Robin she remembered.

He seemed neither surprised nor pleased to see her. Prison had not dampened his restlessness or made him any less self-centred. For a while he would not sit down but paced up and down, shifting his shoulders under a worn brown doublet which he wore unhooked. He was much thinner and his eyes burned above hollowed cheeks. He ought to be pleased with his reflection, thought Isabel. Never has he looked so romantic.

'Have you brought me oranges?' was his first question.

'No. I haven't. I've brought nothing but this letter from our cousin Susannah Thewing. She gave it me when I left Oakshott.'

'I sent a message to father for oranges.'

'Father doesn't know I'm here.'

Instead of praising her boldness he clasped her upper arms for a moment and hissed: 'Is there news?'

'I know nothing. That's why I came.' She had said the right thing. Suddenly he hugged her again and for a moment there was the old delusion that he had some affection for her. The embrace was so unexpected and so welcome after many loveless weeks that she started to cry. Robin warmed still further and played the older brother by settling her by the fire and pouring wine.

'Prison must be a shock to you, Izzie, but of course I'm used to it now. And I comfort myself by thinking of all the great men who have been here before me. You know, at least twenty of us in here are Catholic. We can hear mass once a week and pray together every day. It's like a holiday.' He had the knack of always making her feel disadvantaged.

Isabel's tears were almost dry but she made a great fuss of mopping her eyes so she could watch him over the lace edge of her handkerchief. He seemed almost happy. Perhaps as a prisoner he could plot and dream of being a hero unchallenged. She recognized the blaze of enthusiasm in his eye, the eager smile and low, passionate voice. This was sparky old Robin, the obsessive sword-fighter who could never give up, even when he was losing.

'Catesby is dead,' he said. 'Robert Catesby. A quick, heroic death from a single shot. How completely right for him. Catesby. I can't believe he's dead. You never met him, did you? If you'd seen him, Izzie, you'd not forget him. I never laughed so much as with him. He made you feel as if there was brilliance in each moment, as if life was brimful of excitement. He could have done anything. It's hard to bear his death. We were so close. He was like a brother.'

Isabel, whose memory of Catesby was of a par-boiled head on a pole, found her sympathy fading rapidly. 'It's said his plot was doomed from the start, yet because of it priests are being hounded simply for existing and it looks as if they'll clamp down even harder on Catholics. Well done, Catesby. And don't you think he's a lot better off than his friends in the Tower? I'd rather be shot quickly than executed, wouldn't you?'

'His death was holy. When he died his lips were resting on a picture of the Virgin Mary.'

'I wonder how he managed that,' said Isabel unkindly.

'Everard Digby and the rest will be just as glad to die for such a cause. But you know they won't just hang, Izzie. These Protestants are monsters and treat them as traitors. Do you realize what they do to a Catholic they find guilty of treason? First he's hung, but not quite enough to lose consciousness. Then he's cut down, laid on the block and castrated. You will have no idea of the agony, Isabel. They wish to destroy his manhood, you see, to show that his chance of fathering Catholic children is gone for ever. Next they hack out his heart, dwelling of the soul, and the organs are burnt on a fire that's been lit before the victim's eyes. Finally the body is chopped into quarters and sent to four corners of England to be displayed as an example. Such is the compassion of Protestants.' Was there gloomy envy in Robin's tone?

'And what about their wives and children? Should the conspirators not have thought about them before they started on this wild scheme? Think of poor Lady Mary Digby and her two little boys.'

'Isabel. We can't consider human love.' He put the tip of his finger on Susannah's letter and twirled it round. 'We're asked to give up everything. Everard made his sacrifice willingly. *Justorum animae in manu Dei sunt, et non tanget illos tormentum malitiae . . . Exsultabunt sancti in gloria.* The souls of the just are in the hand of God, and the torment of malice shall not touch them. They say he'll die on 30th January. I'll be praying for him.'

Isabel did not like him spouting Latin so glibly, nor translating for her. It may well be, she thought, that Digby and the others will rest joyfully in heaven but what about the chaos they have left behind for us to deal with?

'Hung, drawn and quartered,' said Robin. 'A traitor's death. Traitor or martyr? Which? Martyr, martyr. And you know what I keep telling myself? Digby is dying for me. Did you know that he only heard the full details of the plot about a fortnight beforehand? I think if he'd refused to join Catesby

I would have been the thirteenth conspirator. It could have been me. As it was, I knew something was going to happen. I knew I had to have horses ready but I was never sure why.' He beat his fingers on the stone sill, a petulant boy left out of the game.

I know why they didn't include you, Isabel thought, you're wild and desperate like Catesby, but I believe you would squeal at the first hint of pain. And Digby had money, lots of it, while father keeps you penniless. Catesby needed cash. 'I suppose you know mother is a prisoner because of you.'

They spoke so low that to a listener their voices would have been drowned by the lick of flames in the hearth and the unhappy cries and murmurs from the prison below. 'Not in prison. She's lodged with some alderman near Westminster. Don't worry, Isabel, I'm able to keep abreast of everything that happens. We use the juice of oranges and lemons to write to each other. Invisible ink.'

'Is there nothing you could do that would help free her?'

'I pray, Isabel. I pray.'

'You must do more. You are responsible. How can you bear to think of her locked up for your sake?'

He shook his head and looked at her pityingly. 'Hush, hush, Isabel. You should learn patience like the rest of us. Mother knew what might happen. She'll be at peace.'

Isabel squeezed the handkerchief tight in her hand. 'Father Garnet, what happened to him?'

'Not taken.'

'The others?'

'Some priests. None I know well, thank God.'

'The priest they call Father Peter Carisbroke?'

'Him. He won't get caught. He's like Gerard, an old hand. He knows every hiding place from here to the Scottish border. My God, these Jesuits. What a life they lead. I could have been a Jesuit.' Robin threw aside Susannah's letter and gathered up Isabel's clenched fingers. 'Izzie, stay strong. We need you. Keep praying. Ours is a glorious cause. Try not to be sad.'

'I am sad. All this seems a terrible waste of men's lives.'

'Father's got to you. I knew he would.'

'He has not. I thought it out for myself. Catesby was playing a game.'

'You forget that the difference between success and failure is a hair's breadth. If we'd succeeded we would be heroes now.'

From somewhere he had acquired a gold crucifix and a set of rosary beads fashioned out of hardened citrus peel. He made her kneel down and pray with him though she was cold as ice, despising his relish of secret letters and hopeless conspiracies.

Before leaving she kissed his cheek and whispered: 'Please, Robin. If you reply to Susannah, tell her where I am. I am not allowed to send letters but I do so want to be kept informed. I must do something to free our mother.' But she knew that this plea had fallen on deaf ears. Robin would never include little sister Isabel in his distorted world.

Released from the Clink she ran gasping into daylight and breathed with joy the choking fog of wood-smoke that hung in the little alley leading down to the river. It was low tide and traffic was confined to a channel between muddy beaches strewn with debris.

For the first time in days the sun had emerged and was sinking low. Isabel imagined a long gallop home with her mother across the flat green fields of Cuddington. How could anyone be willing to give up their life for a man called Catesby and a half-baked plot?

Or was the sunset the eye of God smiling encouragement on the prisoners in the Tower?

Chapter 7

By dark everyone in the Hoxton house knew that Mistress Isabel had been to visit Robin and the servants avoided her as if she were infected by plague. Margaret had buckets of scalding water brought up and insisted that she and Isabel scrub themselves from head to toe. She then lay prostrate declaring that the day's experiences had destroyed her and thanks to Isabel she would be sent away. Isabel sat by the fire and awaited punishment. Sir William didn't come.

Next morning she stitched at yet another bodice while Margaret languished fully dressed on the bed. At noon Sir William was heard at last in the hall and a few minutes later the quaking Margaret was summoned, soon to reappear in much higher spirits with the news that Isabel, fortunate girl, was to be taken by her father to see the Twelfth Night masque at Whitehall.

The timing of this outing was so strange that Isabel was left reeling. She had braced herself for blame and outrage but was now to face a very different ordeal. A masque at court. It seemed that her father expected her to mix with Protestants who had locked up her mother and would soon execute Everard Digby.

She hadn't worn a farthingale for days but now her body was encased in steel bands and a long busk thrust into the front of the corset to flatten her chest. Layer upon layer of petticoat, cold as snow, fell over the metal hoops then yards of satin skirt were pleated and the folds pinned in place one by one. The white silk bodice, unwillingly embroidered by Isabel with roses, was laced so tightly that her lungs seemed to stick to her ribs. She was faint with exhaustion by the time the laborious process was finished.

And yet she couldn't resist glancing in the mirror at the crease between her breasts forced by the new bodice. A jewelled band, worn once by Thomasina, was fastened in her floating hair and a small white ruff tied round her neck to frame her jaw and tickle her chin.

Sir William handed her into the carriage and travelled inside with her. She flinched at his touch and avoided his eye but no mention was made of the Clink. He was dapper in gold quilted silk, padded, buttoned and knotted so elaborately that there was no reaching him.

At Whitehall Isabel's mind ticked bright and clear under a dreamy view of herself in a fantastic palace, head held high, beaded slippers pushing at the hem of the white gown, tragic Mistress Isabel. Here it was crowded like yesterday under Bishops Gate but this time people were slow-moving; there was a murmur of cultured voices; the flow and tilt of voluminous gowns; the gleam of pearl droplets, broad white foreheads and the fuzz of hair and beards; lace, satin, bulging sleeves; high-pitched laughter; slippered feet on shallow steps; soaring ceilings painted with more plump, smiling faces and bare flesh; cold oval eyes; the brush of a moustache on Isabel's fingers, the dip of her own curtsey and the friction of her clothes.

Sir William had timed their arrival so that he had only minutes to wait for the king. When James made his entrance Isabel saw an unremarkable man with hunched shoulders and a wary face quenched by showy clothes. If Catesby had his way, she thought, that man would be dead.

Hymenai, written to celebrate the marriage of the Earl of Essex, was so extraordinary that other preoccupations were driven from Isabel's head. Even God was crowded into a corner. Every element of the masque was unexpected. Music was discordant, dance disorganized, costume diaphanous, poetry an odd mix of rhetoric and lyricism. Actors emerged like magic from a revolving globe, smoke billowed and the characters of Hercules and Atlas appeared in the flesh. It was like being fed a meal that bloated the eyes, ears and brain.

'So may their ardors last, So either's strength outlive . . .'

The masque was nearly over and Isabel could have wept for sorrow at seeing a lovely bubble burst.

> *'All loss that age can give,*
> *And though full years be told,*
> *Their forms grow slowly old.'*

But there, it was already gone, leaving her limp with anti-climax and self-loathing because she had sunk like a thoughtless babe into the charm of a play. The surging mass of courtiers now seemed disgraceful, seduced like her by a cheap drama. Where was her determination to be vigilant, her desire to make every moment an offering to God?

Isabel, she scolded, you're as frivolous and changeable as a heretic.

'I've been watching you, Mistress Isabel, and I think you rather enjoyed our masque.' A young head bowed low over her hand, clean, nut-brown hair resting on a ruff of starched lawn.

'Isabel, may I present your second cousin, Francis Bourne.' Sir William stood at the young man's elbow and smiled on Isabel with unusual warmth.

Bourne kissed her fingers; Isabel dropped a curtsey and was prodded in the thigh by the point of her bodice. She straightened her knees, staggering under the weight of farthingale and embroidered satin. Here, produced from nowhere, was her intended bridegroom, the much heralded second cousin. So this was the reason for tonight's outing.

'I did quite like the play,' she said coolly.

'Oh, faint praise, Mistress Isabel.' Bourne laughed a little too loudly, showing good teeth. 'Tell me what you really thought.' He tilted his head to listen more carefully as if she were the only person of importance in the room. A strand of feathery hair fell over his pale ear.

'I thought it poetic and I loved the costumes. But I didn't like myself for enjoying it. In all the three hours I learned nothing that mattered.'

'Ah, so you share your father's desire to find the proper

value of things. But Mistress Isabel, theatre can't be judged simply by what you think you've seen.'

'Why not?' She was rather confused by the attention both Francis Bourne and her father gave every word and found her new cousin's features hard to read. First she saw one thing clearly then another which didn't quite match. He seemed open but his face was full of angles, the eyes light blue and rather close-set, merry but underneath watchful. His mouth was generous when he smiled but disappeared inside his beard when he was serious. And she wasn't sure of his voice which had an extra layer, almost as if he were reciting someone else's words.

'Let's not concern ourselves with masques for a moment. I don't count masques. Too much amateur acting and obsession with machines. Not that I don't care about machines because I do. I love them. No, I mean real theatre. Have you ever been to a real play, Mistress Isabel?'

'I don't think so.'

'What are you thinking of, Sir William? Your daughter's education has been sadly lacking.' Her father grunted and Isabel saw that his eyes had glazed. Francis Bourne was certainly a brave young man to scold her father even in jest. 'The real theatre for me is all that matters in life. Don't you think poetry and performance are a celebration of the best in us?'

She was fascinated by his mouth that spoke with great energy, revealing the glisten of those fine teeth. He was sure of himself, almost like a priest. Her smile faded. He is wrong, she thought. What is the point of a play? All the hours spent on that masque, all the words written and learnt, the music, the dancing, should have been directed to God.

'Mistress Isabel?' Again he ducked his head to take a closer look at her face. This time she turned her head to one side and wouldn't meet his eye. Her father, she noticed, was already deep in conversation with someone else. 'My one ambition is to write for the stage although of course I've considered many other possible careers. My interests are varied, actually. Navigation – ask me any question you like on that subject, I'm an expert. Painting. Alchemy. Now there's a thing. What do you think, Mistress Isabel? I believe there's certainly proof that any substance can change into something else. Look at a caterpillar, look at water and ice or rust on metal. I spent a lot of time experimenting when I was a student. But I always come back to the theatre in the end because in a play we can show what we are. Theatre grips me more than anything. I've written play after play but nobody takes them on. I would even pay to have one produced. I've offered to act the lead myself and provide an audience. At Oxford my fellow students used to perform the odd scene but since then, nothing. What do you suppose I'm doing wrong?'

She couldn't help laughing. He had a way of lifting one eyebrow and twinkling at her that was unlike her usual treatment by young men; Robin, her Thewing cousins and of course all the priests she had ever known including Father Carisbroke.

'I think it could be that they're too long,' he added. 'Usually four hours' running time. Too many characters. I can never get my cast less than forty. And verse is tricky, making it scan, finding the right words.'

By now she was laughing so much that her ribs struck her busk. Her father glanced across and looked gratified.

'Minor problems,' Bourne said, waving an airy hand. 'Why do you laugh? You see, I comfort myself by the knowledge that when you're as hopeless as me, you can only get better.'

'I don't see how you can fail, Mr Bourne, if you're so determined.'

Bourne's lips were so close to her ear that she could smell a musky fragrance in his beard. 'I am determined, yes, and I understand that you also number determination among your many excellent qualities, Mistress Isabel. I think you are very brave but very sad. Take care, my dear cousin.'

'I don't understand.'

'You must be patient, Mistress Isabel. All will come right in time.' But they were suddenly surrounded by other young men and with a further light kiss on her hand Francis melted away, as if he had been only the dream of a cousin. In his

94

place came Sir William with his unfocused smile. Isabel felt the heavy grip of his hand through the silk of her sleeve.

On the homeward journey leather curtains were drawn across the windows of Sir William's carriage to blot out the frosty January night. The interior was stone cold and with every lurch the curtains swayed aside and moonlight flashed in. Sir William's face appeared and disappeared in the gloom, his skin grey, his eyes fixed on some point above Isabel's head. He seemed calm, even sleepy and she could hear his steady breathing when the horses halted for a moment.

Francis Bourne flickered in her mind's eye like an image from the masque. She could grasp only an elusive impression of him; the intense blue of his doublet, an elegant hand, a laugh and a warning. All her life he had been a threat, the future mapped out by her father. Now he was flesh and blood. One moment he had seemed frivolous, the next too solemn. And he had known more about her than he should.

Sir William leaned forward and placed his hand on Isabel's knee. The pressure of his fingers sank through the many layers of cloth. Her body ached from the long walk yesterday, hours of nocturnal prayer and the effort of being held taut inside the farthingale. She had to brace herself to each jolt of the carriage.

'Do you remember what I told you once about Francis Bourne, Isabel? When I die, if neither you or Robin lives to bear children, that young man will inherit everything I possess.'

He gripped her thigh so tightly that his hand slid over the flimsy fabrics of her gown and was hooked by a steel hoop. There was alcohol on his breath and his clothes smelt of the court; perfume, polish, the crush of hot human flesh.

After a moment he released her and sank back on his seat. His voice was light and low as he repeated Bourne's question. 'What did you think of the masque, Isabel?'

'I liked it, father.'

'No you didn't. You despised it. You thought it frivolous and worldly. I heard what you said to him. You looked at the audience and decided you were superior to everyone else there.'

'No.'

'Because you are like your mother. I see her in you. That witch.'

Her attention had drifted away from him but she awoke abruptly to the realization that she was in danger. Stanhope's hatred for Thomasina was shocking. Crossing the carriage with a spring he sat beside Isabel so that his weight on her huge skirt pinned her to the seat. His hand came up and plucked at her face, pinching the flesh of her cheek between thumb and finger. 'Where did you go yesterday?'

'I'm sure you know. To the Clink to see my brother.'

'My God, I can trust no one, not even my daughter. They will take everything I possess. The penalties for what your mother and brother have done are crippling me already. They've stripped Cuddington. You saw. And they have begun to add up all the years she refused to go to church, let alone the masses that must have been said at Cuddington. Nobody will talk to me at court.'

'I'm sorry, father, but I thought you knew she was a practising Catholic and that secretly you sympathized.' Her lower eyelid was wrenched down by his thumb so that her eye was dry and sore.

'Sympathize. God help me, I loved her. I turned a blind eye thinking it would do no harm if she wanted to save her own soul and maybe mine. But now I see her in you. You're not sorry for my suffering. You would disobey me again tomorrow and the next day if you felt you had to. Let's try. Promise me you'll give it all up. Promise me, Isabel, that you'll forget all about being a Catholic and instead be an obedient daughter.'

'I shall try to be an obedient daughter, father.'

He released her cheek and instead cupped her burning face in his cold, scented fingers. His breath came and went on her chin and his eyes seemed sorrowful in the grey light. 'Yesterday they found and arrested Nicholas Owen, your Henry Garnet and two others. I wonder who these moles and parasites will betray under torture? What members of this family will have their names dragged again through the mire because they sheltered these men, heard mass or conspired with them to murder their king? Aren't you ashamed, Isabel, that our family name may be linked with theirs? Tell me you're sorry.'

Two others, he had said. Father Peter then. Was Father Peter taken? She touched her father's hand and whispered: 'What were the names of the two others they caught? Do you know?'

In the white light of premonition she saw what would happen. He slid his left hand down on to her throat to steady her head and drew back his right. The slap of his palm cracked across her ear and hurled her face against the carriage door. She got herself upright only in time to receive a second and third blow from his fist across her cheekbone and temple. Her neck couldn't support such violence and a ligament tore as her head swung sideways. For a moment she didn't know where she was or even if her head was still attached to her shoulders. When she put up her hands she expected her skull to crumble under her fingers.

Sir William returned to his seat opposite. Isabel sat absolutely still while pain surged in and out of her ears and her brain seemed to bleed inwardly to her neck. She couldn't see properly, only darkness.

Through the shattered fragments of her consciousness she heard him say: 'You are my only hope. I told you what I would do if you disobeyed me. This is your fault.'

They reached the house in Hoxton at last and Sir William jumped from the carriage, full of energetic concern for his daughter. 'Very tired . . . Help her upstairs.' Michael Latham's face loomed into view. She tried to warn him that her head would split apart if he lifted her but the words wouldn't reach her mouth and she was swinging through space while the candelabra in the hall swayed crazily, a portrait of Sir William fell towards her and a balustrade multiplied again and again.

'I'm so sick,' she murmured into Michael's arm and he quickened his pace.

Sir William was waiting at her bedroom door. She closed her eyes and felt the soft horizontal of her mattress rise up beneath her.

'You may be quite sure, Mistress Westward,' said her father, 'that my daughter will not be visiting her brother again.'

Chapter 8

For weeks after the masque Isabel lay in bed with piercing headaches and fits of dizziness. From her window she watched the sullen skies blown by a sour east wind and questioned the teaching that men were made in the image of God.

At the end of January Margaret confided that eight conspirators including Guido Fawkes and Everard Digby had been executed. During February she gave frequent bulletins about the progress of Garnet's interrogation in the Tower. In early March she brought news that he had at last admitted to knowing about the plot all along because he'd heard it through the confessional. 'Guilty, guilty of treason. He could have told the government about it but he chose not to,' cried Margaret, moistening the end of a length of silk between pursed lips. 'Oh, and did I tell you, Isabel, that another of those dreadful men is dead? Nicholas Owen. Thank God.'

Isabel bribed her maid and learned that Owen had died under torture, though he had neither admitted to being part of the plot nor given away the location of any hiding places. She kept a vigil for him but her prayers were swamped by rage with Catesby, the unrepentant Robin and even her priest who had given his blessing to a scheme that led to the horrible death of a holy and faithful man. Of all those on pilgrimage the previous summer, Owen had said least and prayed most.

Towards the end of April an invitation came for Mistress Margaret Westward and Mistress Isabel Stanhope to attend a small party at Fitzroy House. Since the widowed Lady Fitzroy was a close friend to the queen and moved at the very heart of London society, Sir William gave his consent with alacrity.

Isabel was decked out once more in her best ivory silk and when Margaret began her own finicky preparations, asked permission to walk in the garden. The skies had cleared at last and the wind dropped but Isabel shrank from the sweetness of the air and looked away from tender buds because she couldn't bear their innocence.

But she was not alone in the garden after all. Thomasina, with Sir William at her elbow, had suddenly emerged at the top of a flight of steps leading up to the house. Mother and daughter faced each other in the glare of sunlight, Isabel trapped within the immense skirts of her gown, Thomasina huddled in a dark cloak despite the heat of the afternoon.

'Your mother is on her way home to Cuddington,' said Sir William. 'I thought you would like to say goodbye.'

Isabel was already on her knees at her mother's feet. Thomasina's distant voice trickled through her hair. 'You are looking very grown up, Isabel. Almost a lady.'

Of course, she disapproves, thought Isabel. She assumes I'm happy to be dressed like this. Still holding her mother's hand she leaned forward to kiss her cheek. 'Mother, are you well?'

Though Thomasina's eyes were dull her skin was a good colour and she had gained some weight. 'I am. Thank you. Everyone has been as kind as possible.'

'Was it terrible to be locked up? Why have they let you out? I wanted to visit you. Did you get any of my letters?'

Thomasina's soft hands fluttered up to Isabel's face. Her fingers seemed to know where her daughter had been struck though the bruises had healed. Uncharacteristic tears brimmed in her green eyes. 'I wasn't locked up exactly. It was all very pleasant. House arrest. But I wasn't named by Father Garnet or anyone else, even under torture, so they have no reason to keep me.'

'Torture. Nonsense,' put in Sir William. 'Garnet was certainly not tortured. This is an humane government. He confessed of his own free will. These Jesuits. I notice his silence only lasted as long as there was a chance of the plot's success.

The silence of the confessional meant nothing to him once it was matter of saving his own skin. Garnet. Puppet of the Spanish.'

Thomasina said: 'I'm hoping your father will bring you home to Cuddington in the summer. I am banished from London, you see, as a condition of my release.'

'Can't I come with you now, mother?'

Thomasina put her mouth to Isabel's cheek in a long kiss. Her whisper was no more than a breath. 'I am so proud of my girl. You have been very brave.'

Margaret was hovering with Isabel's gloves. She dropped a succession of uncertain little curtseys to Lady Thomasina – how deferential should one be to a self-confessed enemy of the state, a practising Catholic? – deeper bobs to Sir William. 'Your lovely daughter . . . safe in my care . . . such a privilege . . . Don't you think, Sir William, Isabel and I ought to be gone?'

Isabel forced her fingers into the tight gloves while Thomasina stood motionless, as if still in her prison. Her power was all gone. She had brought no comfort to Isabel except an assurance of her love, which always had a patchy quality like sunshine among clouds.

The late Sir James Fitzroy had amassed a hefty fortune in the textile trade during the reign of Elizabeth and built a mansion opposite Arundel House, one of the sprawling palaces backing on to the river. Although the Fitzroy residence was on the less fashionable north side of the Strand, behind the gabled frontage was an imposing entrance hall and a white reception room graced by scantily clad statues. Isabel, with her head full of her mother, was bewildered by these opulent surroundings. Here was the same glittering assembly she had last encountered on the night of the masque, the same smiling mouths and calculating eyes.

Lady Arabella Fitzroy, widow of Sir James, was so be-ruffed that she could barely move her head which appeared to be perched, neck-less, on the frothy disc of starched lace.

She had an oval face, plucked hairline and sleepy eyes. The tapering fingers she raised for Isabel's kiss were limp. 'I think you will be a new star in our firmament, my darling child. You have your mother's brow.' Thomasina had been dangled within sight and snatched away. She must already be ten miles from London. How cruel of Lady Arabella to mention her.

A delicate index finger hooked Isabel's chin. 'Never droop,' said Lady Arabella. Her heavy lids sank as her languid gaze fell on Margaret Westward. 'Everyone talks about your exquisite needlework, Mistress Westward, and your appreciation of music so I have reserved you a place close to the harpsichord.'

Margaret was dazzled. Her lips were pressed tight to contain her pride and she shook her head and curtseyed, overwhelmed by this unexpected attention. After all, as she never ceased to tell Isabel, she was only a very poor relation of the Stanhopes. Her minute hand was tucked under Lady Fitzroy's stately arm and the two sailed off, a little rowing boat tugged by a great ship. 'Isabel, wait here. In a moment my niece, Blanche, will take care of you,' called Lady Fitzroy, tossing the words over her shoulder like crumbs to a sparrow.

Isabel was adrift in the great room, disorientated by the sudden flaring of candles lit one after another amidst fountains of cut glass. The harpsichord struck up with a trill of notes and Margaret was installed beside an elderly dowager in the first of several rows of seats.

'Isabel Stanhope? Come on.' The inaptly named Blanche had black hair and a bright, high-pitched voice. She walked with considerable determination up a shallow staircase over which hung portrait after portrait of Fitzroys present and past, the ladies holding tiny gloves, a little dog or a fan, the men more glamorous still with their pearl buttons and bejewelled daggers.

'An awesome crew,' said Blanche whose own wide-open eyes and brisk movements suggested that she would never stand still long enough to join the ranks of her ancestors on canvas. 'Sea-faring. Or rather, merchants. I can't imagine a Fitzroy ever setting foot on a boat.' She paused in front of a portly gentleman dressed in fur-trimmed robes and with a distinct air of resignation about the eyes. 'My uncle Sir James Fitzroy who built this house. Lady Arabella is one of the wealthiest widows in London. There's always a queue of suitors.' She swung her forceful gaze from Sir James to Isabel. 'You do realize why you're here?'

Before Isabel could answer her escort had marched on upwards to a low-ceilinged room furnished with a laden supper table. Up here the harpsichord was a mere trickle of sound and voices were muffled by deep casements and heavy panelling. 'Here we are. I think you know my great-aunt Lucy.'

Isabel put her hand to the door frame for the great-aunt was none other than Lucy Morton, last seen an eternity ago in the upper room at Coughton. 'Don't look so aghast, Isabel. Have I aged that much? Blanche, fetch us some wine. Isabel and I shall take a little walk together.'

Off they set, round the darkly panelled room with its two bay windows, through the next little ante-room to yet another parlour thronged with people, back across to the supper table, round and round, Isabel leaning on Lucy's stalwart arm and taking occasional sips from a glass of red wine.

'Lady Fitzroy is a church papist and you know what that means. Staunch Catholic but careful not to draw attention to herself. She trots off to church once in a blue moon and has sworn the Oath of Allegiance but underneath she's rock solid. Very helpful. All kinds of people meet here right under the nose of the court.'

They made another slow circumnavigation of the rooms. 'I have a message from your grandmother who has had a very hard time since November. She sends her love. Oakshott was ransacked but they found no priests, though of course some had been hiding there. Instead they arrested the tutor, Nicholas Turner, who's been in the Castle Prison ever since accused of teaching the Catechism.'

In another age Isabel had moved from prayer to prayer through the quiet passages of Oakshott fretting under the iron fist of her grandmother and the dubious intellect of Nicholas Turner. Now Lucy had brought them so close that

Isabel could see vividly her grandmother with folded arms and thin lips defying the pursuivants to ask the right questions. She could smell Turner's wet breath.

'What about my cousin Susannah?'

'Ah, now the Thewing family is to be all broken up, except of course that your Aunt Teresa will stay at Oakshott. Your cousin Alan is at school in York and to everyone's great joy has suddenly announced that he intends to enter a seminary in France or the Netherlands. His brother Edmund will arrive in London shortly. Lady Fitzroy has promised to introduce him to a friend in the wool trade. And Susannah? Your grandmother has scraped together just enough to send her abroad to St Omer. She expects to join the Poor Clares in a year or so.'

So Susannah was to withdraw into the haven of a contemplative convent and would beat Isabel once again on the path to perfection. One mention of her name and the sins of malice and envy piled up, just like old times.

'Isabel, your father let it be known that you unwisely drank Hoxton water and were taken ill but another, more worrying story is also in circulation. We couldn't write to you either way. Any letter might have been intercepted and made things worse for you or your mother. We have relied on you to stand firm. But there is a priest here today who'd like to speak to you. Will you see him?'

'I can't confess. I'm not ready.'

'Nevertheless. Sit here. Wait.'

In the window was a low carved bench with a cushion of dark blue velvet. At one end sat a young woman in a gown of reddish brown brocade, deep in conversation with Blanche Morton. The woman's face awoke a whisper in Isabel's memory. Where, where had she seen those attentive eyes before? Blanche had her back to Isabel but her small fingers gestured vigorously, her black hair was tossed backwards and her voice with its confident, fluting edge was quite penetrating. She appeared to be arguing with the lady who only smiled in response and then took Blanche's darting hand.

Meanwhile across the Strand in the courtyard of Arundel House the last of the afternoon's sunshine glossed the harness of a patient horse and a maid in a green apron stood dead centre on the cobbles surrounded by men who were laughing greedily and nudging closer. Isabel wondered how it must feel to be such a woman, an unthinking heretic, flirting in the sunlight.

To Isabel's left was a narrow door. After a few minutes a woman came out of it and Lucy Morton made a slight gesture to Isabel who rose and went into a narrow passage beyond. She heard the click of a latch behind her.

At the far end was a small room in which a further door, disguised by heavy panelling, had been left ajar. It opened on to a steep flight of steps and at the top there was a choice of two doors. Isabel pushed back the nearest.

She was standing within three yards of Father Peter Carisbroke.

At once she realized that the invitation to a party at Fitzroy House had led her here as surely as if they had knotted a thread round her neck and reeled her in. First had come the note so eagerly received by Sir William, then her mother's kiss in the Hoxton garden, the lazy authority in Lady Arabella's brown eyes, Blanche's casual friendliness and the surprise meeting with Lucy Morton.

'Isabel. You are like a small bird in my conscience. When I am at my most weak, you fly out of some dark corner.'

In the five months since she had seen Father Carisbroke the flesh had been sloughed from his face so that he was all sharp planes and polished bone. She was so shocked at the sight of him that the wine glass, clutched like a life-line, shook in her hand and splashed a red stain on her silk skirts.

The room was furnished as the bedroom of an upper servant. There was a bed, a table and under the window two plain chairs. A candle had been lit, for this was the darkest side of the house. Father Carisbroke's familiar breviary lay on the table. He took Isabel's hand and guided her to one of the chairs and they sat so close together that his knees touched the fullness of her gown.

Question after question tumbled through her head. How dare he come here, less than a mile from the Tower where the government would love to have him locked up. How had he hidden? Where had he been? Why hadn't anyone told her he was safe?

Carisbroke was an expert. He knew how to cup a girl's soul in the palm of his hand and turn it round and round, inside out. 'You're shocked and still recovering from terrible injury. Don't try too hard. Say what lies deepest. Take your time. God will give you the right words.'

He must be dying. How could a human frame live with so little flesh on the bones? His hands lay folded on his lap, the knuckles and finger joints yellow under thin skin, veins knotted over the concave brittleness of his wrist.

'A few square meals and I'll be right as rain,' he said. 'Lady Fitzroy will set me up.'

The minutes were spraying in all directions like sparks and still Isabel could find no words.

He took the glass from her tense fingers and set it on the table. Candlelight jumped across the smeared rim. 'I was like Lazarus leaping out of the tomb. For eleven days I lay in a priest hole so small I couldn't stand upright while they searched the house around me. One of the ladies of the house fed me warmed honey through a straw pushed between my hiding place and the kitchen. Since then I've been on the run. I was named, you see, because I knew about the plot. They want my blood. I don't fear death but I know I have more work to do first.'

She sprang across the room away from him. If you are going to put yourself in such danger, if I have to keep on and on tormenting myself about your safety, then I don't want you near me, she thought. I don't want the anguish of caring for you.

'No one will find you with me. Don't worry.' So now he believed she was afraid of being caught with him. If he knew that it was her reckless expedition to the Clink that had led to her father's punishment, how could he doubt her courage?

She found her voice at last. 'How can you be sure we're safe? Everyone seems to be watched by someone else. How did you and Lady Fitzroy know what my father had done?'

'Not many households are watertight, Isabel. Especially not your father's. You must trust me. I'm an expert on security or I wouldn't be alive. Now, would you like to make your confession?'

'I would not.' Her young voice struck the room with shocking emphasis, startling them both.

'I see.'

'I am not in a fit state.'

'Then there's a beginning.'

'Have you not, for one moment, had any doubts about what you gave your blessing to in the autumn?' Her words were pressed flat and hard, as if between two sheets of glass.

His face had the carved beauty of Christ on the cross, marked by suffering and certainty. 'Of course I have doubts, Isabel, but this is an ugly world sometimes and it is my job to save souls, by whatever means. I have watched good Catholic men and women lose their faith and descend into heresy almost without noticing. The secular pleasures of their neighbours and friends corrupt them and there aren't enough priests to protect them through the sacraments. I have to think of future generations and the health of the church. Catesby's plot failed and he is dead. Nicholas Owen died at the hands of his torturers. In three days Father Garnet will be killed though neither he nor Owen had any part in the plot, indeed tried to prevent it. I have lost friend after friend. But you see, in some ways I think we didn't fail. We have forced people to face up to the responsibility of their belief. We have shown the true evil of government agents who hound innocent men to death simply because they are Jesuit priests or sympathizers. We have exposed hatred and prejudice.'

'You have given them an excuse. You have played into their hands. All Catholics seem guilty now, one way or another.

He looked at her sorrowfully. 'Is that what your father tells you?'

'I've worked it out for myself. Of course you wouldn't mind dying, even on the scaffold. Martyrdom is easy for you. You think you are God's servant. You pray and pray and you think you hear Him telling you what you should do. But it's too dangerous. How can you be sure the voice you hear is

God's and not your own ambition, disguised? If you had one flicker of doubt about Catesby's plot you would never be able to lift your head again. That's what I think.'

There was a long silence. 'I asked to see you especially because I was afraid of this, Isabel. I knew you had been separated from all your friends and I feared for your soul. When I first saw you I thought you could do much for the church. I wanted to reassure myself that you stood firm.'

Isabel watched him, bewildered. This was the face that had haunted her memory, these same luminous eyes. But surely he was using the cheap trick of flattery to keep her in line. 'You mean you don't trust me.'

'It is not a matter of trust. I believe God has a special purpose in mind for you. The church can't afford to lose you to a Protestant marriage.'

'If I matter so much, how can you doubt the strength of my faith?' But the more self-critical part of her mind that had been silent during this spate of anger at last found a voice. What are you saying? He will never care for you after this. Be quiet. Be quiet. Ask his forgiveness.

She must have looked stricken for he got up and took her hands. 'The Powder Plot was discovered. Whether or not it was ill-conceived, it is in the past. You'll be pleased to know that I've had similar arguments with priests in my own order, Isabel. Some of us think the beast in men can only be eliminated by force, others have more faith in verbal persuasion. But you and I shouldn't quarrel. I find that your spirit is far from crushed and that's good. Girls like you and Blanche Morton, of whom I also think very highly, have been schooled by women of the most astounding spirituality and devotion. Your grandmother. Anne Vaux. Lucy Morton. Some of you will become Catholic wives and mothers in your turn. But you, I think, will want to leave all this and abandon your body and spirit to a life of contemplation. Can you imagine greater happiness?'

The simplicity of the picture he painted drew a thick path of yellow light across the plain little room and out into the future where in her convent cell Isabel, perfect at last, flung herself forward as a vessel of God's love.

But in the meantime she had to live in the world. The vision faded and she was aware once more of the clandestine nature of this meeting, his long, steady hands pressed over her cold fingers, his fervent eyes.

Still she didn't smile at him but stood bolt upright while he gave the blessing. She couldn't forgive him for forcing her into the role of onlooker while he melted out of her life again into unthinkable danger. I want to change places, she thought. I'd rather be the hunted. Then I wouldn't have to bear this terrible burden of anxiety for him.

Her eyes were level with his chest and she noticed that down the front of his doublet was a long row of tiny, cloth-covered buttons. She thought of his fingers fastening each one and he seemed to her unbearably fragile, with the ordin-ariness of his daily dressing and undressing placed alongside the huge recklessness of his schemes and dreams. Leaning forward, she rested her head against him.

Her brow was pressed to one of the tiny buttons and the anger and mistrust of the past months flowed out of her. If he loved her, if he thought she was good enough, all was right with the world again.

His fingers moved through her hair. The weight of his palm drew her closer and his thumb made three tiny strokes from the bottom of her neck to the hollow at her hairline. Her breath was caught by the motion up, up. It was as if her heartbeat depended on his touch. She was nothing but the strip of flesh under his thumb.

He put both hands on her shoulders and set her at arm's length. 'There's a young woman in this house you should talk to if you have the chance. Her name is Mary Ward. She wears a plain, reddish dress. And Isabel, don't forget to pray for me.'

Isabel backed away. Before she was out of the room he had sat down at the table and picked up his breviary.

The interview had lasted less than half an hour but in the public rooms on the first floor everything had changed. A new tide of people had come up for their supper and the windows had been flung wide. Isabel edged her way to the staircase and walked slowly down towards the white salon where the harpsichordist was playing one of her favourite motets.

On the half-landing she made a prolonged study of the portrait of a long dead Fitzroy lady whose under-skirt hung smooth as a bell, embossed with gold lozenges and flowers. She wore a pomander dangling from a jewelled girdle. Isabel peered at the near invisible brush-strokes which so carefully reproduced the silken twisted strands on the tassel and tried to compose herself.

It was like emerging on the wrong side of a mirror. In the tiny room with Father Carisbroke she had spoken thoughts kept hidden for months. She wanted an hour with him, a day, a year. Perhaps it wasn't too late to go back for one last word.

'Mistress Isabel Stanhope. Now there's a lucky chance.' She was looking down into the delighted face of Francis Bourne. 'But why should I be surprised to see you here? Lady Arabella has a way of finding out the most decorative people in London.'

He had broken her bubble of yearning. His pale green doublet was artistically unbuttoned at the neck and had a pearly sheen that made him a wand of soft colour. Isabel descended the stairs very slowly, conscious of the splash of red wine in her ivory silk. Her petticoats slipped over the steps and her hand skimmed the balustrade, yet she was still in the upstairs room with her priest.

Bourne bowed low over her hand. 'Actually, it wasn't chance. I heard you would be here and I wanted another glimpse of my cousin, even if I did have to put up with the harpsichord, an instrument I can't stand. And I need to keep in with Lady Fitzroy. She's the wealthiest woman I know who likes the theatre and playwrights. I was hoping she might commission a play.'

He tucked her hand over his arm and led her to an alcove beneath the muscular marble knee of a young Greek warrior where they were safely on view but set apart from everyone else. 'Please don't tell me you play the harpsichord, cousin. I couldn't bear the disappointment.'

'Of course I do. I've been very well brought up. And I'm certainly not your cousin.'

'Second, third, fourth cousin, whatever.'

Isabel was not so befuddled by recent events that she forgot to wonder about the true reason for Bourne's appearance, a Protestant in a house which harboured a Jesuit priest. She could tell that people were alert to his arrival. Occasionally bows and smiles were exchanged but he was certainly not greeted with unreserved pleasure.

Perhaps he had been sent by her father to keep an eye on her.

Since they were safely out of earshot Bourne began a roll call of everyone he knew in the room, their name and status and his opinion of them. Isabel had never heard characters held up for inspection like this, summarized and then dismissed. Previously in her life people had fallen into categories; servant or equal, labourer or courtier and, more importantly, Catholic or heretic. Among the Catholics were the ones she loved, the ones she hardly knew and those she tried to love but couldn't.

Lucy Morton was now seated in the back row of chairs with Blanche and the other woman in the striking red gown. 'Ah, Blanche,' said Bourne. 'A very determined young lady but then she would be, she's a Morton. What a voice, poor love, very shrill. Do you know the lady seated beside her? Mary Ward. Niece to the late lamented Wright brothers who as you know lost their poor heads and a lot else due to their involvement in the you-know-what plot. Mary, Mary, quite contrary. She and I once had a heated discussion on the best path to perfection. She's all for contemplation, prayer and holy acts while I'm for science and experiment. Out of the fire, Mistress Isabel, comes regeneration. Of one thing we can be quite sure, Mistress Ward isn't here to listen to the harpsichord. Nothing so frivolous. She's a catcher of souls.'

Isabel kept quiet. Mary Ward. Her name, spoken also by Father Carisbroke, now had a ringing significance.

What a good front we all put on, she thought, every Catholic in the room must be mourning what has happened in the past months but none of us shows it. Bourne was insufferably glib and she had no idea where his true sympathies lay. But suddenly, without changing his confident posture or amused smile, he dropped his voice. 'How is your mother, Mistress Isabel?'

She stared blindly out into the room.

'Mistress Isabel?' He lowered his head and looked into her face, all teasing gone. She scrabbled for a reply. Carisbroke had said there was a Catholic sympathizer in her father's household but who kept Bourne up to date? Oh, there are so many layers to people, she thought wearily.

'Isabel. Isabel.' Lady Fitzroy and Margaret Westward were upon them in a flurry of skirts. Bourne was wafted away by Lady Fitzroy while Margaret made a series of excessive curtseys and drew Isabel apart. 'You've missed all the best music. He played my favourite Morley ballad. I did want you to hear it. *"My bonny lass she smileth, when she my heart beguileth . . ."* Ah, that song. Have you been at supper all this time? I think I'll just run up and see if there is any tongue. I love a lean piece of tongue. Come along, dear. You might like a little wine. I think we could allow it before we go. Isabel, Isabel,' she dropped her voice to a whisper, 'I hadn't realized you were sitting with him until Lady Fitzroy pointed it out. I feel so ashamed. Never, never be alone with a man, even in public. Have you any idea how bad it looks?'

Father Henry Garnet, alias Mr Farmer, leader of the Jesuit community of England and Wales, had been found guilty of treasonable conspiracy and was to be executed early on the morning of 3 May. The government set the date back two days to avoid May Day which generated too much pagan carousing.

Sir William, who was making every effort to rehabilitate his good name at court, stated his intention of taking a front seat in the audience, although the king had left town and therefore would not witness his subject's loyal presence at

112

the execution. Nevertheless, Stanhope left before 6.30 a.m. to avoid the crush, very smart in a grey velvet doublet and knee-breeches, a sheaf of documents tucked under his arm and a sober black cloak slung over his left shoulder.

Isabel had learnt her lesson and knew better now than to implicate anyone else in her acts of rebellion. Telling Margaret that she intended to walk in the garden, she put on her old cloak, slipped past the kitchen and sculleries out on to the paved courtyard, ducked under the arch to the stable block and walked away very fast towards London. Half an hour would see her safely under Bishops Gate and into the maze of city streets.

Today her feet were clad only in thin leather shoes with cork heels which gave her pace but not protection from the mud. Her skirts and cloak soon grew heavy and a wet wind blew across the fields on her right where the sails of great windmills whirled feverishly. Isabel felt disconnected with the world and unsteady. The previous night she had forced herself to stay awake from midnight until five to pray for the soul of Garnet and she hadn't eaten since breakfast the previous day.

If I suffer too, he might not have so much pain, she thought, though such weak legs were not ideal for carrying her away from Hoxton at speed.

May 3rd in the church calendar was the Feast of the Finding of the Holy Cross and Garnet would certainly see the significance for his own martyrdom. He would pray all the time, even as he lay down on his back to be tied to a hurdle but how would he, such a clean, dapper little man, bear the indignity? His head would bump on the cobbles and the crowd would jostle to see his bare feet raised from the ground by the jolting movement of the horses.

Isabel, forbidding herself to look behind in case she was being followed, set up a chant in her head: By the sign of the Cross, deliver us from our enemies, O God. The breeze tossed her skirts and sent her skimming under Bishops Gate where she could be anonymous.

But here was a new problem. Garnet was to be executed in St Paul's churchyard. From her window in Hoxton she had studied the cathedral's blunt tower but she had no real idea how to get there. She struck off at random down a lane opposite Leadenhall Market, heart in mouth at being unchaperoned among the thrusting London crowd. She sensed that a tide of people was gathered near St Paul's and that she was not alone in her haste to get there.

In the end she found herself too far south of the cathedral and had to work her way back to the churchyard. There was a huge crowd even this far from the scaffold so she skirted round to the left until she could see the very top of a long ladder propped against a horizontal bar. Certainly there was no danger of being spotted by her father whose seat in the stands was invisible. People were furious that they could hear and see nothing even though Garnet's hurdle had arrived more than quarter of an hour ago. Complaints were made about the lack of seating space and the fact that the authorities had built the scaffold so tucked away in a corner of the churchyard.

Isabel closed her eyes. What must he be thinking? Hemmed in by the massive walls of St Paul's and this avid crowd, did he remember that less than a year ago his feet had trodden the empty green hillsides near Holywell? Or perhaps he saw this journey as yet another pilgrimage, the last.

Behind Isabel every open window was filled with a crush of spectators drawn by a ghoulish desire to see the butchering of a notorious villain, the wily Jesuit equivocator. But Isabel sensed a restraint in the crowd, a pulling back from too loud a condemnation of Garnet. Perhaps in their hearts the old faith still tugged or something of Garnet's goodness whisked above their heads.

On Isabel's left two young men were talking about Garnet's dilemma. Should he have revealed to the authorities what he heard in the confessional? Of course, said one, of course, if it would have saved lives. No, no, thought Isabel. If a person can't trust a priest to keep quiet what hope is there of redemption? How will we ever dare confess our sins?

She had not expected the execution to take so long. Who cared about the formalities at this late stage? But others in the crowd knew better. They would be trying to get him to renounce his faith even now, someone said, although there was a general consensus that nothing would move Garnet.

But suddenly Garnet was in view and must be standing actually on the platform of the scaffold. The crowd shifted and Isabel had a clearer glimpse of sturdy upright posts and the ladder. Someone else moved and this time she saw the block, two foot high, and a brazier in which bright flames danced.

Garnet looked frail and cold in his black cloak and his voice wafted back and forth in the wind. 'Catholics to be quiet . . . souls in peace . . . send them help . . . His glory.'

'Anne Vaux,' yelled a voice from the crowd. 'What was it like in her bed? Snug, was it?'

A few people laughed, most looked uncomfortable.

The priest said something more then ducked out of sight again and there was a marked increase of tension in the crowd.

He is so alive, thought Isabel. How can they kill him?

When he next appeared he was wearing only a white shirt sewn so tightly down to his knees that he had trouble climbing the ladder. Isabel felt helpless in her separation from him. She, fully dressed, would turn in a few minutes and walk back to the house in Hoxton. There she would eat, pray and sleep. He, shivering in the wind, would take perhaps four more steps in his life.

When Garnet was high on the ladder she pressed her hand over her eyes. His voice came more strongly this time because the crowd was completely silent. He was praying in Latin, familiar words spoken by all Catholics at the end of the day, as well as the end of a life. '*In manus tuas, domine, commendo spiritum meum . . .*'

There was the faintest creak of wood and rope and a general movement forward. Isabel, who was no longer at the back of the crowd, felt the pressure of a hundred other bodies. And then there was a shout, a scuffle and the rope was no longer swinging randomly from side to side but held taut. 'They've got him by the heels,' someone said. 'He'll be well and truly dead by now. Lucky bastard.' Disappointment hung bitter over the crowd.

Isabel raised her head, freed her right hand and made a sign of the cross in a small, deliberate gesture of solidarity. Perhaps nobody saw. In her mind's eye she watched herself; Isabel Stanhope with her young hand touching forehead, breast and shoulders.

Oh, Father Carisbroke, please don't die like this.

The rope was dangling loose again so Garnet's body must have been cut free. The crowd edged closer and closer and there was a faint rip of cloth.

Raising her fists and elbows Isabel fought her way out. People were so absorbed they scarcely noticed her frantic efforts but she emerged at last in a tiny lane and worked her way southwards to the river. By now Garnet's shift would be a heap on the scaffold and the straw sprayed with his blood. The wind was much stronger and blew a pungent, wet spray on to her face when she came to a wharf and flung herself against a wooden hut to draw breath. Garnet's dead legs sprawled and in the executioner's hand a dripping knife was raised high.

The grey waters were so ruffled and pulled by the wind that oarsmen rowing against the tide were hardly making headway at all. Garnet's death had made no mark here. No one else was thinking about that knife. Isabel crouched against the hut and crushed her hands between her thighs. Robin's ghoulish account of execution rang in her head and would not allow her to hide. The image of it hurt and fascinated, making her mouth water and her stomach turn. The executioner would hack through Garnet's most tender, hidden flesh, dangle it before the eyes of the crowd and toss it into the flames. Isabel could hear the hiss of entrails in fire.

If they caught Carisbroke, that's what would happen to him.

Isabel's head fell backwards and she gazed up at the massed grey clouds. Garnet's soul, like a strong-winged bird, must be flying up and up. Hush, Isabel, it's all over. Hush. Nothing can injure him now.

After a while she detached herself from her rickety shelter. She must somehow find the way home and face the consequences of having been out on her own for several hours. And some odd looks were being cast in her direction by workmen on the wharf.

But for the first time she became aware of an unfamiliar weight against her hip and sliding her hand deep into her pocket felt the soft corners of a leather-bound book.

She didn't own such a book. Certainly it had not been in her pocket when she left the house. She gently opened the cover and wafer thin pages rippled across her fingers. There was no message, no inscription, no clue as to who had left it.

The Imitation of Christ. Thomas à Kempis.

Garnet was dead but Isabel had stepped forward from his slaughter with this new talisman, like a needle freshly threaded. Whose elbow had brushed hers? What friend had stood so close that his hand had touched the cloth covering her hip?

But as she walked on she was overcome by weariness. Just for once, whispered a persuasive little voice, wouldn't it be lovely to go home and forget all this? Wouldn't it be good to be free of the clinging tendrils put out by the church?

Chapter 9

In early August 1606 the court of King James was engaged in an orgy of festivities to celebrate the visit of Queen Anne's brother, Christian of Denmark. For a week or so even sedate Hoxton residents were caught up in the extravagant show of ostentation by the English court. Cannons were fired to mark the arrival of the Danish party and there was an unwieldy procession through London witnessed by Isabel and the awe-struck Mistress Westward. Days of sport and pageant were to culminate in the installation of Christian as a Knight of the Garter followed by a play in the Great Hall at Hampton Court arranged with breathless haste. According to Sir William, both monarchs were finding the cost of so much fun for so many people a great drain and Christian had decided to cut short his visit.

Sir William insinuated his way on to most of the royal jaunts, returning at night from bouts of hawking and tilting in a furious mood because sport bored him. Nevertheless these high-profile attendances paid off. His sin by association with treacherous Thomasina and Robin had clearly been forgiven and he was given some responsibility for organizing the final ceremonials.

Out of the blue he invited Isabel, with Margaret as chaperone, to attend the play at Hampton Court. Isabel was deeply suspicious of this and other signs of leniency. Not only had Sir William never mentioned her expedition to witness Garnet's execution but he now allowed her regular excursions to town and even to send and receive letters from her mother.

At eight in the evening his barge carried Isabel and Mistress

Westward from their temporary lodgings at Richmond to the water-gate at Hampton Court. Margaret had sewed herself a new under-skirt to wear with Isabel's cast-off ivory silk and the red wine stain was cunningly disguised by elaborate piping. Isabel, who had grown at least an inch since Easter, felt all elbows and knees beside her tiny chaperone. It was like being a stork escorted by a neat little coot. On the long walkway leading to the palace she marched ahead of Margaret, her skirts scraping the gravel path. The sky to the west was a violent orange and she saw herself as if from a distance, a young, white-necked girl in glossy skirts, for ever alone.

A year had gone by since she had left Oakshott to begin her pilgrimage. Nowhere could present more of a contrast to the dank chapel at Holywell than the Great Hall at Hampton Court hung with tapestries which would have made Martha Canton swoon. 'Priceless,' breathed Margaret, 'only brought out for special occasions.' Here, under the gilded ceiling, courtiers dripped jewels. Isabel wandered like a lost child through a forest of luscious fabrics. Last summer she had been one of a tight-knit circle of loved friends, now she was anonymous except to Francis Bourne who had of late become an habitual if unreliable escort.

'The playwright is over there – bald head – dark blue and cream doublet. See him? Not a gifted actor, goes for the more minor parts so he may not be performing tonight. He's a rich man despite being a writer, one of the few, my ideal in fact. If you'll excuse me, Mistress Isabel, I'll just have a quick word – see if he'll read a scene from my latest play. I think it'll interest him because it's all about whether animals have souls . . .'

Off dashed Francis but he was soon diverted by a couple of Danish courtiers who hailed him like an old friend. As usual he seemed to know everyone; must have a quick word here, a joke there. It was impossible to hold his attention for long.

The heart of Holywell had been a pool of holy water, clear as air; here the focus was a high dais draped with gold and crimson. Then the scarred Saint Winifred had presided, petrified above stone steps; now in came the kings, poor James dwarfed by his much sturdier brother-in-law and even by his wife, a stiff puppet in the weighty burden of her gown. Alcohol had obviously been flowing freely, for James staggered as he reached the podium.

A year ago prayer for Isabel had been like breathing. Now once the play began poetry strummed ruthless fingers across her most bitter memories. Three witches with crabbed hands oversaw a mesh of bloody destruction. Ambition and greed were the themes of this drama and Isabel saw Catesby, Digby and Garnet corrupted by the playwright into grotesque shadows behind Macbeth and his lady.

Afterwards Bourne reappeared at her side. 'Shall I take you on a tour of the palace, Mistress Isabel? You'll see why the noble King Henry took such a fancy to it. Come away quick or we'll get embroiled in the supper crowd and sometimes ladies have lost their skirts in the crush here.'

Warm evening air blew through the elaborate state rooms, agitating a thousand candles which banished the evil universe of the play by their brilliance. But Isabel wasn't fooled. Here was yet another illusion: that the king was an heroic monarch deserving of this graceful place, the expensive paintings and sculptures a fitting background to his noble figure. The play world had been replaced by a real world ruled by squalid King James with his grimy fingernails and suspicious eyes.

Isabel knew now that nothing was as it seemed. Displayed in her latest gorgeous dress, face framed by a gossamer ruff, she was outwardly an obedient daughter to the courtier Sir William Stanhope but actually she had kept true to her faith and was deeply disobedient to him. Beneath her corset against her bare flesh she had taken to wearing a knotted length of rope that lacerated her skin and served as a constant reminder that her life was dedicated to God and she must not be seduced by the pleasures arranged by her father. And in the inner pocket of her petticoat she carried the little brown volume given to her so mysteriously on the morning of Garnet's execution. It was the only tangible proof that her other world had ever existed, the one physical link between herself, Carisbroke and all the rest. She imagined his long index finger sliding between the cover and the first page, his blunt, beautiful nail resting under the opening lines:

> OF FOLLOWING OF CHRIST AND DESPISING OF ALL
>   WORLDLY VANITIES
> Our Lord saith: he that followeth me goeth not in
>   darkness.

The gardens were lit by tiny lanterns and among the trees strolled other courtiers stirring the night air with murmurings and occasional laughter. Bourne led Isabel into a sunken garden which had a gate at the far end opening on to a path beside the river. The perfume of warm hedgerows and lavender bathed her face and the starry sky was innocent and soft. The taint of the play and of her own deceptions slid away and for once she lived fully in the moment with the breeze swaying her great skirt and knocking back her ruff.

They came to three little steps, skirted a sundial and crossed the garden where one side was a mirror image of the other. Ahead was a small rose arbour sheltering a bench where a couple sat close together. At first, in her gentle, drifting mood, Isabel barely glanced at them but then she saw that the man's hand was buried in his companion's bosom and that her fingers were thrust between his thighs. Slowly Isabel and Bourne drew nearer and again Isabel's shocked eyes were drawn to the gleam of pliant flesh above the woman's bodice. And she, far from resisting the man's writhing fingers, was turned inwards, her arm flung diagonally across his body so that her dainty cuff of white lace ended in the folds of his breeches. Neither noticed Isabel or Francis Bourne. The man's loose-lipped face was thrown back and the woman's mouth was fastened on his ear.

Isabel's tranquillity was shattered. Her body had lost its calm, rhythmic movement through the garden and the play world whispered again, words hot with meaning that had not touched her before.

> Hie thee hither,
> That I may pour my spirits in thine ear,
> And chastise with the valour of my tongue.

Bourne, nonchalant as ever, closed his hand over Isabel's eyes. 'Avert your gaze, sweet maid. Next time I'll bring a bucket of water. These gardens are notorious. Don't worry, I won't take you much further. Do those ridiculous little slippers hurt your feet?'

She ought not to be alone with him though she had grown used to his company now and thought of him as a boyish, rather frivolous relative. But here in the gardens there were no distractions, no darting aside to have a word with someone else. Isabel felt the fumblings of the couple on the bench as a hot pressure on her own body.

Watched at a discreet distance by liveried servants they had passed through a succession of gates and were out on to the path beside the river. Grasses grew like soft fur on the opposite bank and willows trailed their feathery branches. A pair of swans, as if posed for Isabel's benefit, lifted their small white heads and sculled quietly downstream.

'I never want to see another play,' Isabel said childishly.

'I thought you'd gone very quiet. Of course it was disturbing, as it was intended to be, I'm sure. A nasty warning for would-be regicides. But not just that. An appeal to everyone with a conscience, even our great king. Shakespeare is the best but I hate him for his talent. He probably wrote that play in a matter of months. How does he do it?

> *all our yesterdays have lighted fools*
> *The way to dusty death*

I wish I could write even one line as good as that.'

'I'm glad you're not him. I'd rather not be a successful writer if I produced such a cruel play.'

Black river water lapped the bank and the swans made an inexplicable turn and began to sail back towards them. Isabel felt she had crossed a boundary into a world where different rules applied. The rope was knotted tightly round her waist so that by this late in the evening, with the corset laced over it, her body seemed belted with fire. Yes, she was pledged to serve God but here she stood beside an heretical young man with warm hands and glittering eyes.

'Isabel, when first I made myself known to you it was

because you were my distant cousin and I had been taught to think of you as a possible wife. Very expedient to marry the Stanhope heiress, I thought, egged on of course by my family. Don't be surprised by my frankness. My dearest girl, I would never lie to you.'

She half heard him. Her skin felt thin as membrane so that when the breeze touched her hand the nerves vibrated along her wrist. He had edged closer still and slipped his arms round her waist. The knots in the rope bit and her flesh twitched.

Now, Isabel, now is the time to move. But she was locked into the moment.

Isabel, Isabel, cried the small voice in her head, what are you doing?

Bourne's lips touched her bare shoulder between bodice and ruff. 'Don't be afraid. I'll keep you safe. I won't do anything to hurt you. I know what you are. I know where your sympathies lie, and those of your mother and grandmother.'

She tried to see his eyes. 'But I don't trust you.'

He held her face. 'Trust me. Trust me. I won't harm you but I will protect you from your dangerous friends.'

'What dangerous friends?'

He brought his head closer and his breath smelt of mulled wine. 'I could sympathize with your cause, Isabel, were it not for the stranglehold of Rome. It's all a matter of who's paying whom, you see. Nothing is as simple as one man believing one thing, another something different. Not at the highest level.'

'What happens at the highest level has nothing to do with me.'

'No, my little girl. That's why you should marry me one day. You could keep your faith, and I would keep you safe.'

Carisbroke, in a plain wool robe, passed swiftly among the reeds on the opposite bank. She saw his face, lean and calm-eyed. Bourne's legs flattened her skirts against her thighs. His arm had drawn her inwards and his nose gave hers a playful nudge. 'Dearest Isabel, I think if I could win you I might even write better plays.'

She could no longer see the river, only Bourne's eyes. His smile caught her wandering attention and her thoughts dissolved. Her body was so glad to be touched that she edged closer and closer, as if folding into a father's loving arms. When Bourne kissed her forehead she turned her face to receive more and more kisses. Her hand went up to his silky hair and pulled his head down to kiss her mouth. His lips were so tender and lively she forgot he had a beard.

Bearded men waiting for bad news in a silent chapel. Bearded heads pierced by sharp poles.

Bourne left a trail of kisses along her upper lip, gently, gently. 'Tonight, I only ask again that you trust me. I will never put any pressure on you. I would wait decades for you. Do you understand me?'

Together they would sail away into a future where there were no more partings from the ones she loved best, no more silent days, no more lonely nights. She looked up and saw his loving eyes and crooked smile. He wasn't like the man in the garden whose fingers had clutched at the woman's breasts as if to pinch them into his possession. Instead he took strands of her hair, one after another and stroked them back over her shoulder.

Her small voice said. 'I'll never marry, Francis.'

'I'll not say another word. But remember, whatever you do I'll be always on your side. I'm your knight. Send me on any quest, my lady, and I'll gallop away to do battle with dragons for you.' Once more he was Bourne the would-be dramatist, everyone's darling, and the night was again just a drowsy backcloth to the aimless gliding of the swans and the lazy breeze. He held out his hand. 'Mistress, Isabel, may I escort you back to your father, perhaps by a different route? There's a pond garden, a knot garden, an avoid-Margaret-Westward-at-all-costs garden. What is your fancy?'

She wished their walk would last for ever through avenues of topiary and walled gardens with moonlight trapped in circular ponds; the glaring whiteness of a statue or a carved bench; the preoccupied or curious faces of other couples and ever closer the parapets and turrets of the palace, with yellow light streaming from every window and hundreds of courtiers let loose on food, wine and their adult world of gossip and ambition.

Sometimes Isabel thought she saw the little figure of Margaret in her second-hand ivory gown, tripping through a gateway or under a tree. Sometimes she seemed to hear her own name whisked beneath a pergola or across a silvery strip of water. She paid no attention.

This is what I want now, she thought. I want to run night after night through open spaces. I want always to hear music somewhere in the distance. I don't want to be ashamed of laughter. I don't want my life to end behind a grille.

On the brief journey back to Richmond along the river Sir William said how pleased he was with the evening. He folded his hands and pom-pommed a little tune to himself. Margaret Westward, however, was not at all happy with Isabel, who had so nimbly kept out of sight.

Neither of them noticed the tears trickling down Isabel's cheeks and on to her wrists. Moment by moment she was more deeply struck by the terrible thing she had done. It was the vision of herself that was so wounded, the little nun on a thorny path to the convent. And in its place came a scarlet woman, like the one who had sat so shamelessly with her lover on the bench in the sunken garden.

Her behaviour with Bourne was above all a terrible betrayal of Father Peter Carisbroke and the vocation he had awoken in her. What would he think of her?

Jesu, if you want me to give all this up for you, then please tell me clearly.

Isabel. You will hear what you want to hear. You have blocked your ears but you know what has been asked of you. Listen. Listen.

I don't want to listen. I want to remember Francis Bourne's kisses. I want to think about what he said to me.

Temptation. Lust. You hardly know him. He's the one your father wants you to marry. How can he be the answer?

Love. Love.

*

Margaret Westward fell asleep quickly, having maintained an oppressive and uncharacteristic silence as she undressed her charge. Afterwards Isabel knelt by the window and tried to pray. Somewhere in the night Bourne was riding back to his father's little town house near Westminster.

She had decided to trust her future to Thomas à Kempis so she opened a page at random and read:

Desires ofttimes set thee on fire and hugely stir thee; but consider whether thou be moved more for my worship or for thine own profit. If I be at the root thou wilt be well content whatever I ordain; and if there be anything of thine own seeking that is hid privily, that it is that letteth and grieveth.

TWO

Mary Mary

1609

Chapter 10

One advantage for Isabel of paying a visit to Francis Bourne's family in Bedfordshire was that Margaret Westward suffered agonies during their stay.

Francis Bourne's mother, Philippa, had compounded the misfortune of being born the daughter of an impoverished branch of the Stanhopes by marrying for love John Bourne, then an eighteen-year-old steward. But Bourne's career had been meteoric and at forty-eight he was bailiff to an outstandingly successful merchant, Lionel Cranfield. Astute investment and the swift accumulation of land had made Bourne wealthy enough to own two properties, the narrow town house frequented by his oldest son Francis when in London and the grandly named Startsdon Old Hall near Bedford which was in fact so new that it was still permeated by the smell of freshly sawn timbers. Since the autumn of 1606 Isabel had been a regular visitor to Startsdon and by September 1609 was chief guest of honour.

The Bournes fell over themselves to make Isabel welcome because unless her wretched brother Robin was released from the Clink she would be heir to her father's fortune. If she bore a son, the boy would inherit and Sir William's land and property would pass out of Stanhope hands for ever. However, if there were no male offspring, the land was entailed to Francis Bourne through his mother. The best solution to everyone's ambition, therefore, would be the marriage of Francis Bourne and Isabel Stanhope, for their progeny would have pure Stanhope blood running in their veins and could legitimately take the Stanhope title.

Twenty-six-year-old Francis was the oldest Bourne child

and nine-month Cecily the youngest. Mistress Philippa Bourne, now in her early forties, had been continuously pregnant since the age fifteen, though luckily for the over-strained premises at Startsdon almost half her children had died in infancy. Of the remaining eleven most surged in and out of the house and garden in a flurry of grubby petticoats and breeches, one girl had married a local squire and two boys worked with their father on the land. Only Francis, the heir, had received a formal education. His resulting desire to be a playwright coupled with his inability to earn money had dissuaded his parents from sending any of the others to school. After all, they would only learn how to be poor.

The Bourne children had taught Isabel how to play. On her first visit she had sat with Margaret in Philippa's parlour wondering how she could stand a fortnight at chaotic Startsdon. All the young Bournes worked hard and the daughters of the house had to bring up their siblings, help in the dairy and clean the bedrooms. But they could not leave Isabel alone. Her dainty shoes and gorgeous gown enchanted them and they crept up to take a look, then retreated as if scorched by her beauty. On the second afternoon a plump three-year-old climbed into her lap, presented her with a couple of marigolds and invited her to help make raspberry jam in the kitchens.

Once she had learnt how to enjoy the Startsdon summers they became Isabel's holiday from conflict. For the rest of the year she must behave outwardly as her father's heiress but in secret pray like a nun. Her vocation was kept alive by rare contact with recusants at Fitzroy House and even more occasional visits to Cuddington where her mother was obsessed by Robin's imprisonment. Sir William had his daughter watched night and day.

But at Startsdon the only spy was Margaret, incapacitated by her shuddering dislike of the entire household. In the evenings Isabel tried to salve her conscience by explaining Catholicism to the Bourne girls. After their talks there was no time for private prayer because sleep came too easily after a day of boisterous human contact, fresh air and physical activity.

Even Francis did not intrude much. He was often in town and when he came treated Isabel like a sister, never attempting to touch her as he had at Hampton Court. But everyone understood that when she was sixteen, Isabel Stanhope and Francis Bourne would be betrothed.

So in September 1609 a visit to Startsdon was arranged to coincide with Isabel's sixteenth birthday. But Isabel, withdrawn into a spiky bundle on the opposite side of the carriage to Margaret Westward, was in no mood for festivities. Instead she was conscious of a slow burning coil of disenchantment. The inside of the carriage was gloomy and the drive through miles of dripping woodland agonizingly tedious. She felt nothing but contempt for Margaret, herself, her father and Francis Bourne. She hated being nearly sixteen and so listless.

When they turned into the muddy drive at Startsdon Margaret pointed out that each gatepost was now mounted by a ferociously snarling stone lion. A clutch of children had tumbled out on to the steps and behind them, vast in green satin, Mistress Philippa Bourne had emerged and stood jigging her latest child, sickly Cecily, on her hip. There was no sign of Francis.

Isabel slumped deeper into the cushions. It wouldn't do to look too keen.

The door was wrenched open almost before the carriage had stopped and the bony face of Deborah, aged thirteen, appeared. 'Isabel, Isabel, we've been on the look-out since three. Where have you been?'

Margaret tottered out among the gaggle of children, was swept by effusive Mistress Philippa into a breast-crushing embrace and stood swaying on the step with her hand to her forehead. In a few minutes she would find an excuse to beat a retreat to her allocated room at the top of the house. Not that there was much seclusion there. Startsdon Old Hall, like its owner's finances, was constantly undergoing expansion and hardly a room was entirely finished. The family was used to the reverberating bang bang of a hammer or the sawing of planks as yet another bay was knocked out or a wing added. Even so there was a shortage of space so

Margaret had to share with the housekeeper, a fearsome affront to the dignity of both.

Meanwhile Isabel unfroze fast. The children were irresistible and, as Philippa had explained well before they were over the threshold, Francis and his father were away on business until the following evening so Isabel could relax her guard.

'What it is, Mistress Isabel, it's high time Francis knew how to negotiate a land deal. He takes no interest in my husband's work but I'm sure he's got a good brain somewhere.' Philippa propelled herself forward with her elbows, beneath one of which was tucked the unfortunate Cecily. Her voice, always several degrees louder than necessary, rebounded from the cornices of her tumultuous parlour.

'So tell me, Isabel, how is your dear mother?' asked Philippa, dropping her voice a little to mark the fact that Thomasina's faith had put her beyond the pale.

'Not well when I saw her in June.' No two women could be more of a contrast than Philippa Bourne and Lady Thomasina Stanhope. At Cuddington Thomasina, weakened by vigils and fasts, wandered solitary from room to room, fading rapidly as the years passed and still her son remained a prisoner. Meanwhile here at Startsdon the earthy Philippa Bourne had dumped Cecily into a pile of mending while she darned a stocking; her bodice seeped milk and her assembled children sprawled over the furniture or hung across the window ledges.

'And your brother? Cecily, put down the scissors. There now, I warned you before they'd give you a nip. Never mind, don't cry. There, there, my lamb. Let's go to cook and find some sugar water.' Up leapt the mother with the stocking somersaulting over her great skirts and off she went to the kitchens, leaving the field clear for the children to pounce on Isabel and drag her upstairs to the room she shared with Deborah and her elder sister, Dorothea.

These two girls had collected knowledge like magpies, eavesdropping on their brothers' sketchy education at the hands of various ill-informed tutors. Deborah, lanky and impulsive, raged about her lack of reading matter but had acquired a small shelf of books supplemented each year by Isabel. Shy Dorothea was the family artist. One tutor, more gifted than the rest, had taught her the rudiments of mixing oils and understanding light and now she painted miniatures of anyone prepared to sit for her. On her first visit Isabel had pronounced that Dorothea certainly had an eye for perspective and had subsequently been treated as chief art expert and critic by the adoring young painter.

While the latest acquisitions and achievements were displayed to Isabel and the younger children led her up and down the passages to show off the building work, her London reserve was gradually worn down. After half an hour she felt restricted by her city clothes and off came two petticoats, her farthingale and boots. Then, led by Deborah who had the longest legs and the boldest eye, away they all ran barefoot across the lawn, leaping the ditch between garden and home farm, across the stubble field and into a tiny copse where they were beyond shouting distance even of Philippa.

Of all Isabel's followers, the most dedicated was fourteen-year-old Dorothea who had a round face, dense complexion and flat brown hair. She was an untidy girl, already heavy-bosomed like her mother but with a moist weight to her lips and a dreamy watchfulness to her eye that had stopped Isabel in her tracks when she first took the trouble to notice her. Dorothea, with her pregnant silences and deep sighs, bore a disturbing resemblance to Susannah Thewing but was unlike her in that she worshipped the ground Isabel trod.

Through Dorothea Isabel had learnt the intoxication of power. She could make Dorothea miserable by ignoring her and bring a light to her eye simply with a smile. On that first afternoon, mellowed by the strawy September sunshine that had at last broken through, Isabel was feeling kind.

Dorothea's special responsibility was for the hens who had a low barn to themselves. Each morning she let her charges out into the courtyard and gathered the eggs, each evening she had to chivvy the wayward brood back inside. Sometimes Isabel helped, sometimes she didn't. By late afternoon the warmth had gone from the fields so she was ready to wander back to the house and tend the hens.

The barn had kept the heat of the sun and the bitter smell of poultry was overpowering at first. Isabel kilted up her petticoats and moved from one nesting shelf to the next searching for eggs, though most had been collected in the morning. High on the straw stack was a nest Dorothea had missed and there was a little cluster of three cool eggs.

Isabel lay down with them pressed to her chest, turning them softly in her fingers so that the shells grated against each other. There was a dragging on the straw as Dorothea pulled herself up to lie close by. As usual, Isabel was both pleased to have the company and furious with Dorothea for being so clumsy.

'Are you all right, Isabel?'

'Of course I'm all right.'

'You seem a bit distant.'

'Whatever do you mean? If I was any closer I'd be lying on top of you.' The roof had been built of uneven, overlapping planks and there were sparkling glimpses of blue sky. Dust quivered above the girls' heads. Dorothea, pink and rumpled, had straw spiking over her shoulder. 'I'm just a bit confused,' Isabel said more kindly and smiled. But she didn't want to play their usual game of sophisticated Isabel and rustic Dorothea.

'Why?'

'Who knows.'

'Are you looking forward to seeing Francis? I am. Did you know one of his plays might be performed at a proper theatre?'

'I didn't know about that.'

'He's been waiting so long for this chance. He's never given up. And now two things will happen at once. His play and you. Aren't you excited?'

Isabel closed her eyes. 'Yes and no.'

'Why?'

Isabel chipped out words one by one. 'I can't expect you

134

to understand because you're not a Catholic, Dorothea. I've told you before that I have a vocation to be a nun. But at the moment it is impossible. My father would never give me money for a dowry and I can't cross to the continent without funds.'

Dorothea's salivary whisper came again in her ear. 'I've tried to imagine what it would be like to do nothing all day but pray and pray.'

'It is my dream. Oh, Dorothea, you have no idea what you're missing by not being a Catholic.' But Isabel was becoming increasingly uncomfortable with this conversation. She no longer had any idea what she wanted. Her faith had been eroded by years in the wilderness of her father's house.

'Tell me, tell me,' said Dorothea.

'As I've said, the most important thing is the presence of Christ in the Eucharist. He is there at communion and enters each one of us. And then there is the confessional. We believe in the priest's power to forgive us.'

'What is it like, to confess your sins?'

'What is it like?' She looked into Dorothea's damp face and heard the rustle of straw under her breast. 'It isn't easy. It's learning to admit the darkest secrets of our hearts, to let the priest see what we are truly like.' The intense days at Oakshott were a too distant memory. What had this moment under the barn roof of Protestant Startsdon to do with those momentous conversations with Father Carisbroke?

Religious fervour had seeped away leaving only a memory of something vital. Isabel was too repelled by the clenched figure of Robin in the Clink, unrepentant and unrelenting, his eyes as fanatical as ever, always plotting, refusing to acknowledge any allegiance to the crown. And then there were sermons preached by other Catholic priests, dubbed Appellants, who put the case for appeasement and compromise. What was the king, they argued, but the secular head of the country? Where was the conflict if the king had jurisdiction over the body and the Pope supremacy over the soul? Nothing was clear to Isabel any more.

'Poor Francis,' said Dorothea.

Yes, poor Francis, for I despise him too in a way, thought

135

Isabel. He has been so patient. He has kept me amused and occasionally rescued me from Margaret Westward. But he never has much time for me, is always in a hurry, always has someone else to meet. 'Oh, don't worry,' she said, 'I expect I'll have to marry him. I don't seem to have any choice, do I? And then I'll be a Bourne too.'

'I shan't ever marry,' said Dorothea.

'Why not?'

'I just have no idea of myself married. I couldn't imagine being like mother.'

Oh but, Dorothea, thought Isabel, you'll be just like your mother. I can see those big bosoms feeding a whole clutch of children. She put her face closer to Dorothea's and her cheek was jabbed by straw. The desire to inflict pain tingled in her fingertips. 'What else do you propose to do? What is your body for otherwise? Have you started to bleed yet?'

Dorothea nodded. Yes, Isabel could imagine her bleeding like an over-ripe plum. Oh God, how dismal life was, how dreary the conversation she'd had with Margaret who had hustled her into the darkest corner of the bedroom in Hoxton as if to discuss a contemptible secret. 'It'll happen every month now, Isabel. Thank goodness it didn't soak through to your farthingale. Be more careful next time.' She had pressed a fistful of torn rags into Isabel's hand. 'Clean yourself with these and rinse them afterwards in cold water.'

Another secret then, stored in the red petticoats of every woman. Even Anne Winshawe? Even the Virgin Mary? No wonder Saint Winifred had recoiled in horror from the arms of her lover if she had shared Isabel's sudden understanding of female flesh as being rankly composed of disgraceful secretions. Each morning she watched Margaret Westward encase her small breasts and waist in a tight corset that made her rigidly geometric. Margaret's imprisoned body said as clearly as her compressed lips: Don't look here for softness. I have put an end to all that.

Only the thought of the convent solved for Isabel the problem of what to do with her body. There it would be shrouded in layer after layer of black cloth, an unwieldy vessel in which the soul must live through its owner's short life.

Slam would go the grille on choice. Slam, on desire. Slam, on confusion.

The convent was out of reach. If Isabel refused Francis she would condemn herself to a future without substance. She noted rather petulantly that once she had been withdrawn from the tight network of her grandmother and friends, they seemed content to let her go. If Carisbroke was alive, why had he made no effort to contact her, if dead what was the point of bothering anyway? So much for the saving of souls, she sometimes thought, they obviously don't care much for mine.

How often do you want to be called, Isabel?

Once, by Father Carisbroke at Oakshott.

Twice in the holy waters of Winifred's Well.

A third time by Father Carisbroke in the servant's room at Fitzroy House. Isn't that enough?

But that was all before Francis Bourne. I was shown no other option. Now, I want a clear choice and I don't have it.

The eggs turned against her skin. The world had shrunk to an unkind conversation in the barn of a half-built country house and all the days of mortification and self-sacrifice had gone for nothing. Over the years Isabel's prayers had grown emptier, unanswered and undisciplined. Perhaps her young, ardent self had been just a foolish girl who had substituted love of God for the human love never found within the conventual walls of Cuddington or Oakshott.

'When I marry your brother I'll be able to share everything that happens to me with you,' said Isabel. Dorothea nestled on her side and cupped her cheek with her hand. Her ponderous gaze dwelt lovingly on Isabel's face. She had not noticed any irony.

'So won't that be nice?' Isabel sat up so violently that she banged her head on a rafter. She threw back her right hand and let one egg go hurtling across the barn. It shattered on a beam and sank down the wooden slats, the yellow yolk trailing transparent slime. The waste. The waste. At Cuddington every scrap was gathered up at the end of a meal and carried in baskets to feed hungry mouths in the village.

'Don't, please, Isabel. What's the matter?'

Smack went another egg after the first.

Dorothea put out her hand and gently took away the last. Isabel stared at her for a moment then closed her long fingers over the egg. At first Dorothea smiled uneasily but then the pressure increased so that the egg was crushed with a slow crackle and spilled out messily over Dorothea's skirt. 'You see what I'm really like, Dorothea? Who'd have me for a sister?'

Isabel laughed, scrambled down from the shelf and ran.

Even after supper the next day, Isabel's birthday, Francis and his father were not back and Isabel was in a frenzy of disappointed expectation, defiance and relief.

There was no peace to be had at Startsdon except on the attic floor beyond the servants' rooms where Isabel had once discovered an airy cavern under the eaves. Lit by a triangular window cut in the gable, it would have accommodated a perfect priest hole. The attic was a soothing place though not entirely insulated from the shrieks which accompanied the children's bedtime in the rooms below. The knee-level window gave Isabel a good view of the drive and even of the lions on the gateposts. She sat with her thighs crushed to her chest and thought sadly of her jagged moods and the way her mind had jumped and speculated unhappily all day. It was so easy to make a raft of good resolutions when safely alone.

September 8th was the feast of the Birth of the Blessed Virgin Mary and Isabel knew by heart the prayers said by Catholics on that day. 'Beata viscera Mariae Virginis . . . Blessed is the womb of the Virgin Mary, which bore the Son of the Eternal Father.' But the prayer cracked on the shallow saucer of her skull and had no resonance.

Francis was coming. Isabel recognized the jaunty feather on his high-domed hat as he and his father rode down the long stretch of lane between the village of Startsdon and the house. He leaned forward occasionally to pat the mottled grey neck of his horse, as if urging it on.

Isabel didn't move.

The gates were flung open and Francis rode between the snarling lions. A squeal from below suggested one of his sisters had also spotted him. He scanned the front of the house and his gaze went up and up as if drawn to Isabel until he caught her eye, whipped off his hat and made an elaborate bow. She smiled to see him so light-hearted and tapped her fingers on the glass. Then he was out of sight under the wall of the house.

Ten minutes passed. She judged his movements. The horse must be handed over, his father helped to dismount and his mother and numerous siblings embraced.

If he comes to me in the next two minutes I shall marry him. Otherwise, not. She began counting the seconds, cheating to elongate time. Still he did not come. She hitched her skirts and knelt up. Perhaps he hadn't seen her from the drive after all or was so indifferent he couldn't be bothered to come.

There were hurried footsteps in the servants' passage and a shoulder was thrust against the thin planks of the door.

They had never been so cut off from other people before. Francis was out of breath and seemed very assured in his crimson riding clothes and with a sheen of sweat on his cheek. Isabel's long shadow fell on his feet and dusty light spilled over her shoulders. It was as if they paddled in sunshine.

He took her hand and pulled her upright against his chest.

'Was it my mother's conversation that drove you up here? Or were you hiding from me because you knew what I was going to ask?'

Her indecision hit a wall of surprise. The hostility was crushed out of her. He was usually restrained when he kissed her hand or cheek but now she was scooped tight against the thick brocade on his doublet and he kissed her forehead and mouth.

Sparks flew through long channels in her limbs. His flesh had a new texture, salty and moist. He tasted of woodland and evening sky and the softness of his lips melted her mouth into a deep sigh. They sank down until she lay across his lap.

'Marry me.'

She couldn't answer. His fingertips trailed across the square of naked flesh under her ruff and skimmed the edge of her bodice.

'Marry me. If you marry me, I will do anything you want for you.' Soft kisses were dropped on her earlobe, cheek and eyelid. 'I will become a Catholic. Isabel, I've been waiting for you.' The tip of his tongue dabbled the crease under her nose to her upper lip. His warm right hand worked softly across her waist.

'I don't know. I don't know.' Images flickered in her head. Hampton Court and a stranger's hand in a white bosom, a swan's smooth turn in the black river, a glimpse of estuary beyond an ocean of young grass and an upwards flight through icy water in Winifred's Well. The flat of Francis's palm pressed her stomach through layers of cloth and her flesh clamoured. A slender priest with incandescent eyes darted through a hidden doorway and, on the night the pursuivants came to Oakshott, the child Isabel curled among warm, crumpled sheets in an unseen room smelling of male sweat. Francis's hand scooped up a fistful of petticoats above her knee and she clung to the back of his neck.

'I know you, Isabel, more than you think. Listen. I'll have plenty of money from my father and yours will agree to anything if you marry me. Think. A Catholic household, Catholic children, the priests we could help.'

He drew back his head and his eyes were dazed like a sleepwalker. She jumped when his fingertip stroked the back of her knee. Her voice struggled through a swollen throat. 'I don't understand why you are so different now.' She was spinning on the touch that trickled on her inner thighs.

'I waited for you.' He put his mouth to her ear and his words tiptoed on his fingers and dabbled her navel. 'I know every inch of you, Isabel. I have learnt you. Under my finger is your womb and these strong ribs are built to protect your lungs and other organs. I have studied how the blood flows in your veins and how with each beat of your heart it pulses onwards. We know so little even about ourselves we are blind to what we see, Isabel, but we could find out together.' The palm of his hand made slow rotations on her stomach. Words of prayers she had chanted every day of her life – *Ave Maria . . . Confiteor Deo omnipotenti . . . Gloria Patri . . .* – stuttered in her mind. This was not what was planned.

'Listen, Isabel, you could keep your faith. I wouldn't mind.' The upper part of her body was constricted by tight lacing, the lower half exposed to the late evening sunlight. Isabel saw herself a second Lady Arabella Fitzroy. In a disguised chapel candles flickered and a host of starving priests came flocking to the shelter of Isabel Bourne's labyrinthine chambers. She would brandish the torch of Catholicism even as she lay with Francis in the downy pillows of her marriage bed. Her father was wreathed in smiles. Excellent Isabel. My good daughter. And her mother Thomasina's cool embrace would link her into the sisterhood that united the great Catholic houses of England.

But there was an icy shiver of doubt even as she kissed him again. St Winifred was petrified with revulsion in her breezy chapel. Robin breathed his stale air and said: No, no, no to the rest of his life. Mortification, sacrifice and pain were the way of salvation.

'Marry me. Marry me.' She wanted to climb under his skin and dive into the warm haven of his flesh. The hair on the back of his head was swansdown and her legs fell open under his weight. 'Dear God, Isabel.'

Somebody knocked twice on the door. Francis pulled her petticoats over her legs. She scarcely recognized his face which was soft-skinned and bruised with love. Generally he had an actor's capacity for rapid readjustment. The door was fumbled open and Dorothea stood peering from one to the other as musky air emptied itself through the doorway. Isabel read in her astonished eyes a fearful memory of yesterday afternoon and the self-importance of one who has sensational tidings.

'I've got bad news for you, Isabel. Your father's here. You have to go home now. I'm afraid your mother's very ill. Dying. Oh, Isabel.'

Chapter 11

Apall lay over Cuddington. On arrival Sir William, who had scarcely spoken a dozen words during the journey, went immediately to his library leaving Isabel and Margaret to face a series of closed doors. Isabel, wrenched from Startsdon, subjected to two more days' drive and now abandoned in the entrance hall, had forgotten how adult her home was and how silent.

Mary Bonniface appeared on the staircase dressed in a black gown which did nothing to soften her dour features. She took them to the parlour where the light of many candles caused their faces to spring from darkness. Margaret was nervous as a mouse, doubly intimidated by the hostile Roman Catholic Mary Bonniface and the hovering proximity of death.

'Anne Winshawe has arrived,' announced Mary. 'I wrote to let her know Lady Thomasina was sick and she came while your father's been fetching you. He can't abide her so he'll not be pleased.'

Margaret shrank still further at the thought of being under the same roof as that notorious recusant, Anne Winshawe, and even Isabel quailed. Her grandmother's presence explained why the house was smothered by an invisible cushion of restraint.

'How is my mother?'

'Very sick. Unlikely to last until morning. It's a good job you came when you did.' Mary had kept her face averted from Mistress Westward but now glared at her. 'A girl will see to your things. You'll want your bed.'

Once Margaret had gone Isabel was shown a little softness.

'We'll go up to her now. I'd like to say she'll be glad to see you but she's not conscious. Your father can't bear to be in the room with her which is why he went for you himself I suppose, to be out of the way.' Mary gave her a quick kiss. 'She needs all the prayers she can get but not necessarily of Anne Winshawe's kind. In my opinion that woman has allowed far too many Jesuits into her life.'

Two candles burned on either side of the bed and between the meagre flames Thomasina lay under the embroidered canopy with long strands of hair trailing over the quilt. Her shoulders were covered by a tightly-drawn sheet, her neck was propped on high pillows and her hands folded on her breast. There was a shocking yellow tinge to her sunken cheeks and her nose and eye sockets were unnaturally prominent. Martha Canton sat on her left, Anne Winshawe on her right. Both held rosary beads, Martha's of wood, Anne's of garnet.

I wonder what my father will think of this arrangement? thought Isabel. I suppose he'll have to turn a blind eye because she's so ill. She dared another look at her mother and saw that life was a bloodless flicker in Thomasina's throat.

There was a fierce fire in the grate and the shutters were closed. Thomasina had a growth in her abdomen and the intimate nature of this complaint was signalled by a series of mysterious china receptacles ranged about the room. The stench of diseased female flesh was so strong that for a moment Isabel thought of the Clink.

Anne did not acknowledge her granddaughter's arrival but Martha shot her a shy smile. They had reached the fourth decade and whispered in unison. *Ave Maria, gratia plena, Dominus tecum, benedicta tu in mulieribus . . .*

'Ave Maria, gratia plena . . .

'Ave Maria, gratia plena . . .'

Thomasina's brow clenched. Her hands clawed the sheet and Anne Winshawe, without interrupting her prayer, folded them carefully back in place.

Isabel, conscious that she brought in her clothes the breezy smell of late summer, looked on with mounting horror. The figure in the bed with the translucent, fluttering eyelids could not possibly be Thomasina. No wonder she was dying. How could she breathe under the weight of so much heated air and stifling prayer? She should be on her feet, ranging the house with her head full of contemplation and good intentions.

Anne Winshawe on the other hand was little changed. Her thin hair was scraped back under a plain white headdress and her pink chins rested neatly on a small ruff. Otherwise she was in black. Her features were as composed as ever and she prayed with her usual high-pitched certainty. This, to her, was but another trial among many. In fact, Isabel realized with dreadful clarity, even the mortal illness of a beloved daughter was just part of the bread and butter of Anne's life, another stepping stone to heaven.

Still Anne refused to notice Isabel.

'*Pater noster, qui es in caelis . . .*'

Isabel remembered that when she had returned in disgrace from Oakshott after the argument with Nicholas Turner she had sprung across this room into Thomasina's arms, and the canopied bed had provided a blissful refuge. She walked to the window, opened the lattice and breathed deeply in the night air. The candles flickered.

Without missing a beat of the rosary Anne rose, shut the window and returned to her seat.

Isabel said: 'Please may I speak to my mother?'

Anne nodded.

'I want to speak to her alone.'

Anne's frigid eyes met hers. Isabel could read the thoughts sliding across the front of her mind, though her lips still intoned: '*Sancta Maria, mater Dei . . .*'

Naughty, spoilt child. My goodness you've changed.

Yes, I have changed. I don't want to be a part of this passive acceptance of death. I'm more interested in life now.

' . . . *et Benedictus fructus ventri tui . . .*'

My dear girl, said Anne, speaking through the rosary beads draped between her manicured fingers, I'm sorry to find you still so rebellious. And don't think I can't see what you've been up to; the print of a man's lips is on your mouth and his fingers have left their mark on your body. Unchaste.

144

'I want to speak to my mother alone.'

Suddenly Martha got up and trod softly to the door. Mary followed, and then at last, stiff-backed with disapproval and still chanting, Anne Winshawe. The door closed behind them and the candle flames dived and righted themselves. Isabel again unfastened the window and stood with her hands on the stone mullion, rather frightened by the ground she had won. What was she to do with this half-dead mother?

But slowly the nightmare subsided. The firelight was mellow on the white satin of the canopy and her great-grandmother's flowers emerged clear as ever. Isabel lay down on the bed, slid her hand under her mother's neck and drew her closer. The smell of stagnant flesh wouldn't go away and there seemed to be nothing of Thomasina in this weak bundle. What a contrast to Francis Bourne's muscular body, his passion.

'I'm looking for the bee, mother, and the ladybird. Yes, I see them. There they are. They remind me of summer.' Had Thomasina ever noticed these dainty insects or were her thoughts always turned inwards to the task of perfecting her soul? Isabel was struck by the loneliness of her mother's life, brought up by saintly Anne within the constraints of Oakshott, then whisked away by William Stanhope for the sake of her ancient name and impenetrable beauty to be kept a prisoner of her faith all these years at Cuddington.

Will my life be like hers if I marry Francis? she wondered. In this quiet chamber a needle sharp as glass had traced gentle flowers across the draperies. Thomasina's body had locked with her husband's in this same bed where other Stanhope women had been plunged into motherhood. The complication, the piercing and dragging of female flesh, the turmoil of being possessed. And each next day the fine needle had resumed its steady path, forget-me-nots, rosebuds, love-in-a-mist.

She pulled the edge of the sheet from under the mattress, released Thomasina from its grip and gathered her so close that her chin rested on her mother's bony shoulder.

'Can you smell the beginning of autumn, mother? I can.'

Her mother fluttered like a small bird, relaxed and sank

145

deeper into Isabel's arms, her breathing soft and regular as a sleeping child's.

The canopy insects and flowers flickered in and out of focus as the candle flames trembled in the breeze from the open window. Isabel's weary body came to itself again. She turned her face into her mother's dank hair and remembered Bourne's salty skin and insistent hands.

Was that embrace the cause of this disease? Had a vengeful Christ noted their illicit kisses and with a twitch of His right hand struck Thomasina down?

There must be a link, or why had Isabel been transplanted so swiftly from the arms of one to the deathbed of another?

Anne Winshawe and Sir William were at loggerheads over the question of whether or not a priest should be brought to Cuddington to give the last rites, though few words were spoken between them because of course Sir William was not prepared to admit that Catholic priests existed in England at all. When they met during his reluctant visits to Thomasina's room, Anne would say in a dispassionate voice: 'A deathbed wish should never be denied.'

Or: 'There is no need for you to be present when the priest comes.'

Or: 'I will attend to all the arrangements.'

Sir William didn't reply. He was uneasy that so little could be done to relieve his wife's pain and impatient at being kept waiting for something as unprofitable as death.

Two more days dragged by. The only diversion was Mary Bonniface's treatment of Margaret Westward whose bell was never answered and who was fed the most meagre portions. Margaret stayed in her room except when forced to appear at meals when she favoured Sir William with her admiring attention but kept a wary eye on the door in case yet another Catholic walked through it.

Only Martha Canton was sympathetic to Isabel. One morning when they were together in the garden Isabel heard news of her Thewing cousins. Alan was now at a Jesuit seminary in the Spanish Netherlands and Edmund, who had been taken under the wing of Lady Fitzroy, was already making his mark on the wool trade. Isabel noted that though he must have been in London often, he had never bothered to seek her out. She thought of the unpromising hours spent in the schoolroom at Oakshott with snuffling Alan Thewing and said: 'Fortunate boys. Who would have thought it?'

'Certainly Alan's vocation was a surprise to us all. Teresa is a mix of pride and terror. As you know, the chance of a Jesuit surviving more than a few months in this country is very slight. And we can now boast that another, secular priest was formed at Oakshott. Nicholas Turner will be ordained in a year or so.'

'Nicholas Turner a priest.'

'So we are very quiet, except of course for your Aunt Teresa who never gives us a dull moment.'

But here the conversation was interrupted by a visitor. Lady Joyce Whitfield, wife to Sir Richard, the justice who had dealt with Thomasina after the Powder Plot, was huge, bumptious and oozing prosperity. Recusant money, Isabel decided, fines, confiscations and bribes from families such as ours. Lady Whitfield's greying hair, wired and padded to rise an astonishing foot above her brow topped a crimson gown trimmed all over with rustling black appliquéd leaves.

'Your poor mother. She's had a terrible life. Could I just run up and take a look? We may have something in the pantry at home that would do the trick. Well, perhaps tomorrow. I could call again tomorrow. She must have been under such a strain all these years.' Lowered voice, inquisitive pale blue eyes.

'You mean since Sir Richard came and arrested her,' said Isabel.

'Poor man. That type of work doesn't come easily to him. Fortunately he brought her to me so she was among friends. He's in London now, in fact spends most of his time in London these days. He's got deeper into the law. I'd be in town myself except that my daughter is about to produce our fifth grandchild.'

Isabel escorted her to the door and watched as she heaved

herself into the carriage and was driven away. Happy Lady Whitfield had no scruples but rode from one pleasure to the next with just a quick diversion to Cuddington so she could carry news of that blighted household back to her friends.

Yet she is damned, thought Isabel. Is she? If not, there's no justice for my mother who has put all her eggs in the basket of our one true faith.

Meanwhile in the sickroom other battles were being fought. Sometimes Thomasina was plunged into such pain that her eyes opened wide with terror and Anne prayed louder to muffle the screams. Usually the patient didn't stir.

Anne and Isabel were not on speaking terms. Before Isabel's arrival Anne had been the director of her daughter's death but Isabel broke all the rules, even refusing to pray with the others. Instead she kept up a defiant litany in her head. She detested their lack of resistance and couldn't understand how her own feelings for her grandmother had undergone such a change in four years. At Oakshott she had thought Anne a saint, excusing her bitterness and bad temper as strength of character. Isabel had felt it a fault in herself to be critical. But now she saw an old woman entrenched in a rigid faith, wrong-headed, selfish and over-mighty.

After an hour in the sickroom Isabel would burst out and take gasps of the fresher air beyond, only to encounter the closed door of her father's library. Inside that sacrosanct place sulked Sir William Stanhope, another intransigent soul who manipulated people for his own ends. Isabel understood that her father and grandmother were alike and for the first time recognized the impulse that had caused Thomasina to marry Stanhope. She had been mesmerized by the part of him that was like Anne Winshawe.

It rained, the kind of soaking rain that comes in a vertical downpour, lets up to allow a sudden burst of glistening sunlight and then rains again. Riding or walking were out of the question, the drying-room was a fug of wet wool and servants had a constant dampness about their shoulders and calves. Isabel ranged from one room to another watching the rain bounce on the brick paths outside. She crept up to her mother's chamber, along to her own, down to the little parlour near the front door, back to the window, tormented by the way her mother's illness had hacked through the brief minutes of intimacy she had with Francis Bourne at Startsdon.

There was a figure out walking in the rain. Five minutes earlier, when Isabel last looked, the drive had been empty. The woman was hooded and cloaked but moved as if the driving rain did not touch her. Even through water and the thick glass in the parlour window her eyes met Isabel's and she smiled.

She came unhesitatingly up the steps and the bell jangled faintly behind the stairs. A servant scurried in response, a door was opened and the house went quiet again. Isabel went on looking out at the rain.

It was as if a firm hand had been placed on her shoulder.

Quarter of an hour later Isabel was summoned to the library. 'Nobody knew where you were. I've been searching for you all over the place,' said the maid. 'A friend of yours has come from London. She's very wet.'

The woman had taken off her cloak but her skirts were soaked from ankle to knee. She wore a taffeta over-gown and a fine embroidered linen petticoat but no ruff, a wise precaution in weather that would have softened any starch. Her light brown hair was plaited into a coil, unornamented and also damp. Yet she stood away from the fire, her head cocked to one side. Isabel knew exactly who she was.

Sir William seemed oddly displaced in his own library. 'Isabel, this is Mary Ward. She is staying near Alcester with friends of Lady Fitzroy who asked her to call here and enquire after you and your mother.'

They had been under the same roof together twice before, in Fitzroy House and somewhere on the way to Shrewsbury when Isabel had glimpsed Mary fleetingly through an open door. Isabel had heard her name spoken by Father Carisbroke and Francis Bourne and it was whispered sometimes in the few Catholic houses her father allowed her to visit. Mary was still a youngish woman – twenty-three or four – with a slender body and heavy-lidded eyes. Her gaze was concentrated like that of a swordsman who calculates several moves ahead.

Her composure fragmented Isabel's self-possession. There was no tension in her mouth or hands and she wore her clothes as if she were unaware of them. The library, with its many layers of history and ownership, was irrelevant to her.

'I'm very glad to see you again,' said Mary and her voice exactly filled the space between them.

'And I you.' Isabel had the vertiginous feeling of being too near the parapet of a high building. She remembered that at Lady Fitzroy's she had envied Blanche Morton for being deep in conversation with this woman. Now she was shaken by the implications of their encounter here at Cuddington under the eye of her father. 'My mother is dying. My grandmother, Anne Winshawe, is with her.'

Mary nodded.

'I'm afraid this isn't a very peaceful house to die in,' Isabel said. Her father moved to a table and picked up a document. 'I'll take you up to her if you like.'

They walked in silence across the hall, Isabel a couple of paces ahead.

'Father Carisbroke asked to be remembered to you. I last saw him a few months ago in St Omer,' said Mary.

His name was a blade of fire. It had the power to change the density of air and the colour of darkness. Isabel turned back. 'Why didn't you let the carriage bring you to the door? You are so wet.'

'I like the rain. And I like to see the whole of what I am coming to. You remember Father Carisbroke?'

'Yes.'

'He has a very high opinion of you.'

I understand, Isabel thought, that you are pulling me back into his net. *The Imitation of Christ* was still folded in a petticoat at the bottom of an old trunk and lay in her mind, a dark brown, portentous rectangle. 'My grandmother will do nothing but pray. She never pauses except to sleep sometimes or eat. Of course we must all pray. But I want my mother to die peacefully, not so filled up with other people's words that she has no space for her own. And my father hates being here at Cuddington and detests the praying. He's not a Catholic.'

'Isabel, what does your mother want?'

'I think, above all things, my mother would like there to be a priest.'

'Then I shall have one brought.'

Mary Ward let it be known that she was happy to take a hand at the nursing so a servant was sent to a house near Alcester for her clothes.

She appeared at supper in an ornate ruff and with a ruby necklace glinting on her breast. Anne Winshawe, who had unusually offered to eat with Sir William, was nervy in Mary's presence and more approachable. Beside her sat self-effacing Martha with an attentive glimmer to her eye. Isabel, intercepting an exchange of smiles, wondered how this alliance between Mary Ward and insignificant Martha had been sealed. Margaret Westward obviously thought that Mistress Ward was a true lady for she had dressed with extreme care, hoping perhaps that Mary would sympathize with her predicament among so many treacherous Catholics.

Mary's presence altered the mood completely. She reminded Isabel of Francis's most celebrated actor friend, a man who had only to lift a finger for the theatre to fall silent. They shared a scorching inner energy, as if a careless word might set them on fire. Yet Mary was serene and while the actor had encouraged attention by his extravagance, her gestures were unremarkable.

'You have been staying with Lady Fitzroy lately, Mistress Ward?' asked Sir William.

'Among other kind friends.'

'Who? Who do you number among your friends?' Either

he was on the alert for influential contacts or he was sounding her out for, as Isabel well knew, he was faintly uneasy
about the magnificent but enigmatic Lady Arabella Fitzroy.
Meanwhile Margaret's brows had reached her hairline in the
expectation of hearing a famous name.

'Sir William, you can't expect me to reveal the secrets of
the queen's intimate circle. But I can tell you that the talk
at the moment is all very dull, all money. The queen is being
asked to retrench.'

Mention of the Catholic queen was a double-edged sword
but Sir William had been steered deftly on to a subject very
close to his heart. 'And quite right too.'

'Do you think James will be forced to recall parliament?'
asked Mary.

Having at last found someone prepared to take an interest
in politics, Sir William began a long discourse on the state
of the king's finances, the iniquitous raising of customs duties
and the need for economies at court. Mary ate slowly,
listened attentively and put astute questions. But eventually
Stanhope remembered she was just a woman and turned
the conversation. 'Your own family? What is your history?
I don't know any Wards.'

'We are from the north.'

Anne Winshawe pushed her chair back from the table. A
servant sprang forward to help her up. 'I have neglected my
daughter long enough,' she said, thereby leaving a discon-
certing trail of guilt in her wake. Isabel caught the trace of
a smile in Mary's eye. Margaret exclaimed: 'Oh, I know the
name Ward. A very old name. Very old.'

An hour later a gangly Irish priest arrived. The bed-chamber
was cleared of its paraphernalia of sickness and a little table
set out for the anointing. Anne Winshawe submitted to all
Mary Ward's arrangements with uncharacteristic docility and
took up her post in silence at Thomasina's head.

The whole household attended except Margaret who had
a room at the far end of the house. Servants clustered in the

little dressing-room and outside in the corridor. Isabel knelt with her grandmother, Mary Bonniface and Martha while Mary Ward, being neither a relative nor an intimate, kept her distance beyond the circle of light. The next day Isabel was to hear it rumoured that Sir William had left his bedroom door ajar so that he too could take part.

'*Illumina faciem tuam super servum tuum* . . .' The priest's soft Irish lilt was a reassuring caress but somehow this was not an easy picture to have of Thomasina, who belonged not in light but in shadow.

By dawn Thomasina was dead. The fire had been put out, the hearth swept, the shutters latched, the casements fastened and clean linen folded round the corpse. The priest had gone and the servants were in bed. Anne Winshawe had been led to her room by Martha and Mary Bonniface slept in her truckle bed by the door but Isabel still held her mother's hand, as if by her grip Thomasina might be prevented from disappearing in body as well as soul.

There was a small rustling of skirts. Mary Ward's eyes were black with exhaustion but her smile as bright as ever. Where had she spent the small hours? Together they glided down the stairs and along the servants' passage to an outer door.

In the mossy courtyard cobbles were soaked by heavy dew and a feeble sun struggled through a film of cloud. The air was quite sharp and cut across Isabel's stale cheeks.

To the west of the house paths wound through a small shrubbery to a hedged vegetable garden. Beyond was a stretch of wilderness where pheasants were bred, and then the fields of the home farm. Mary Ward linked her arm through Isabel's and clasped their hands together. As they walked their skirts gathered a burden of moisture. Isabel was washed by morning, projected forward by the energy of the other woman's stride.

They came to a closed gate and silence, pale as the sky, opened between them. Isabel felt the weight of it like a blanket. I don't want this, she thought. I want to be released from the pressure of my grief, not forced deep into my head. Fiercely she unlatched the gate and walked into the wilderness which was a small copse of spindly trees and dense undergrowth.

She said violently, 'I'm going to marry Francis Bourne. We're as good as betrothed.'

No answer came from Mary Ward.

'Tell your Father Carisbroke that, will you? I'll marry Francis and then I'll be free of you all.'

Silence.

'I don't want to be hounded like this. I've made my choice and I'm going to marry Francis. My father will be so glad. I know you'll deny it but you've been after me since you arrived. Even at my mother's deathbed I knew you were waiting for the chance to take me. Well, weren't you?' Tears spurted from her eyes and nose. 'I would so like to be more sorry that my mother is dead. I should so like not to have shared my mother with God all my life. I have never felt so alone. Don't tell me I'm not alone. I ache. I ache. I am so lost, Mary.'

A pheasant burst shockingly from the undergrowth. Isabel sprang back but Mary didn't move. Insubstantial and calm-faced in the thin morning air, only her skirts swayed in the slight breeze.

Silence re-established itself, bred in the forested plains of central England, washed clean by dew. Birdsong perforated it at intervals, like pins through muslin.

'Who is hounding you, Isabel?' Mary said.

Isabel's head was too heavy and her throat fell back until she saw the hazed sky through a canopy of fading leaves.

'God will never give up on you, Isabel. He'll never let you go however hard you fight.'

'How do you know? How can you know?'

'I remember seeing you in Lady Fitzroy's house. I couldn't get near you but I wanted to. I knew that you and I would be important to each other. But you were too young then and I was about to leave England. Isabel, I am an expert on uncertainty.'

'I don't understand what you mean.'

'You are expecting to be sure. You think everything will all of a sudden be simple. Well it won't. I know. Five months ago I was in a convent in Gravelines with the English Poor Clares. I thought I'd be there for life. Now look at me.'

'My cousin Susannah Thewing is there, I think.'

'Yes. I knew your cousin Susannah.'

'What happened? Did you give up?'

'I didn't give up but I couldn't go on. There is a difference. I understood that not changing course is a matter of pride sometimes. In the end humiliation, how something might seem to others, is part of what must be surrendered. God works beyond these considerations. I always thought I knew what I wanted. I could never imagine myself married when I was a child. I wanted to be a nun though nobody else was keen on the idea. Even my confessor, Father Holtby – now the revered head of the English Jesuits – even he was trying to persuade me to marry. Bear Catholic children, he said, that is the best service you can do our cause.'

'How did you dare tell him he was wrong?'

'There was no resisting my inner conviction. Only the convent. Only a life given body and soul to God. So in the end I got my way. When I arrived in Flanders three years ago I thought I was close to heaven. Like you, I had been forced to worship in secret at home. Over there everyone shared my faith. I was certain that I would find a contemplative convent and be welcomed with open arms. I thought it would be simple. But the convents were over-crowded with English refugees like me. When eventually the Poor Clares let me join them they said it must be as a lay sister. I must go begging every day to support my sisters inside the enclosure. As you can imagine I was shocked to the core. My vanity was hurt. For heaven's sake, I, a lady, was expected to beg like a poor country girl with no dowry and no education.'

I don't want to hear this, thought Isabel. I don't want to hear that Mary Ward has taken a series of wrong turnings. I want her to be clear. If I have to jump, I want to jump cleanly.

'I'd never served anyone before except when I chose to as a kind of penance. I'd not known poverty or hunger. Instead of an undisturbed life of contemplation I had to travel long distances and talk to dozens of people every day. It felt utterly wrong. Now I see it was completely right.'

'You say that because you want it to be true. You don't want God to have led you astray.'

'I was weak and God made me strong. I thought I had bad health but He showed me I could overcome sickness if I was working for him. He taught me not to be deflected by people who jeered at my accent or my clothes or who answered my request for food with a fistful of rotten vegetables. I came to know the streets of St Omer like the back of my hand. I learnt how to read the weather, to speak out fearlessly, to crush my fear of being rejected or disliked and to deal with the little crumbs of admiration that came my way, which are just as distracting. Hardly a waste of time, all that. And then I was shown that a new foundation needed to be set up.'

'Shown. Shown?'

'It was something I had really known all along, but not seen. An uncovering.'

'By God?'

'By God. It became obvious to me that English women like myself and your cousin Susannah should not have to enter foreign convents where nobody speaks our language, not even the priests to whom we confess. Once I saw that, there was no time for prevarication. I had to raise money and write letters, make contacts, get permission. We rented a house in Gravelines, near the coast and furnished it with straw mattresses. Five nuns were sent from the convent where I'd been a lay sister in St Omer to act as founder members, abbess and novice mistress of our new foundation. They arrived in a closed carriage escorted by three Franciscans, wrenched from the enclosure in which they had expected to spend the rest of their lives and transported to another but they didn't complain and nor did they snatch at a glimpse of the outside world. They simply took up the threads of their religious life again. Their world was so contracted that the town they had driven through scarcely existed for them. That's what I wanted for myself, to be free at last of all the complications of secular life. I couldn't help rejoicing that I'd created a little English nest for myself and other women like me.

'So I flung myself into the life of a novice. I woke at midnight to say the Divine Office and spent hours and hours on my knees. The rule of St Clare allows one meal a day and no meat. I could feel my body thinning into transparency and it seemed to me every day I flew higher and higher towards God. It was as if my life had become the essence of itself and soon all that was left would be a small white flame of prayer.'

A bee was crawling lazily up a fold in Isabel's gown but she didn't take her eyes from Mary's face, the clear skin on her forehead, the contour of her upper cheek and the perfect, palest pink ellipse of her eyelids.

'I never slept for more than two hours at a time because I was so hungry. I would wake in the small hours and every minute would be separated from the next in its own grip of cramping pain or cold or even despair. There was no future that would be any different from the present and no memory that mattered. Each day a new phrase of the Gospel would unfurl itself from the others and make itself understood, like a flower from a tight bud. If I'd had one such revelation a week I would never have stopped rejoicing. I treasured every minute gift of God's creation because I had time to understand it. I could scarcely breathe with excitement when I thought, if I can achieve so much in so few months, what will I have become in years?

'And then abruptly my days in the convent ended before I was professed. I was annihilated by God. He struck me down and plucked me upright again, wiped me clean and filled me with His light. He told me to leave the convent he had earlier asked me to found and serve Him in some other way. So I have come back to England to await my next move.'

Isabel was outraged. Surely an inner voice which urged the abandoning of a vocation ought to be treated with deep suspicion, especially given the harsh conditions of a Poor Clare convent.

'It was like being split into fragments, every bone broken,

every drop of blood separated from the next. And afterwards I wasn't the same. I could no more resist what I had experienced than I could ignore being pierced by steel or burnt with a flame. Do you understand?

'My confessor, who was deeply upset by my change of heart, pleaded with me to join another order, maybe the Teresians. So I read the life of Teresa of Avila. I admired her spirituality but was unmoved. I came back to England and certainly I find that I'm needed here. I have a gift, I know it, though one I'd rather be without because it leads to trouble. I know that when I speak, people listen. If I want something to happen, it often does. If I enter a house where the Catholic faith has been suffocated and God ignored, I can re-ignite the flame. I believe I can uncover similar gifts in others and make them work for God.'

'But what about those nuns you left behind in Gravelines? You set up the convent for them. You had a responsibility to them.'

'No, Isabel. I love them and pray for them but I am not bound to them. Each woman chose to join the order of the English Poor Clares, not the order of Mary Ward. They have a mother superior and excellent spiritual directors to guide them. I was only one among several unprofessed there.'

'So, you've rejected marriage and left the convent. There are no other choices.'

'None that you or I can see at the moment. But there is another way. God has something else in mind for me.'

The morning had deepened. In an outbuilding a metal tool clashed on stone and a male voice shouted. Isabel imagined a hushing up, a guilty glance round, that there should be such loudness when Lady Thomasina Stanhope lay dead in her room upstairs. In a few minutes she and Mary must go back and the shuttered house would close round them, the beginning of mourning.

'I shall be leaving in a couple of hours,' said Mary.

'For London?'

'And then Flanders again.'

An impulse was struggling through Isabel's mistrust and

grief. Until the words came she had no idea what they would be. 'I should so love to go with you.'

'Perhaps one day, when I know for sure where I'm going and when you're not needed here.'

They began to walk back together, barring the gate, skirts and shoulders brushing occasionally.

There. A door left ajar. The invitation on which a life pivots.

Chapter 12

Two days after his wife's funeral Sir William left Cuddington and a week later a letter arrived ordering Anne Winshawe and her entourage to depart immediately. He had found out that when dining with Mary Ward he had supped with the devil. Of course he had realized after the first night that she was a Catholic but not that she had a name for wreaking havoc among wavering recusant households by encouraging love of the sacraments and luring young girls into foreign convents. For this deception he blamed his mother-in-law.

Margaret watched Isabel with ever greater vigilance. Letters were read, servants searched, private conversations forbidden. Even Francis Bourne was not allowed to speak alone with her when he called soon after Thomasina's death. The proprieties, said Margaret, must be observed and Isabel after all was in deep mourning. Mistress Westward was taking no chances. Who knew what her charge might do to overset the wedding plans?

Meanwhile Sir William was busy petitioning for his son's release, this time on the grounds that Robin should be allowed home to grieve. The subtext of his request was that with Thomasina safely out of the way her son was in less danger of going astray. His application was again refused.

Then rumours came that Sir William was intent on wooing a rich young widow for himself. During his brief visit at Christmas the pressure on Isabel to marry soon was insistent. No wealthy Protestant could be won by a widower with a disobedient Catholic daughter and a son in the Clink accused of treason. If, however, that daughter was the wife of the delectable Francis Bourne she would turn from liability to lure, for Bourne was a great favourite at court and had desirable family connections with Lionel Cranfield, rising star of finance and commerce.

Isabel, caught between the sugary condolences of Margaret Westward and incessant visits from Joyce Whitfield and other neighbours suddenly keen to ingratiate themselves with a household cleansed of Thomasina, paced the gardens in an agony of grief and anxiety. But beneath her sorrow was a clenched fist of determination. She used the silent hours spent sewing mourning gowns or alone in her chamber to armour herself with prayer.

In February Francis brought two of his sisters to stay in nearby Warwick. Isabel and Margaret received them in the library, now largely disused. The chairs had been set at a formal distance from each other, the windows deeply shrouded in muslin. Neither of the Bourne girls had visited Cuddington before and at first sat stiff as dolls in their best gowns, Dorothea in grey, Deborah pale blue.

Francis had subtly adapted his dress to suit his new status of lover and Deborah, who could not be kept down for long even by sober Cuddington, pointed out the modifications with a sisterly eye for the ridiculous. 'He must love you, Isabel. Ever since you left Startsdon he's been wearing one of your ribbons in his hat and open-necked lacy shirts. Mother says he looks like a fool.'

'I'm an artist,' put in Francis. 'I know nothing of fashion. All I care about is words.'

'Look at his gloves,' cried Deborah. 'Pansies, see, on the gauntlet. What next?'

'Well, Mistress Isabel, soon I'll have no choice but to smarten up,' said Francis. 'I have bowed to pressure and entered the world of commerce.'

Isabel had insisted on wearing her newest black silk gown for this occasion, so encrusted with seed pearls that it rattled softly when she moved. Its shoulder wings and deep ruff kept her sealed up tight and Bourne could not come near her. Only the very tips of her fingers reached past the wheel of her farthingale. From behind this barricade she watched him coldly and tried to understand the girl in the attic room who had returned his seductive kisses.

That was another Isabel, since discarded. Her replacement was rigid as iron but the sight of Francis was an unwelcome reminder of her lapse. And her heart was untrustworthy. His sudden lop-sided smile shook her aloofness and the affection of his sisters was very touching.

'My new play, *Persephone*, has suffered a set-back. I had been promised it would be put on at Blackfriars but suddenly funds weren't available and now the management has said they're not happy with the mythological theme. They prefer histories. So for the time being I've given in to my father and am working with his master, Lionel Cranfield.'

'How marvellous,' put in Margaret, diligently winding silks. 'Lionel Cranfield.'

'I shall continue to write but soon I shall have a wife and household to maintain so I must be more serious about money. I need a town house for my lady and I want her to be proud of me. So I've gone into the starch trade.'

Deborah snorted.

'You see the lack of respect they treat me with at home, Isabel. Starch is a lucrative business, according to Cranfield. I am to spend some time in London and some in Europe investigating the markets there and the state of our competitors. I'm hoping my new wife will come with me on my travels.'

Isabel turned a ring on her middle finger and gave a small smile.

'He's going to put together a library for you, Isabel,' said Deborah, her thin face eager and unguarded. 'Already he's started collecting books.'

Dorothea was silent. There was an uncomfortable bond between her and Isabel formed by their unequal friendship and the incident with the eggs in the chicken barn. When Isabel glanced up at last she saw that Dorothea was looking very tidy and sober with her hair brushed smooth and a long stomacher contorting her unfashionable figure. Her gaze was infused with loving sympathy.

Before he left, Francis gave Isabel a leather pouch contain-

162

ing a pendant of amethyst droplets. She held it up to the light and as it rotated each gem swung from a separate little chain. 'You could pin it in your hair or your ruff. Do you like it?' She couldn't avoid his eye any longer and was disturbed by what she read in his face. How awkward and terrible it would be to discover that he really loved her. But it was impossible to tell with Francis which was a truthful expression. 'I wish you'd trust me, Isabel. I wish you would say if there is anything I can do for you.'

She shook her head and turned away to exchange awkward kisses with the girls. Throughout this interview she had managed to seem entirely preoccupied by grief for a dead parent and was well aware that she had quenched the girls' pleasure at visiting her.

I have no choice, she told herself fiercely. It is kinder in the long run to make them think less of me.

In April 1610, Sir William settled the financial arrangements with John Bourne and decreed that Isabel's wedding would take place in July. Isabel and Margaret were summoned to London.

Margaret, who detested the isolation of Cuddington where she was terrorized by Mary Bonniface, began a frenzy of packing but Isabel shut herself in her mother's room and lay for hours under the canopy. The soft tentacles of her future were pulling her away from this safe, female enclave. Goodbye. Goodbye, my poor mother.

The intricate embroidery spoke a clear enough message to her now. Break the thread, Isabel. Break.

Four days later she and Margaret reached London where Isabel continued her punishing programme of self-denial and prayer. For years she had neglected her faith but now must be so resolute that no amount of violent persuasion could make her waver. Her nerves jangled with excitement. Once more she was in tune with the church and all the people she loved and admired the most; Mary Ward, her mother, Father Garnet, Father Peter Carisbroke. Meanwhile she

163

appeared docile and allowed herself to be measured and discussed by Margaret's cronies who had infested the house to help with the sewing.

Lady Fitzroy called, aristocratic and glacial. Isabel met her in a downstairs room where Margaret sat stitching a translucent muslin cuff. Cool as February, Arabella pressed her petal-soft cheek to Isabel's. 'I see you have put your hair up, Isabel, surely a little premature?' Her eyes were marble, her fingers limp and her gown of ruby satin glowed in the dim room with gaudy lack of feeling. Gold thread glinted on the under-skirt and her cushiony bosom swelled above the jewelled edge of her bodice. 'Isabel, see who I have brought with me. It is your cousin, Edmund Thewing. I couldn't keep him away.'

When Edmund kissed Isabel's hand a waft of perfume issued from his jerkin. He was transformed from a bored and subversive boy to a languid gentleman, glamorous in trunk hose so short they scarcely covered his buttocks. Margaret's eyes popped.

'I remember you well, Edmund.' Isabel decided that she disliked him as much as ever. He was all gloss; dark eyes and lashes, silky beard, tapering white fingers. 'I thought you were a merchant of some sort.'

'The trouble is I can't let Edmund go. He's become so useful at managing my affairs,' said Lady Fitzroy.

Now there's a thing, thought Isabel. Edmund, useful. She shot a glance from one to another wondering what was behind this unlikely liaison but Edmund wandered to the window and Lady Fitzroy's impassive eyes gave nothing away.

She had come to offer both condolence and congratulation, she said, though her attention was not focused on either for long. 'Mistress Westward, the quality of your needlecraft is unmatched, exquisite. But surely you need more light?'

The visit dragged on. Lady Arabella's conversation was airy and trivial. She had salacious gossip about the king and his Scottish favourite, Robert Carr, whose meteoric rise and expensive tastes had caused dismay in the queen's circle. And she longed to see Francis Bourne's play performed at last but alas, she'd heard that it had been put off yet again. Oh, great heavens, had Isabel never been to a performance in an outdoor London theatre? But she must, she must. Such an experience was unmissable. In a few weeks, maybe, as a treat before the wedding.

At this Edmund, who had been silent, woke up. 'We adore the theatre. Never miss a play. I strongly recommend you go some time, Isabel.'

But now, having run out of conversation, the visitors departed, leaving not a single suspicious titbit for Margaret Westward to relay back to Sir William.

Martha Canton, dressed from head to foot in stifling black, was sent from Yorkshire to represent Anne Winshawe at Isabel's wedding. She was greeted with hostility by Sir William and considerable jealousy by Margaret because of her superb needlecraft. However, Martha was such a mouse that no one could regard her seriously as a threat for long. And the hideous task of embroidering a black veil for Isabel, black silk thread on black voile, had been left very late so Martha was ushered into an insignificant corner and set to work.

Gradually the festivities were stepped up. The shutters were opened and the house came out of mourning. Isabel was encouraged to wear a dress of deep blue instead of black. She appeared at court again in company with Francis and met her father's widow, a thin-haired woman with an unfortunate nose and wary eyes who clung to Sir William's arm with girlish dependence and gave Isabel a mean little smile.

Margaret pushed hard for the proposed trip to the theatre. She was starved of society and Lady Arabella had promised that if they sat high in the gallery they would be among the most influential and seen by everyone. Isabel was outraged. How could she possibly attend a play less than a year after her mother's death? No. No. She and Martha would stay home. Let Margaret go if she wished. Sir William replied furiously that if she was marrying Francis she must learn not to despise his pleasures. Of course she should go to the theatre.

So once more Isabel set off through the crammed and noxious streets of London, this time in her father's carriage and accompanied by Margaret Westward, Martha Canton, whose rabbity eyes were huge with alarm, Michael Latham and a maid. In the stifling heat of the dark interior, the women fanned themselves furiously.

They crossed the river in Sir William's decorative and upholstered barge, thereby avoiding crowds on the bridge. Isabel kept her eyes firmly on the south bank which floated mistily through the dense gathers of her veil. Somewhere to the right of the sturdy tower of St Mary's church her brother lurked in his high prison room. She had not been allowed to visit him since her return to London.

The interior of the Globe was bewildering. Isabel had been isolated for so long she could not get used to the crush of spectators and the great mass of moving fabrics. The circular galleries rose like a fortress and overhead skittish clouds sped across a blue sky. Sunlight, when it emerged, was painfully bright but edged abruptly by black shadow and the painted marble pillars and mock plaster caryatids had been created with an unrestrained relish for colour.

Isabel remained aloof from those who jabbed their heads forward to look into her veiled face. She climbed a narrow staircase, up, up to the highest level and sank on to a bench at the very brink of the gallery with her toes hanging over empty space and her breast pressed to the restraining bar. A little to the left but at a distance was Edmund Thewing, nonchalant in saffron velvet, a lady on each arm. He gave his cousin an uninterested nod but didn't trouble himself to approach.

Francis Bourne, like every other member of the audience, seemed like a player to Isabel, real and not real. She saw his face appear round Margaret's shoulder, the slightly contrived lock of hair hanging over his forehead, the crooked smile that sprang up on the right side of his mouth and slowly pulled at the left, the uncomplicated pleasure at seeing her. He fell to one knee and his lips touched her gloved hand though she felt only the faintest breath of warmth through the soft leather.

He whispered: 'I wish I could see your face. I'd love to watch you watching a play again.'

'I hope the play will be more interesting than my face.'

'Seen it before. A strange piece but plenty of suspense. The audience will love it. I wonder where your sympathies will lie?'

Her heart was beating so fast she could hardly speak to him. A sharp elbow was pressing her ribs. She smiled at him and hoped he could not see her eyes through the veil. Someone from far below shouted up so he hung over the balcony and waved vigorously. He was reluctant to leave Isabel but couldn't resist getting closer to the stage.

There came a fanfare, a sigh of fading conversation and a quickening of tension. Isabel's hands sweated into the lining of her gloves.

Dear God, keep us safe.

> *Gentle Isabella,*
> *Turn you the key, and know his business of him:*
> *You may, I may not; you are yet unsworn . . .*
> *He calls again; I pray you, answer him.*

Her head jolted up. Who had called her name? She expected the audience to stare at her but they strained towards the stage where a boy actor was dressed in the dark gown of a novice nun. And there was Francis right at the front, arms folded as if to say: I'm such an expert. I know how this is going to unfold. Nothing will surprise me about this play.

> *bring me to the sight of Isabella,*
> *A novice of this place, and the fair sister*
> *To her unhappy brother Claudio.*

Isabel shook so violently that her spine struck the knees of the man behind her. She turned first to Margaret then Martha but both were immersed in the action.

> *the hideous law . . .*

'Isabel. Be calm.'

Under whose heavy sense your brother's life
Falls into forfeit

'What about Robin? Won't it make matters worse for him?' Isabel murmured.

'You're not responsible for Robin.'

Sometimes the play retreated so far that Isabel thought she was all alone with her future pressing on her eyes and roaring in her ears. Sometimes she was startled back into the present and a torrent of phrases would become crystal clear.

Then, Isabel, live chaste, and brother, die:
More than our brother is our chastity.

Dear God, prayed Isabel, let this be the worst trial of my life.

She glanced again at Francis and saw him laugh. The sight of his exposed throat and open mouth reassured her. So this staged duplicity amused him; the twists of the plot, the misfortune of women fighting their way through a conspiracy of sin and seduction, had made him forget all about her. And yet she sensed he was aware of her. He was deeply self-conscious, and an actor. He knew she watched him because he was watching her, in fact had been alert to her throughout the play.

Her hands could hardly reach together to applaud for the air seemed to bounce between her palms. The audience turned in on itself and became an ants' nest of a hundred different purposes. Francis was already weaving his way through, had disappeared under the gallery and was now close to her again.

'What did you think, Isabel? I told you that playwright was a genius. A much more accomplished production than the first time I saw it. Will you come and meet a friend of mine? John Fl –' But they were separated at the head of the stairs. Edmund Thewing and his ladies were in the way, a throng of admirers had caught up with Francis and Isabel's maid, overwhelmed by the crush, staggered against Michael

168

Latham. Isabel's elbow was caught by a steady hand and she was drawn down the steep steps.

'Take off your veil. Put this on instead.' There was a tug on her hair, even while she stumbled downwards, and the black veil was replaced by one of white which floated to her knees. When they emerged, blinding sunlight was diffused through snowy cloth. 'Walk fast, Isabel. Don't resist me.'

Their feet slithered in an alley dark as a cavern. A plain little carriage with shuttered windows waited for them and was set in motion almost before they had closed the door.

In the stuffy half-light the two women spoke in nervous whispers.

'I think we have half an hour to be clear of the city. They will waste time looking for us in the crowd.'

'I almost feel sorry for them.'

'You have cause.'

Nothing more was said. Isabel gripped Martha's hand. At last she was calm, her head emptied of all thought but the process of getting away. Fifteen minutes later they sat in a rowing boat, heads down, faded red cloaks hiding their clothes. The currents bore them swiftly under the central arch of London Bridge, tossed them about in a sudden turbulence then released them into calmer water beyond. The Tower slid by and Isabel tensed her shoulders as if its thick walls had the power to draw her into their confines but the oarsmen pulled strongly and they flew down river with the tide until the city had thinned into the odd jetty or small settlement and flat empty marshland stretching away on all sides.

Near Woolwich a three-masted ship was moored, flying the Flemish ensign. A few last bales of wool were being winched aboard and a ladder was thrown over its side. Isabel flung her hand on to its narrow rung, hoisted up her skirt and began to climb. Her feet tangled in her petticoats and her body swung out over the Thames but she was pierced with joy. At last, at last to act, to spring into life. She turned gleefully and offered her hand to Martha Canton. On deck they were met by the captain himself who spoke little English but made several obsequious references to the generosity of

169

one Lady Fitzroy. He ushered them down another steep ladder and tucked them away in a tiny cabin. A thousand planks of wood shifted in the water and the busy ship went on with its work.

They laughed, cried and clasped each other's waists. It was a moment of soaring triumph and thanksgiving.

By nightfall the ship had sailed to the mouth of the Thames. Isabel stood under the stars and thought she was cupped in the palm of God. Francis, whose latest obsession was astronomy, had taught her that beyond what she could see were more and more stars, and that the night sky was yet another world that men looked at with eyes blinded by ignorance. 'Isabel, there are men who do nothing but watch the sky. They find patterns in the stars and subtle movements. When we have learnt how to read the sky what now is darkness will be unfolded as space between a wonderfully coherent composition of light.'

The ship was fragile, riding the gentle swell under the vast sky. I was born for this, Isabel thought, the time between the leaving and the arriving. She suddenly had a perverse wish that there was no one ahead of her, no hand reaching out to grasp hers, no Mary Ward or Father Carisbroke. How wonderful to sweep forward for ever like the ship.

But somewhere under her feet Martha Canton was at prayer. Nearby in a state-room a senior member of the French ambassadorial staff, official passenger on this vessel, was entertaining the captain. Tomorrow or the day after that, depending on the wind, they would reach Flanders and be flung forward into a new world.

Chapter 13

M ary Ward had a multitude of friends and supporters. She was a magnet for the frustrated, the bored or the committed English Catholic who had no niche in a religious order, the priesthood or among the noble families worshipping at home in England. The Spanish Netherlands teemed with young Catholic males hot from school in Douai so Isabel and Martha Canton were met in Gravelines by two ardent young men who handed them into yet another carriage and served as out-riders on the day's journey to St Omer.

Isabel had been prepared for dramatic incident but there was none. She was sped on her way by fair winds and quiet roads. God was smiling on this daughter who had at last obeyed His call. She was hollow as a bell, a receptacle for new sensation, every minute further from persecution and the marriage to Francis Bourne from which she now shrank. The old life was sloughed off.

Nothing disappointed her, neither the unremarkable fields of crops in exactly the same state of ripeness as at home, nor the fact that labourers here looked very much like their English counterparts with no visible sign of the untainted Catholic blood flowing in their veins. This was the promised land where the wrenching pain of believing body and soul in a prohibited faith was over at last.

It dawned on her that dozens of Catholic priests must have travelled this same road on their way to speedy martyrdom in England. Father Garnet had seen these same wide skies and lush plains but all his years of prayer and study had culminated in arrest and a few tortured steps to the scaffold.

And Isabel now had a bond with him for there was no going back on her decision. If she ever returned to England it would be as a subversive like Mary Ward, a resistance worker armed with a quiet smile and petticoats.

Her companion rarely spoke. The practicalities of the journey weighed heavily and she never relaxed her guard. Isabel had certainly revised her opinion of Martha whose lacklustre appearance ensured that she was usually overlooked but whose timid eyes and buck-toothed smile hid a woman of needle-sharp wits and cool audacity.

'Martha, do you wish you were me, going to live in St Omer with Mary Ward?'

'I'm very happy at Oakshott.'

'But you must surely have longed to be more active all these years.'

'I'm not the adventurous type. I only do as I'm told.'

'Mary Ward would say that your talent for subterfuge is God-given and shouldn't be wasted. Think how useful you could be in London helping priests and visiting prisons. Don't you find your life at Oakshott too limited?'

'No. I'm content.'

'But if you were me, would you have chosen to go to Mary Ward? Don't you think she is amazing?'

'Isabel, I could never be like you.'

'I want an answer.'

Martha was not used to giving her opinion. Again Isabel wondered how such an unpromising exterior could house so fine a character.

'What I certainly do envy,' said Martha at last, 'is that you'll be among brilliant and devout English Catholic women. The calibre of those who have joined Mary is a great tribute to her. Mary Poyntz for instance, is descended from the Earls of Pembroke and Cornwall and her cousin Winifred Wigmore is remarkably learned, fluent in at least five languages. Blanche Morton you already know.'

'You've not answered my question about Mary Ward. What are you holding back?'

'I think your grandmother would have preferred you to have gone to the Teresians. She's read a great deal about

Teresa of Avila. It's what she would have chosen for herself, the contemplative life, no possessions.'

'She could have entered a convent when grandfather died,' said Isabel sharply.

'She had a duty to Oakshott.'

'I can't imagine grandmother in a convent. She couldn't have kept the vow of obedience. But what does she think of Mary Ward?'

'Your grandmother is always suspicious of other strong women. Do you remember the argument you had with Nicholas Turner? Certainly she used it as an excuse to get you and a string of horses south to Cuddington but she really was furious with you for criticizing Turner. She had picked him out and decided that she would sponsor him for the priesthood. Who were you to cast a slur on her judgement? So though she admires Mary she mistrusts her. She sees that young women like you find her very compelling and that her work is of great benefit to the church in England. But there is a fine distinction between a visionary and a heretic. Mary Ward is close to the edge.'

'What can be heretical about the work she's doing? She has simply founded a community of celibate English Ladies. Her work educating the daughters of English Catholic families is already legendary.'

'The question is whether she will be content to stop at that.'

'Whatever do you mean?'

'Isabel, my job is to extricate you from your engagement, not to cast doubts on your decision.'

'You should have told me you had reservations about Mary Ward.'

'Your grandmother wanted you out of your father's clutches. Mary Ward has many friends and impeccable credentials apart from her rather unfortunate tendency to change course. She may succeed, she may not. Certainly she can do nothing alone and is dependent on girls like you taking the plunge with her. You may be at the start of a foundation that will be of importance to the Catholic church. On the other hand, the whole thing might disintegrate in a

173

matter of weeks. Who's to say? It's a risk. Isn't that what you wanted?'

The landscape had changed from fields and forests to heavily cultivated market gardens. Cottages set in plots of cauliflowers and potatoes were bordered on all sides by canals. They passed a hooded monk stooped over a row of beans like a print in a forbidden book.

Occasionally St Omer's churches were visible above a cluster of sloping red roofs. For an hour the carriage lumbered along lanes which must have constituted half a day's walk to Mary Ward on her tortured begging expeditions as a Poor Clare. 'Shall we go to the cathedral first? Shall we see what it's like to be in a Catholic church?' Isabel said.

'We're expected in the Rue Grosse.'

'Ten minutes. Just to convince ourselves of where we are.'

They lurched over cobbles into the heart of a tightly packed town. As Isabel stepped from the carriage she felt significant, like one of Francis's actor friends making an entrance on stage.

But she preferred not to think of Bourne and her desertion of him. Instead she gazed up at the soaring cathedral which in England would have represented terror and exclusion. When she put her hand to the massive door it fell back on well-oiled hinges. Inside there was black inner space and then another door, as if the interior were reluctant to reveal itself too suddenly.

The ceiling floated above three storeys of arcades and the sunshine slanting through hidden windows bleached stone tracery to the colour of whipped cream. Isabel wheeled under pale arches and jewelled light filtered by stained glass. She was drawn across broad flagstones to an aisle edged with wrought-iron railings. A dozen side-chapels were painted and carved in a feast of sacred images and stories. Statues sparkled with gold, crimson and indigo.

She couldn't pray. The brilliant colours, the fretted stone-

174

work, the bustle and the murmur of French voices seemed all wrong. She was stupidly home-sick for the little chapel in the roof at Oakshott with its sparse candlelight and the knowledge that God waited quietly in the space between the roof tiles and the edge of heaven. When a bell rang she flinched. Bells in England summoned people to Protestant services or informed them of war or plague. Here they rang jubilantly just because mass was beginning.

Martha knelt near the door, too humble to penetrate further. Her prayer world continued its peaceful cycle whatever the circumstances. She was more unshakably rooted in her faith than anyone Isabel knew, except perhaps Mary Ward. Martha was invincible. The exuberant trappings of a cathedral could not swamp her, nor the threat of Sir William Stanhope's rage when he discovered who had made possible his daughter's escape.

The pews were now flooded by a buzzing, casual congregation, wealthy ladies in vibrant gowns sweeping to the front, the poor shuffling to the back. A priest decked out in glistening robes processed behind rows of men and boys in crisp surplices. Two women in the pew ahead gossiped through a mass said at break-neck speed. Isabel, who had not confessed and therefore could not participate in communion, watched with mounting disillusionment.

To her right, on an abutment between two chapels was a small, stone panel, a relief of the Virgin and Child. Isabel glanced at it once, then again. A cat was curled at the Virgin's feet, its head snug against her skirts. The baby, tightly swaddled, rested one fat palm on his mother's wrist, the other on her breast. The fingers of the Virgin's right hand were parted to offer her exposed nipple. She was very young, wavy-haired, happy, perched on a bench with an ox pressed to her back and an ass raising its head above hers. At any moment it seemed, the girl would tuck the baby under her arm, leap to her feet and rush off, sending the cat flying.

'*Credo in unum Deum, Patrem omnipotentem, factorem caeli et terrae . . .*'

Here was the Virgin Mary presented as a local girl with sturdy peasant's hands, paused in her busy life to nurse her child. In St Omer everyone was part of a great unity. Peasant, artist, priest and aristocrat were of one mind. Catholic.

Mary Ward's house on Rue Grosse stood at the corner of a narrow side-street. It was broad, high and of local stone with green shutters and a sternly ornate door set between two pairs of ground-floor windows. Though by now it was early evening the street was still bathed in sunlight. When Isabel put her hand on the weighty knocker there was a breathless pause before the door was pulled back and she stood face to face with Susannah Thewing.

Outside motes of dust danced through golden light. Within, the air was very still. Susannah wore a dark, narrow-skirted dress and her hair was scraped back under a nunnish cap. She did not smile but put out her hand.

This wasn't right. A crack, like a lightning streak, opened in the crystal vision Isabel held of her future with Mary Ward. No. It couldn't be. She'd last seen Susannah five years ago in their shared room at Oakshott minutes before Isabel's sudden departure. In the half-light between two windows Susannah had hung back and spoken not a word of regret or farewell. Wasn't she supposed to be safely locked up with the Poor Clares?

Susannah's fingers felt thick and small. Their cheeks touched, Susannah's peachy smooth and cold as if it had absorbed no sunlight that day.

Find words, Isabel told herself. She won't.

'I had no idea you were here, Susannah. I thought you were in a convent in Gravelines.'

Martha, equally surprised, embraced Susannah with much more affection.

The hall was tiled in plain black and white. Doors on either side were shut. Susannah led the way up a staircase which swayed a little under her deliberate footfall. Her sweat smelt exactly as before and she had awoken precisely the same feeling of antagonism. Isabel knew that she would not have left England had she known Susannah was here.

Susannah turned so suddenly that Isabel's face nearly collided with her huge bosom. 'Did you give my letter to your brother.'

'What letter?'

Susannah was panting, tiny beads of moisture visible on the shelf of flesh above her thick upper lip. Her pupils, fixed on Isabel, dilated and contracted as she waited for her to remember.

'Oh. That letter. Yes, I gave it to him when I visited him in prison.'

'Is there no reply?' The brown eyes were brothy with hope.

'None that I know of.' Susannah, I'm not even sure if he opened your wretched letter. It was years ago.

'The community is in chapel. Will you join us?' Susannah softly opened a door and stood aside for them to enter a bare-floored room where twenty or so women faced a small gold crucifix. The quality of quiet was smooth as milk.

The house was so crowded that the English Ladies slept three to a room, separated from each other by makeshift partitions. Isabel shared with Susannah and Blanche. Her tiny cell was furnished with a straw mattress, a crucifix and a chair. Everybody else went to bed quickly but Isabel, unused to managing her own clothes, shuffled about in the gathering darkness conscious that her clumsy movements jarred the rule of silence. She lay down at last, crossed her hands on her chest and considered her predicament.

From the moment the front door had opened and Susannah's lugubrious face appeared, nothing had gone as planned. Isabel, anticipating a heroine's welcome, had imagined herself seated at Mary Ward's right hand during dinner and drawn into the glad embrace of the community. But Mary was in Brussels visiting the Archduchess Isabella Clara Eugenia and the other women, though friendly, were too busy to pay much attention to Isabel. And as the English Ladies ate only once a day there was no evening meal. The regime in this house was more rigid even than at Oakshott and here Isabel did not have the privileged status of Anne Winshawe's grandchild.

First in the pecking order of Rue Grosse was the inner circle of five women who had first come with Mary Ward on her trip across the Channel to found this new community. Then there were more recent disciples like Blanche and Susannah. All these slept in cells on the attic floor and kept to the austere rule of the Poor Clares. Next came the boarders sent from England to receive a Catholic education. These young girls occupied neat beds on the second floor. In the basement slept the servants who had accompanied their mistresses from England.

The straw mattress was soon crushed flat and though it was August Isabel was cold under her thin blanket. The street outside was quiet but occasionally there came the sound of other town-dwellers, a drunken shout, a clatter of horses' hooves, laughter.

Most disturbing of all was the presence of Susannah who as Isabel's appointed mentor had clung to her side all evening, bulging-eyed, competent and humourless. Now she was inches away, on the other side of thin board. If Isabel stayed with Mary Ward she would condemn herself to a life-time under the same roof as her cousin.

Next morning at eleven Isabel was called to an interview with Winifred Wigmore who had been put in charge during Mary's absence. As the only meal of the day was taken at noon she was desperately hungry. Furthermore, having passed a near sleepless night she had been roused at four to attend chapel. The sanitary arrangements were rudimentary and a queue formed in a damp yard outside the only privy, called by the monastic name, reredorter. This brave euphemism did nothing to detract from the horrors within.

Winifred met Isabel in a plain little room known as Mary's parlour. She had white skin, delicate gestures and a sweet smile. Isabel, in no mood for platitudes or piety, prepared to do battle. The pair watched each other for several moments.

'Whatever you were expecting from life here will probably have been over-turned already,' said Winifred. Her voice had the quiet authority of one born into a very old family and her fingers were slender and dainty.

Isabel was at once on the defensive. 'I had no fixed ideas.'

'Good. It's best to start with an open mind.'

'I have, I have an open mind. But I do have some concerns. You all seem so well established that I wonder if I'm needed here at all.'

'You've probably found, like the rest of us, that you have more need of the community than the community has of you. And we're so used to keeping quiet about our vocation that it's quite salutory to discover there are others like ourselves.'

No, thought Isabel. You under-estimate the problem. This is not what I wanted at all. I find that I have come to the worst of all worlds; a convent with none of the benefits of an established order; a domestic house with all the deprivations of a convent. 'I'm glad there are others like me,' she said. 'Blanche Morton, for instance. I'm very pleased to see her. But I was surprised about Susannah Thewing, my cousin. I thought she'd joined the Poor Clares.'

'So she had. But when Mary left, Susannah felt she must follow her.'

'I would have thought Susannah ideally suited to the life of an enclosed order.'

'Possibly. I'm sure it was not an easy choice for her. You've probably found out already that life in this house is very demanding. We expect our women to serve the community and teach as well as pray. Of course Susannah is a great asset to us because as you know she has many gifts, particularly with the sick.' Isabel could scarcely argue with such fulsome praise, though she wondered how Winifred, who was supposed to have such a towering intellect, could have been taken in by Susannah.

Winifred had a small mouth with corners turned up in a perpetual smile but her wide-set eyes were steady and observant. 'You'd be wrong to think you're not needed,

Isabel. We understand that your French is excellent and that you share Martha Canton's talent with the needle. Our school lacks a competent sewing teacher so we're hoping you will take your first class this afternoon.'

I didn't come all this way to teach needlework, Isabel thought, horrified.

'We are trying to establish a three-year curriculum not only for the English girls who board here but for local children. Mary thinks girls should have both practical and intellectual skills. If they have the means to independence they will be of more value to God.'

'But I thought Mary trained girls from English Catholic houses. I was expecting to teach Latin and French.'

'The way forward has yet to become entirely clear. Our work with English girls is very important but we must also make ourselves useful to the town. St Omer has so many religious houses that if we become a burden people will turn against us. And hasn't a poor mason's daughter the same right to understand the Word of God as the child of an English lord?'

During the months spent planning her escape from England Isabel had anticipated that she, in complete contrast to the wet-lipped Nicholas Turner, would dispense classical knowledge with staggering authority to a row of high-born English maidens. When her pupils returned home to marry and bear children the memory of saintly Mistress Isabel would live on in their hearts and her name would become a byword.

A bell rang and Winifred got up. 'Give us time, Isabel. For all of us, the process of undoing what we are and becoming someone better is very hard. Don't expect too much too soon.'

When she was alone Isabel stood in the tiled hall and looked at the heavy entrance door.

Francis, where are you? If you came for me now I would fall on your neck with joy.

*

180

Martha Canton, who had absorbed herself into the little community with her usual genius for self-effacement, left after three days. She was to travel with an English family to London where she would be met by Anne Winshawe's carriage. Isabel stood in the gritty street with her skirts tangled against her legs and her eyes sore. 'Please don't leave me here.'

'I'd love to stay.' When they hugged Martha's bony frame was tough as iron and her neck smelt of all the clean, neat things Isabel associated with her; skeins of silk, the interior of a work-box, the stiff creases in starched fabric.

'Please don't go.'

'I'll write to you but I don't think you'll need my letters. You'll be very happy here.'

'Oh please, please wait a few more days. I'm not sure I can bear it without you.'

'Isabel, give Mary Ward a chance. This was your choice. I know that you will never fail if you're determined enough.' She set Isabel firmly aside and the steps were kicked away.

Isabel ran after the carriage but it was an unspoken rule that Mary Ward's English Ladies should not draw attention to themselves so she pulled her veil over her face and walked straight-backed to the house where she resumed her sewing class. 'We'll use black thread for the border. Remember how I taught you to make an invisible join. Hold the canvas very loosely or the fabric will bunch. We want a stitch no longer than the tip of your little fingernail.'

Desperation built in her throat.

Chapter 14

A month after her arrival in St Omer Isabel was still floundering. When she woke in the morning her first thought was that she wanted to go home. She day-dreamed of meat dinners, sweet puddings, feather beds and hot water. Her prayers were dominated by longing for sleep. In the schoolroom she was bored, her veneer of loving kindness a sham.

So, she thought, neither Father Carisbroke nor Mary Ward cares that I am here. To them I am just one among many. She expected that Francis would come soon and rescue her in a carriage with cushioned seats. Every day she went through the motions of participation, hoping that something would happen.

The other women seemed to have no doubts. They found laughter in trivia and greeted each other with what seemed to Isabel unnecessary affection. Not since Oakshott had she experienced company of her own age and then the only candidate for friendship had been Susannah. Here were a dozen young women but she didn't know how to like any of them except perhaps Blanche Morton.

At twenty Blanche had two significant accomplishments. The first was an effortless soprano voice, the second a gift for figures and both were of great value to the English Ladies in Rue Grosse where she proved to be an excellent music teacher and accountant. But Blanche was dangerous for she could be outspoken and cruel. If one of her pupils behaved foolishly her dark eyes would go cold. Once, when late for chapel, she had nudged Isabel and made a mock-penitent face at Mary Poyntz's blameless back. She regularly broke the rule of silence and was impatient with Mary Ward's long absence from the house. Yet she could be loving and honest, quick to forgive, witty and full of remorse when at fault. She spent every spare moment in contemplation or study.

Compared to Blanche, Isabel felt pallid and insubstantial. She hated her own uncertainty and thought that Blanche's friendship could save her by sweeping her along in a ferment of activity and emotion.

Mary Ward was due home on the first Tuesday of September and on that day Blanche, with Isabel as chaperone, was sent to an English family newly arrived in town who wished to discuss the practicalities of one of the girls joining Mary Ward's community. The Huntlys, acquaintances of Lucy Morton, had taken a house in Rue des Clouteries barely five minutes walk from Rue Grosse. It was mid-afternoon. Steamy heat rose from the surrounding marshes and plagued the quiet streets with flies. The dirt in St Omer had a different quality to that in London and gave off a vegetable rather than fleshy tang. Animal and human carcasses were disposed of more efficiently here and the gutters drained into low-lying land beyond the town.

Nevertheless Isabel suspected that her mud-spattered skirts were unlikely to please the Huntlys. Blanche told her that the younger daughter, Cordell, would bring a large dowry because the family, though known recusants, had managed to keep hold of a sizeable fortune.

Two female Huntlys sat together in a stifling parlour, mother swaddled in black velvet and a figure-of-eight ruff so deep it buried her ears, daughter in a farthingale of greyish blue to match the unhealthy shadows under her eyes. The pair looked half-starved, pale lips unsmiling, fair hair scraped back from white brows and pale-lashed eyes. Cordell's companion, a young French girl who was to accompany her into the chosen religious community as a lay sister, was much more promising with fiery hair partially quenched by a white cap and green eyes which never left Blanche's face. In her obscure corner she was a little darting flame while the Huntlys, stiff and long-waisted, were stale as bog-water.

Lady Huntly had the high-pitched voice of a much younger

woman. 'Your Aunt Lucy sends her love, Blanche. We have come to St Omer because Cordell insisted. Everyone, including your Aunt Lucy, is talking about Mary Ward. What can you tell me of her?'

Isabel began to sweat in the airless room. She fixed her eyes on Lady Huntly's face and had the now familiar sense that her head was floating apart from her body. Hunger was such a habit that she had forgotten how it felt to be healthy and was tormented by headaches and fits of shaking. This was a rare moment of relaxation for nothing was required of her. Blanche was giving confident, well-practised answers to Lady Huntly's interrogation.

Though actually, thought Isabel, I should be praying for the soul of this prospective candidate.

But do we really want her? We haven't space for any more women in the house.

'I wonder if you could set my mind at rest on a couple of points,' lisped Lady Huntly. 'I've heard that you women teach Latin and allow the girls to act in plays. Surely that's not right.'

'We do teach Latin,' said Blanche, 'because Mary Ward believes that we should be able to study the Scriptures for ourselves.'

'It is surely priests' work to interpret the Gospels. We must rely on their reading.'

Isabel drifted into the conversation. 'But how much better to go to the very source of our faith.'

Lady Huntly's eyes swivelled. 'And you are . . . ?'

'Isabel Stanhope.'

'Ah yes. My dear girl, you're the talk of London. No wonder you look ill. What a tragic life you have had. And now I see your father has come to St Omer to bring you home.'

Shock darted through Isabel's ribs. Sir William in St Omer? At once the very idea that he would not follow her seemed absurd for he was a man who kept close control of all his possessions.

Blanche cut in hastily: 'Plays are a wonderful learning experience if the subject matter is right. By watching and

184

performing in a play the girls are taught a dozen lessons at once.'

Isabel was in London on the day she escaped from the Globe. She saw her own quivering figure in her father's barge and then Francis perched near the stage with his head thrown back in laughter. 'Acting gives confidence and teaches eloquence. Women who join us must not be afraid to speak out,' Blanche said.

To Isabel it seemed that the other life, the one she might have led if Francis had kept tight hold of her arm that afternoon in the Globe, was only the distance of an outstretched hand away. If her father was here, might it be possible to regain it?

'. . . expect a dowry when Mary Ward, as I believe, has no clear rule,' Lady Huntly was saying. 'The arrangements you have at the moment must surely be only temporary. You girls won't be allowed to gad about town for ever.'

Blanche's posture had changed. It was now clear that Lady Huntly had no intention of sending her daughter to Mary Ward and that she had summoned them to provide fodder for gossip when she returned to London.

'I've heard that Jesuit priests come to your house, even seminarians. Is this true?'

'My cousin Susannah has received a visit from her brother, Alan Thewing, who is studying at the English College,' murmured Isabel.

'How interesting. What a lot of freedoms you all seem to have.' Blanche got up abruptly but Lady Huntly hadn't finished. 'As you can imagine I have other orders to visit before I make up my mind. Cordell is very gifted and I don't want her vocation wasted.'

Blanche flung her veil over her face and dropped a curtsey. 'All Mary Ward's ladies are gifted. We already have linguists, musicians, mathematicians, needlewomen, theologians and brilliant teachers. You will know the names Poyntz, Babthorpe and Wigmore. Are you sure, Lady Huntly, Cordell could hold her own amidst such women?'

Neither of the Huntlys accompanied them into the entrance hall but the red-haired companion darted ahead and blocked their way. She was very self-assured, unafraid of breaking the rules by addressing them directly in faltering English. 'Even if Mistress Huntly doesn't join you, I should like to,' she said and kissed each of their hands. As her head ducked forward, a small band of bright hair flashed in the grey light.

Instead of heading for home Blanche marched towards the city walls and began a brisk circuit of the town. Isabel followed though she feared the crowded alleyways and sudden bursts of jarring noise this far from the centre. St Omer had two distinct sides; the prosperous district where wool and tobacco merchants lived and traded, and a squalid underbelly who took no part in the religious or commercial life of the more respectable classes. Suddenly the street was filled with men, noisy, jostling, awash with alcohol. They peered into the English women's veiled faces and blew smacking kisses but were repelled by their crucifixes and black gowns. Penniless Spanish foot-soldiers had roamed the streets of St Omer in ever-increasing numbers since their country's truce with Holland. Because there was no war nobody wanted them.

When the men had gone Blanche said: 'I commit about a dozen sins a minute when I'm with someone like Lady Huntly.'

Isabel leaned against the old stones of the city wall. By breaking the silence between them Blanche had made an unmistakable gesture of intimacy. 'I think you were justified in speaking as you did.'

'The thing is, Lady Huntly is quite right. We have practically no money. No one pays us anything except the English boarders and occasionally some wealthy family looking for a fashionable charity. Yet we spend more every day on donations to the poor and teaching materials for the local girls. Parents will only pay dowries if they know their daughters are joining a reputable order. Mary says she's still waiting for direction. We live like Poor Clares, we are highly regarded by the town but we don't yet know what we're doing here. It can't go on.'

'Put like that,' said Isabel, 'I wonder anyone stays.'

'Why do you stay?'

'I don't know. I don't know if I can. And now apparently my father is in St Omer so I may be forced to go home.'

'Well, I shall stay because I think Mary Ward will have to jump one way or another soon or she'll run out of funds and I'm interested to see what happens next. She's got herself into a corner, you see. She resists enclosure because she wants to train us up and send us home to England as missionaries. And she certainly doesn't want to belong to an existing order, like the Ursulines. She'd hate to lose her autonomy. But she'll have to be careful. The church won't put up with anything too revolutionary.'

'You sound critical of her. If you are, is it right that you should be with her?'

'Oh, I tell her what I think. She likes people who speak their minds. I have my music. I feel as if I matter. God help me, I don't want to be stuck behind a grille all my life or married to some lunatic back in England. And two months ago I made the Spiritual Exercises. After that, there was no going back.'

They walked on and were soon back in less hostile streets. From shops near the market square came the smell of money; tobacco, wine, perfume, coffee, cheese. The passing of English Ladies caused a stir. Isabel wondered whether Mary was naively unaware that instead of making the English Ladies seem modest, her insistence on restraint actually increased their mystique. The residents of Rue Grosse were unmistakable in gowns that had an elegant simplicity compared to the bunchy elaboration of local fashion. Everybody watched them all the time, perhaps waiting for a slip-up, something wild or extreme. Sometimes they would turn a corner or emerge from a church and notice a discreet stepping aside, a sliding away of eyes and a pretence at indifference. Information oozed in the gutters and rumbled away from town disguised in cart-loads of cauliflowers. Almost anything could be bought in St Omer, including news of the English Ladies.

In Rue Grosse the entrance door opened before Blanche had a chance to knock. Susannah had become the self-appointed gatekeeper and knew everyone's movements. There was a glimmer of interest in her normally inscrutable eyes and as Isabel stepped into the hall she said: 'Your father's in Mary's parlour.'

'What about Mary? Is she back?' demanded Blanche.

'Yes.'

'Is she with him?'

'No, in chapel. Isabel, you're to go straight to him. He's been waiting over an hour.'

He will kill me, thought Isabel.

Leaning with folded arms against the parlour door was Michael Latham bearing the signs of travel; a stained leather jerkin and hair crushed by many hours under the heavy hat now lying on the floor at his feet.

Isabel always used to think Latham had a kind and generous face but had since decided that he was no friend. He had the heart of a heretic and a craven loyalty to his master. Had he not carried her upstairs after her father's beating without a single gesture of sympathy or astonishment though the side of her head had been swollen and pulpy?

Blanche stood behind Isabel's shoulder and Susannah watched from the bottom stair. Neither seemed to understand the physical threat posed by Sir William. How could Mary Ward let her face him alone?

Latham stepped aside and held open the door. Isabel walked through and it closed softly behind her.

When Isabel and her father had last met in Hoxton she was just emerging from mourning and her gown had been of dark blue silk embroidered with flowers and scrolls of a lighter shade. Her hair had been piled in soft, high curls threaded with a sapphire and gold chain once belonging to Thomasina. Now she wore black and her head was covered by cap and veil. She was much thinner and her eyes were huge and shadowed with lack of sleep.

He seemed to have trouble identifying this sober figure as Isabel and did not immediately cross the room. She had time to catch a flicker of doubt in his eye and a glint of silver in his hair, to breathe his cloying perfume before he was upon her and had gathered her into his arms. His embrace was full of uncomfortable textures.

He did not release her immediately but took her face in his scented hands and his thick-lashed, smiling eyes looked into hers. She put her palm to the panelled door for support.

Sir William had chosen to play the role of loving but injured parent, the sword hanging low at his hip signifying reckless haste to get here but Isabel wasn't fooled. There was no grime on his boots and his hair was just combed. He had taken the time to groom himself carefully.

'At least I don't have to speak to you behind a grille. I suppose I should be grateful for that,' he said and chuckled affectionately, as if his daughter was playing at a game of nuns. 'I have come to take you home, Isabel. Shall we go?'

Isabel knew she could be forced from the house. Latham was at the door and despite his pampered fingers Stanhope was strong. She sat down on one of two rush chairs. 'I'm sorry to have put you to the trouble.'

'No trouble. No trouble. So, shall we go?' He held out his ringed hand.

She thought of walking with him past Blanche and Susannah, out into the evening and away. That simple. But this prospect was deadening. The England that had seemed so glittering and fertile in her night yearnings now felt like a trap. 'I'm afraid it's too late. I must stay here.'

'Isabel.' He pulled the other chair close and sat knee to knee. 'I was to blame because I made it impossible for you to confide in me. The death of your mother was a blow. I drove you away by being too hasty. Forgive me. We must all begin again. The kind of step you have taken here can't be made rashly. It must be carefully thought out. Let's go home and reconsider.'

'It's a step I have thought about all my life.'

She expected the thin trickle of his patience to run out at any moment. 'But Isabel, did you think of the implications of your coming here? Did you consider what it would do to your family? What about me?'

She was waiting for a word of love. 'I suppose I expected

you to come for me,' she said, 'and I wonder it took you so long.'

Her cool voice riled him but she wanted to provoke an honest response so she could cut him cleanly away. 'You are not my only consideration,' he said, and the disguise of paternal tenderness slipped. His spittle fell on her cheek. 'By the time I found out you'd gone we'd lost hours. I had the theatre searched and every ship from London to the coast. I don't suppose you have any idea how much an undertaking like that costs. Margaret Westward was useless. I sent her packing and had Robin interrogated, thinking he might be behind your escape but of course it was your grandmother all along, the bane of my life. My own marriage plans are in tatters as a result of all this. Bourne is distraught.'

'Is he?'

'Stricken with grief. Who can blame him. He's disappeared completely, probably into the clutches of his playwright cronies. Thrown up his chance of employment with Cranfield.'

'I wonder he didn't come to St Omer himself.'

'So were you testing us all, Isabel. Was that it? What a risk.' He was knife-sharp because he knew how his own mind worked.

'It was a risk. It continues to be. But I made my choice.'

He put the back of his hand to his eyes. 'Isabel. You were not free to make the choice. You can't see the wider picture. You are in danger and I must save you.'

'Danger. What could be more dangerous than being a practising Catholic in London?'

'Better to fall into the hands of English justice than Dutch or worse, Spanish. I cannot bear to see my daughter a puppet of the Spanish.'

Her head jolted up.

'Ah yes, I've had a long look at your Mary Ward who I'm told is just back from Brussels. Why do you suppose she's being given so much encouragement by a Habsburg monarch who cares nothing for the English? Because she's is a valuable tool, part of their offensive. Can't you see? You're helping coerce local children into the faith of their ruler,

Archduchess Isabella. But what will happen to you all when the wind changes and things get nasty in St Omer? Mary Ward has chosen quite a precarious spot for her little nest. A Protestant Dutch Republic to the north and in the south the French, who last year assassinated their Catholic monarch. And within a stone's throw of Brussels are German princes frantically clinging to whatever faith they happen to be, Protestant or Catholic. *Cuius regio, eius religio*, Isabel. The prince dictates the religion of his subjects. What has that to do with conscience? When war breaks out, as it surely will when one of the big Catholic powers or some haphazard Protestant alliance intervenes, your little house will be eradicated.'

'Nevertheless, our way forward is clear.' And indeed, the more he spoke, the clearer it became.

'I passed the Jesuit College on my way here. What ostentation. Their own printing press even, churning out prayers and propaganda. Do you think it's a matter of coincidence that you have been made welcome in a town where the Jesuits have such a foothold? They're all using you, Isabel. It's very clever. Indoctrinate the future mothers through the good offices of Mary Ward, and feed these devoted Catholic women back into England.'

'We think for ourselves. The Jesuits help us but they don't force our hand.'

'They watch every move you make. They give you a little bit of rein but just you wait, if you step out of line they'll pull you up short and strangle you.'

'Oh, I don't think so.'

'For God's sake, Isabel, I beg you to come home. All this is killing me. The Bourne money would have saved us from bankruptcy. I may have nothing now to pass on to my son but debts.'

'I hope Robin is treated no worse because I am here.'

Suddenly his temper broke. 'Your brother Robin is out of the Clink. He signed the Oath of Allegiance two weeks after you left. What do you think of that? He suddenly saw there was nothing more to be gained by staying there.'

'Why, why did he sign? Did you make him?'

He took her by the upper arm and dragged her upright. 'The way has become clear for him to inherit everything. The fashion has changed and he'd rather be rich and idle than a prisoner of conscience. So much for your Catholic brother, Isabel. You broke his resolve.'

It was at this moment that Mary Ward made her entrance, leaving the door ajar behind her. She bowed gravely to Stanhope who released Isabel and braced up to this new enemy. Neither Isabel nor her father had seen Mary since the morning after Thomasina's death. The sight of this grave, slender woman was quite unexpected and very different to the richly dressed young lady who had talked so knowledgeably of politics at Cuddington.

'I have come to take my daughter home,' said Sir William.

'How kind. I hadn't realized she wanted to go.'

'You have split our family apart.'

'If your family is split I am very sorry but I don't think it was my doing.'

Sir William howled. 'She's mine. She came without my permission.'

'Would you have given it?'

'I would have expected her to do her duty.'

'She has done her duty.'

'If she stays here I'll not give a penny for her upkeep. If she stays I'll make sure your name is dragged through the dirt in England.'

If she stays . . .

He had lost and Isabel knew that the chance of going back was now gone. He would not take her by force because she was no good to him as a captive. But if he had uttered one word of affection he would have broken her.

She and Mary stood side by side and watched him go. He raised an elbow to fend off her embrace. The room readjusted itself, shedding the angry male presence.

Mary sat down at the table. 'I have been thinking about you on the journey home, Isabel. We must find someone to give you conversation lessons in Spanish. We need at least one fluent Spanish speaker if we are to make any further headway at court.'

Isabel wished there had been no outing with Blanche Morton that afternoon, no conversation under the city wall. She would have liked to have greeted Mary with an untroubled conscience. 'All these weeks I have not known what to expect when I saw you again,' she said. 'The last thing I thought was that you would want me to have Spanish lessons.'

'None of us knows what to expect. We can only make ourselves ready for the unexpected. You have a brave heart, Isabel, and it seems to me that Christ never chooses the really timid ones to do His work.'

A small miracle began. The interior of the unremarkable house in Rue Grosse became beautiful to Isabel. Even in austere Oakshott there had been tapestries, portraits and panelling but here the bare bones of the house were exposed, the plastered walls were creamy white and the misty windows uncurtained. The rooms were cleaned with passionate vigour so that the curve of the balustrade and the oak surface of the refectory table had a waxy amber glow.

Isabel now noticed harmony in tiny things. In chapel she would study the long curve of a veiled woman's shadow or the drapery of her gown, the complexity of gathers meeting the smoothness of a taut bodice. White light flowed through two high windows above the stairs and pooled on the black and white tiles below.

Mary Ward allowed herself to be directed by God with an abandon that took her in directions no other woman would go. To be near her was like standing beside a hot flame contained under thin glass.

Suddenly, as she crossed a landing, praised the clumsy work of a slow pupil or sat down to dinner, Isabel would experience a flash of pure joy. I am happy, she thought.

Chapter 15

In the autumn of 1611 Isabel received a terse letter from Robin announcing the death of their father. She had no time to reflect on her newly orphaned state for that same week an epidemic of measles struck Rue Grosse. One morning a girl in Isabel's sewing class uncovered a hot red rash on her wrist. Two days later five more children were absent and a couple of English boarders had been taken ill. Everyone watched for the next victim.

It seemed to Isabel that ever since her father's visit to St Omer the English Ladies had been circling calamity, the peaceful rhythm of their daily life a calm prelude to an approaching storm. Life sometimes seemed horribly precarious, a thin veil flapping over the abyss. A woman who caught a cold on Sunday might be dead by Friday. A pupil might be breathless with the expectation of a new baby brother or sister one week, in mourning for her mother and still-born sibling the next. If even a Catholic monarch like Henry IV of France could be murdered nothing was sure, except Mary Ward's conviction that she did God's work.

Now, as if triggered by Sir William's death, the forces of disease and dissent broke over them. They were stalked by poverty and indecision. Though parents refused to pay dowries to an institution that had no papal approval, the policy of free education for local children continued. In the streets and churches of St Omer too many rival religious orders struggled in an unholy competition for funds from royal and influential patrons.

The measles crept through the draughty rooms like a large, invisible hand grabbing a child here, a woman there. Isabel, who had been infected as an infant, shared some of the nursing with the French girl who had worked as companion to Cordell Huntly the previous year. Originally called Véronique, she had now taken the name Praxedes, after a Roman saint. Despite her fanciful name Praxedes seemed at first to be an asset to the English Ladies, being hard-working and pious. At recreation she always sat by herself and if spoken to raised startled eyes as if roused from deep meditation. She confided in no one.

Even after penances and prayers, Isabel continued to make harsh judgements of her companions. She had become finely tuned to all their moods and earlier euphoria had given way to moments of cynicism. Praxedes was easy to read. She had a way of making herself significant by assuming insignificance. Her smiles were rare and she skimmed from place to place like a shadow. To make time for more prayer, she slept only two hours a night and the flaming hair that always escaped just a little from her cap was a poignant and beautiful contrast to her huge green eyes and fragile white skin.

Isabel, just eighteen, and Praxedes, sixteen, kept the sickroom vigil between midnight and 3 a.m. By the fifth night Isabel had sunk into a grim state of wakefulness that bordered on black despair. This helpless witness to suffering was all too reminiscent of her mother's death. She hated to see children in pain and blamed the crushed conditions in the house. If they had been properly funded, had bought the new premises that were always being hinted at or at least had built a second privy, perhaps the girls would have been safe. She even found herself wondering, as Anne Winshawe would have done, whether this was a punishment from God for the obstinate refusal by Mary Ward to accept enclosure and the rule of a conventional religious order.

Praxedes mouthed: '*Misit Dominus, verbum suum, et sanavit eos . . .*'

'We can't go on like this,' Isabel interrupted suddenly.

She was shot a wounded glance but there was no reply for she had broken the great silence of the night.

'We are killing ourselves and our pupils. And for what?'

Praxedes smiled and went on with her prayer.

The room was lit by single candles placed at the end of each bed. Sick girls moaned and stirred their limbs against the sheets. On the mattress nearest Isabel a child drew noisy, dragging breaths. The stench was hellish for there was a constant struggle to keep back the tide of excreta that accompanied disease. Bowls and pails had to be carried up three flights of steps, hot water was in short supply and soap was costly. Each clean sheet was a triumph. Was this what God wanted for his daughters?

Of all the women Susannah was the most efficient. After all, she had spent her girlhood at the knee of Anne Winshawe and there was little she didn't know about remedies for fever. While Praxedes prayed over the patients Susannah made masks for aching eyes and applied salves to itchy skin. And she protected herself by eating every scrap she could lay hands on at dinner, strolling in the yard during recreation and never missing an opportunity to sleep.

Five adult women caught measles, among them Mary Ward. One night in chapel she knelt too long at prayer, her face ashen and her eyes half blind. The next day she was carried to the guest-room which at least had a comfortable mattress. Within thirty-six hours her fever was so extreme that a priest was summoned to give the last rites and every healthy woman in the house gathered to say goodbye.

The plain canopy framing the bed seemed to Isabel like some dreadful parody of the lit stage in one of Francis Bourne's theatres. Mary's prone figure had one arm thrown to the side in an attitude of abandon and her face was the same unforgettable yellow as Thomasina's on the night before she died. She was oblivious to the chorus of merging female forms at her bedside, skirts pressed so close they were indistinguishable, mouths distorted by tears.

Then Isabel's eyes fell on the priest at the head of the bed, seated well back with just his hands and face lit, and gazing directly at Isabel.

Peter Carisbroke. Here at last. Cutting through the nightmare with a sweet, slow smile. The five years since they had met in the servant's room at Fitzroy House slipped away as if that meeting had led seamlessly to this. His black biretta, perched on a side-table nearby, was a clear-cut, substantial shape amidst falling drapery and flickering shadow.

The candles flared and Mary Ward was revealed as defenceless as any mortally ill woman. Usually she wore a plain veil and high-necked gown but now her hair was bunched on the pillow and her small breasts rose and fell under the white cloth of her shift. For the first time Isabel sympathized with her completely as a young woman, fragile and suffering.

Three days later Mary was a little better and the women were called to the refectory where they found her seated at the centre of the long table, grey-skinned and heavy-eyed. Isabel thought she was foolhardy to have got up so soon.

The meeting began with a prayer of thanksgiving but there was a breathless quality to the responses, an understanding that the community had been to the very edge of a precipice.

Mary's voice, however, was reassuringly steady. 'Two days ago I lay in bed feeling extraordinarily peaceful. Then I distinctly heard a voice say: *Take the same of the Society of Jesus.*'

It was clear that to the original five companions, the fact that Mary had another vision was not news. Mary Poyntz was smiling as if to say: I've already given my blessing. Winifred Wigmore was very watchful, waiting to see how the others would react.

'I don't understand,' said Blanche.

'The next words were: *Father General will never permit it. Go to him.* And then I knew. We are to adopt the Formula Instituti of the Jesuits. It's so simple I have to laugh. All these years I've been groping to find the way forward and the answer was here all the time.'

Isabel said gently: 'Don't you mean we are to live by the Jesuit rule, which is perhaps not so very different to what we do now.'

'I mean the Formula Instituti as approved by Pope Paul III in 1540 and again by Gregory XIII in 1584. We will adopt it at once and seek papal approval for it.'

There was a disbelieving silence. Mary's idea was breath-takingly ambitious. They might just as well ask the Pope to ordain them as priests.

Winifred, whose cosy figure would have looked quite at home in a country house parlour with a clutch of infants at her skirts, now proved herself a revolutionary. 'So this will be our new way of life. We must now live by the Jesuit rule. We will be wholly committed to this community, or Institute, which will be subject only to the authority of our foundress, Mary Ward, and the Pope.'

'But if we're not recognized by the Pope,' exclaimed Isabel and was ignored.

'We will defend and encourage the Catholic faith under the three solemn vows of poverty, chastity and obedience.

'We will confront heresies and immorality wherever we find them.

'We will prepare adults and children to receive the sacraments. We will attend public sermons whenever we can and help priests wherever we are. We will care for prostitutes and prisoners, the sick and the dying. We will enable girls to become good mothers, nuns in conventional orders or members of our institute. As we grow in number and our influence spreads we will send our women to every corner of the earth, particularly England where we're needed so much.'

Blanche's brown eyes were snapping, her lips tight with incredulity. 'This will never be allowed. Surely you realize that since the Council of Trent all women's orders have had to be enclosed. There will be a huge scandal.'

Isabel remembered that when Mary Ward had talked of visions in the copse at Cuddington she had acknowledged their inconvenience but acted on them straightaway. Her only concession to Blanche's argument was a slight, appreciative smile. 'I've no doubt, Blanche, we shall cause a stir. But as you know I have been seeking enlightenment for many months and I now realize that God has been steering me in this direction all along.'

'The Jesuits won't let us use their rule,' Blanche said, her voice even more strident. 'They're already reluctant to be confessors to a women's order because they fear for their reputation.'

'I know. God told me they wouldn't like it. But we must go through the motions of asking them.'

'Why bother if we're destined to fail?'

'We shan't fail. It will be lack of vision in those who stop us that will be the failure. We have the highest authority for our work. Human approval would simply make life easier.'

'But what if the Pope refuses to accept us? He receives inspiration from God.'

'The Pope is advised by men,' said Mary and suddenly the tension was released by laughter.

Blanche's disbelieving eyes swept the assembled group of women. 'If we fail we shall look like fools.'

'As foolish as that most notable failure, Jesus Christ, who was arrested and crucified between two thieves. You see, God is a genius. Why re-create something that has already been successful? The Jesuits have become an unstoppable force for good. We shall be the same.'

Chapter 16

There was no hiding from winter in St Omer. Fires were
lit only in the teaching rooms, water froze overnight
and the women suffered from chilblains, sores, fevers
and colds.

At the end of November Isabel began retreat. For the next
thirty days she would speak to nobody but her priest and spend
every waking hour in penance and meditation. The Spiritual
Exercises were an ordeal not everyone survived. After weeks
of introspection and confession some women were so broken
they fled St Omer for ever. Others like Blanche and Mary
Ward emerged radiant, their faith honed to the strength of
polished steel. Whatever happened, Isabel would not be
unchanged. Ignatius Loyola, founder of the Jesuits, had
designed the Spiritual Exercises to make a difference.

Responsibility for reshaping the retreatant's soul fell to the
spiritual director and much depended on who was appointed.
Some women had suffered at the hands of bored priests who
despised the female sex, believing that a woman's soul could
never fully conceive God. Others were over-protective, sentimental or savage.

Since Mary's illness Father Peter Carisbroke had become
a regular visitor to Rue Grosse. He taught at the English
College in St Omer and was responsible for the printing press.
In fact he was still a menace to the British government,
arming Jesuits with piles of prayers and pamphlets and sending his pupils across the Channel ablaze with zeal, eager
to die for their faith. Yet he suddenly found time to hear
confessions, say mass and give the Spiritual Exercises for the
English Ladies.

But Isabel perversely did not want him to lead her retreat. It seemed to her that he had no right to take up Mary Ward's cause again as if on a sudden whim. Mary needed consistent, selfless allies among the Jesuits and Isabel knew that Carisbroke lacked both these qualities.

Besides, their relationship from the very first had been unequal, she yearning and confiding, he elusive. He clouded her judgement and absorbed her attention. Now she would be expected to strip away layer after layer while he, her mentor, remained buttoned up tight, a professional in the science of souls watching her squirm under the glare of his scrutiny.

On the first morning she waited in the room allocated to retreatants, a cubbyhole behind the chapel with a disproportionately high window overlooking the street. Outside all was scurrying movement as clothes, scraps of foliage, charred embers and a pigeon struggled and twisted in a strong wind. Women were buffeted across the cobbles with their skirts blown between their legs and cloaks flying. Only Isabel was still, shivering behind the ill-fitting glass.

A woman sheltering in a doorway opposite had her surcote tweaked up by a strong gust revealing pattens and sturdy ankles. Her large, pale face was barely visible within the shadow of a deep hood but she seemed to be staring up at the house.

The next moment, when two more people joined her, a man and a woman, Isabel stepped back abruptly for there was no mistaking the man's plumed hat, the tilt of his head or his casual elegance. The other lady, much thinner than the first, was dressed in bright, untidy layers of clothing and had a bony face and staring eyes.

Deborah Bourne, Francis and, in the shadow of the porch, Dorothea.

Isabel crept a little closer to the lattice. Francis Bourne?

The window had lozenge-shaped panes so bevelled that her view of him wavered. When she tried a different angle the shape of his face changed. By now her nose was pressed to the glass and her palm made an involuntary hammering.

Her memory of Francis was of laughter and tenderness but

now his eyes were bleak. He stooped to hear what Deborah said and offered each sister an arm. As they walked rapidly away only Dorothea looked back.

He couldn't have seen Isabel, surely, or he would have made some gesture of recognition. She remained crushed to the glass as if to draw him back, needing one more look. All these months she had kept him sealed up, not daring to shake out his memory. She wanted to be repelled by him but felt only a dismayed longing to explain herself and beg forgiveness.

She sank down and covered her face. Though it wasn't unusual for English travellers to take a look at Mary Ward's notorious establishment it did seem very odd that Bourne should bring his sisters abroad. This small room now felt like a hiding place. While she crouched shaking, the Bournes had blown round a corner and away.

The chapel door opened, swift footsteps approached the altar, paused to genuflect and then came nearer still.

Part of Isabel's consciousness followed Francis Bourne into the Market Square.

Instead here was Peter Carisbroke. The skirt of his black soutane fell smoothly from a loose, narrow belt and above the high neck was the merest flash of a white collar. His skin was aglow with health, his beard and hair neatly trimmed. She thought of telling him who she had seen but kept quiet for he was unsmiling, all priest, not a chink showing of the young man who had leapt through Aunt Teresa's herb garden.

He motioned her to sit down on a bench under the window while he stayed by the door, folded his hands one on the other and spoke to her as if she were a small congregation. 'During these Spiritual Exercises I will visit each day to hear your confession, discuss your reading and lead your meditation but I can only be your guide. It is up to you to make a good retreat.'

For the first time Isabel noticed the glimmer of an accent which placed him further north than Anne Winshawe, perhaps at the very border of England and Scotland, for the vowels were lilting, the final 't' of *retreat* emphatic.

And then her mind pulled away again. Across the windy street she had seen Dorothea Bourne's upturned face gleam within the folds of a hood and Francis's dismissive gaze.

Carisbroke paused, waiting to regain her attention and his air of patronizing forbearance made her defiant. 'In the first week,' he said, 'we will contemplate how we reject God through sin. Are you ready to make a general confession?'

Why was he treating her as if they were strangers? It must be obvious that she was upset.

Again she saw Francis Bourne and his two sisters walking into the teeth of the wind.

She was armoured from Carisbroke in the clothes of a religious woman, a dark gown and gauzy veil which fell like a cloud across her cheek. Isabel these days at least carried herself like a nun and had learned to repress outer signs of strong feeling.

So, she decided, I'll be as cold as he is and see how he likes it. Our relationship shall be priest and penitent, our meeting-ground the mutual desire to be perfect in the eyes of God.

Carisbroke now sat hooked over, as in her memory, with his brow resting in his hand.

She knelt straight-backed before him and shut off her emotional self.

'My greatest fault is still that I stand too far apart and watch. I want to be fully inside each moment, to offer it entirely to God. But all the time there is a double self, one acting, one watching. I believe I am not alone in this.' Indeed, I'm sure you know exactly what I mean, she thought. Your vanity dominates this room. You have adopted the posture of a priest over-burdened by the receiving of sin but you can't fool me. It's just the face you've chosen for today.

'This tendency must be curbed. You are soon to take your simple vows, the second of which is obedience, the third chastity. If there is a part of you that remains undisciplined you can never be either obedient or chaste. In order to be reborn in Christ, the rebellious part of you must die.'

His eyes still had their astounding clarity, like spring water, and his face had retained its sculpted planes. She had experience of more faces now and knew that his deep forehead gave him exceptional beauty. Time had compressed his mouth, the lips were firmer but still sensual and a tiny irregular indentation, like a crescent moon, had formed itself across the space between his brows. There was a complacency about his face, a settling into itself that had not been notice-able before.

'But you once told me this critical faculty of mine was valuable to the church,' she protested. 'That's what I find confusing. You Jesuits, for instance, are noted for the quality of your individual thought.'

'We start with a clean sheet. We wipe our old selves away during the course of these exercises and climb down to a state of nothingness. And then, as we rebuild in the image of Christ, we find that our intellect is not dead but recharged for God.'

'How can you be sure that your new being is God, not self-directed? Heretics insist that God has spoken to them but we call their visions false.'

'You must be guided by your spiritual director, appointed by the church.'

'But that's you.' And I don't trust you. In the past your judgement has been grievously at fault. You manipulate me and so far, every time you have so much as crooked your finger, I have come running.

'Spiritual directors, ghostly fathers, are ultimately appointed by God,' he said, as if giving the last word. 'Now, which of your sins do you consider to be the greatest?'

She paused rebelliously for a while. 'The sin of doubt. Of doubting authority.'

He smiled faintly. 'Every time you fall into this sin you must strike your breast and ask for grace to be forgiven. Every time. You must crush this failing.'

I don't know that I want a part of me to be killed if it's protecting me from the likes of you and my father, she thought.

'And now,' he had the actor's ability to create tension. First a pause, then a summoning of strength as if for physical exertion and a long assessing look at Isabel. 'You must face up to the full horror of your sins. As you lie prostrate imagine yourself as a polluted river flowing down a beautiful mountain. Everything in your path is poisoned and finally killed. Grasses, wild flowers, butterflies, birds, mammals, all become sterile or die because of you. That is your first subject for meditation. You are vile and you infect everything you touch.'

There he sat brandishing an invisible whip and judging her evil.

For anyone else I might do it, she thought. For Mary Ward or any other priest, even my poor little seminarian cousin, Alan Thewing. But not for you. I despise you now.

He waited a few more minutes then abruptly left the room. When the street door below banged shut she jumped to her feet and watch him stride rapidly across the cobbles, pause to greet some merchant's wife then disappear, just like the Bournes.

She held her ground, pretending to amuse herself by looking at passers-by.

He offered to be my spiritual director because he wants to see me humiliated, she decided.

And then she thought: He chose to come because he loves me.

He came because he fears for my weak and sinful soul.

It just happens to be his turn.

Once this last reason had occurred to her she could think of no other. To Carisbroke then she was just one of a number of religious women whose confession it was his duty to hear. By resisting him she was in fact resisting God. If she refused the Spiritual Exercises she could make no further progress in the religious life but would remain vulnerable to sudden upsets like the sight of Francis Bourne and his sisters.

She dropped to her knees. The palms of her hands touched the floor and she lowered herself until her breast and cheeks were pressed to wood. Her arms were flung wide, her legs spread-eagled under her skirts.

Mary Ward has made this act of self-abnegation. My grandmother, Martha Canton, Carisbroke himself. Don't fight it, Isabel.

At first she dozed. It was strangely comforting to be for once without work or the call to regular prayer, to be lying prone with her cheek, breasts, pubic bone and thighs finding the hardness of the floor. She reconsidered her encounter with Carisbroke and decided that she had nothing to regret for she had kept her self from him. She would do what he said but she wouldn't weaken.

The sound of children's voices filtered up from the room below. A bell rang and in the street a young baby began to wail. Isabel's neck ached and a muscle in her shoulder burned. She estimated that only ten minutes had passed. He had asked her to think of a mountain stream flowing with poison but instead she wished to be with her little class in the sewing-room below, walking briskly along the airy street outside or giggling with Blanche in the store cupboard.

A poisoned river. Isabel had visited every church in town and grown used to the work of Flemish artists who painted local landscapes into the background of religious subjects. In a portrayal of the Annunciation, for instance, through an open window behind the Virgin's head could be glimpsed Flemish fields, a pale sky and the silver curl of a river.

For a while Isabel meandered through this peaceful landscape but then found herself seated on the side of a hill near Holywell across the valley from other pilgrims who plodded on and on into the distance. Her feet were a mass of blisters but now she realized that not just her feet but her whole self was running with sores. The springy grass around her was shrivelling up and the sheep on the nearby hillside stumbled as their thin legs buckled under them. A butterfly fell as if shot by an arrow.

The other women came and went in the chapel nearby. They sang a litany and said the office. Isabel picked out each voice: Susannah's sibilance, Blanche's trilling soprano, Mary Ward's confident prayer.

I have never loved Susannah. I never can. I never respected my father or my brother as I should. With Francis Bourne I was lustful, abandoning myself to desire. It was my fault, not his. And then I betrayed him and his sisters. I slighted Martha Canton until I saw how useful she could be and I neglected my mother in the last years of her life. Since coming to St Omer I have allowed my pupils to irritate me and I have indulged in gossip with Blanche. We slander Praxedes and make cruel jokes about Mary Poyntz. Despite committing myself to Mary Ward I still question all she does.

By nightfall she couldn't have moved if she tried and her joints were fixed at their unnatural angles. But in any case how could she face the agony of knowing that she killed all that she should love?

The next day Carisbroke came back. Well, she thought, let him see that I have carried out his instructions to the very limit.

'Get up.'

She didn't move.

'Get up.' His toe kicked her elbow. 'Get up. This is hysteria.'

Her body plucked itself upright though her neck was a column of fire where the muscle had been wrenched.

'It is not enough to suffer physical pain. You should be confronted with the terrors of hell. You are lost because sin has condemned you to an eternity of suffering.' And so the second day began without a shred of pity or praise.

She did all he said. At night during the great silence, she took the discipline using a small birch cane on to which were tied three lengths of knotted rope, in the freezing seclusion of her cell. Kneeling by the mattress she opened the neck of her shift and bared her neck and shoulders. The flick of the birch would be heard clearly by Susannah lying only a few feet away.

Her body objected to the first, tentative lash but she made her hand work until her back sang with pain and a trickle of blood ran into her shift. She thought her misery would be cauterized by violence.

Later she pushed aside mattress and blanket and lay on the floor shaking with shock and cold. She felt filthy, a collection of blood, bones and wicked thoughts, and recalled the arrogant Isabel who had begun this retreat.

*

By the start of the second week Isabel's body was an assembly of pain. For eight days she had fasted, slept for less than an hour at a time and knelt through hour upon hour of meditation. But though shaken with the chill of failure and rejection her heart was still closed up tight to Carisbroke.

But now his tactics changed. He smiled and made jokes. When he came in the morning he touched her shoulder or took her hand, encouraged her to eat properly and sleep well. Both his manner and the material he gave her for reflection were softer. It was like being led into sunlight. He told her to walk slowly round the little room as she prayed or to wrap herself in a blanket.

She watched him all the time. This approach was well known. After initial harshness the confessor softens up so that in the relief of being treated kindly the penitent breaks down and gives every last inch. Well, not Isabel. You are too transparent, Father Carisbroke, she thought. Nothing you do is genuine. I shan't give you what you want.

As he left on the last day of that week Carisbroke produced a copy of *The Imitation of Christ* and marked a chapter for her.

'But I have this book already. You gave it to me. Don't you remember?'

'Of course I remember.'

He had forced her out of her corner. She said: 'I was actually quite angry with you then. I was so sickened by what I'd seen that I wanted to be left alone by the church. And how did you know I would be there at Garnet's execution?'

'We kept our eye on you to keep you safe.'

'I couldn't understand why you had to be secretive, why you couldn't have shown your face to me?'

'I should never have been among that crowd. There were spies everywhere. In any case, I was just the messenger. Nothing mattered but that you received the message.'

'I think you enjoy stealth. You wanted to intrigue me.'

There was a long silence before he laughed boyishly, the first spontaneous gesture he had made in a fortnight. 'Isabel, you see everything in terms of your own self. After all this time you still believe you are at the centre of the world and everyone operates purely for your benefit. I am trying to teach you humility and still you've got it all wrong. You want your life, your standing in the world, to be enhanced by service to Jesus Christ. It should be the other way round. Isabel should serve Christ, not Christ Isabel. Everyone you meet, including me, you want to possess. You want us to revolve about you, live only to be in your consciousness, as if we had no other function than to serve you. You think like a pagan God.'

'No, no, all this applies to you. If this is what I am, you've made me like it. You've made me mistrust love of any kind, so I have to hold on to the tiny offerings I get. No wonder I don't know how to love God if I am treated like this by His priest. You made me love you. You relied on my admiration, my love, your personal influence over me. And then, when you had caught me, you pushed me away and disappeared from my life. What kind of a lesson in love is that? How am I to serve Jesus Christ if I have to defend myself from disappointment all the time?'

'Isabel, priests are human. They must have friends. I offered you friendship.'

'Or was I just another conquest?'

'You loved me because I told you what you wanted to hear. I offered you something that your soul had craved all along. When I first met you in your grandmother's house you were waiting to be called.'

'It's not as simple as that. You get in the way of God.'

She wondered if he understood what had happened. He had slid a knife under her defences and prised her open but in return he was betraying more than priestly interest. He had marked her out and been aware all along of what he was doing to her. And now, did he see how their relationship was balanced on a hair's breadth? This probing of each other's hearts was too interesting.

He drew back his head a little and narrowed his lids as if appraising her. 'You refuse to see me as anything other than your own personal priest. Believe me, I work with many people and I behave in the same way with them all.'

'Then you feel nothing for me? You said just now you had offered me friendship.'

'Isabel, I know little about human love except that I feel pleasure in being with some people, less with others. I never had brothers or sisters. When I was ten I was taken to the gallows and made to watch my father hang because he was a Catholic. I make no ties except to God. But I know that I can exercise a strong influence over people, and I use this gift to do God's work.'

Very well, she thought, let's try you out. If you're so lacking in feeling, let's see how you deal with my next confession. I will trade the admission you've just made for my most secret crime.

'There is one more thing, Father. Francis Bourne. I have not yet confessed the truth of my relations with him.'

As soon as the words were out she understood that she had done something irreparable because she had been right all along. Carisbroke remembered every detail of their former relationship, every touch, every word spoken. She was not after all a minor member of his vast flock but Isabel, Mistress Stanhope, whose presence cut through his priesthood like a knife through butter. All this she recognized by a flicker of movement in his neck, the wounded realization in his eye.

She scrabbled to recover ground. 'I was betrothed to him last year, as I'm sure you knew. I never told him that I planned to come here and I regret it deeply.'

'You have no cause for regret.'

'Last week I saw him in the street. Perhaps he followed me here. What should I do if I see him again?'

'You won't. He's gone from St Omer.'

'You knew, then?'

'We are alert for English visitors. The English government monitors all our movements.'

'But what do you know of Francis Bourne?'

'No. You tell me.' He had his fingers to his brow so that his face was covered.

'He kissed me. I desired him.'

'Did he seduce you?'

'Seduce me? No, I was only too willing.'

He was watching her lips. So, she had finally reached him. The tables had turned. 'Did you lie with him?'

210

'No.' She sank back against the wall and closed her eyes.

'Bourne,' he spat suddenly. 'You should never have let that man near you. I thought we'd reached you in time. Of all men.'

'But he's a good man. He seemed to love me. I regret the pain I caused him.'

'Men such as Bourne feel no pain.'

'How do you know him?'

'Never trust him, Isabel. Never let him near you again. I can't give you absolution until you promise to reject him utterly.'

'I have rejected him. I no longer love him. I never thought of him until I saw him from the window.'

'Have you torn him from your heart completely?'

'I have. I have. But why are you talking about him like this?'

'Because he's a man who would sell his best friend to the highest bidder. He hates Catholics, whatever he might have told you. How do you think he lived so well in London on the allowance his father gave him? By buying and selling secrets. Never trust a playwright. They need influential friends too much.'

Her memories fluttered like birds and rearranged themselves. She thought of Bourne at the masque and in Fitzroy House, waiting for her at the foot of the staircase. He had known all about her, ensnared her by his kisses and almost lured her into an ambitious but loveless marriage. She rocked forward and cried. Wrong, wrong, wrong again, Isabel.

She was held by strong arms. Carisbroke smelt of the soft worsted fabric of his soutane and the incense burned at mass that morning. He put his hand to her face and pressed her cheek to his chest. As she sank deeper against him her tears flooded over his long fingers.

The last days of the retreat, in contrast to the first, were all to do with the consuming love of God.

Isabel's resistance drifted away like a puff of smoke. Deeper and deeper she tumbled until she was swallowed up.

She was Mary Magdalene pouring oil on to the feet of Christ.

She was Veronica wiping His streaming brow.

She was all the saints who had ever died in His name, a fall of pure water, her body and mind rinsed through and through.

At the end of the retreat Carisbroke kissed her cheek. She smiled, sister to brother, full of gratitude that he had brought her so far.

'Isabel. Stay a while longer and talk to me.'

They sat on the bench by the window and she decided he must be exhausted by the process of receiving sins and issuing forgiveness. She remembered how her mother had once enclosed him in a fierce comforting embrace at Coughton Court and wished she could do the same.

'I think one day you will leave me far behind, Isabel.'

'No.'

'Yes, you will. Your Mary Ward has ambitious plans. This business of adopting our Jesuit rule is a strange and worrying development. You must keep her steady and use your influence.'

'Those plans will not take us away from you and the other Jesuits, but alongside you.'

'I understand she is soon to open two new houses and that one will serve as the novitiate.'

'If we raise the funds, yes.'

'I want to keep you safe, my special girl. I want you to know that I hold you very dear. Do you remember the kind of mutual support Anne Vaux and Father Garnet had for each other? I sometimes think we are destined for a similar future.'

They sat together in the pale light of the December afternoon and she wondered how the angle of a cheekbone, the slant of a forehead could be so lovely and hurt her so much.

'Don't be too fixed,' he said, 'be open. Test that everything you hear is God's will.'

'I am dedicated to Mary Ward. It's very simple.'

'Yes.' He left a space after this word so she could hear its precise intonation. *Yes.* Not affirmation but resignation. 'But be careful, Isabel. And write to me.' His smile was tender and his eyes dropped love like warm wax to her very soul.

'*Yes.*' He had turned a word of agreement into a question that planted a seed, like a black speck, in her newly cleansed heart.

THREE

Galloping Girls

1617

Chapter 17

Anne Winshawe died in January 1617 and Martha Canton, released from her duties as companion, asked to join the English Ladies. This left Teresa Thewing in charge at Oakshott until such time as her elusive elder son Edmund chose to take up his inheritance.

It was decided in Rue Grosse that Susannah should visit her grieving mother, and that Isabel, who had not yet prayed over her father's grave, should accompany her as far as Cuddington. Mary Ward was always looking for opportunities to send women on missionary work to England but they must have a cast-iron excuse. The authorities in St Omer asked no questions when they signed travel documents but English officials were less tractable.

However, by the end of April their passage had been arranged and the cousins were chaperoned across the Channel by Lucy Morton, close friend of Lady Arabella Fitzroy whose credentials as companion to Queen Anne made her difficult to thwart. They were met at Rye by a smart carriage bearing the Fitzroy crest and driven west to Horsham through the succulent greenery of dense woodland. Lucy owned a safe house for priests in London and could not be spared for long so they parted company with her and began the journey north, sheltering at night in drowsy farms and manor houses whose owners remained stalwart Catholics.

Only the most dedicated and devout in Mary's Institute were sent to England; their mission to shore up the faith of the wavering, to prepare the converted for the sacraments and to educate and encourage young girls in their vocations either as mothers, nuns or, in exceptional cases, future members of the Institute. Cloaked in whatever disguise was most appropriate, servant or fine lady, Mary Ward's companions must move among the cynical, the disaffected and the treacherous.

The women had been schooled always to devote part of themselves to prayer. While in the company of heretics, whether eating, dancing or gossiping, they were to have their hearts set on God. Isabel's chosen text for the journey, the story of the Israelites' flight from Egypt, was a favourite of Mary Ward's. What was there to fear when God controlled even the sea? On the voyage from the Spanish Netherlands to England, Isabel had felt like a flung stone. Exhilaration and terror were mingled in the realization that she was in physical danger again after so many years in one small, safe town.

'Tell the sons of Israel to march on . . .' said Yahweh.

In the hedgerows sunlight glinted through hawthorn and there was a clamour of birdsong. Isabel was chock-full of exuberance. She was returning home to Cuddington a professed religious, experienced teacher and scholar.

It was then that Moses and the sons of Israel sang this song in honour of Yahweh . . . 'Yahweh, I sing: he has covered himself in glory.'

Throughout the journey the women kept closely to their rule, though during the hour of recreation when they were supposed to talk to each other conversation was decidedly sticky. For Susannah the Jesuit ideal of divine indifference came very easily.

'I'm glad you'll see Cuddington at last,' said Isabel.

Susannah gave a tiny huff of breath through her nostrils, the closest she ever came to a smile.

'Of all the people for my brother to choose as chaplain, why did he pick on Nicholas Turner? Father Turner, I should say.'

'He's a great intellectual, apparently.' Susannah's instinct for putting Isabel in the wrong was unerring as ever.

Isabel missed Blanche Morton who would have recognized at once that Nicholas Turner was a parasite that fed on devout Catholic families. But Blanche had not so far been sent to England.

'And you haven't seen my brother Robin since Holywell, of course. Do you remember him at all, Susannah?'

An internal hand kneaded Susannah's doughy features and produced expression. 'I remember. I remember your brother.'

So that was how the land lay. Isabel recalled too late Susannah's letter tossed carelessly across the table in Robin's prison room.

'He sounded enthusiastic about my visit when he wrote so perhaps he's mellowed. Certainly he's indicated that there's plenty of work for me here.'

Colour came and went in Susannah's florid cheeks and again the flesh near her mouth managed the shadow of a smile. Isabel closed her eyes and sank with relief into the less rocky byways of her communion with God.

When at last they came to the broad straight drive leading to Cuddington Isabel abandoned nun-like restraint and craned forward. She saw uncut grass and the stain of last autumn's leaves under tossing trees. The grounds seemed shrunken and the house huddled forlorn and damp-bricked beneath gathering cloud. Here Thomasina had spent her last years in prayer and Isabel had first spoken to Mary Ward. The house should be shining, not sulking.

Perhaps the estate found its new owner, Sir Robin Stanhope, former prisoner of the Clink, somewhat unsympathetic.

Nobody came out to greet them. Faced with locked entrance doors Isabel was dazed by the collapse of time. For a moment she was the little girl quelled by the sight of her abstracted mother ranging from pantry to parlour and her father terrorizing the household from the library, his lair.

Mary Bonniface appeared at last. 'We expected you earlier,' she said.

Isabel blessed and embraced her as a dear friend but Mary shrugged herself away, unimpressed. 'Your brother's in the library. Whether he's ready to see you or not I don't know.'

The interior was clean and the old wall-hangings and rugs carefully maintained but the atmosphere was listless. There was no lady of the house now to put heart into the servants, bring flowers from the garden or sew fresh covers for worn chair-seats. And the flame of Thomasina's prayers had long gone out.

In the chilly parlour Isabel stood at the window to look out over the neglected drive.

That's where I first saw her, she thought, through rain.

At the end of half an hour Isabel's certainty had frayed. She had planned to greet Robin with a kiss, a prayer and a series of gentle questions about his spiritual health. But of course he would never allow her to dictate the terms of their meeting. Even though she had been absent eight years she must be patient until Mary Bonniface came again and escorted them into the presence.

Dead centre of the library, hand on a chair-back and dressed in black from head to toe, stood Sir Robin Stanhope. Blue eyes beamed guilelessly into Isabel's with brotherly affection. 'My dearest sister.' He was framed between windows and held a quill in his left hand as if disturbed in the midst of pressing business but he took her fingers and bowed, favouring her with the sight of his rippling golden hair.

He then passed on to Susannah who stood lumpen in the doorway, flesh quivering under its layers of grey cloth. For their journey to England the women had shed their plain black gowns and decked themselves out in frills and farthingales again. Susannah was at her least prepossessing when encumbered by braid and lace. The effect on her of Robin's proximity was extraordinary. Her breathing now was an unsteady sucking at the air.

'Shall we pray together?' he asked, taking their hands and drawing them close. 'Let us offer thanksgiving for your safe return and for the soul of our dear grandmother, Anne Winshawe.' When he sank to his knees and began the Pater

Noster Isabel had no choice but to follow. Isabel, professed religious, had expected to take the moral lead but big brother Robin had adroitly pushed her back into the shade. She was a fool to have expected anything else. As if Robin Stanhope would be chastened by years in the Clink and an undignified climb-down in the form of his signature on the Oath of Allegiance.

She wished they could be honest, or at least abandon the desire to impress each other. But Robin was busy establishing his pose of grieving son, forbearing brother of wilful young sister and austere Catholic country gentleman. He seated himself in a chair by the hearth and motioned Isabel to do the same. Somewhere among the confusion of furniture at the edge of her vision Susannah sank down and the stays in her under-bodice groaned.

The library had never recovered from the vandalism inflicted by the pursuivants and its heyday as the luxurious domain of a London gentleman was long over. No fire burned and no candles were lit. Isabel wondered whether these were necessary economies or if Robin had developed a taste for austerity during his years in the Clink.

'So tell me,' he said, 'how is life in St Omer? We hear great things of you all.'

'Good, very good. The community is growing so fast that Mary is even thinking of opening a house in another town, Liège. We are able to offer the girls so many more skills now; ethics, astronomy, bookbinding, curtain-making even for some of the local children. You see we try to give our poorer pupils a trade so that they will never have to beg or sell themselves.' Robin's lip jerked with disapproval but, as Isabel was determined to prove, the practical ladies of Rue Grosse did not mince words or shrink from the truth. 'Latin is at the heart of all our studies.'

'I'm amazed your pupils should want to learn such arduous subjects.'

'They understand Latin is the key to the Scriptures. And of course we also study rhetoric because we must be able to put our case, even to priests and theologians.'

Robin tilted his head in a familiar posture of belittlement.

'I hear you've had some trouble with the authorities.'

'Only about our constitution but I'm sure we'll soon reach agreement with the bishop. The sticking place is always enclosure. Nobody can understand why we won't accept it.'

'And how is our friend Mistress Ward?'

A warning sounded abruptly in Isabel's head. 'I didn't realize you knew Mary Ward well enough to call her your friend.'

'Oh, everyone knows Mary Ward, even those of us who have only met her a couple of times. Whenever she comes to England we hear all about her achievements. She visited me in prison, you know. Brought me a book, as I remember, and prayed with me.'

'Do you regret those lost years?'

'How could I? I dedicated them to God.' But they were in the Clink again, Isabel the visitor, he the captive. Stale air clotted between the uneven floorboards of his stark little room. Neither she nor Mary Ward would ever be forgiven for seeing him in the martyr's prison he had later abandoned.

'I'm sorry I wasn't reconciled with father before he died.'

'There was no possibility of reconciliation. He never recovered from his last interview with you, I'm afraid. It cut him to the quick.'

Isabel set this accusation aside to deal with later. 'But you at least were with him?'

'Nobody was. He died alone in his bed. At least we assume alone.' A flash of malice sparked in his eye. 'The funeral, as I remember, was not well attended. I'm afraid our father had few friends at court. A lot of people blamed him for losing their money on unwise investments and I'm afraid your little escapade was thought very disreputable. One way or another the king had lost all patience with him. I hope you realize, Isabel, that there's not much money. I have salvaged what I can but I had to sell a lot of land because the estates were heavily mortgaged. Oh yes, sometimes I wish that I too could set sail for the religious life and leave all this behind. But no. Duty must be done. I'm even having to consider marriage to one of the Bourne girls.'

'What?'

'My first choice was Dorothea.'

He crossed his arms over his chest and planted his elegantly shod feet wide apart, aware that he had shattered her composure. Robin married? The idea was extraordinary. She had thought of him as a celibate knight of the church, too hard at core, too devout to marry. How was it that all his life Robin ducked and dodged yet always bobbed up righteous.

'My father suggested the match, particularly as it made the Bourne family some reparation after Francis's disappointment over you.' There, a direct hit. 'But as you are doubtless aware, Dorothea had other plans for her future.'

'I'm not in touch with any member of the Bourne family.'

'Really? Well, you'll have plenty of opportunity to renew your acquaintance with Dorothea, I'm sure. Rumour has it that she intends to join Mary Ward. Her poor family has little cause to think kindly of your community, Isabel. You should watch out for them. However, I have been able to console them by offering for the hand of the third girl, Deborah. In return for the title and our family name they have made a very generous settlement. The Bournes and Stanhopes ought to be united. John Bourne now farms a number of taxes as well as half of eastern England and in the unlikely event of all Deborah's numerous brothers remaining childless our heir will inherit both the Stanhope and Bourne estates.'

Isabel wondered what the fleet-footed Deborah Bourne thought of this scheme. 'And Francis Bourne. Have you discussed the matter with him?'

'Francis Bourne is rarely in the country. He is not in any case a man I would wish to spend time with.' Suddenly Robin turned to Susannah and gave her a conspiratorial smile. 'Alchemy, astrology, other antics. Did you ever meet Isabel's betrothed, cousin Susannah? A man of many tastes, some less commendable than others.'

So disturbing was the effect of his brilliant eyes on Susannah that Isabel would not have been surprised to see the flesh within her cousin's voluminous gown melt like jelly. She decided that quite enough damage had been done already. He had let fall one startling revelation after

223

another so that all her good intentions had been blown away.

Rising swiftly she shook out her skirts and Robin sprang to his feet. Her first impression that he wore sober mourning had been an illusion and in fact he had become quite a foppish dresser. A huge bow fastened his breeches beneath the knee and his doublet was overstitched in a pattern of drooping flowers. In his right lobe a gold crucifix glinted and a chain studded with jet beads was woven into the delicate lace of his collar. 'You'll say Matins with us, I hope. We have turned the old barn into a chapel. And we weren't sure whether you'd share our meals or not. You women might have strange rituals of your own.'

Cuddington was apparently run on a shoe-string these days. Formerly a multitude of servants had underpinned the quiet routine of the house; there had always been someone in the linen-room, crossing the stable yard or stooped in the kitchen garden. Now many of the outer reaches of the house were unpeopled and the few servants left were strained and hurried. Even the kitchen was deserted except for one cook and a couple of boys. Mary Bonniface managed the skeleton staff with a sullen blend of resentment and martyrdom.

Yet in certain areas there was evidence of lavish spending. In the rooms used by Robin, the dining parlour, chapel and the new gallery linking it with the ground floor of the house, were some extraordinary acquisitions. He had developed a taste both for Italianate portraits of full-blooded boys with cherubic lips, and intricate battlescapes depicting forests of lances, torn flags and split bodies. At intervals athletic bronzes were displayed, nude figures frozen in savage acts of destruction and in pride of place above the new black marble fireplace was a life-sized portrait of the late French king, Henry of Navarre. Such a secular collection seemed to Isabel a strange choice for orthodox Robin.

Perched on an easel was a portrait of Sir Robin Stanhope himself. Isabel, who had studied a painting by Rubens in

St Omer Cathedral, thought the picture stiff and old-fashioned for Robin was posed hand on hip with the Stanhope crest above his head. He wore a white doublet spotted with green embroidery, the combined colours of hopeful youth, and on top, to mark his tragic history, a sober black jerkin bristling with pearls. In the background, as if through a window, was a view of Cuddington and on the lawn two figures, one Robin, the other possibly Nicholas Turner, engaged in a sword-fight.

The chapel itself was recklessly ornate, proof that there must be only loyal Catholic servants left at Cuddington or pursuivants would have come long ago to rip it apart. And in the midst of the silk altar cloths and jewelled statuary stood Father Turner, gorgeous in a chasuble of embossed green satin, grown a little portly but as moist-fleshed as ever. Isabel was sure that through the incense she could smell him, mushroomy and pluvial.

At dinner Robin sat at the head of the table flanked by his priest and his sister, with tongue-tied Susannah next to Isabel.

Nicholas Turner's eating habits had always made Isabel queasy. There came a soft gulping from his side of the table as mouthfuls were broken off by cheesy teeth and worked between flaccid gums. Before every utterance he gave a sliding glance at Robin. 'Mistress Stanhope, here we live so secluded that we are always anxious for news.'

'I believe that you trained at Douai. Don't friends there keep you up to date?'

'I dare not write often. It would put us all in great danger.'

'You say the office here openly enough. I thought priests in England were still in hiding. We hear stories of them travelling at dead of night to perform the sacraments.'

Turner's glance met Robin's and clung awhile. 'I am particularly blessed to be among loyal friends here but such is the threat to my life that I can never leave the estate.'

'You must fret to be more active.'

'Like your Jesuits,' he gushed. 'Is it true that in St Omer the Jesuits have been instructed by their superiors never to come past the door of your house for fear of corruption? That must be a blow.'

England was, as Isabel had been warned, a world of smooth tongues and perfidious hearts. A priest like Nicholas Turner, determined not to put his neck on the line, was bound to be hostile to the militant Jesuits. Why should his cosy faith be sullied by pain and conflict?

'Some Jesuits, like Father Gerard, are our greatest allies.'

'They must be pleased that now they're established in Liège Mary Ward is thinking of opening a house there too.' Isabel had mentioned the Liège scheme to Robin less than three hours ago. Information had been passed on with worrying speed. 'How do the Carmelites and Teresians feel about your swelling numbers? It must be hard for them to swallow, girls from such good families flocking to join Mary Ward.'

'All the other orders benefit from our work because we encourage so many girls to join the religious life.'

In came more food, pork, jellies, capons, sauces. Isabel's temples throbbed and fibrous meat caught in her throat. The English Ladies would never draw attention to themselves by refusing food but this sudden glut of elaborate dishes was sickening. Robin packed quantities away between his glistening lips. 'Mary Ward seems to have the Habsburg court under her thumb. You must be very well off financially,' he said suddenly.

'The archduchess is a dear friend but has many other demands on her purse. You've obviously been asking questions about us, Robin. I hadn't realized you took such an interest.'

'Oh, I have many friends among the Catholic community in St Omer. You don't have the monopoly, Isabel. Remember, the likes of Father Peter Carisbroke and John Gerard were my intimate companions long before you came on the scene. But nobody mentions whether Mary Ward has any French followers. I would urge her not to rely too much on the Spanish. They have never been trustworthy despite what the Jesuits say. Do you get money from the French? Are there French among you?'

'We have one or two French women, of course. A lay sister, Praxedes, for instance.'

'Ah. The French. Our great hope. What a country.'

Susannah was watching Robin hungrily, her fork poised between plate and mouth. He met her eyes and gave her a wistful smile. 'Don't you wish, cousin Susannah, that our old antagonism towards the French could be gone for ever? What allies we would then have.'

Because the fire was unlit no window had been opened. A thousand heavy meals had left their after-smell in the drapes and Isabel's hands were clammy with nausea.

'I wonder did you see our dear little Princess Elizabeth ride through the Spanish Netherlands on her way to the Palatinate? Poor Catesby. I'm glad he wasn't alive to see his would-be puppet queen wed to a Protestant,' sighed Robin and passed Isabel a dish of marzipan. 'Of course now his precious daughter is married to Frederick, James has a stake right in the middle of Europe. There's bound to be a war, Isabel, as you must know, and the English will side with the Protestants. I wonder if that will clip Mary Ward's wings?'

'We're not interested in politics. All we're concerned with is the saving of souls and the spreading of the faith.'

'Is your Mary Ward really above politics? I doubt it. She couldn't be so naive. Perhaps I can help out, Isabel. It's dangerous to be ignorant. We'll have some talks. Europe is a hazardous playground for you at the moment.'

The marzipan had been shaped and painted to impersonate strawberries and plums but the colours had a greyish sheen. Isabel's tongue was clagged in sugary clay. A few minutes later she excused herself and everybody rose. Nicholas Turner, suddenly nimble, whisked round the table and drew back Susannah's chair. 'We have neglected you, Mistress Thewing. You've told us nothing of yourself or your brothers, my other gifted pupils.'

Her large eyes dilated and within the tight bodice her flesh strained. She was caught between Turner and Robin, who smiled encouragement along the table. 'Your brothers, Susannah. How are your brothers?' he asked kindly.

She ran the tip of her wet tongue along her upper lip, unable to drag her gaze away from Robin. He smiled and she stared until at last he got up, flung a casual hand round her shoulders and helped her to the door. 'Your brothers are worth ten of me, don't you think? I hear news of Edmund sometimes. Everybody loves Edmund. He has the Midas touch. I understand he's become quite a pet at court, especially with dear Lady Fitzroy.' Did Isabel detect a salacious glint in his eye? 'And the other one?'

'Alan,' prompted Turner.

'Is a priest,' murmured Susannah, her gaze still locked on Robin's face. A trickle of sweat ran from her smooth hairline, past her ear and into her ruff.

'A priest. Of course.' He took her hand and enclosed the knuckles with his lips.

She stared down at him and her mouth fell open. 'A Jesuit. He came to London last month.'

Isabel, who had been watching this tableau with considerable distress, suddenly woke up to the fact that Susannah had been dangerously indiscreet. The movements of Jesuits were always kept secret. Indeed Robin seemed to recognize the mistake for he put his fingers to his lips and hushed soothingly before kissing them both goodnight.

The English Ladies got up in the small hours to say the litany together and afterwards Isabel couldn't sleep. She had a sense of being outside and beyond herself, neither the girl she once was nor her new incarnation as a religious. The deep quiet of the surrounding countryside disturbed her and finally she began to pace the room and the stretches of passageway beyond.

Long ago, in darkness, she had heard Carisbroke's voice as she peered down at a cluster of men in the hall. Tonight no moonlight shone through the casements and no candles burned in the sconces. Portraits on the stairs were black rectangles, dense as obsidian.

Once inside the library she fumbled from window to window, opening the shutters to let in a glimmer of dawn.

You were here, Peter Carisbroke, but we never discovered you, neither the pursuivants who hated you nor I who love you.

Her fingers trailed the shelves again and the mantelpiece but they held no secrets. Everything in the room was solid; books, chimney breast, carvings. She unlatched the hidden servant's door in the panelling and crept in pitch darkness to the first floor. To the right was the silent gallery of family portraits, Thomasina and all the other Stanhope women with their heavy-lidded, oracular eyes and skilled fingers.

But instead of visiting these selfless ghosts she went back to her mother's chamber, intending to pray in the old dressing-room chapel. The door opened on well-oiled hinges and she turned to close it behind her. Only when she was several paces inside did she realize her mistake.

Grey morning light fell across the bed where Robin lay on his back with one arm flung above his head and his nightshirt thrust up above his navel exposing naked legs and genitals.

He was like a sculpture, sinewy and tough, a survivor, his prone body sprawled under Isabel's beloved canopy of airy insects and flowers.

Beneath Robin and on the empty half of the bed the sheets were crumpled and a mound of pillows lay under his elbow. It was as if he had flung himself down exhausted after a fight. His penis, snugly at rest on his upper thigh, winked at Isabel.

She backed away but Robin's eyes had clicked open and in their sleepy depths was triumph.

Back in her room she closed the door, leaned heavily against it and laughed. God, she decided, had given her a sign clear as daylight. This insular, self-seeking life at Cuddington was rotten. In the name of an outlawed religion Robin wallowed, making his own rules, pandering to his own needs.

Two days later the rickety Winshawe carriage that had taken Martha Canton south to London collected Susannah from Cuddington. As only Isabel was there to say goodbye, only she saw the glance of anguished hope her cousin gave the dark hallway in case Robin should trouble himself to come out.

In the weeks that followed Isabel was kept very busy. She made herself a plain little altar in an alcove of her bedroom, an act calculated to improve her relations with Mary Bonniface who softened considerably and admitted her to the circle of servants and local people who had remained faithful.

Robin and his chaplain in fact received plenty of visitors, an assortment of fanatical young men who now pinned their hopes on a match between the good-looking but unreliable Prince Charles and a Catholic princess. Some of them had even financed the sending of emissaries to Spain to flatter the Infanta into a betrothal. Robin, who of course favoured an alliance with France, was always deep in argument about the conflicting merits of the French and Spanish. Isabel was sorry to see him so dogmatic but her sympathy was tempered by frustration. She had realized that he was not short of money at all and pointed out that with his resources he could do much, both for the poverty-stricken tenants on his estates and for Catholics abroad.

Her advice was more welcome elsewhere for the Catholic underworld was flourishing in the Midlands despite the set-back of the Powder Plot. Lady Mary Digby, widow of Everard, was staying with her friend Mary Throckmorton at Coughton Court where mass was still said regularly. Both were eager to meet Isabel, companion of the celebrated Mary Ward. But though she joined their litanies and had long talks with a number of young ladies who were brought some distance to meet her, she found the atmosphere in the house oppressive.

These women rarely left the seclusion of their estates and their faith hung about them, burdensome as the black gowns of satin, net or brocade that muffled their limbs and accompanied all their movements with a scraping chorus. White faces supported dense, wired caps and from their belts hung keys and crucifixes. Tears came readily. They were tense and nervy and their anguished prayers heaped softly against the old glass and surged over the ancient furniture, stilling the air and misting the sunlight.

Lady Digby's boys had long ago been taken from her and

farmed out to irreproachably Protestant families. She still talked obsessively of the Powder Plot and the way her husband had pranced so heedlessly into treachery and intended murder.'

Isabel saw her other self in these women, the Catholic wife groping her way to salvation through good deeds and whispered rosaries. By contrast she felt like an exotic bird flown in through an open window, wings dusted with the glamour of another country. She was part of the turbulent memories of Coughton and her coming created a ripple of excitement, an echo of the days before the Powder Plot when anything had seemed possible.

Near the end of Isabel's visit a memorial service, prefaced by a trip to Sir William Stanhope's grave, was arranged by Robin. Sir William's ambivalence towards religion was signalled by the fact that a grandiose stone plaque had been erected in his honour within Cuddington church though his body shared a tomb with his wife who was buried discreetly in a newly enclosed corner of the churchyard. Sir William had designed a miniature temple in the classic style to cover them both. The inscription, composed by himself several years earlier, was part in Latin, part English and dwelt much on his inestimable services to the king.

Isabel had a posy of forget-me-nots and violas but these humble flowers were overshadowed by the towering white slabs of the tomb. She pressed them between iron bars in the locked gate, prayed for her father's soul in purgatory and gave thanks for the part he had played in bringing her to Mary Ward. She had realized that a childhood of neglect and cruelty had in fact been an excellent pathway to the religious life.

On the way home, hoping that Robin might be softened by this period of shared reflection, she tried to talk about money. After all, he carried a gold-tooled Italian Missal which must have cost a small fortune.

'Robin. When I leave I hope to take my dowry back to Mary Ward. How much can you give me?'

'I'm up to my eyes in debt.' He always talked faster when money was mentioned.

'Perhaps we could sell some of father's paintings or books. They're not to your taste I shouldn't think.'

He was puffy with outrage. 'They must be kept in the family.'

'Our community has supported me all these years. For the sake of our family pride, we must give them something.'

They were within the boundaries of Cuddington and at the far end of a walk, shambling towards them with his idiosyncratic, heavy-heeled gait was Father Turner.

Robin's eyes had re-focused. 'If Mary Ward had been a little more conventional I might have managed a small payment but if I give you money now I shall only be letting myself in for more expense in the future. Your community might fall apart in a few years and then I'll have to support you again or pay another vast sum to have you accepted into a more conventional order.'

'Robin, a few hundred pounds.' She looked pointedly at the crystal crucifix which hung from a gold chain on his breast. 'Then if you won't give me money, will you at least help us. I was wondering, what happened to the house in Hoxton?'

'I keep it on in case I go to London.'

'What about the servants, do you trust them?'

'Michael Latham is there. You no doubt remember him. He is completely loyal and a good Catholic.'

'Are you sure? He kept it well hidden while my father was alive.'

'Nevertheless, I trust him.'

'Then could you let us borrow the house? Our London community is always in danger of discovery. We need somewhere else, just in case. Hoxton would be ideal.'

Turner had reached them and made a complicated half-rotation that brought him behind Robin's shoulder.

'Think of my reputation, Isabel,' cried Robin. 'I'm trying to re-establish the family name. How will it be if the government finds I have given my town-house to Mary Ward's women?'

'We'll argue that you had no idea I invited them there. After all, I have a right to stay in our father's house.'

She was shot a look that said: You have no rights and don't you forget it.

Nicholas Turner, head cocked to one side, now brought himself level and rested his hand on the small of Robin's back. 'No one need know that you gave your permission.' Isabel was astonished by his cooperation until he added: 'The house is an expensive encumbrance at present. I believe that if Mary Ward's ladies moved in they would have to pay rent. Every little helps.'

Chapter 18

At the end of October, chaperoned this time by Mary Bonniface, Isabel was driven to Hoxton in Robin's second-best carriage. The house in Spital Fields where the community had lived for some months had come under surveillance so over a number of days, in twos and threes, the English Ladies had moved to the Stanhope house in Hoxton.

For Isabel this was the truest homecoming she had ever known. A spell at Cuddington had dented her self-assurance but in the Hoxton house where she had once been so lonely, she tumbled into delighted arms and recovered the joy of being among Mary Ward's companions. With these women, courageous, highly organized and inspired, the doors of the spirit were flung wide open. She slept with three others in the room used formerly by her father where the walls were hung with unsuitable paintings of bare-breasted goddesses, fat Cupids and lustful swains with a wisp of drapery at the crotch, but the women were too exhausted to care. Isabel was cupped by the quiet breathing of her friends.

There were three other notable additions to the London community. The first was Martha Canton, past her mid-forties and stooped by a life-time of sewing in dim corners but even she had the air of being on holiday, light-hearted and engrossed, all misgivings about Mary Ward shed.

Cousin Susannah, just arrived from Oakshott, had gone into retreat for five days to recover from the strain of a summer spent with her unpredictable mother.

The third newcomer was Dorothea Bourne who had crept

up to the front door early one August morning and begged to be let in. Normally she would have been sent at once to Mary Ward in St Omer but for the past year she had been suffering from a haemorrhage of the womb and was now too weak to get out of bed.

We should never have taken her, thought Isabel. We can't afford passengers. The knowledge that she would encounter this member of the Bourne family each day was very disturbing.

Dorothea had been given a small room on the first floor and Isabel was shocked by her appearance. Formerly so robust, she was now pale and wasted. When she saw Isabel her eyes filled with tears.

'I have been longing to see you ever since I heard you were in England,' she said.

The contrast between Dorothea's pleasure and her own ambivalence made Isabel understand for the first time how it must feel to be Mary Ward, admired by so many friends and followers. The gap between the ideal of perfection imposed by others and a sense of personal fallibility was very painful.

'I owe all this to you,' Dorothea continued, taking in the house and its residents with a weak movement of her hand. Her head rested on Isabel's shoulder and her body was a clinging encumbrance.

'Dorothea. Please.'

'Your example and courage brought me here. I'm not sure the rest will thank you, though.'

'Your family must find this hard to bear.'

'Oh, they won't miss me much. We are so many and they have been saved the trouble of my illness. Deborah is to marry your brother so the title will come into the family one way or another.'

Isabel was not much reassured. Robin's warning rang in her ears. The Bournes had become powerful and were unlikely to overlook Dorothea's sudden conversion. 'I'm surprised your brother Francis allowed it.'

'I was a coward and waited until he was out of the country.'

Worse and worse, thought Isabel as she left the room.

The only consolation was that this was an excellent test of endurance; under one roof were Susannah and Dorothea, the two women she found it hardest of all to love.

Mary Ward's London community was run by Susan Rookwood, a woman who in less charitable days Isabel might have found too impenetrable. Susan's astute mind and unflappable bearing were exactly suited to her situation in Hoxton where the women were resistance workers in a hostile city. Her brother Ambrose had been killed for his part in the Powder Plot so she was well used to subversion.

The community's cover, that they were a group of impoverished gentlewomen thrown together by necessity, seemed so transparent to Isabel that she expected the house to be shaken apart by pursuivants at any moment. After all, no ordinary gentlewomen received priests in the small hours. Father Alan Thewing, for instance, stayed for a week, leaving the house each evening at dusk to visit the dying or new born, pitching his slight frame into a dangerous world and creeping back before dawn to rest and hide. Sometimes the women gathered local people to an upper room for mass or welcomed a motley collection of visitors from beggars to aristocratic mothers and daughters come to seek advice. Every day they went out in pairs and worked with the sick and imprisoned.

But Isabel learnt to trust Susan's team whose vigilance never faltered whether they rubbed shoulders at glittering receptions with smiling government officials and Catholic aristocrats or dressed as tradeswomen to hand out bread, money and prayers to the poorest of the poor on the London streets.

There were seven ladies living in the house and nine lay sisters posing as servants. Michael Latham had moved into the stable block. Isabel wanted to befriend him again, or at least reassure herself that he was as loyal as Robin had suggested, but he gave her no opportunity. According to

Susan, though, he had been of great help in ensuring that the house was secure for the English Ladies.

An inner chamber on the second floor had been made into a chapel and an attic room was always left in readiness for a priest or refugee. The back staircase was concealed at the top by an unpleasant portrait of Sir William wearing an extravagant peascod doublet, and in the basement by a hinged wooden partition coated with plaster and whitewash. Escape was possible through a high window in the cellar covered by ivy on the outside, into a bed of shrubs and out of the garden gate which gave on to a series of alleys and eventually the fields beyond Hoxton. A couple of Catholic households near Cornhill had agreed to take the women in at short notice should the need arise.

The house buzzed. In Sir William's day it had been dead; too big, too luxurious, too self-regarding. Mary Ward's women had brought it alive.

On a freezing Tuesday in late December word came from Lady Arabella Fitzroy that Lucy Morton was ill and had been carried to Fitzroy House where she was asking for the English Ladies. Lady Arabella suggested Susannah for her nursing expertise and Isabel because she was an old friend.

Enclosed with this note was another sent care of Fitzroy House and written in a spidery hand that made Isabel shudder. It was from Margaret Westward who wrote that she was now living alone in a small house close to New River Head and would much appreciate a visit from her former charge.

Some time was spent debating how Margaret had discovered that Isabel was in London and what motive lay behind her letter. At length it was decided that the invitation posed no greater risk than any other though Isabel insisted on going alone. If it was a trap, only she would be caught.

For protection she wore the rough woollen dress of a minor servant, a hooded cloak and the stoutest boots the household could supply. She let herself out of the door beside the pantry and entered a garden numbed by frost. Her glove stuck to ice on the latch of the gate and her warm breath smacked freezing moisture on to her face as she took a field path towards the lane running west under motionless windmills. Occasionally a giant sail groaned.

To her left were clusters of houses in the outer suburbs of London. Despite prohibition on sprawl beyond the city walls Hoxton was no longer a village set apart but was linked by new houses to Moor Fields and the London Wall. A fat cloud of smoke hung over the city. Even this far north Isabel could smell the sourness of burning waste.

The New River Head was a reservoir recently opened to supply clean, piped water to the city. Today its outer reaches were frozen solid but its ambitious scale and the perfection of its brickwork hinted at a cleaner, more rational London than the one Isabel had left years ago. Close by, Margaret's little house was crammed tight in a row of five, its dimensions a perfect match for its diminutive incumbent. As Isabel knocked vigorously a black cat appeared and nudged her calves.

A scrap of a girl no more than ten showed her into a panelled parlour while the cat whisked out of sight up a crooked flight of stairs. There was a pervasive smell of melted wax. In the heat of the cramped room Isabel flung back her hood and presented a face agleam with the desire for reconciliation.

However, waiting by the hearth was not Margaret Westward at all but the even less welcome figure of Francis Bourne.

When he stood up his physical presence engulfed her. He had grown substantial and tough. Hefty shoulders strained the quilted brown velvet of his doublet and a thick beard shot through with grey thrust against the soft folds of a small ruff. Too tall for the little parlour, he stooped to avoid a jagged rafter. Mistress Westward's meagre bits of furniture were dwarfed by his weathered hands and spurred feet. Isabel was frightened because she could see no chink in him, no softness in the eyes or liking for herself.

And he was an actor, well prepared for this meeting whereas she had been entirely wrong-footed. He seemed much older than his thirty-five years and watched her from beneath half-closed lids, the corner of his mouth tweaked up in a smile that had none of its former mischievous charm.

Isabel had not spent eight years under the discipline of the religious life for nothing. A decade ago she would have reacted angrily to such deception but now she merely untied the hood of her cloak and let it fall to her shoulders before dropping a deep curtsey.

Bourne did not bother to take her hand. 'Don't worry, Mistress Stanhope. You are well chaperoned. Margaret Westward is indeed in the next room, though she refuses to see you. Besides she's much too busy. I'm afraid that when gentlewomen are thrown on to the streets they must resort to all kinds of unpleasant ways of earning a living.' His voice, stripped of its theatrical cadences, was soft but emphatic.

Isabel was dimly aware of unsetting elements to the room aside from the pungent smell; a large book lay on a high shelf between a little glass box and an engraving of some mythical animal with contorted limbs. The thick diamond panes of the deep-set window let in the merest puddle of light.

'I hadn't realized you knew Mistress Westward so well,' she said calmly.

'Oh we're old friends. Since the day you ran away, in fact.'

Despite her training a little shiver of rage vibrated along Isabel's spine, more because of her own foolishness than his deception. Here she was closeted with the very man she had been warned by Carisbroke to avoid. 'You should have written to me yourself. I would have come.'

'Would you? I couldn't be sure but I knew you'd find the chance of doing your duty by Margaret Westward irresistible. It must be hard for a holy woman like you to live with the knowledge that your antics made someone destitute.'

'I wonder how you discovered I was in London.'

'I wonder.'

The most distressing change in Bourne was the way his face had now moulded itself into that of a cynical courtier. Though his hair still flopped over his forehead there was less of it. His nose seemed more aquiline and a long diagonal crease from nostrils to lips was paralleled by pouches of flesh under his eyes. It was a face that had endured many wearisome experiences. And yet those straying locks gave her hope. There had been a time when she might have reached up and swept them aside. Perhaps the memory of their former intimacy would soften him. Certainly her body refused to forget. She was vulnerable in her skimpy servant's dress, as if he still had the right to reach under the fabric and touch her skin.

'I'm sure you realize that I only wished to speak to you because of Dorothea. You're my last hope.' He must have noted her surprise. No thought of Dorothea had entered her head. 'We know that she is very ill though she seldom writes. I want you to persuade her to go back to Startsdon. My parents are beside themselves with worry.'

'Dorothea assumes you are glad to be rid of her. And my brother says your parents are happy that at least Deborah is prepared to marry him.'

'It's true my parents are obsessed by the idea of a title and they don't mind which girl marries one. After all, it's you and not Robin they blame for Dorothea's defection. Incidentally, I can't imagine Robin's best pleased with you either. Dorothea would have made a much more tractable wife than Deborah.' His lip twitched on one side and she sat down abruptly, a move that brought her level with his upper legs, so close that she could make out the plain stitching on his garter. He smelt of horse and spices, quite different to the muted female scents she was used to.

'Dorothea is very happy,' she said. 'I promise that nobody is keeping her against her will.'

'She left because of you. She worships you. When the family was cursing you for running away from our marriage she wouldn't come out of her room until they agreed not to vilify you in her hearing. You could make her change her mind.'

'So was it her idea to come to St Omer that time?' she asked suddenly.

'St Omer?'

'Your visits to the town are noticed, Mr Bourne. Some say

you take an unusual interest in the movements of Jesuit priests there.'

'I might have made a slight detour with the girls on the way to Spa once. Dorothea said she wished to take the waters. She never asked for anything in her life before so how could I refuse her? But I think really she wanted to find you.'

He actually seemed quite fond of Dorothea so Isabel said gently: 'She is in excellent hands.'

He moved away so swiftly that the tip of his sword caught on her chair-back. As he was now in front of the window the room was dark except for firelight. 'She has no roots in Catholicism. I can't bear to think of her rattling the beads of a rosary. Spouting Latin. Praying for a Borghese pope.'

After a considerable pause Isabel said: 'It's just as well we didn't marry. I had no idea you had such a violent hatred for the Catholic faith.'

'What happens when Mary Ward is hung and her community broken up? What will become of Dorothea then? You think there's a new leniency towards Catholics in England. There's no such thing. These days parliament is stuffed with Puritans who dislike Catholics even more than the king does. Nobody will support you. I don't want to see Dorothea dragged into prison.'

'She would consider that a small price to pay.'

'Don't give me platitudes, Isabel. Look at you. I remember I could once read every thought in your head but now you are the same as all fanatics, Catholic and Puritan. You're so sure of yourself. Be careful, Isabel. Don't trust a soul. Mary Ward has few friends here in England and not many in Europe. You behave like fools. Oh, I know you think martyrdom is a great death. You Catholics set huge store by the next life and your rewards there. But this life matters, Isabel. Wake up.'

'I am awake, Mr Bourne, I am sure of my chosen path. I don't waste time wondering how to live. What about you? I wonder what you have been busy with of late? What is your latest craze, Mr Bourne? Astrology still?'

He watched her for a moment in the uncertain orange light. 'Not astrology. Astronomy. Science. The pursuit of knowledge. Galileo, he's the one. I'm going to try and meet him in Italy. Perhaps my next play will have a star-gazer as its hero. Galileo studies the planets and tracks their movements across the sky. He wonders. You and I are not so far apart, Isabel. We both spend our lives wondering.'

'Believing.'

'Ah yes, you have become such an expert in your field of speculation that you call yourself a believer while I merely dabble.'

'Dorothea said you'd been abroad this summer. Where this time?'

'Here and there.'

'And who do you work for now? My father told me you'd left the service of Lionel Cranfield.'

'Oh, I went back soon enough. Cranfield has risen to the dizzy heights of Master of the Wardrobe though he won't be long in favour, I fear. He's trying to persuade our great monarch to cut down on drink and candles in his palaces. That won't make him popular.'

'So you travel on Cranfield's behalf?'

'I keep my eye on the competition. Yes. That's my job. We don't want cheap pepper or starch imported into the country except on our ships. Nor must a European war get in the way of trade. You have registered, Isabel, that England will side with the Protestants when the king's poor little son-in-law, Frederick, gets kicked out of Bohemia? As he will. Then what will happen to you all?'

Am I to blame, she wondered, for the way he is now? Or was his former sweetness of character just a sham? 'Everyone warns us that we won't last long in a war. We'll see.'

'So you won't help Dorothea? You'd all be much safer if you got her out. She can't be moved quickly so she'll slow you down if you have to decamp.'

'Is that a threat, Mr Bourne?'

'It's a piece of advice. I'm told your Mary Ward is expected in London soon. Archbishop Abbot, the great and the good, has said she does more damage than six or seven Jesuits. I've no doubt the lady would take this as a compliment but don't you see how they'd love to arrest her?'

'You are remarkably well informed.'

'What I know, Isabel, others know. You're living in a fool's paradise if you think any of you is safe in Hoxton.'

'We like to be fools.' She gathered up her cloak, pleased with this last rejoinder. 'Mr Bourne, has it occurred to you why Dorothea and so many other young women join us? We are sick of the self-seeking, faithless world of the court. We want to make a difference. Isn't that something to be applauded?'

In the hall she delayed for a moment, then flung open the little back door. She had an impression of a dense interior, the beams hung with drying leaves and shapeless garments, every surface cluttered with bottles, jars and pots. By the window stood Margaret Westward, the hidden listener, sprung backwards in haste, diminutive as ever but much aged and full of hate.

'Margaret.'

Margaret turned away her face.

In Isabel's ear came Bourne's whisper: 'You could buy her forgiveness. It's the only way, but I don't suppose you've enough money.' His breath was warm and his beard touched her cheek. She walked hastily to the door but he stopped her again, took her by the shoulder and pressed her against the wall.

His face was on hers, nose against nose, mouth on mouth. 'Isabel. I knew a woman once who was a shiver of white heat. Where has she gone?'

She stood shocked, mouth half open, eyes wide, then ducked away, wrenched open the door and ran from the house.

The morning beyond was very silent and strange. Frost still hung in the air though a phantom sun floated in a grey haze. There were people about in broad hats and thick cloaks but the landscape lacked solidity, like the cold oils on a Dutch painting. Everyone seemed isolated from each other. Isabel hurried home on the fringes of a vast, unfriendly London and knew that her footprints had scorched an indelible trail across the frozen ground.

Chapter 19

A visit to Fitzroy House required elaborate preparation. Clothes, like everything else in the Hoxton community, were a shared resource. Yellow ruffs were reportedly in fashion so Isabel was decked out in a dyed concoction of starched muslin above a low-cut green bodice. The unfortunate Susannah meanwhile was laced into a borrowed gown of staggering ugliness, black with tufts of white pulled through slits in the fabric.

The sense of alienation Isabel had experienced at New River Head returned the moment they were inside Lady Fitzroy's carriage. London on a pitch dark winter evening was without quarter. Inside the city walls pockets of open space had been swallowed up by houses shoddily built to accommodate layer upon layer of new families; Huguenot and other Protestant refugees from the continent and labourers from the north or east of England lured by the promise of easy money. The government, ever fearful of riot and plague, tried to keep down the population by strict building regulations but nobody took any notice. Teetering second- and third-floor bays were supported by frail pillars so that the houses were like trees in a thick wood struggling up to the light. Through stinking mud ploughed too many ill-shod feet and the wheels of too many carts.

Fitzroy House had been modernized. Marble heroes still patrolled the alcoves but the ceilings were now decorated with a host of cavorting cherubs while some of the stiffer family portraits on the stairs had been replaced by sober Dutch still-lives and Italian interiors with religious themes: John the Baptist's head on a plate and Christ with the woman

taken in adultery. Across the polished floors paraded the
wealthy and the influential, for Lady Arabella kept open
house on Tuesday evenings and the queen was a regular
visitor. Isabel had a dizzying sense that these people in their
circular skirts or puffed breeches had been here all through
the years since her last visit, twirling for ever under the
chandeliers with the colour of their silks and the arrangements of their ruffs an ever-changing kaleidoscope of movement. Tonight singers had been hired and periodically the
babble of voices was underpinned by the convoluted out-
pouring of a madrigal.

Lady Arabella had taken to wearing a ruff the size of a
cartwheel and her hair was pulled back in a high frizz which
arched her brows in an expression of perpetual surprise. The
lids of her drowsy eyes, however, had sunken still lower.
'Dear Mistress Stanhope. A yellow ruff. How courageous of
you. And you still in mourning for your grandmother. Never
mind, there is someone who wants to meet you. Susannah
Thewing. At last we meet.' She kissed the air an inch from
Susannah's plump cheek and whispered: 'You will be amazed
by the wonderful surprise I have waiting for you. Not one
but two brothers.' She flicked her fan, intricate as a dragonfly
wing, and a maid came forward to escort Susannah away.

'Dutch or Italian, Mistress Stanhope, whose art do you
favour? I hear you've been speaking to Francis Bourne?'

They stood beneath an Icarus braced for his fall to the
ocean, dark features bewildered above a taut body. Lady
Arabella's index finger moved a fraction to indicated the
signature. 'Palma Giovane. So much more extraordinary
than Holbein. I never know what to think about Francis
Bourne, Isabel, and that's unusual for me. I have been at
court long enough to know my mind on most people. I hope
you weren't too open with him.'

'I wondered how he knew I was here.'

'Everyone knows everything in this community. Francis
stays on the fringes among his theatrical friends but I'm sure
there are many who are willing to tell him what he wants
to know.'

'Is that why you asked to see me, Lady Fitzroy?'

'And to tell you that there is bad news from St Omer. Mary is so short of money that she is planning a fund-raising visit to London herself. Ah, here is your cousin Edmund Thewing. Just the person.'

Edmund had grown quite fleshy and had the full, pouting lips of a spoilt child. His doublet and breeches were of ivory satin and he wore a girdle embroidered in gold and silver, dotted with strawberries and pearls. Isabel suspected that many hours must have been spent in front of the mirror to achieve such a practised twinkle in the eye and a dimpling of the cheek. She was surprised that Lady Fitzroy had not yet found a more useful favourite.

There was no doubt, however, that he was the most attentive of gentlemen. His mistress had schooled him well. Isabel's hand rested on his bejewelled sleeve and together they paraded the length of the room until they were very close to the singers. Edmund smiled on all, urbane and charming but with just a hint that he was doing the room a great favour by being in it. Familiar faces drifted past Isabel. A towering arrangement of white hair decorated with bobbing plumes was surely Lady Whitfield, eyes a-bulge with curiosity.

Isabel was not grateful for her cousin's gallantry. She felt no more fondness for him now than when they were children and wondered why he wasn't with Susannah instead. It also quickly became apparent that though his manners were impeccable, his mind was elsewhere and he was hiding considerable agitation. There was tension in his arm, he blinked too often and held his head too rigid.

'The truth is, cousin,' he murmured under the cover of a piping boy soprano, 'Lady Fitzroy hates talking about money. She leaves it to me. It's said that Mary Ward is to open a house in Liège. Can we help? Lady Fitzroy is eager to be part of a project that has at its heart the welfare of Catholic girls.'

'Edmund, I am hardly the one to approach. As far as I know I shall be in England for several years.'

'She's concerned, however, that there seems to be an attempt by Mary Ward to link herself with the Jesuits.' The 'J' of Jesuits was stuttered, as if the word pained him. Isabel was amazed that he would risk the name in this company. 'We don't think this is the right way forward.'

'You surely don't expect me to comment on that here,' and Isabel moved deliberately back into the crowds. Many heads were turned their way. It would be widely known that the lady in the tasteless ruff was Isabel Stanhope, disgraced daughter of Sir William and a member of Mary Ward's notorious institute of scandalous nuns.

Former acquaintances moved in and out of her orbit. Lady Huntly, an unhealthy network of blood vessels prominent in her staring eyes, came close to take a better look and gave her a frigid nod. A man in dark blue silk pushed back a strand of hair from his eyes but was gone before she could look his way. Her heart lurched.

The public side of Fitzroy House was fantastical and over-heated but Isabel later stepped again through the secret door which led to the other world, silent and restrained, where once she had met with Carisbroke.

Lucy Morton on the bare-foot pilgrimage to Holywell had been a strapping woman who had plunged unhesitatingly into the freezing waters of the well. Less than a year ago on the crossing from France she had seemed equally robust, as courageous and wilful as her niece Blanche. This evening she lay on her deathbed.

Susannah had removed her over-skirt and ruff and settled into her old competence. Near the bed was a young, flaxen-haired priest with white skin and a short, high-bridged nose. Alan Thewing, the latest Jesuit arrival in England, was certainly in demand these days.

A table was set for communion. Lucy's body had rejected all nourishment for five days now and she was a wisp, ready at any minute to disappear altogether, too weak to speak Isabel's name or squeeze her hand. Apparently she had caught this disease while visiting a struggling family near the river in Southwark and it said much for Lady Fitzroy's charity that she should harbour anyone with such a virulent infection. Many would have turned even a close blood relative away.

'*Si ambulem in medio umbrae mortis, no timeo mala . . .*'

Isabel had heard Father Thewing say mass a number of times and wondered if Lucy Morton was comforted by this nasal recital. No doubt the presence in a confined space of both his sister and his cousin, neither of whom had shown him much sympathy in the past, did little to reassure him.

Father Thewing's fingers trembled as he raised the host. Susannah lifted Lucy's head from the pillow, the sick woman's dry lips patted on the white disc and her feeble grey tongue drew it in. That she could swallow at all seemed like a miracle.

But even as Thewing gave the blessing Lucy's body drew itself together in a bout of dreadful coughing. Susannah sprang forward with a bowl and the host was vomited back in a trickle of black bile. A thin tear ran down Lucy's old cheek.

Nobody knew what to do but after barely a second's hesitation Susannah dipped finger and thumb in the bowl, took the host and placed it between her own lips. With her free hand she crossed herself, then murmured to Lucy: 'There has been no desecration. You have simply shared a precious gift with me.'

Father Thewing, after a moment's amazed silence, resumed his prayer. Lucy sank against the pillow with a shaky smile of gratitude.

Isabel forced Susannah out on to the narrow landing. As she couldn't bear to get too close to that poisoned mouth their conversation was conducted in tense whispers. 'You must be out of your mind.'

Susannah bent her head and said nothing.

'You should not have done that. Do you want to kill yourself? She caught that illness just by being in an infected house so you don't stand a chance. I presume you'll come back to Hoxton and expect us all to look after you.'

Susannah turned on her a ponderous gaze. 'I had to do it. It was the Body of Christ.'

'No. No. You did it to prove how self-abasing you are. You did it for you. You have never done a truly generous thing in your life.'

The two stared at each other in horror. The world was splintering apart with outrage and jealousy.

Isabel broke away and plunged down the steep stairs and out into a narrow passage leading to the courtyard.

I am still mad, she thought. There is still a streak in me that won't be schooled. I travel a small distance along the path of the religious life and then in an instant I become once more a wild child. Will I never be free of this demon?

She had no cloak and rushed in bitter wind along crazy back streets fogged with the smoke from a thousand hearths. Within minutes her fingers were almost too cold to untie the tapes of her ruff. Shaking violently she tore off her moonstone headdress. It scarcely mattered to her whether she ever returned to Hoxton. She would rather fly for ever along these friendless alleys.

By the time she had recovered a little she was under the walls of St Paul's. Among the huddled crowds she saw the phantom of a scaffold and heard the creaking rasp of rope on wood. She wore only slippers and the soles of her feet felt every cobble, every crack in the pavings. Her extravagant skirt was filthy with London mud.

But she was on familiar territory and her bruised feet carried her along the old route home through Cheapside to Bishops Gate. She moved as one possessed, straight-backed and sightless. Her exposed neck was a column of ice. Across Spital Fields sudden gusts rattled the ropes anchoring sails of windmills that all day had been still. Ahead small beacons of light marked the beginnings of Hoxton.

On the biting wind came a memory. Isabel was riding with her mother through winding lanes near Cuddington. Every time she thought they were close to home the house slipped again behind another copse, another hedgerow. At last they were under the high gateposts and ahead was the long drive to the house. But instead of silence and rest, ranked horsemen awaited them.

Abruptly Isabel turned off the road and on to a field-path

that would take her behind the houses and through the garden gate to her father's house. The wind shook her skirts and tried to fling her off course.

The garden, usually so peaceful, was full of activity. Susan Rookwood in a dark cloak stood at the gate and a procession of silent women crept towards Isabel. 'They're at the door. They say they want to search the house. We've fastened the gates to the stableyard but we can't hold them for long. They've heard a rumour that Mary Ward is in the country. We think as they can't have her, they'll go for Dorothea.'

'Why?'

'Money. Her father is richer than anyone else's. He'd pay the most to get her out.'

Of course they would want Dorothea. The Bourne family was wealthy enough to pay generously for this sham of an abduction. Francis Bourne had spelled it out for Isabel only that morning. He might as well have said: Give me Dorothea or we'll come and take her. After all, the search of a recusant household gave a legitimate, even praise-worthy excuse for this violation.

'It would kill her,' said Martha Canton who was not prone to exaggeration.

'Will you be able to get her to Cornhill?'

'Michael Latham has borrowed a horse. Just a few more minutes is all we need.'

With hands shaking so violently that she struck her own neck and cheek Isabel re-fastened the despised yellow ruff, replaced the headdress and marched into the house. By now hammering on the entrance door was deafening.

She flung open the door with a vigour that caught the men on the step off-balance.

'It is very late and as you see I have only recently come in,' she said. 'Whatever is the matter?'

Martha Canton was at her shoulder, an elderly companion gibbering with fright. Isabel's tongue produced arguments formed by a childhood spent between ambitious Sir William and unbending Lady Thomasina while Martha, wailing, pleading and tearing at her mistress's sleeves, had doubtless played a similar game at Oakshott more times than she could remember.

The pursuivants were led by a heavy-set man with cumbersome lips and lower eyelids pulled down by fat cheeks. His laboured sighs and slow speech intimated that it was a great bother reasoning with a couple of Catholic women but for form's sake he must go through the motions.

His most pressing concern was for Isabel to give up the key to the courtyard door so that they could unlatch the yard gates. 'I'd love to, if I only knew where it was. Martha, please try and help. Could it be in the dresser, do you suppose? Or the cabinet in my father's old room. If only I'd been more careful with it.'

The limited patience of the pursuivants was running out. They knew that the women were slipping through their fingers like sand. At last Isabel and Martha were thrust aside and the men let loose in the house.

In the old parlour Sir William's map of London still hung over the hearth. Here they brought the English Ladies who had failed to escape, each in her nightgown, innocent and bewildered. Not Dorothea, who must have been spirited away. But the pursuivants found plenty of booty: Latin Missals, a rosary, a crucifix and a leather bag containing three little pots of oil.

'Who is responsible for these?'

'I am, of course. This is my father's house,' said Isabel. 'What do you expect from the daughter of Lady Thomasina Stanhope? All these are mine.'

'I presume these oils belonged to a priest. Has a priest been staying in this house? Has mass been said here?'

Isabel weighed briefly the advantages of denial. How could she best ensure the release of the other women and a speedy end to the search? 'I often entertain priests, though I can assure you there is none here now.'

She was studied for some moments by fish-cold eyes. 'To shelter priests is treachery.'

'I have never understood why. Certainly I am very fond of my king.'

Let's get it over with quickly, she thought.

Now it seemed to her that a day begun with a false message from a former lover had always been destined to end in imprisonment.

Chapter 20

A little after ten the following morning Isabel was
ushered into the august presence of Sir Richard
Whitfield, examining magistrate at the Guildhall.
Flanked by lesser officials, he sat on a dais behind a great
table while she stood in the middle of the coldly tiled floor
between a couple of armed guards. Whitfield was muffled
up in a fur-trimmed gown and though his ruff was askew his
opulent garments gave him a distinction he had not possessed
when younger. However, when she later edged forward
a little, Isabel noted that his shoulders were flecked with
drifts of flaked skin and his beard had become straggly with
age.

Despite his lofty position, Whitfield was hard-pressed to
hide his triumph at Mistress Isabel's appearance before him.
She had been kept all night in a small locked room and
looked like a prostitute with her stained skirt and low-cut
bodice. By her admission that priests were welcomed at the
Hoxton house she had given up the right to humane
treatment.

In any case, there was no mercy to be had at Whitfield's
hands. He was too tucked up in his great office, too wounded
by a youth spent scrabbling up the slippery rungs of promotion and embittered by the knowledge that he would now
never reach the very top. His complexion was dusty and he
had lost most of his teeth. Isabel imagined them breaking off
one by one in wads of tobacco.

She wondered dazedly whether an exchange of pleas-
antries would help. Perhaps she should say how glad she'd
been to see Lady Whitfield at Fitzroy House the previous

night but decided such familiarity would dent his dignity and make him even less sympathetic.

Whitfield laid out the physical evidence against her in a precise row, making tiny adjustments to each item, straightening the books and forming the rosary beads into a circle. The man was a terrible fidget. He'd spent his life on the watch for lucrative opportunities or the chance to bend an influential ear and could never be sure that in the next room, at another meeting, someone wasn't bettering him.

He would have been mortified to learn that Isabel in fact considered him of little importance compared to the other things on her mind. During eight hours of solitary confinement she had grappled with a number of emotions, the most powerful being guilt because she knew all this could have been avoided. She even wondered if she had willed it upon herself. After all, she had known from her interview with Bourne that the raid on Hoxton was bound to happen but had said nothing to her companions. Vanity had convinced her that he would never betray a woman he had once promised to love.

Or perhaps she actually wanted to be condemned, the ultimate test of faith and a pathway to martyrdom that had been marked out by her childhood idol, Margaret Clitherow.

The true seriousness of her predicament made little impact at first. Women were not often executed because to do so might glorify the Catholic cause. And prison held few fears for Isabel. She had been schooled in hardship and solitude and this interrogation was chicken-feed compared to the severity of the Spiritual Exercises.

Her gaze kept flying up and sideways to the lancet windows and vaulted ceilings.

On this very spot Father Henry Garnet had stood during his trial.

Not me, she thought, this can't be me, and her soul seemed to flutter to the darkest corner and hover there, watching.

What happened to Garnet could never happen to me. I'm not important.

Important enough for the Guildhall.

Sir Richard Whitfield was not doing well. As the defendant

was both female and known to him, he was striving to show the assembled court that this was a sheer waste of time. But despite himself he was drawn into the proceedings because he was irritated by Isabel's air of calm abstraction.

'Yes, I own that breviary, I use it every day to say the divine office.'

'Yes. I own that Missal.'

'Yes, the rosary is mine and the little wooden crucifix.'

'Yes, as I said, if you found that leather bag in my house it suggests that a priest must have visited at some time.'

'I've not signed the Oath of Allegiance but I deny that I have shown disloyalty or treachery to the king.'

'Neither my brother nor his servants were party to what I was doing.' She saw Robin and Nicholas Turner as the painted figures in the corner of the new portrait at Cuddington, sparring on the lawns. At least this escapade would give them something to discuss during their indigestible dinners.

Whitfield made a great fuss of refusing bail and airing dates of a pending trial but had little further opportunity for throwing his weight about. The case was a formality.

Isabel was seized by her two guards, one of whom fingered the side of her breast as he grabbed her upper arm. By the door they stood back to allow the next defendant through and at that moment she was finally jolted out of her dream state. Supported on either side by hefty gaolers limped the apologetic and dismayed figure of Father Alan Thewing.

Isabel had to wait in her cubbyhole until late afternoon while other prisoners were committed and a wagon brought, so it was evening before they lurched off past St Paul's, up Ludgate Hill and along the Strand to the Gatehouse Prison in Westminster. She looked away from Fitzroy House and instead watched the smoky sky between rooftops, heartily regretting her borrowed finery of shiny embossed satin that felt like slithery sheets of ice against her arms. Her skin was raw inside the corset that should have been removed hours ago and her waist could not bend under the long stomacher. Every jolt of the cart made her aware of some constricted organ or limb.

At least Alan Thewing wore serviceable clothes of thick worsted, several sizes too big. He quivered like a clubbed rabbit yet managed to smile.

'Did they come for you at Fitzroy House?' she whispered. 'Was anyone else arrested?'

'Outside. They were waiting when I left. Someone must have tipped them off. Of course I had everything with me, my stole, the chrism, a purificator. And they knew my name.'

Understanding broke on Isabel like a fever. Carisbroke had warned her that Bourne was a spy. Had he not visited St Omer, training ground of the English Jesuits? He must have had the Hoxton house watched and seen Thewing emerge from there. At Fitzroy House she'd noted a dash of dark blue silk and a lock of hair swept from a man's eyes. Father Thewing was a juicy catch compared to Isabel Stanhope. Fresh from the continent, ripe with information about safe houses, fellow seminarians and loyal English Catholics, he would be interrogated until squeezed dry and then hung, nine years of training snuffed out in a moment.

Well, Francis Bourne, how do you sleep at night?

Isabel watched her cousin's face with its transparent white skin, downy beard and ever-open mouth. She had never taken him seriously and yesterday during her interview with Francis Bourne had not given him a thought. But through her negligence she had brought him down. She should have warned him.

In the prison courtyard Thewing was dragged away with the other male prisoners and Isabel was left to the tender mercies of the warden's wife, bony and curly-haired, torn between her respect for Isabel and pride at her own exalted status within the prison. As no bribe had yet been organized by Isabel's friends, no concessions could be made. Agile hands searched through her hair, removed the spangled head-rail that had somehow stayed in place all day and cast it into a basket. Next came the ruff, lace cuffs, pinned over-skirts and farthingale leaving her in bodice and petticoats. The forlorn heap of discarded finery did nothing to appease the warden's wife for though carefully restored by Martha Canton, it was all second- or third-hand and of little value. Finally, when the shoes and stockings had joined the pile and the woman had run her hands the length of Isabel's thighs, an iron chain was locked on her wrist and by it she was led like a dog across a courtyard and through a low door.

The first shock was the quality of cold inside the prison, quite different to the knife-sharp wind on the streets. Although braziers had been lit, the thick walls licked up heat and seeped freezing moisture into shadows so impenetrable that Isabel thrust out her hands to push them aside. She made herself smile into eyes that watched her passing with the slack interest of those who would rip the skirt from her hips if she happened to fall down among them. Her bare feet trod slippery brick floors or uneven boards. They passed from one black chamber to another and through a slit on to a steep spiral staircase. Though Isabel stooped, the outer wall, leaning inwards, pressed on her hair.

Of all the horrors of prison, this was the worst; the inexorable drop from one step to the next, the narrowness of the treads so that only Isabel's heels had contact with anything solid, the walls thrusting in upon her as if to say: Go down, go down and never come up.

At the bottom was another long passage with grotesque shadows leaping across the stones and low voices weirdly echoing from hollow spaces within the blank walls.

At last, in a far corner, the gaoler groped along the wall for an iron ring and locked her on to it. 'That should keep you right and tight, little Catholic. You'd better start praying.'

'Why am I being put here? Surely I'm entitled to a light or a mattress.'

'No special orders. Female prisoner. This is where we put them until after the trial.'

When he left so did his lantern, swaying out of sight as

he peered randomly from side to side. What remained was a glow from a far-away brazier and the mournful light of one or two candles burning in distant cells.

Isabel had never known such darkness. The prison seemed a panting, ice-cold cavern stuffed with pitiless human beings. There were no windows this far down so she would have no idea of when morning came. Her eyes strained, her weight was on one elbow driven against the stone floor and the iron ring cut deep into her wrist. She could not swallow for the volume of darkness blocking her throat and felt her mind shrink to a tiny speck of terror which cried, No. No. No, but never made a sound.

Her body clamoured with needs that had never before gone unanswered except through choice.

Make me warm.

Give me something to drink.

Let me lie down on a clean mattress.

She was watched. There were eyes in the darkness. She stood up cautiously and the chain unravelled itself and tumbled to the ground with a shockingly prolonged jangle of metal.

There had been a terrible mistake. No woman of her rank ought to be subjected to such conditions. She struggled to decide which of her enemies had ordered this treatment for her. Sir Richard Whitfield certainly couldn't forgive her for being of a truly old family, its position in the world unassailable despite its faith. But much more frightening was Francis Bourne.

She had never considered the implications of what she had done to him until now. When she thought about him it was of someone essentially shallow, not easily touched. He had seduced her but she had expunged that episode in the confessional with Carisbroke and then set it firmly aside. Now it seemed that Bourne, on the other hand, had not forgiven her for deserting him. Her rejection of him had festered. He had waited and watched until he could set his trap. Only if she'd agreed to use her influence on Dorothea would she have been spared.

What kind of a man was he, to kiss a young girl in an attic

room and then, when she ran from him, wait a decade to destroy her?

Ranked against him were her friends, the community of English Ladies and Lady Fitzroy, but they had little power because they were Catholics operating beyond the law and must choose their battles carefully.

And Carisbroke. How soon would he find out what had happened? Would he keep a vigil for her night after night until she was released? She tried to bring him closer but her prayers were too insubstantial to wind their way up the spiral staircase and out into the open air.

Lord Jesus Christ, Son of God . . . She was so cold that the prayer was frozen out of her skull. *Lord Jesus* . . .

A hand shot out of the darkness and grasped her fingers, then her lower arm. It worked its way up the frogging on her sleeve and kneaded the bare flesh above her bodice. An expert foot hooked the back of her knees and dragged her down until she lay on her back with the woman seated astride and clutching a fistful of hair.

'What do you want?' panted Isabel.

'What have you got?' Her assailant was clamped on to her chest; the woman's skirts, reeking of urine and stale female secretions, covered Isabel's mouth.

'They took everything,' she cried. 'I have nothing. I am a Catholic, a nun. If I had anything I would give it to you.'

The woman's calloused hands rubbed across Isabel's eyes. 'Nuns don't cry.'

'This one cries,' and suddenly Isabel twisted her hip so violently that the woman was flung sideways: 'Leave me alone. Get me out of here. Get me out. I can't bear it. Don't touch me.'

The woman scrabbled to regain her dominance by tearing at Isabel's hair. Two remaining combs were clawed out and stuffed down the front of her own bodice. She clasped fistfuls of petticoat and wrenched it off, twining it round her shoulders with one hand, gripping Isabel's throat with the other. Next she went for Isabel's legs, thudding her knee between her thighs.

Animal cries issued from Isabel's throat and the tiny part

of her brain that still watched was amazed by her own noises and the fierce physical battle in which she was taking part. Again and again she slapped at the woman's face and kicked out, wailing shrieks resounding through the stone arcades of the prison until there were moans and curses from far away telling her to be quiet.

Finally she was on her knees, then had regained her feet until she was able to kick out at the woman's face. Her attacker retreated and crouched close by. 'Well you surely ain't no nun,' she said.

Isabel paused mid-scream. At least she was warmer, her skin smarting from the woman's blows. 'I am a nun, or like a nun. My life is given to Christ. That's why I'm here. I've committed no crime.'

'That was quite a performance for a Catholic, nun or no nun,' said the woman. 'Catholics usually cringe when I go for them.'

'You've fought with other Catholics then?'

'I fight with anybody. It keeps me amused.'

'I'm glad to hear it. But have you nothing else?'

'Nothing.'

'I could help you survive, even in this place. Christ could help you.' Isabel felt a stirring of hope. With every passing minute she was returning more to herself. Even here she must work. Perhaps this lost soul had been waiting for Isabel to redeem her.

The other woman's face, a blurred collection of nose, eyes and mouth in the intense gloom, was brought close. 'You, my little madam, can help nobody. Look to your own soul, darling, and don't bother with mine.'

'I do bother, I do . . .'

'No. It's all prayer and counting your sins with you. I want shoes on my feet and a meal on my plate.'

'Mary Ward, the founder of our . . . My friend Mary Ward wants every woman to have . . .'

'Don't give me words. You'll be gone tomorrow. They'll make a nest for you among the Catholics upstairs. We hear them singing sometimes and it makes me mad.'

'Is it because you're left out? You could . . .'

'I hear those songs and I understand that once those people sat in a quiet place and were taught music. I think, why did nobody sing for me? If that is God, doling out singing to one child, silence to another, don't lead me to him. I'd rather blind chance than such wickedness in a God.'

'I will pray for you,' said Isabel.

'Don't. Don't pray for me.'

Isabel didn't sleep that night. She wrapped herself up tight in her remaining petticoat and huddled against the wall with small movements all around her, rustlings, snufflings and moanings.

Oh, Peter Carisbroke, is this enough? Are we now equals in the eyes of God?

Mistress Isabel Stanhope, as her wrestling partner on the first night had predicted, was promoted rapidly, brought up through the prison hierarchy until she found herself in a relatively snug cell, her companion a robust mother of eight doing a routine stint in gaol for insisting on having her latest babe baptized a Catholic. Each morning they were allowed into a neighbouring room with a grid in the ceiling through which they could hear Alan Thewing on the floor above say mass. Isabel watched his feet move across the bars, heard the familiar invocations, sang the responses, and understood the rigorous nature of the Jesuit training and why Mary Ward admired it so. Though effectively still a novice, Father Thewing had been moulded by theology, prayer and the Spiritual Exercises to be indifferent to his physical condition. Despite the initial disadvantage of a timid and reluctant nature, he had forced himself into a state of certainty.

He would be dead within weeks. To the authorities, Jesuits were like ants. Stamp on one and three more emerge through another crack. In less than four years, thirty additional priests had arrived so that there were now estimated to be around a hundred in the country.

A stream of ladies came to see Isabel. Martha Canton, an expert prison visitor after years ministering to the needs of

Anne Winshawe, brought soap, clean water, paper, ink, quill, food and a copy of *Spiritual Combat*. 'I won't be here again as I'm being sent to St Omer. We're all praying for your release but we suspect you won't be here long. The Spanish Embassy is practically next door and the ambassador will be furious that yet another Catholic lady has been arrested. How can our king hope for a Spanish match if Catholics are so badly treated in this country?'

Next came Susannah, on her way to see her brother, Father Thewing. She was not best suited to cheering the afflicted because she had so little to say.

'How is Lucy Morton?' asked Isabel.

'She died.'

'You suffered no ill-effects then after that night?'

'None.'

Oh for goodness sake, Susannah, help me out, thought Isabel. I'm trying to make amends. She brought her mouth very close to her cousin's ear which was half tucked away under a white cap. Susannah's best feature was her dense, clear skin, and the way her dark hair sprang from a smooth hairline. Her clothes had a freshness that was entirely lacking elsewhere in the prison. 'Send your brother my love. Tell him I'm sorry.'

'Why must you apologize to him?'

'It's my fault he was arrested. Francis Bourne had him watched because of the grudge he bears me.'

Susannah's face underwent a most unexpected change. She laughed, revealing small, white teeth and delivering a series of slow, deep chuckles. 'There are other people who influence the way things happen, Isabel, apart from you.'

Five days later the warden's wife arrived in person to announce that Mistress Stanhope was to be released without trial. But now Isabel found herself in the extraordinary position of not wanting to go. Prison life was very straight-forward. It was easy to do right when movement was restricted and there were few distractions. She shared out her possessions to fellow prisoners, bade her cell-mate an emotional farewell and asked to see her acquaintance of the first night.

'Whatever for? It's against regulations. You won't want to go in those cellars again.' But Isabel, re-established in her rank of lady, was not to be denied.

Susannah had brought her a plain grey dress, the skirts of which she lifted fastidiously as they made their way down to the bowels of the prison. She faltered only once, under the grid where Father Alan Thewing said mass. Reaching up her hand Isabel slotted her fingers through the metal. My dear cousin.

The spiral staircase proved to be much more functional than she remembered and there was a lantern perched in a niche to light the way. Even the squalor of the cellars seemed less nightmarish. Perhaps there had been a sweeping out and a mopping down.

In the corner briefly occupied by Isabel the warden's wife flashed her lantern about and revealed three iron hoops riveted to the wall, a scattering of limp straw and a broken chamber pot.

'Where is she, the one who was here?'

Dark eyes winked triumphantly in the smoky yellow light. 'Oh, her. If I'd known it was her you was after I could have saved us the trouble. She was hung yesterday. Theft from an employer. Two sheets and a tablecloth. Didn't stand a chance.'

The winter sunshine was so brilliant in the courtyard outside that Isabel raised her arm to shield her face. The prison dropped from her shoulders like a dragging cloak. Two women stood at the gate, Susan Rookwood and Mary Ward.

Isabel ran across the cobbles like one possessed, taking deep breaths of cold, bright air, laughing and crying, covering her eyes with her hand. The shock of freedom coupled with this wholly unexpected reunion with Mary were too much. How dare she appear in the precincts of the Gatehouse? Surely they would all be followed and re-arrested.

Mary wasted no time on sympathy. 'Much has happened in your absence,' said she, as if scolding Isabel for being unavailable. 'Susan has done well to re-establish our little community at Hungerford House which the family has kindly loaned to us. The gardens are neglected and the rooms much too big but its central location makes it ideal and Dorothea Bourne seems to have rallied nicely since she's been there.'

'Well,' remarked Isabel shakily, 'we might just as well pitch camp right in the middle of Parliament Square. We could hardly be closer to Westminster Palace.' The nerve of Mary and her companions was breathtaking. Crushed one day, they popped up the next. Imprisoned, they leapt free. Or perhaps there was something to be said for living as if the law simply didn't apply. Eventually the authorities might be worn down by the chase and give it up.

'You must be wondering why we're not heading home now,' said Susan with unusual sharpness. 'Mary wants us to go with her to Lambeth Palace.'

'Lambeth Palace. Mary?'

'As you've probably heard, Archbishop Abbot wants me arrested so I thought I'd save him the trouble by paying him a visit. We'll tell him that it would be more polite not to send his men for us in the dead of night. Morning would be better.'

'Why take such a risk?'

By now they had crossed Old Palace Yard and were heading for the river. Isabel, still afraid of being snatched back into the Gatehouse, huddled into her cloak and pressed closer to Susan but Mary was in holiday mood, almost dancing with glee. 'I think it degrading for an archbishop, even of an heretical church, to spread ill-founded rumours. He ought to have facts on which to base his arguments. I'll give him a few.'

'If you go to the archbishop he'll have you arrested.'

'I don't think so. He prefers to see me as a criminal and would rather catch me red-handed with a priest in my house than sitting quietly in his own parlour.'

'He won't agree to meet you, then. He certainly won't

deign to argue with you. You're a heretic and a woman. He's the Archbishop of Canterbury.'

'I think he will listen. There must be some good in him. If I could only see him I'm sure I could convince him of our excellent motives. What a chance, to speak with such an implacable enemy.'

The ferryman rowed across a river skittish with tiny, ruffled waves. Isabel threw back her hood and raised her face to the sun. There was logic in Mary's behaviour. The English Ladies committed no crime that she would acknowledge and secrecy suggested guilt. Mary's power lay in her blazing conviction that she did God's work. Persecution, imprisonment and even death itself were unfortunate but minor obstacles.

The harsh winter light reflected from the water was not kind to Mary who looked much older than her thirty-three years with a sickly complexion and sunken eyes. Her intense concentration, the ability to be absolutely present and yet focused on God seemed too powerful a quality to be contained by such frail flesh.

'I am taking you back with me to Liège, Isabel. I need you there. You have excellent French and are more persistent than most.'

Isabel forced herself to pay attention. Clearly, there was to be no wallowing in recent trauma. 'I've heard so many rumours that I wondered if you would still go ahead with the Liège project. Should we really be buying another house when we can hardly make ends meet in St Omer?'

'We must. We can't rely on the income from just one house. And our friends in St Omer may not remain faithful for ever. The Catholic government in Prague is under threat. If it is over-turned, if war breaks out, we are at risk so we must find other toeholds in Europe. Liège is the answer. Its prince-bishop is Ferdinand, brother of Maximilian of Bavaria who I think could be a valuable friend. And more importantly, Father Gerard is building a Jesuit College for further study there. It's vital that we stay close to sympathetic Jesuit friends.'

'But can we afford another house? Is it wise?'

265

'It's not wise and we can't afford it. Nor will we until women who join us pay proper dowries. That won't happen until the Pope gives us his blessing. He will never give his blessing until we accept enclosure. We will not accept enclosure. Find me a way out of that conundrum.'

'Compromise. Accept some form of enclosure. Draw up a rule that will satisfy the authorities. Once we've been ratified we can make a difference from within. You're asking too much of a church that has always been set against change.'

'I know what God asked me to do. I look at you and all the other women and I think if we were behind an enclosure our own souls would be cosy enough, but who else would we save?'

'Prayer . . .'

'Life is a prayer. Women can pray and work in the world, as men can.'

Isabel remembered the woman in the prison cellar. What good had prayer been to her? Action, yes. Yes. 'I will, of course, go with you to Liège.'

'And then perhaps to Rome.' The glint in Mary's eye was dreaded by those of her companions who sought a quiet life. 'We will have to go to Rome ourselves, I fear. People have written petitions for me and all kinds of messengers have scurried to the Pope on our behalf but our letters always fall into the wrong hands or get forgotten. There are men in Rome trained to pick holes in the written word. I think if I could meet the Pope face to face he would give me what I want.'

'How will we get to Rome without money?'

'I've no idea at present. But I'm sure we'll find a way.'

By a small tilt of her shoulder, a slight withdrawal, Mary indicated that the subject was closed.

Lambeth Palace, with its towers and crenellations, was horribly like a fortress. The archbishop was not at home. By now the women were high as kites and stood about among fellow petitioners in a small waiting room, cracking jokes and speculating about what the archbishop would do when he heard they'd come.

At last Mary said: 'Well, he'll be sorry he missed us. What a chance he's lost.'

'He won't believe you were really here. He'll never think you had the nerve unless you leave your signature,' whispered Isabel. She took Susan's hand and drew off her little diamond ring.

With the jewel Mary cut her name in the window.

Mary Ward.

She then turned to Isabel. 'We mustn't waste any more time here. You smell of the prison. Tallow. Worse. We must boil your petticoats and give you a bath. It's high time you were home.'

Back across the river they rowed with the wind buffeting their veils and Westminster Palace blurred by smoke under a delicate blue sky.

It is Mary's gift, thought Isabel, to make things happen. From one day to the next my life is transformed.

On the wharf was a solitary horseman. Even from a distance they could tell that the huge black horse was restless and that the rider wore a short grey cloak with a purple lining.

When the women were handed from the barge one by one, Isabel was placed firmly between Mary and Susan and they walked steadily up the jetty. Mary gave Francis Bourne a courteous nod as she passed, Isabel didn't look at him.

The horse switched its tail against a nearby post and threw up its head with an energetic shudder of muscle and leather. The women walked on.

'Isabel.'

Mary's bony elbow clenched her arm. The low sun shone on her face and she thought of Father Alan Thewing's feet, clad in slippers sewn by Susannah, crossing the grid in the Gatehouse.

'Isabel.'

They had turned a corner. Her head was full of red heat. She was sick. Susan clamped her arm tighter still and dragged her forwards. After a few more steps it became clear that he had not chosen to follow them.

FOUR

Praxedes

1621

Chapter 21

In London the resolve of the English Ladies had been rock solid, their resourcefulness and energy generated by the scorching spirituality of community life. They faced problems and hostility at every turn but came home after episodes of intense physical and mental activity full of stories and jokes; excited, indignant and motivated.

But in Liège their objectives were not so clear. For a start they had the cumbersome maintenance of two large houses, the first a day-school on Mont St Martin, the other a newly refurbished mansion used as the boarding-house for English girls half a mile away on La Pierreuse.

The money for this latest house had originated from a very peculiar source and one for which Isabel took some credit. Edmund Thewing, thanks to Lady Fitzroy's patronage and his eye for a lucrative deal, had become a successful merchant adventurer and seemed surprisingly eager to share his wealth with the English Ladies by securing them loans. As his sister Susannah had never been given a dowry and his brother, the Jesuit Alan Thewing, had been slaughtered in 1618, he argued that by donating funds to Mary Ward he was making some amends to both.

Thewing had become quite a familiar figure in Liège, trotting into town on a highly-strung white horse, the azure jewel on his breast proclaiming that here was a man of substance. Because he was too long in the body and short in the leg to ride well, people had learned to be wary of flying hooves but always smiled or bobbed a curtsey when he passed by. No beggar's cupped palm was left empty when Thewing was in town. He had shed his London persona of languid courtier and instead was always in a hurry.

His schedule was breathtaking; breakfast with the mayor, Jean de Merlemont, a mid-morning glass or two with some influential prelate seeking advice on the progress of the war, half an hour in church, an inspection of the building he had helped fund for the English Ladies, and possibly an audience with the Prince-Bishop Ferdinand. Even the Protestants, tucked out of sight in the back streets but kept busy by lucrative trading agreements with the Dutch to the north, had a good word to say for tolerant Mr Thewing.

But the money he pledged the English Ladies went on property, not living expenses. For these they were thrown back on their own resources. Local girls recruited to the day-school on Mont St Martin spoke only French and were inclined to be giggly and ungrateful while the young women sent from England were fearful and bewildered. In Liège there was a convent on every street corner so the competition for vocations was fierce. The locals, while appreciating free education for their daughters, were grudging in their voluntary contributions to the English Ladies.

So Mary Ward's companions were in danger of losing heart. They had beautiful buildings but were always hungry, even though the stringent rules regarding food had been relaxed and they were supposed to eat regular meals. The original team was now spread between houses in St Omer, London and Liège. Worse, despite the opposition of most of her friends, Mary was currently on a round trip to Trier and Cologne where she was intent on setting up two more establishments. 'Has she even thought how they are to be financed and staffed?' Blanche demanded. 'Does it occur to her that she's only welcome in these places because of the war? Catholic princes are falling over themselves to please their citizens. What could be a better way of winning popularity than providing a free education for girls?'

The only unequivocably good thing that had happened in Liège was the arrival of a relative of Mary Ward's so distant that she'd scarcely known of his existence. Robert Wright was a melancholy young man with a rope tied round his breeches to stop them slipping off his bony hips. He never smiled and the most attractive feature of his lugubrious face were eyes of forget-me-not blue.

Robert had sold all he possessed to come to the service of Mary Ward whose work he'd heard of in London. By the time he'd been a day in Liège he'd proved an invaluable asset to the English Ladies who adopted him as odd-job man and messenger. He was devoted to Mary, lived in an adapted outhouse and quickly became the uncomplaining butt of jokes and source of stability in an unfriendly town.

By the window of the community's parlour in the house on Mont St Martin the light was good but the temperature low. March that year was bitterly cold and always wet. During recreation Isabel sewed black sashes for the latest intake of novices and her needle disappeared into four layers of fabric with precise, steady thrusts. Her feet were crossed at the ankle under a heavy skirt, her hair, held by a small cap, was coiled in a warm weight at the nape under a veil.

Blanche leaned against the wall close by, arms folded, eyes snapping. As book-keeper, she had grown haggard with the struggle to keep them all from starvation.

The parlour in this Liège house was strangely resistant to the women. It refused to accommodate them but seemed rather to endure their presence. The walls were plastered an unpleasant greenish yellow and the hard rush-seated chairs stood about on the terracotta tiles in a formless pattern that never allowed for relaxation or comfort. The fireplace was too small and unless they spoke in whispers the noise level under the vault-like ceiling became intolerable.

Nevertheless, all seemed peaceful enough, with most of the women clustered round Dorothea Bourne who had been commissioned by Winifred to paint a series of canvases telling Mary Ward's life-story. Paintings, said Winifred, would be universally understood and their sober account of Mary's work would scotch all the damaging whispers about her failure as a Poor Clare or visions bred of hysteria.

The problem was that Dorothea, whose skill as an artist

had not developed much since girlhood, had been given the job simply because although she'd lived far longer than anyone expected she was still too sick to do strenuous work. Her appointment as artist and record-keeper had caused jealousy. Though loved, Dorothea was too withdrawn to be much liked, yet she now had access to Mary with a regularity that was denied most people.

Praxedes had learned to paint during her time as companion to Cordell Huntly but had refused to pick up a brush since the pictures had been commissioned. Called on to admire the pictures she had paused in the act of writing a letter, one fragile hand resting on the paper as if to hide its contents. Although she had the pearly complexion of the red-head, Isabel found her very unattractive. The glance from her greenish eyes, darkened by too much night prayer, was a little too cautious, the arching of her brow too contrived.

Isabel snipped her thread and unwound a new length. She was so familiar with these women that she could anticipate thought and action. Even the pace of their breathing, the idiosyncrasies of their digestive tracts, the degree of suffering they endured during menstruation were known to her. The texture of their skin was as much a fabric of her life as the close woven cloth of her own winter robe.

Blanche's mouth was compressed by concentration, short dark hairs emphasizing the firm line of her upper lip. No amount of inner discipline would keep Blanche quiet. If she saw fault she must comment. She was ruthless with herself and couldn't understand compromise in others. 'You see, Dorothea, the figure of Mary is far too small. I know you're trying to get perspective but that's ridiculous. You've made her look like a dwarf.'

'It's a wonderful painting,' said Praxedes softly. 'So imaginative.'

'But Dorothea is supposed to be showing Mary at home in England as a small child. That's not an English interior. Surely you remember how things look at home? The lattices are diamond-shaped. The ceilings have low beams.'

Even from her seat at the window Isabel could tell that the perspective in the picture was inaccurate and the likeness of Mary poor, but she said nothing. Blanche would probably tell her off later for being too wary of conflict.

Dorothea never reacted to what anyone said except to smile and apologize. She owed the women such a debt of gratitude for taking her in that she was apparently incapable of irritation.

Praxedes returned to her letter. 'I was just thinking that usually in a painting all the shadows lie in the same direction.'

At that moment the door was shoved open so violently that later a gash was discovered in the plaster where the knob had struck the wall. Those women who had been clustered near the table leapt to their feet.

It was as if the devil had entered the room.

Plague was rife in Liège. The rain-laden wind that so unsettled the hungry women on Mont St Martin flurried the thin breeches of soldiers hobbling into town with slashed limbs and bleeding heads. Raging with pain and hunger they brought stories of bloody skirmishes in Bohemia and the Palatinate between Habsburg forces and their Protestant enemies. In the soles of their inadequate boots, their fever-thickened saliva and under their filthy fingernails, these homesick vagabonds carried all kinds of infections from influenza to dysentery, syphilis to plague.

One such soldier had blown into a warm inn near the heart of town and got drunk at the table of the large-hearted and respectable master cellarer, Giles David. Three days later the soldier was dead of plague. Now, after one more day, Monsieur David, also infected, had staggered from his bed and made his lurching way along the steep lanes of Mont St Martin with some idea of reaching the church at the top where he remembered hearing angelic singing the previous Sunday. Instead, delirium had blasted him up the scrubbed steps of the late Canon Thenis's house, rented by the English Ladies since their arrival in the town four years previously. Compared to the squally streets, the interior was very peaceful. The sick man had veered across the swept hall floor and into the parlour.

Giles David wore only a shift and a pair of grey breeches undone at the waist. His body was so puffed and seeping with plague that it was impossible to tell what he usually looked like. Flesh seemed to have boiled up within itself and in places burst through the skin or collected in shiny hot pustules the size of a fist. His eyes were slits, his swollen tongue flicked mucus from his lips and he stank of vomit and shit.

The women, some of them very young, knocked over chairs to avoid his flailing arms. '*Sauvez moi*,' he rasped over and over again. '*Sauvez moi, les religieuses anglaises.*'

Isabel's first thought was that Susannah ought to be here. After all, she had held a bowl unflinchingly under Lucy Morton's dying mouth in Fitzroy House. But Susannah was in the house on La Pierreuse where she looked after the boarders.

The man lunged at Dorothea.

Since her spell in the Gatehouse Isabel had a special loyalty to Dorothea, who had to be kept alive if only to spite her brother. Never must Bourne be given the satisfaction of telling the world that the privations of life with the English Ladies had killed his sister. And now here was the plague, panted into Dorothea's sallow face.

Stepping hastily between Dorothea and the sick man, Isabel said: 'Praxedes, fetch Robert Wright. See if he can find out where this poor man has come from. Monsieur, we'll take care of you. You're safe here.' The wet sleeve of his shift slithered under her fingers as he strained away from her. 'Hush now. Hush. You're safe with us. Monsieur, we are religious women. We can't care for you in our house but if you tell us where you live some of us will nurse you there. Come with me.'

But he had twitched himself out of her grasp and was away across the hall and out into a cruel drizzle. A crowd had gathered at a safe distance and a distraught woman was toiling up the hill in search of her husband. Isabel took one arm, Robert the other and they escorted him home.

276

On her way back, with Robert loping behind at a discreet distance, damp, clean air blew in Isabel's face. Her initial satisfaction with the way that she had dealt with the matter faded fast. She and Robert now would have to lock themselves away until all fear of contagion was over. And she couldn't shake out of her head the idea that Monsieur David would never have got into the house if there had not been discord between the women, a rift caused by the paintings. The plague victim had inserted himself into the crack.

In Liège the English Ladies had little contact with the Jesuits, very few of whom were prepared to say mass for them or hear their confessions. Rumour abounded about the proximity of Mary Ward's house on La Pierreuse to the Jesuit College next door. The wall of the college facing their house was windowless so that no priest would be corrupted by the glimpse of a woman undressing but this didn't prevent whispers in the cosy shop-fronts of the lace-makers further down the street. As a result, Father Gerard had been sent to Genoa because he was far too anxious to help Mary Ward and there had reportedly been a flurry of letters from Vitelleschi, the Father General in Rome, instructing other Jesuits to keep their distance.

So Isabel saw nothing of Carisbroke though he divided his time between Liège and St Omer. Now very senior among the Jesuits, he lectured in philosophy and managed the printing press. He was a source of comfort that was closed to her though she felt an increasing need of his counsel.

She was haunted by the memory of the parlour door flying open and Monsieur David's grotesque figure appearing among her friends. In her reconstruction of the moment she again waited that split second for the others to react. Blanche had remained motionless by the wall and Praxedes sank her face in her hands as if to blot it all out while Winifred had begun to draw the younger women away from danger. There had been no united response.

When Mary came back she presented the women with a

brand new idea. Because the Institute had still not been confirmed by Rome, for the sake of everyone's security there must be an interim measure, a civil contract to be signed by each professed member which would commit her totally to Mary Ward. Afterwards, in celebration of the contract and Mary's safe return from her travels there was to be a small party in the courtyard of the house on Mont St Martin to which even the prince-bishop was invited.

The signing ceremony took place privately at the beginning of May. In the parlour the chairs were arranged in a stiff horseshoe and under the window sat Mary and Winifred with the parchment and a quill on a table before them. Isabel was placed near the centre of the semi-circle with her back to the door. Since Monsieur David's intrusion the floor, walls and furniture had been scrubbed and some of the wood had not yet recovered its waxy gleam. The only decoration was a crude painting of the Virgin holding in her arms a spiky Christ-child and through the open window came the sound of preparations for the party. A table was scraped across paving stones and novices were laughing.

Winifred, the scribe and administrator, read aloud: 'Out of gratitude to the Institute for accepting and training her, each woman must promise to remain in it, despite any opposition and difficulties that might occur. She must never wish to leave, or influence others to harm the Institute.'

The women were called up one by one, in order of seniority. Mary Poyntz stepped forward immediately, seized the pen and signed with a flourish. Next came Susannah, her face hidden within the folds of her veil. Her signature was small and emphatic.

Blanche Morton stood up and approached the table but her hands remained clasped firmly together. 'I can't sign.'

There had been a sense of festival in the room, of joyful ritual. Now everyone went still. Consternation blotted out the chinking and rustling from the courtyard outside.

Mary was confident in her role as leader, contemplative and spokeswoman, though she worked best through personal interview or letter. Blanche's refusal to sign immediately diminished Mary because she was an expert at pitting herself against a hostile world, not at being the oppressor.

'Do you want to tell us why?' asked Winifred. She had talked the contract over with each woman beforehand and given them every opportunity to object.

Isabel couldn't see Blanche's face, only her small waist and neat shoulders. She felt a special entitlement to be hurt by this sudden turn of events because though she and Blanche were close friends, Blanche had never confided that she would refuse to sign.

Blanche's voice was steady but a little more high-pitched than usual. 'How can I be sure you won't ask me to do the impossible? I worry that I may resign the right to exercise my individual conscience. I belong to the Catholic church and acknowledge the Pope and his bishops as my spiritual leaders. Though I share your desire to have the Institute confirmed I don't think this contract is necessary.'

Isabel could hardly bear to look at Mary. How could she stand resistance even from among her own, hand-picked women? She looked very frail, her complexion papery, her head trembling a little on its slender neck, but she still smiled faintly. 'Don't you trust me?' she asked.

'I do trust you.' Isabel noted that Blanche's elbows jerked inwards a little, the only visible sign of stress. 'But is it that you don't trust me?'

Mary's smile widened. 'Of course I do. But I don't trust events, and the pressure they may bring to bear on us all.'

'So what will happen if I don't sign?' asked Blanche, suddenly impatient.

'We told you. There is no compulsion to sign.'

Blanche moved forward, took Mary's hand and pressed it to her lips. 'It's my conscience. Of course I'm loyal to you. But I want to be part of this Institute voluntarily. I joined it of my own free will and I don't want to lose that impulse. I don't need the threat of a broken promise.'

Isabel was next. She had been looking forward to this moment which seemed to her an obvious next step. Not to sign would be a fatal holding back that would always be a factor, like a twinge from an old injury.

Afterwards the women sat silent again and waited for

Praxedes. But Praxedes didn't move. She folded her top lip over her lower and kept her eyes down. 'I prefer to follow my own conscience. Like Blanche,' she said at last.

There could be no easy retrieval of the situation. They all stood and prayed together then filed out to join the party in the courtyard below. But Isabel gripped Blanche's lower arm and held her back. For the first time she wondered whether she really loved this woman whose searching, critical nature had now led her to hurt Mary Ward.

'Why didn't you sign? Was it really to make a point or do you plan to opt out some day?'

Blanche lifted her head and turned away.

'If it was to make a point it was very cruel. Mary will suffer because of it.'

'It was because I know too much about what's going on.'

Isabel sank down on to the chair left by Mary Ward. Sunlight shone on her neck from the courtyard window and she moved her cold hand into it. Blanche perched beside her, so close that Isabel could smell the starch on her clean cuffs.

'Have you any idea of how much has been spent on wine for this party?' asked Blanche.

'It'll be worth it. Mary wants people to see us celebrating our work.'

'We have no cause to celebrate.'

'I don't know. These days the fact that anyone comes back safely from a journey, let alone Mary, is surely good news.'

'Isabel, we haven't paid a bill for the past six months. I now avoid a certain route through town because I know the butcher will come out and shake his receipt book at me.'

'Why don't you pay him?'

'Every stick of furniture we possess is mortgaged. The houses in St Omer have been lending us money month after month.'

'But I thought they had nothing to spare.'

'Precisely.'

'Surely our friends . . . Edmund Thewing.'

'Edmund Thewing.' Blanche began to gesticulate with her right hand, clenching the fist and making small, tense movements of the lower arm. 'All Edmund Thewing has done is borrow money on our behalf. We've paid him back what we can afford and more. But do you know what? Today I received a note informing me that not a single guilder has gone into the hands of our real creditors, the ones who loaned him the money.'

'I don't understand.'

'Nobody would give a mortgage to a group of women. We needed a man of substance like Thewing so we trusted him blindly.'

'But why hasn't he paid back the money?'

'I don't know and I almost think it doesn't matter. Can't you see what's happening to us? We have nothing and we owe vast sums. We keep on recruiting new members but their families won't pay us any money because we've no sanction from Rome. If Mary carries on like this we'll be on the streets.'

'Well, what choice do we have?' asked Isabel, turning her hand back and forth in the light so that her fingers were translucent. 'Mary does what she has to.'

'There are other choices but she's terrified of losing face or of having her wings clipped. If she would only be a little diplomatic she could have the church eating out of her hand. Imagine it, an order of high-born English Ladies prepared to teach, led by the noble Mary Ward. I sometimes think she's too proud, too full of herself to accept anyone else's directives, even the Pope's. What a convenient vision hers was to a woman of her type.'

Blanche's criticism was shrill, a fundamental undermining of Mary's character. Isabel got shakily to her feet. 'I wonder you stay,' she said. 'I really do.'

Blanche followed her to the door. 'That's why she trusts me and all of us. We have no other choice. There's no going back. If she goes under, so do we all.'

There was quite a throng in the courtyard, though no sign of the prince-bishop. The English Ladies had achieved a little colour by training ivy up the walls and planting a few geraniums in pots but as usual the finery of local grandees outshone nature. The first person Isabel saw was Edmund Thewing, today resplendent in crimson criss-crossed with gold brocade and accepting wine from Robert, who was making an ungainly attempt at being a footman. As Thewing approached her Isabel caught a waft of civet and when he bowed over her hand sunlight glinted from his dark crown. She judged that the warmth in his eye was somewhat forced.

'My dear Mistress Stanhope. Sometimes when I look at you I remember the schoolroom at Oakshott and how your little tantrums were the only thing that kept me amused, God help me. Then, at Fitzroy House I thought you were a gem created for a London salon. Now I see you in your element. Both you and my sister. You are . . . perfect. You shine here.' He pursed his lips at the end of each sentence, possibly to emphasize the dint in his cheek above his beard. In fact there was no sign at all of Susannah who would have used any possible excuse to avoid a social occasion.

'Edmund, I have been talking about you with Blanche Morton. She tells me we are heavily in your debt. In fact we are in debt to everyone.'

He shook his head and smiled a little more. But he didn't like the comment and rocked back on his heels. 'Don't you worry about owing me money. It's nothing. I would do anything for you.'

'I expect you know our finances are as precarious as ever.'

'Who, in this uncertain world, can be truly sure that they have wealth enough?'

'I should like to think you are, Edmund.'

He glanced over her shoulder and pressed his hand on her forearm in a gesture that was both intimate and dismissive. 'Mistress Isabel. I'm here in part to say goodbye. I have business in Prague and Munich.'

'How long will you be gone?'

'Who can say when there's a war on? The demands of trade insist that we gamble with our personal safety.' She supposed that his rueful smile was meant to convey selfless courage.

'What do you trade in these days, Edmund?'

'Oh various, various. Liège, as you know, is famous for its foundries. Knives, locks, chests . . .'

'Firearms.'

'Yes indeed, the finest armaments in Europe. We must be grateful for Liège's political neutrality, or we could expect some momentous explosions.' Discomfort was making him foolish.

'Forgive me if I speak out of turn now but I know that Mary Ward has had a very exhausting time of late. Can you reassure me that at least she has no cause to worry about our finances? Is everything in order?'

His affectionate eyes said: Silly little nun-woman. Bothering your head about things you can't understand. 'Of course. Of course. Only today I handed all the papers over to your Mary Ward. The house on La Pierreuse is now entirely in her name.' Again his gaze shifted and he gave a small wave at someone else, the mayor perhaps who was deep in conversation with Winifred Wigmore. Popular Edmund Thewing must move on.

Isabel, watching him weave from brightly lit patches of courtyard into shadow, wished she'd never set eyes on him.

Chapter 22

The chapel of the house on Mont St Martin was per-fumed by beeswax, newly carved wood and late spring flowers, its back wall dominated by a painting pre-sented by Edmund Thewing, an Adoration of the Magi crowded with gesture and incident, the Virgin a bosomy matron wearing a modern gown of rose satin with a low-cut bodice. Although an interior wall had been demolished to create more space the chapel was already too small for the burgeoning numbers in Mary Ward's Liège Institute and in the summer months was inclined to be stuffy.

Isabel regretted the necessary lack of spontaneity that accompanied every element of life in Liège. When the bell rang for prayers the women filed in row on row, professed at the front, then the lay sisters, servants and novices. There was none of the joyous bundling into chapel that had been a feature of the early years in St Omer.

For the Litany of the Blessed Virgin sung twice a week at seven in the evening, Blanche stood at the front facing the little altar and chanted the invocations. Her singing voice was at variance with her penetrating speech for it had a purity which suggested a gentle, yearning spirit and Isabel found herself swimming more and more peacefully into the old mantra.

> *'Sancta Maria. Ora pro nobis,*
> *Sancta Virgo Dei Genitrix, Ora pro nobis . . .'*

There was a shuffling in the row behind, a withdrawal of concentration. Blanche's voice soared.

> *'Sancta Virgo Virginum . . .'*

A low moaning underpinned the chant, catching at the silence between cantor and choir.

'*Deo gratias,*' sighed a voice. '*Deo gratias.*'

When the litany was over the community usually remained on its knees for a period of silent prayer then drifted away one by one. Now they were riveted by the drama taking place in the fifth row.

Further long moans, passionate and profound, rippled the veils of women schooled not to be distracted by minor incidents. But after ten minutes of this sighing and groaning even a saint would have been tempted to crane her neck and find out what was going on.

Directly behind Isabel knelt Praxedes. Her back was arched, arms held rigidly at each side with the palms up, face directed towards the ceiling. Bluish eyelids were half closed over trembling eyeballs and shudders ran from breast to knee. The unearthly moaning seemed to issue from deep in her abdomen and her lips were drawn back in a grimace somewhere between pain and pleasure.

Isabel's first thought was that Praxedes was experiencing some kind of sexual spasm. Then she understood that she was witnessing religious ecstasy.

Although Praxedes had hitherto been an exemplary member of the Institute, this current behaviour was somehow unsurprising. Isabel recognized in Praxedes a deeply self-conscious nature, ever on the watch and perhaps by no means as undesigning as she liked to appear.

Mary Ward had not looked round and Isabel swiftly resumed her own prayers though the disruption continued in the pew behind. Winifred genuflected and left the chapel followed shortly by Isabel who went to the courtyard and took long gasps of evening air. She reached up her arms to the luminous turquoise sky as if to cleanse herself of the charged atmosphere in the chapel.

Praxedes had not emerged from her trance by supper-time and the community was tense and subdued. Isabel whispered to Blanche: 'I'm amazed she hasn't had one of these turns before.'

Blanche stared at her. 'What do you mean?'

'She's a typical candidate for hysteria, don't you think?'

'What makes you think this isn't genuine?'

'Because Praxedes, of all people, is the one most likely to go into a trance. This sort of thing often happens in communities of women. She's found the perfect way of gaining everyone's attention.'

'I didn't realize you were an expert on this type of religious experience,' said Blanche coldly. 'You are very quick to make a judgement.'

A group of women kept a vigil with Praxedes that night and so were there to witness her sudden release from possession. They wept together and prayed until dawn about what they called the great insight bestowed on her during ecstasy. All the next day Praxedes was to be found in chapel, resisting her new status as visionary by making feeble gestures heavenward as if to say: I never wanted this to happen.

If questioned her huge eyes would brim but she'd speak with authority. 'We must give up any idea of adopting the Jesuit rule, and agree to enclosure. I know my revelation comes from God, but why, why did He choose me?' In the afternoon she was suddenly transported again and therefore not available for further discussion.

Around her clustered an ever increasing number of women eager to latch on to this new visionary. They pressed close, murmuring their own spontaneous prayers and giving little cries of thanksgiving. Blanche knelt apart and refused to look at Isabel. The work of the house was badly disrupted as novices crept into corners and asked each other who they thought was right, Praxedes or Mary Ward. The seepage of power caused by this momentous event was almost palpable.

The next morning it was announced that Mary, not wishing to place undue pressure on anyone, had gone into retreat. Winifred and Blanche took advantage of a pause between trances and escorted Praxedes to the church of St Servais where hasty arrangements had been made for her to be questioned by a group of senior churchmen, one of them Father Carisbroke, to test the integrity of her vision.

Isabel stood at an upstairs window and watched them go. Praxedes, who had fasted for over twenty-four hours and not slept, stumbled between upright Blanche and calm Winifred.

A few minutes later Isabel's attention was caught by the plodding figure of a woman dressed in black and rolling from the hips as if reluctant to bend her knees too far. Susannah had done the unthinkable and broken her routine to walk down the steep slope of La Pierreuse, through the heart of town and up Mont St Martin in the middle of the day. Moments later she appeared at Isabel's elbow.

The cousins didn't look at each other but from the corner of her eye Isabel could see Susannah's profile; the rounded forehead and chin, the dense skin and protruding eyes and lips, rather like those of the buxom Madonna in the chapel.

'What do you think about all this?' asked Susannah.

'Need you ask what I think?'

The two women stood side by side for some time, shoulders touching.

Two hours later when Praxedes came back her mouth was set in a long-suffering smile. The verdict of the Jesuit fathers was that she had received light from God.

That afternoon Isabel gave the novices a lesson in rhetoric. Usually she stressed to her pupils that they were unique among women because they must break silence if need be and speak out. But today the words died on her lips. If Praxedes had her way rhetoric, like most of the current training for novices, would be redundant. Instead the women would have to study the old conventual disciplines of silence and custody of the eyes.

Carisbroke had given Praxedes sanction. How could he have been taken in by her when one of his most compelling qualities was the ability to read hearts? Surely he must see her for what she was, hysterical, vain and duplicitous.

At last Isabel could bear her own passive acceptance of calamity no longer.

Abandoning her class in mid-sentence she summoned Robert Wright and set off for La Pierreuse, the sun hot on her veiled head and her pace too rapid for the uneven cobbles. The town was just rousing itself from mid-afternoon torpor and there were few people about.

All this will be denied me soon, thought Isabel. Enclosure will put an end to walks and visits. In the walled gardens on either side fruit trees and trellises hung with honeysuckle gave dense shade. Through slits in a gate she caught a glimpse of a sleepy arbour and pots of marguerites. Beneath her Liège was sunk in a fumy yellow haze pierced again and again by the spires of its numerous churches.

At the English Ladies' house on the top of the hill she marched up to the infirmary and announced to Susannah that she required a chaperone. Without a word her cousin untied the apron from her stout waist and followed Isabel and Robert to the neighbouring Jesuit house where their knock created an echoing resonance within. The lofty door was opened by a manservant who stared at them dumb-founded. Over his shoulder Isabel glimpsed an empty hall-way, very austere except for the portrait of Ignatius, right arm outstretched over a host of kneeling congregants, large eyes fixed on a podgy cherub. The painting struck her as smug.

'I must speak with Father Carisbroke. Tell him Mistress Stanhope is here.'

The message came back that if Mistress Stanhope wished to see Father Carisbroke he would arrange to hear con-fessions in St Servais that afternoon.

The cousins walked away, sent Robert home and settled themselves for a long wait in the church.

Carisbroke came at last. Isabel was not watching the door to the sacristy but when it opened she sensed by its brisk release followed by rapid footsteps along the nave that it was he. Between her fingers she saw his trim, black-clad figure, a Missal clasped between his hands.

She allowed everybody else to go in front of her including Susannah, so by the time she entered the confessional Bene-diction was being sung in the Lady Chapel. A half-door enclosed her from the shoulder down and her face was pressed so close to the mesh that when she spoke her lips touched the wire. Carisbroke was at right-angles facing the nave so she saw only his cheekbone and jaw. She did note however that time had scored another small line in the flesh beside his mouth.

Now that she was near him once more she wondered how she had managed to be content for so many years without seeing him.

'Father, I have come to ask for your help.' He inclined his head slightly, as if preparing to receive a list of sins. 'You spoke to Praxedes this morning. There is no truth in what she says. I know you. I know that you can tell a fraud. Why did you not speak out and say so?'

In her head the difference in their status had been erased. They were two souls whose past encounters had been highly charged and unforgettable. Furthermore, her own experiences in England and Liège had toughened her up and made her much more independent in her thinking. She assumed that he would recognize her maturity and treat her as his equal but she saw at once that she had been mistaken. He was playing the part of a senior priest in an order which was now implacably hostile to the irrepressible English Ladies

He wouldn't look at her though his ear was just six inches from her lips as he leaned on his left elbow and rested his forehead lightly on his fingertips, a gesture she recognized from their long ago meetings.

'It is sometimes very difficult to discern the truth,' he said at last, speaking so low that she could scarcely hear him. The organ had struck up *'Tantum Ergo'* and the hymn surged along the nave on a drift of incense.

'I know I'm right.'

'If only the rest of us found it that easy to be sure.' He glanced at her, an almost furtive movement of the eyes which met hers and then looked hastily away again.

She adjusted her tone. 'Father, I may sound arrogant but there is too much at stake here for me to mince words. You must see that Praxedes is false.'

'Must I, Isabel? Do me the justice to have thought this out carefully. If Mary Ward's vision is God-sent she will succeed whatever the odds and this Praxedes episode will soon be forgotten. But opposition is healthy. You shouldn't be afraid of it. Praxedes may be the agent that makes all things clear. She suggests the Ursuline rule. Well, in some ways the Ursulines provide an excellent model for you. And following them will save you wasting more time. The church will never agree to an unenclosed order of women. It's out of the question.'

'You can't truly believe the church is so rigid. Your own leader Ignatius was opposed at first and hated by the very bishops who came to admire him. He went to Rome and convinced the Pope that God was behind him. We shall do the same. We could go to Rome and win over the Pope if only we could heal this wretched faction created by Praxedes.'

'I've obviously been under a misapprehension. I thought you wished to hear my advice. Instead I find myself at the receiving end of a lecture. You women ask too much of us. You damage our reputation again and again.'

His voice was still mild but his posture had become rigid and his face was turned aside. Isabel put her hand to the wire. 'I don't mean to lecture and I do need your advice. Please.'

'My advice is to let events take their course. God will make His will known sooner or later.'

After Isabel had made a very ill-thought-out confession she retreated to the obscurity of a side-chapel dedicated to St Sebastian. In a life-sized portrait above the altar the saint, dressed in a scanty loin-cloth, was round-shouldered and meek despite the fact that his face, breast, belly and thighs had been pierced with absurd precision by a dozen arrows.

I am tired of all these saints and martyrs hanging their heads and keeping silent in the face of injustice, thought Isabel. What is so wrong with action?

But her defiance soon turned to anguish. The interview with Carisbroke had gone badly wrong. Even approaching him had been a betrayal of Mary Ward. Why seek his advice at all? Was it that at last she'd seen an excuse to meet him and that after all these years the desire to impress him still lingered?

But the more she reflected on their discussion, the more disturbed and angry she became. He had pompously intimated that she was seeking to undermine his priestly auth-

290

ority. And he had not bothered to hear her argument. Her twelve years of contemplation and study as a member of Mary Ward's Institute counted for nothing in his eyes.

By what some called a miracle, the crisis was resolved most unexpectedly by the sudden death of Praxedes. On the morning after her meeting with the Jesuits she had a slight fever which by evening had developed into full-blown typhoid.

As was customary the community gathered round to say their farewells. Poor Praxedes, thought Isabel, watching somewhat dispassionately the river of red hair flowing across the pillow, I wonder whether she might have thought twice about having her visions if she'd known she had only days to live.

Blanche whispered: 'We can't afford a coffin. Now Thewing has left town we are responsible for most of his debts. He put all his papers in our name.'

Isabel was so relieved to be spoken to again that she hugged her, but Blanche pulled away. 'This alters nothing. I'm convinced now that Mary Ward is wrong.'

On the day after Praxedes' funeral a group of the most senior professed members of the Institute were called to Mary Ward's parlour. She stood among them as if in too much haste for formality, though Isabel noted that she had developed the careful posture of a much older woman. She made no natural movement of her arms or neck because an impulsive gesture would cause her pain.

'In September I'll go back to Cologne to visit the new community and afterwards we'll set off for Rome. We're fortunate in that Father Carisbroke, who happens to be going there himself, will travel with us as chaplain. Robert will also come. He can act as guide because he tells me he once had a master who spent a year studying painting there. He says we should hire two horses, one to carry the baggage, the other for anyone who's too tired to walk.'

Just four days ago Isabel had said to Carisbroke: 'We could go to Rome and win over the Pope . . .' He had acted with surprising speed to get himself involved. She asked: 'How will you get to Rome? We have no money at all.'

'We'll just have to manage with the little we have. Praxedes' death has been a terrible lesson to me. She was under too much strain. I can't wait about any longer for other people to sort out our affairs. The only way is to talk to the Pope myself. And I want to have a conversation with Vitelleschi, the father general of the Jesuits who keeps sending very unhelpful messages to his priests here in Liège. I think at least he should listen to my point of view.'

'The Pope won't even give you an audience.'

'Oh I think he will. He'll see me if only to keep me quiet.'

The women glanced at each other. This scheme, at a time of such unrest among the Institute, was almost too wild to be taken seriously. Winifred intervened. 'As I've said to Mary, my worry is that we shall be leaving the houses in Liège and St Omer defenceless and under-staffed during our absence.'

'Barbara Babthorpe, Margaret Horde and Martha Canton will be in St Omer and Blanche Morton will be in charge of the houses in Liège. She's more than competent.'

Mary pushes faith too far, thought Isabel. Doesn't she remember that Blanche refused to sign the contract and sided with Praxedes?

'I've picked each of you to come with me for a special purpose; Winifred as my deputy, Susannah to take care of our health, Mary Poyntz as record-keeper and secretary and Susan Rookwood, whom I have recalled from London, to act as first superior in Rome. I shall take you, Isabel, because you're an excellent linguist and will throw obstacles in my path every step of the way, thereby giving me practice for the cardinals.'

There was a shout of laughter but Isabel exclaimed: 'Mary, you are suggesting that we set off in the autumn. A journey to Rome will take months so it'll be winter by the time we get there. What about the war? Think of how dangerous the roads will be. And with only two horses most of us will have to walk all the way. How long will that take? Two months? Three?'

'We shall be pilgrims. Pilgrims are always safe. When I was a lay sister for the Poor Clares I walked up to twenty miles every day and I was quite alone. This time I shall be with you and it will be no more strenuous, except I shall be going forward rather than in circles.'

'Have you discussed this with anyone else?'

'Of course the archduchess tried to dissuade me but has none the less promised to write letters of introduction and instruct her ambassador, Vives, to help us when we get there. Even though Father Carisbroke has offered to come with us, the Jesuits would obviously much rather I didn't go.'

This was probably a ludicrous understatement. Isabel tried another line of protest. 'The houses in St Omer are poverty-stricken. They had furniture seized last week in lieu of a debt. In London we are persecuted. Here we are penniless too. Wouldn't it be better to consolidate what we have?'

'I can't do that except by prayer. I can't give anyone security until I have the Pope's approval. You sound defeated. It seems that you expect me to fail. My view is that a journey to Rome is the only choice left to me. And even if it is the wrong thing, it will have been done for the right reasons.'

By nightfall news of the planned trip to Rome was common knowledge and there was a fresh outbreak of discontent among those who had not been chosen to go. To avert any more trouble Isabel asked Blanche to meet her in the court-yard where they sat together on the steps under the deep shadow of the house. Blanche's hostility was palpable. Her face had been redrawn in sharp lines.

'I'm sorry you're not coming with us.'

Blanche shrugged. 'I wouldn't have gone if she'd asked me. A trip to Rome is sheer madness.'

'I agree.'

'Then why are you going? You should have refused. Why does everyone say yes to Mary Ward?'

'Because she has said yes to God.'

'No. Because you're so intoxicated by change and excitement you have to go for the ultimate challenge, an audience with the Pope. And meanwhile the rest of us will probably die.'

'Do you really think that, Blanche?'

'The one thing that attracts donations is Mary Ward's personal reputation. If she goes she takes even that away.'

'You should say all this to her.'

'There's no point.' Nobody won an argument with Blanche. Words whipped from her tongue, fluent as a rehearsed speech. '*You* ought to listen to me. *You're* not driven by visions. It amazes me that you were so ready to discredit Praxedes but follow like a donkey when Mary Ward snaps her fingers. It's because you feed off people who admire you and now you can't exist on your own. I've watched you, Isabel, from the first time we met. Every step you take, I watch. You surround yourself with people who won't stand up to you. Dorothea. Susannah. Martha. Mary Ward. The only person that matters in your life is you, and how you appear to others.'

Isabel was so surprised she could only reply weakly: 'I have never pretended to be other than what I am.'

'I'm glad I'm not you. I'm glad I won't have to bear the ultimate responsibility for what happens, as you will. You will lose your way through this, Isabel, as surely as Mary Ward has lost hers.'

Chapter 23

On the night before leaving Liège Isabel unhooked a mirror from a little cloakroom on the ground floor and carried it to the chapel where a candle always burned. For the first time in years she studied her reflected face. There were irregular shadows in her eye-sockets, her forehead was lightly furrowed and sunken cheeks gave prominence to a jaw that was formidable rather than delicate.

She decided that she now looked very like her mother, though less sad. The air of pious inscrutability she had once hoped to achieve was certainly lacking. Instead the mouth looked a little amused, prone to asking one question too many, and the eyes were critical rather than kind, on the look-out for difficulties which might not arise.

She put down the mirror and instead gazed at the brave little candle flame.

Isabel Stanhope, self-contained here in her black gown, tomorrow would be a bird on the wing, battered by heaven knew what forces of nature and man.

She thought: I know of no other women who have done this. We are different. We have become different.

The beginning of the journey was a step into the street, a crossing of familiar cobbles and a leaving of town by the road south. The sky was high and white, the wind soft. Robert Wright, six foot tall, lanky and long-faced, was their only defence against malignant forces on the road.

They were to travel on foot at the rate of between twenty and twenty-five miles each day.

The community gathered to see them off and most faces struggled to hide the pain of what was bound to be a prolonged parting. Blanche, now in charge, stood unsmiling on the steps. She accepted Isabel's kiss but would not return it though she embraced Mary Ward at length.

Within thirty feet the narrow street wound to the left and the house of the English Ladies was out of sight.

For the second time in her life Isabel was embarked on a pilgrimage. She remembered how her grandmother had been so anxious about leaving Oakshott when they set out for Holywell and understood now the pressure of domestic and personal ties that must have dogged her. Mary Ward, on the other hand, from the moment they were on the move seemed to grow taller, her shoulders straightening as she sniffed the air and marched downhill. Isabel suspected that the journey to Rome was a necessity for her in more ways than one. This was a side of Mary that she had not seen before, a woman who loved change and new places.

Carisbroke, that most elusive of priests, had announced that he could not be with them after all on this first lap of the journey. He had business in Nancy and had gone ahead but would meet them there and travel with them to northern Italy, the most dangerous part of their trek. He was too much in demand to go at their slow pace all the way.

Isabel was glad. In the confessional at St Servais she had been humiliated by his refusal to treat her as an equal. He had upset the balance of their relationship by watching her step out of line and refusing to follow her.

The first hour of walking was a physical pleasure. Although the women led active lives no one except Susan and the two Marys had left town in years. It was a novelty to stretch their legs and be in well-trodden lanes amidst undulating, neatly hedged farms but gradually lack of practice began to take its toll. Isabel had new wedge-heeled walking shoes so inflexible that by midday her calves were aching and her toes rubbed raw. The thick pilgrim's robe worn for protection by all the women was far too substantial for so mild a day, her starched collar chafed her neck and the high-crowned felt hat tormented her brow by its weight and warmth.

The women pursued their usual disciplines of silent meditation and communal prayer while for hours their road ran through a vast forest and their voices mingled with wind sifting through a million dying leaves. Robert, who led the horses, followed at a little distance with his head down but his blue, Irish eyes always on the next bend.

By the time they were within sight of Nancy twelve days later it was as if there had never been a life before this journey. Prayer, the company of friends, aching legs and the endless road ahead were constants that would now go on and on. It seemed the easiest thing in the world to keep walking the twelve hundred miles or so to Rome.

And Isabel had no desire at all to meet up with Carisbroke. The group had managed perfectly well without a priest and she knew that he would direct her attention to himself in the old, exhausting way. We should do this alone, she thought. Once we are in his hands everything will become unclear.

Mary announced that they would be staying in Nancy for several days as she must write letters of encouragement to her various communities and make further preparations for Rome. She was planning a new petition to hand over in person to the Pope, and the Archduchess Isabella, whose goodwill and patronage were crucial, had to be kept abreast of their progress. They needed more money.

Nancy was very crowded, full of Spaniards following their army north because after a twelve-year truce with the Dutch war had been declared again. Spain was therefore busily propping up its Catholic cousins wherever they were under threat, anxious to cut off Protestant armies and supply routes. The latest target was the little state of Julich east of the Netherlands where the Dutch were garrisoned. So Nancy was buzzing with merchants, tradesmen and other more dubious travellers out to make a fortune from the renewed hostilities. The streets were so blocked with carts and carriages that the prospect of finding accommodation seemed hopeless and Isabel had a sudden fear of becoming mixed up with complicated forces that might somehow carry the English women away from their fixed purpose.

Mary, quite unperturbed, headed for the cathedral. Robert guarded the horses while Isabel and Winifred, by far the best linguists, began their usual search for suitable lodgings.

The inns in the squares and main streets were crowded and expensive, those in quieter areas already full. Gradually they found themselves in less salubrious parts of town. They plunged into dark alleys where floor upon floor of tottering wooden houses piled overhead and the cobbles were as thick with filth as any in London. By now it was almost dark and they linked arms as they shouldered their way towards a small courtyard with a pump at its centre and a patch of evening sky above.

Isabel perched on the edge of the water basin, too hungry and discouraged to go on. 'Where now?'

'Something will turn up.'

A priest had emerged from a narrow passageway and was crossing the square. Isabel caught his eye but looked away quickly, though not before she'd noted his pause mid-stride and a flicker of hesitation. For a moment she was sure he would move on without acknowledging her.

'Mistress Stanhope. Who would have thought it? But then I seem to fall over your family everywhere I turn in Europe. There's no escaping you.' Nicholas Turner, dapper in a long black tunic and white collar, his smile as usual showing too much inner lip and tooth, hung over her hand. Even through her weariness Isabel noted that his hat's jaunty white trim was decidedly non-priestly and that though he was not pleased to see her he was by no means as surprised as he ought to have been.

'Is my brother here then?' she asked.

'Is your brother here?' The hat was turned round and round between his hands. 'In Nancy? Not that I know of.'

She decided not to give him the pleasure of further evasion but instead introduced him briskly to Winifred as Father Turner, her brother's chaplain.

'Former. Former chaplain,' cut in Turner with a modest twirl of his hat.

'Ah,' said Winifred. 'You must be God-sent. A friend in an inhospitable town. I'm sure you'll help us find beds for the night. We seem to have had no luck on our own.'

Winifred, normally a most resourceful women, had evidently decided this was the time to appear weak and dependent but Isabel was already wishing that Turner had avoided them. They were being drawn deeper into his orbit and she was a little afraid of him.

He was equally unwilling to get involved. 'Well, there's my own inn but I'm not sure it's suitable for ladies. I assume there's more than two of you.'

Winifred's trusting smile gave him no choice but to lead them to a grubby little inn in a nearby alley. Isabel wondered whether he had selected such a wretched place out of necessity or meanness. The inn was tiny and smoky, its bedrooms reeked of the privy and unwashed bodies, and its sheets were foul with insufficient airing. Winifred smiled with serene satisfaction upon the chamber Nicholas Turner had booked for himself but now must sacrifice to the English Ladies. 'Perfect,' she pronounced. 'And now you will have to take us back to the town centre or we'll get lost.'

Out they all trooped into the drizzly evening. Turner walked sulkily ahead while Winifred and Isabel propped each other up through the dark lanes. Mary Ward was still at prayer but rose at last and smiled gratefully on Father Turner. Isabel thought with dread of the dirty rooms and probably inedible food that awaited her. The glimpse of an unwashed chamberpot in the darkest corner of the bedroom had given her a premonition of horrors to come.

But the inn was transformed by the English Ladies. Mary was never offended by bad food or foul-mouthed fellow diners. She and her friends sat shoulder to shoulder on wobbly benches and treated this meal as reverently as any other. The difference was that their number was increased by one, Nicholas Turner.

Isabel had learnt to follow Susannah's example and force down all that was placed before her, however rank or badly cooked but Turner, normally so greedy, picked his way through the meal. Afterwards he seemed eager to make conversation with Susannah whom he had once assiduously ignored in the schoolroom at Oakshott. Several allusions were made to 'that saintly former pupil of mine, Alan Thewing,' and here Turner crossed himself and muttered about Alan's tragic martyrdom.

Next Turner asked tenderly after Edmund whom he had met quite recently in Paris.

'Edmund Thewing?' said Isabel sharply. 'Do you know where he is now? We should love to write to him.'

'Oh, good Lord, it's several weeks since I saw him.'

'What was he doing in Paris? War must be good business for him if he's still dealing in arms.'

'Arms. My dear Mistress Isabel, I'm a man of peace, it's no use asking me for details.'

His faked outrage was so tedious that she turned the subject by asking for news from home.

'The news from home. You mean England or Cuddington?'

'Both.'

He took a deep breath through his nose. 'The news is that King James is now giving very serious consideration to a Spanish match for his son Charles. He's had quite a row with parliament about it. They'd rather he fought against Spain than married into it.'

'There have been rumours about such a marriage for years. It will surely never happen.'

'Ah. It just might. Our glorious monarch is always short of money and is trying to avoid war at all costs but since his wretched little son-in-law, Frederick, has been thrown out of Bohemia by the Catholics he has to do something. He thinks the cheapest way of setting all to rights would be alliance with Spain. After all, Spain is very powerful at the moment and could possibly arrange for Frederick to be given back his crown in the Palatinate or some such by way of compensation.'

'And what is your opinion of this policy, Father Turner?' asked Winifred guilelessly. By dint of a network of local contacts and the fact that she made it her duty to read every

300

pamphlet that came her way, Winifred always knew what was going on everywhere in Europe.

Turner folded his hands and replied as if to an ignorant child. 'I think it's a very dangerous ploy and would not even benefit English Catholics. The Spanish are not our natural bedfellows. We should be allying ourselves with France. Ah, the French.' There was an uncomfortable pause caused by Turner's use of the term 'bedfellow' and the extraordinary succulence he managed to invest in the word 'French'. 'You see, Mistress Mary Ward, there'll be no need for your little schools if we are overrun by the Spanish. Jesuits would infest every town and keep us firmly in line.'

'There'll always be a need for us, Father Turner. Nobody else cares about the girls.'

His laugh was a series of exhalations scraped across the back of his throat, thereby producing a great deal of spittle. The women watched him politely but Isabel knew that they must all be thinking about Carisbroke who could materialize in their midst at any moment.

'You haven't yet said what brings you to Nancy,' she said.

'I imagine the same as you. I'm on pilgrimage to Rome.' Horror upon horror. Surely they wouldn't have to travel with him all the way. 'Since your dear brother is now married to Deborah Bourne, Mistress Stanhope, I took advantage of his present happiness to make this long-planned trip. It has been suggested to me by various parties that I ought to come for talks. With the cardinal. You know. But I suppose really I'm acting from pure self-indulgence.' Pure fabrication, thought Isabel. Why really is he here? 'I shall be meeting a friend in Lyons, a priest I trained with at Douai. Not a patient soul, so I'll have to take a reluctant leave of you tomorrow and ride on. He'll be so envious of me because I have met the famous Mary Ward.' He slid Mary a sideways glance, servile and unkind. 'Tell me, when you get to Rome, have you lodgings arranged? Who are your friends there? Can I be your guide?'

As they parted for the night Isabel had the chance to put a more personal question: 'Father Turner, is my brother happily married? Is all well at home?'

'Of course. Why wouldn't it be?'

'I wondered about Deborah, how happy she'd be away from her family.'

'Lady Deborah Stanhope is about to make you an aunt, which suggests happiness wouldn't you think?'

They were barged about by people moving through the cramped room. Robert Wright, as usual destined to spend the night on some too short settle in the kitchen, edged his way past them, stooped nearly double under the low beams. Isabel kept her eyes on Turner's face. 'How did you know we'd be in Nancy? I haven't written to Robin for several months.'

'I met someone in Calais who told me you were off on a journey.' He came so intolerably close that heat from his wet mouth fanned across her face. 'Deborah's brother Francis is in Europe, Mistress Stanhope, and heading for Rome. You should watch your back. I've been told by reliable sources that he doesn't harbour much love for Mary Ward and her little Institute.'

'And who are your reliable sources, Father Turner?'

His mouth pursed up in a soggy smile and he tapped the side of his nose. She went hastily to bed.

Though Susannah had chased bugs from the mattress and aired the sheets Isabel crept warily in beside her and lay wide awake. The walls were of cob, a wafer-thin mix of straw and clay, and the night was full of shouting from the street below and noisy preparations for sleep in other rooms. For the first time in years Isabel was home-sick for some unreachable corner of England; clean, green and quiet.

Europe, she thought, was no longer wide open to the English Ladies. Mary Ward was a fly caught in a web spun by Nicholas Turner, Francis Bourne and others who wished her harm. Their pilgrimage was not so much a huge risk, freely taken, as a risible and hopeless inevitability in which they were to be dogged every step of the way.

Two days after they left Nancy, Carisbroke joined them.

One moment the party was seven, the next nine for he brought with him a dapper male servant and two horses. Everything was immediately different. Carisbroke now led the group, setting the pace by walking a little ahead with his rapid, uncompromising stride, occasionally waiting for Mary Ward to catch up so that they could engage in low-voiced discussion. His servant and Robert Wright were instructed to stay at the back, as if the women were under guard. All prayers were now directed by Carisbroke who also heard confessions and at intervals said mass. At night his officious little servant organized the accommodation.

Either because the company of so many women was potentially compromising or out of an inflated regard for his own status, Carisbroke made no effort to become part of the group. Except in his function as priest, he was unapproachable and Isabel became increasingly resentful. He sapped authority from Mary Ward by assuming the position of leader and spiritual guide.

Isabel avoided him by staying close to the horses but her thoughts were constantly distracted by him. She always knew where he was, even when he was out of sight. Every word he spoke, every gesture he made was registered by her. At night when they were apart she was restless and unhappy. She hated him for this power he had over her, but not as much as she despised and castigated herself.

From Nancy it was a journey of nearly three weeks to Lyons along the valleys of the Moselle and Saône with the weather becoming noticeably cooler. Sunshine seemed to race south ahead of them, unfolding cold weather in its wake.

Their progress remained steady though sometimes the waves of travellers who overtook or passed by were very daunting. Cartwheels kicked up spatters of mud and confident men stirred the air with their straining limbs. Their faces came up oppressively close, bearded, curious and vivid. In their wake they left an after-smell of alcohol, horse-flesh and tobacco and the road was strewn with their debris: manure, phlegm, ashes from their fires, bones from their meals.

However, the real threat to Mary Ward was not fellow travellers but the rapid emptying of Winifred's purse. Every beggar on the road had to be given a little something, food was more expensive in remote places and Carisbroke's man-servant seemed to pay no attention to the cost of things when he arranged beds and meals.

With worsening weather the roads became lonelier and after Lyons their pace slowed. An easterly wind came howling off the mountains and struck their faces with wet air whipped to ice by snowy summits. The women sickened with fevers and exhaustion and took it in turns to ride. They were to cross the Alps at the Col du Mont Cenis and for days they toiled uphill, skirts flung against their legs, hats rammed down hard over their eyes.

One day they lost Mary Poyntz. Towards the end of the afternoon the road passed through a deep forest, mainly of pine but with a thickly tangled undergrowth of thorns and shrubs. For Poyntz trips into the trees were agony because she couldn't bear anyone to know that she had bodily functions and this time she must have gone even deeper to ensure privacy. The others huddled together among the horses except for Carisbroke who stood at a little distance with his open breviary held up to the fading light.

Was he always aloof and self-important, Isabel wondered, or do I see him differently now?

Suddenly Winifred said: 'Mary has been gone too long.'

She had indeed, they realized.

'She's very weak,' added Susan. 'I think she is suffering some kind of flux though she won't say, poor soul.'

They called out to her and Susan walked a little way into the forest, thrashing at the undergrowth to break a path. Dusk had crept forward another notch so that she quickly merged with the trees. Robert raised his mournful face to the brownish grey sky and said it would soon snow.

When Susan came back she took charge. Mary Poyntz had either stumbled too far into the trees and lost all sense of direction, or, if she was ill, had possibly fallen. Either way they must find her quickly before nightfall. Mary Ward and Robert were to stay on the road, patrolling up and down in case Poyntz found her way back, the rest were to spread out but never lose sight of each other. They must shout regularly but not often enough to cause confusion. If they were lost, the moss, growing always on the same side of the trunks, would guide them back to the road. It was essential to act quickly because if she'd gone the wrong way Poyntz could already be more than half a mile into the forest.

Isabel drew her cloak tight round her legs and began pushing her way into the trees. She felt the excitement of the chase as well as considerable irritation with Poyntz for holding them all up. Rome, always a gleaming pearl at the edge of her mind, seemed impossibly far away, a mythical city somewhere in the warm heart of Italy.

Winifred was over to the right, Carisbroke to the left.

'*Mary Poyntz.*'

Darkness seeped through the thorns, under the pine needles and between the bare branches of smaller trees. Isabel's skirts caught on brambles and fallen logs. Far, far up there was an occasional glimpse of dull sky.

'*Mary Poyntz.*'

Carisbroke, who had abandoned his soutane for the journey and wore a plain doublet and long breeches, sprang forwards with his cloak swung up round his shoulders.

Isabel was hobbled by her petticoats and envied his long free legs. She was reminded of the attic chapel at Oakshott where she had seen him come flying over the herb beds, opening chinks in the future for her with eyes clear as water and a slow, tender smile.

'We must go back,' he called suddenly. 'She could never have got this far. Wait there and I'll come over to you.'

She ignored him and shouted again: '*Mary Poyntz.*'

Carisbroke made a number of diagonal lunges and all at once was beside her, gripping her arm. 'Stop, Isabel.'

She was sick of being at his mercy.

'Isabel.' Again he took her arm and pulled her back towards him. This grasping at her body enraged her. She twisted away.

'Isabel. I've been wanting to speak to you.'

'Well I don't wish to listen,' she snapped and recognized in herself the old conflict. All these last days he had seemed to ignore her but in fact had been twitching the thread to wind her in, inch by inch. She tripped up and saved herself by grasping at a long pliant branch which tore through her glove and cut her hand.

There, the split was made. Her reasonable, well-schooled self remained with the scrap of leather on the branch and watched helplessly.

He took her cut hand in his. 'Come back. We've already gone too far.'

'It won't be the first time, Father Carisbroke. Why do you bother with me? When I came to ask you for help with Praxedes you had no time for me at all.'

'Ah. I thought that had rankled. Well, Isabel, we were both vindicated by events. You were sure Praxedes was in the wrong and I said leave it to God.'

She couldn't help smiling at this logic but refused to look at him.

'I have something to ask you,' he said, bringing his face close to hers. His body now acted as a wind-break and the air was suddenly still. She saw the individual strands of fibre in the cord which tied his cloak and her ear was so close to his chest that she heard him draw breath. 'I'm going to Rome for a consultation with my superior, Father Vitelleschi. The Jesuits are planning a mission to the Americas which I may lead. Or, it might be considered safe enough for me to return to England and be the provincial there. If that happens I want you to come with me.'

There was a small rattle in the branches above, the beginnings of sleet which fell like pins on Isabel's hat brim. 'How could I come? As what?'

He was a dream of Carisbroke. The wind had blown them together, out of themselves it seemed, for he had taken the edge of his cloak and thrown it over her shoulders, folding her into the warm tent of his body. The turfy scents of the forest were reduced to woven cloth and all that she associated with him, a hint of sweat, incense and wine.

'I told you before. Anne Vaux. Remember Anne Vaux and Father Garnet. She protected him and was his dear friend. She shielded him by posing as his sister and ran his safe houses for him. That's what I want from you.'

'Why me?'

'I have prepared you from the beginning. I picked you and steered you towards this.'

'But I chose Mary Ward.'

'Mary has given you the perfect training. But you should think very carefully now. She has taken a route that is not compatible with the work you should be doing.'

'So you're asking me to leave her?' She now realized that there was something wrong with his arms which were bent stiffly against her, as if she were a prickly, uncomfortable thing to hold. His mouth was close to her forehead and she sensed that his control was only skin deep. 'Why have you come with us if at the same time you're intent on dismembering her Institute?'

'You see only a narrow picture, Isabel. I have the advantage of understanding a little more. I have been telling Mary how she should approach the Pope. What she certainly should not ask him for is permission to follow the Jesuit rule.'

'But that's the very thing she's determined we must have.' His cloak flapped across her cheek and his fingers clutched her upper arms. She strained up to take another look at his face. 'I trusted you. When I was a child I believed that I'd placed myself into kind and loving hands and that you would mould me into something beautiful for God. But instead you've stunted me. However far I go there's a little bit of me caught up with you. And now you want some kind of maidservant. Is that it?'

She was sure he smiled and that his breathing quickened. 'If you have confused love for God with love for me I am sorry. But I believe we have been marked out to serve each other in some way.'

'Was that all I ever was? A potential servant.'

'Surely you didn't expect any other kind of love? Why must you have so much love, Isabel? God's love is more than enough.'

'I think you would not be touching me now if God's love was enough for you.'

He was inhaling the scent of her skin and his voice was shallow and breathless. 'Isabel, how could you ask for anything else of me? My life has been a long, hard road to what I am now. From the time I could walk I was destined for the priesthood. My idols have always been Jesuits: Loyola, Campion and Southwell. I trained myself to be a fighter and a scholar, first with a tutor, then at Oxford. A Jesuit's training lasts for years and years, the novitiate in Rome, philosophy in Paris, theology in Claremont. I performed the Spiritual Exercises countless times to prepare myself for the mission in England. Do you think I would sacrifice all this out of softness for a woman?'

The sleet was coming down hard but had not yet soaked through the cloak. Isabel fought free of him and held up her face to the clean ice and rain. 'And are you pleased with the way you have done God's work? Does God allow you to do anything for the sake of Catholicism, even the breaking of hearts and the betrayal of friends?'

'If that's what it takes. Remember, we see only a tiny part of what He has in mind for us. Isabel, don't forget what I have said to you. The offer is there.'

'I signed a promise to Mary Ward that I'd stay with her. I despise your offer. I think you're trying to pervert your vows because you've found you need me as much as I thought I needed you.'

Robert Wright was suddenly upon them, having come crashing through the trees with his lolloping stride. 'She's back,' he said and held out his arm to Isabel who took it eagerly and walked off without a backward glance at Carisbroke.

On the morning they left Lanslebourg, the highest village on their route, and set out for the Col, the weather cleared at last. Their feet crunched smartly on frozen snow but the air was so thin that the sun actually warmed their faces. Row upon row of white summits shone under a sapphire sky. The women's black cloaks drifted across this shining paradise and left shallow trails, like gentle brush-strokes.

At Rivoli three days later, Carisbroke and his servant gal-loped away having promised to arrange lodgings for the English Ladies in Rome. Isabel watched until they were specks in the distance. By breaking with him she had cut the final link with the Catholic network that had sustained her all these years, her family, Lady Fitzroy, always Carisbroke. Mary Ward's isolation would be complete as they entered Rome.

Christmas Eve 1621 was fine and cool with the air so clean that even distant hills were sharp as a painted landscape. As usual the two Marys walked ahead, dressed alike in black cloaks and tall hats, Poyntz taller and sprightlier but hesitant, as if she held back each step to keep in time with her idol. Though Mary Ward never flagged, her stride was not easy. It was as if she were pulled forward rather than propelled by her own energy. These days she was often bent double with the pain of gall-stones, her digestive system wrecked long ago by irregular meals, impure water and strenuous activity.

Since Terni they had travelled through rolling hills, each bend in the road exposing a view of forested low country, lake or river. At the top of a gentle incline they stopped. Rome was spread out in the crystal air with the precision of an etching, a perfection of dwellings, cupolas and towers clustered round a high white dome. A silver river threaded its way towards the city in a series of generous meanders.

Beneath the dome rested the bones of St Peter and somewhere in that dense congregation of buildings was the room in which a decision would be made about the fate of their Institute.

If Mary's petition was successful and their status as a religious institute confirmed, they would soon be making their way north again to face a future of fund-raising, training and consolidation. And what if they failed? What if the Pope refused to have anything to do with a women's institution that refused enclosure and the jurisdiction of his appointed bishops?

Whether the outcome was favourable or not, all that Isabel loved most would be gone for ever; this joyful spirit of improvisation, of rushing forward. And even in the short term, from the moment of entry into Rome the intimacy she had with these women would be splintered by the terrible job of living penniless in a mighty city.

Here, between soft hills, the air was sweet and the road empty though ahead and behind there were streams of pilgrims, merchants, soldiers and vagabonds. The future, poised on the quivering plain which held Rome, was all confusion and struggle.

FIVE

Whoever Perseveres to the End, Will Receive the Crown

1622

Chapter 24

For a city dubbed eternal, Rome seemed extraordinarily new. The gloomy arch of the Porta del Popolo, more grandiose and substantial than anything in London, drew the English Ladies into streets simmering with Christmas Eve festivities though Isabel detected few signs of piety among the boisterous crowds.

The women were heckled mercilessly because under the torch light they looked shabby and strange with their dishevelled manservant leading two weary horses behind them. In the Via del Corso mansions reared up on either side. Sometimes an archway allowed a glimpse of a lamplit courtyard with gleaming statuary that would have gladdened the acquisitive heart of Lady Fitzroy. But for Isabel, who had allowed herself to think that the Porta del Popolo marked the end of their journey, this last mile was intolerable. She had pitched herself to travel so far and no further and was disappointed by Rome which seemed too contemporary and the population too secular.

Mary Ward insisted that they find the bridge over the Tiber called St Angelo, a route she had once heard described by Father Gerard that would take them past statues of Peter and Paul and under the walls of the Pope's own fortress. On the Ponte St Angelo, however, the stench of rotting flesh hit Isabel like a recurrent childhood nightmare. Sure enough, haphazard spikes adorned by severed human heads had been thrust into the bridge. The knowledge that none of them had been cut off for being Catholic brought no comfort at all.

Close up the basilica of St Peter was hidden behind its own massive façade. The women were dwarfed by central doors which drew them into a whispering space so vast that despite the light of countless candles and lanterns only the gilt of a distant vaulted ceiling was visible. The translucent air was thick with beeswax, incense, musty clothes, fresh cut stone and more than a thousand years of prayer. Mary walked confidently to a marble rail above steps to the tomb of St Peter. The contrast between the simplicity of the old burial place and the glamour of the modern high altar above it was bewildering. Isabel's thoughts darted into the dome, to her troubling conversation with Carisbroke in the forest, to a craving for sleep and a yearning to feel the right thing now that they had finally reached their goal.

Mary Ward seemed entirely free from such a muddle of preoccupations. Even the aesthetics of this astonishing church were of no interest to her. Here she was, at the appointed time, kneeling before the grave of a most revered apostle. God had brought her here safely, of course.

Carisbroke had promised to find them lodgings within a stone's throw of the Jesuit English College, though Isabel wondered whether this was out of consideration for Mary or so that her activities could be closely monitored. By eight o'clock on Christmas morning the women had been up two hours, prayers had been said, the dusty rooms scrubbed and Mary with her two interpreters, Isabel and Winifred, was ready for a first foray into the city, a trip to the residence of Vives, the Archduchess Isabella's ambassador in Rome.

Robert hurried them along like a bloodhound fearful of losing the scent, pausing only to squint up at street names or allow a cart to pass by. Isabel barged from one obstacle to another, eyes on a city that unfolded itself in crisp sunlight; a crumbling wall, a new fountain, nude males carved in stone and a Christmas Day procession; banners, clerics, fantastic gowns textured in glassy velvets, beads, jewels, lace, and a furious explosion of colour; wine red, berry black, apricot, rose and flame.

The street outside Vives's austere embassy had been swept

314

clear of undesirables and the shutters of all but the ground floor were closed against polluting influences. Robert dragged at a bell-pull and they waited several minutes before the mighty door was heaved open a crack. A servant dressed all in black, stout, harassed and heavy-eyed, took a message, told them to wait and shut the door in their faces. Isabel peered through a tiny chink but could see nothing but an acre of marble floor. After a very long time the man reappeared and told them that Vives would call on them the next day.

Mary thanked him with such a radiant smile that he fumbled his retreat through the huge door.

Although the women had at last removed their tattered pilgrims' cloaks and wore instead neat black gowns, small collars and long veils under wide-brimmed hats, Isabel thought that their appearance was the reason they'd been refused entry even as far as the vestibule. Clothes which had seemed a subtle blend of the religious and secular in Liège here were absolutely eccentric and the crowd parted to watch them go by. No other group of ladies walked the streets dressed in widows' weeds and nunnish headdresses. Mary Ward in particular made heads turn with her potent gaze and yellowish complexion.

Undaunted by this rebuff from Vives they went on a round of further calls. Robert's knowledge of Rome was impressive and Isabel looked at him with new respect. They followed his thin back in its loose doublet and sagging breeches down twisting streets and across the ends of a succession of squares which at first sight were disturbingly similar. Next on Mary's list were selected cardinals: Hohenzollern, a friend she had made in Cologne, Borghese and Farnese, protectors of the Spanish Netherlands and England respectively. But Isabel thought drearily that they were casting seed on very stony ground. The façade of Palazzo Farnese must have contained forty windows. What chance was there of a message from an obscure English woman finding its mark?

In the afternoon the English Ladies clustered together in their little rooms on the fifth floor of the house on Via di Monserrato and kept to their familiar routine of prayer and contemplation but at nightfall they prepared for mass in the new Jesuit church, the Gesù. Mary was determined to establish a link with the Jesuits.

Out they all poured into a city over-ripe with sensation. Dried fruit, screws and hinges, dairy products, leatherware, cloth or pottery spilled from cave-like shop-fronts and old faces peered out of gloomy doorways with a molish blinking of the eyes and a baring of rotten teeth. The smell of ripe cheese was exchanged for one of musty fabric, then stale urine, frying meat and, in a sudden square, a waft of open country. But even amidst dense evening crowds Isabel felt conspicuous. At any moment she might bump into Father Turner, who must be in the city by now.

The Gesu was more a building site than a church. There was scaffolding everywhere and a strong smell of fresh paint. It was so crowded Robert found places for some women in one pew, others in another and Isabel was separated from the rest near the back. Never in her life had she been so surrounded by beautiful boys with clever, besotted eyes and lean bodies. She saw shades of Carisbroke in the austere façade, among the ardent novices and at the exquisite urn holding the remains of Ignatius. This is what formed him, she thought. He has been chiselled out of this same stone into an idea of perfection and has learnt to believe that he can do anything. Here is the world he has never really left.

And there, in the winding procession of priests was Carisbroke himself, robed like the others in vestments of white silk, ranked high among them in the pecking order on the altar, remote and seraphic, so far from the cloaked, trembling man in the sleety forest that Isabel had difficulty linking the two.

No wonder the Jesuits won't let women near them, she thought. Theirs is an order that holds rigidly to the hierarchy of the church. They lock themselves above their congregation with their fluent Latin and glib interpretation of texts which they assume only they have the intellect to understand.

The few frescoes that were finished depicted images of supplicant, suffering women, saints or sinners with draperies ensnaring their feet. Isabel thought of Margaret Clitherow's soft body crushed beneath English stones on the riverside in York. Her brave and doomed protest against persecution was very far from this magniloquent celebration of the mighty Catholic church.

As the women had not been to confession they could not take communion. Isabel's prayer drifted with the anthem. Up, up, up soared the boys' voices – '*Exaudi nos, Domine sancte . . .*' – into the dome, where they gathered depth and came swirling back along the arched ceiling.

'Isabel.'

The whisper came like a puff of black smoke. 'Isabel.'

She quivered as if struck a blow.

'Isabel. I must speak with you.'

Isabel covered her ears. She could feel him now, a slight pressure near her hip and against her shoulder. His many faces flickered in her eyes; Francis Bourne with a lop-sided smile and a boyish eagerness to be great; Bourne's mouth loose with desire under the sloping attic ceiling at Startsdon; Bourne's beard peppered with grey and his eyes bitter in Margaret Westward's acrid little parlour.

She shrank away. The anthem was dying and the Gesù grew still beneath air misted with incense. Her flesh was skimmed with an icy sweat.

The whisper came again. 'You think you can't trust me but trust me in this. Make your petition to the Pope and go home quickly. Get away from Rome. If you'll let me explain . . .'

But she was on her feet, clambering along the pew away from him across the broad skirts of outraged matrons dressed in their festive best. Outside a cold wind coiled dust across the piazza and Robert detached himself from the shelter of a nearby porch. She fanned her face in pretence of a sudden faintness and leaned against a column, glad that she was hidden by darkness and her streaming veil.

We are like insects fallen into a stewing pan, she thought. How do we inspire such fear in them all that they refuse to leave us alone?

*

When Vives turned up the next day his old-fashioned carriage blocked the narrow street and attracted a crush of
onlookers who were much amused by his huge, outmoded
ruff. In their rooms above, the women waited nearly five
minutes for him to climb the seventy or more steps and when
Robert at last ushered him in Isabel's heart sank. So this
crabbed little man was to be the spokesman of a vigorous
new order of women. He must be nearly eighty. It was even
an effort for him to fold his stiff limbs into the offered chair.

The room was now very crowded because Vives was chaperoned by the large manservant who had treated them so
rudely the previous day and who now hovered at the door
as if he might at any moment be called away on far more
urgent business.

When Vives spoke he used the bored delivery of one
embarking on an utterly pointless exercise. 'Our audience
will be in two days' time. You are indeed fortunate to have
such a benevolent and generous patron as the archduchess.
She has been tireless in her efforts to arrange this meeting
and I have received countless letters from her about you.'
His sharp little eyes gazed at a point somewhere to the left
of Mary's forehead while his fingernails made nervous scrap-
ings at the arms of his chair. 'The interview will be in Latin
but I'll give you a summary afterwards of course. Cardinal
Ludovico, the Pope's nephew, will be present, as he always
is. Under no circumstances should you turn your back on the
Pope, interrupt our conversation or make any contribution
unless specifically asked to do so.'

Mary was gazing intently at Vives. She would never question either his competency or his honesty. What was the
point? He was her only access to the Pope. 'You have done
so much for us in a very short time,' she murmured.

Vives made the mistake of catching her eye and her blazing
trust made him gibber with self-justification. 'Letters. Endless, as I've said, between the archduchess, your excellent
patroness, and myself. I told her. I told her. You can only
push this so far. We'll see what we can do. But just for
schools in St Omer. Nothing more. Keep quiet. Say nothing.'

After he had gone Susan Rookwood sprang into action.

Two days. The best gowns were in a terrible state and they had run out of starch for ruffs and head-bands. How would they ever have enough hot water for all three women to wash from head to toe? Mary closed the door of the smallest room and went into retreat.

Isabel allowed herself a moment of intoxicating hope. If an interview with His Holiness could be arranged so easily, surely he must have heard of the English Ladies and especially want to see them. Perhaps their reputation had gone before them.

Through a sleepless night she had pondered Bourne's sudden appearance in the Gesù. Why had he emerged from the shadows again and shown his hand? Well, at this rate he would have his wish. The English Ladies would be travelling north out of Rome on the Via Flaminia by New Year.

But as Vives' coach lumbered the short distance along the Via dei Banchi Vecchi and across the Tiber Isabel began to lose her nerve. The intentions of the English Ladies were made insignificant by Rome, a city so full of churches that nobody had counted them and where seventy cardinals oversaw every area of ecclesiastical life. Why change a system that suited everyone except a group of inconvenient females led by a frail visionary?

Mary, at prayer over the bead of her Paternoster, was blithe as ever. Isabel thought: I love her because it would never occur to her not to do this. Neither prevarication nor small-mindedness are in her nature. I just hope others are as enchanted by her as I am.

They were met under a monumental porch by Vives who looked much more brisk and smart this morning, presumably because here he could show off his familiarity with the Pope. His high, polished heels clicked along gaudy galleries and he occasionally thrust back a liver-spotted hand to indicate they should keep up. Isabel tried to lock the airy passageways in her mind so that she could carry them home to her friends.

The further she followed the striped backs of the servants the more convinced she became that this long trail through the Pope's palaces was a deliberate ploy to intimidate. The only plain thing in sight was the gently swaying skirt of

Mary's robe and the sweep of her long silk veil. Under foot were marble tiles of dove and slate grey and on either side were frescoes showing map after map of Italy. Every time Isabel began to make sense of a painting it disappeared from view as her feet carried her past it. Overhead in the vaulted ceiling arched a hundred more panels. This is too much, she thought. Does anyone ever pause long enough to study them all? If Dorothea Bourne were allowed to wander here for a while she'd learn all she needed to know about perspective.

Dorothea Bourne. That Bourne name again. A sick woman starving in Liège, a new sister-in-law, and a treacherous brother who tracked them across Europe.

At last they came to a series of ante-rooms where slanting light picked out worn patches in their skirts. Young guards with oily noses and downy chins stood expressionless by the door while Vives shuffled from foot to foot and drummed the fingers of one hand on the stiff sides of his puffed breeches. Mary had eyes only for the double doors that would admit them to the Pope's presence. Already she had begun to focus her prayer on him and Isabel felt a momentary sympathy for the pontiff.

When they were at last admitted to the presence, the Pope on his dais seemed as much a fixture as the frescoes on the walls. Pope Gregory XV was sixty-seven years of age and, despite all the pomp of his apartments and person, smelt unmistakably of unwashed male. His old head, clad in a high crimson hat, was framed by the gilt carving on his throne; his knees, neck and wrists frothed with lace and his shoulders were cloaked in crimson.

Vives prostrated himself, sinking little by little to the floor to protect his old joints, and kissed the Pope's ring. When it was Isabel's turn she pressed her lips briefly to the hard, warm stone and prayed: For Mary Ward's sake, let him be sympathetic.

From her position at knee level she saw that another much younger man stood motionless in the background, Cardinal Ludovico, the pope's famous nephew. When Vives addressed the Pope in Latin so rapid that even Isabel struggled to understand, it was as if the words were sucked over the head of

His Holiness and into the formidable brain of his nephew. Isabel glanced at Ludovico again and saw that his focused grey eyes were assimilating information like corn in a grinder. His gaze passed momentarily over her face and then back to Vives. She sensed a withdrawal. After two minutes he had made his decision and wanted them out.

Nevertheless a jovial conversation rambled on between the two old men who nodded occasionally at Mary as if she were a wilful child. The women were left kneeling but Vives was allowed to stand up. He held his head to one side and folded his arms as if to say: Well, you and I both know we're only going through the motions but we'll play their little game for a while.

'Holy Father, here I have Mary Ward who I know you've heard all about. In my native land she's won huge approval for her work, which is the education of young girls to be nuns or mothers, the sacred callings of all women. She wants you to confirm her work in those few schools she has already set up.'

The Pope's gaze had drifted from his ring to Vives' face but in the sudden pause he jerked obediently into speech. 'God supports His church in need.'

Isabel looked at the pontiff sharply and decided that not a word so far had penetrated. The requirement to speak had at least made him stare at them but only with the curiosity of one who has not encountered a woman for some time. After a while his attention drifted away again, this time to the energetic clouds beyond the window. Suddenly, however, he interrupted Vives mid-sentence. 'These women wear odd clothes. What do they signify?'

'They are English,' said Vives, 'and dress as English widows to avoid drawing attention to themselves.' The men allowed themselves a guffaw at Vives' irony. 'Their headdress in particular is typical, I understand.' Isabel thought wearily that at least if Mary Ward was ever mentioned again the Pope's sleepy imagination would summon up the image of a high black hat. There was no mention of the fact that the women's gowns were in fact remarkably like the Jesuit soutane.

Ludovico was looking at her with slightly narrowed eyes.

For a moment she saw a flash of malice behind his careful serenity.

'The thing is, Your Holiness,' continued Vives, 'the foundress is no longer a young or healthy woman. Her Excellency the Archduchess is very worried that unless you confirm Mary Ward's Institute as a religious order all her work will fade away after her death.'

Even Winifred drew a sharp breath at this nonsense and Isabel prayed that Mary's Latin was not up to understanding the insult. Fifteen hundred miles, she thought, and he still calls us frail.

Then she noticed that her reaction had amused Ludovico so she smiled faintly and folded her hands in a more supplicating gesture.

The audience ended with an agreement that the petition would be put to the appropriate committee of cardinals who would look into the matter in due course. No date was given for a final decision. Vives knelt again and they all bowed their heads.

Before giving his blessing the Pope managed one more remark: 'Whoever perseveres to the end, will receive the crown.'

Unfortunately, thought Isabel, Ludovico will persevere as long as us, and I fear his ambitions do not coincide with ours.

As they backed towards the door Mary drew from her sleeve the real petition asking that they be allowed to live like the Jesuits, darted forward and offered it to the Pope. But his fingers failed to work in time to prevent the parchment dropping to the floor. It was picked up instead by Ludovico. The precious document, which represented the culmination of years of prayer and labour, had now fallen into the wrong hands.

Ludovico inserted his index finger into the roll and twirled it playfully. It was even possible that his left eyelid drooped momentarily in the suggestion of a wink.

Chapter 25

By March nothing further had been heard from the Pope or his committee of cardinals and the women were at stalemate. Isabel was not alone in wanting to be gone from the city. Nothing but bad news came from Liège and St Omer where the communities had been sapped by a harsh winter. Poverty had forced many women to go home or join other orders and the few left were hungry and sick.

Isabel's sense of urgency was at times overwhelming. She felt they must get away from Rome before they were stuck for ever. If the money ran out entirely, if the archduchess's goodwill finally expired, they would never be able to leave. And nobody came forward to help them, neither Vives, Carisbroke nor any of the English Catholics who were in Rome. Bourne's warning, or threat, rang in her ears.

Everyone was too busy for the English Ladies. On 12 March the Pope was to canonize no fewer than four saints, among them Teresa of Avila and Ignatius Loyola, reformer and founder of popular and prestigious orders. A century earlier the Catholic church had been brought to its knees by the zeal of Luther and Calvin so it was small wonder it should be wallowing in self-congratulation now. The war was going well for Catholic parties in Europe and from the destruction of the old church had emerged these compelling new saints.

The festivities rolled over the English Ladies in wave after wave of extravagance. They dressed in the least shabby of their gowns and set out to hear mass in St Peter's though there was such a throng it seemed unlikely they would even get into the basilica. For two hours they waited in the square outside while the Vatican's favoured sons processed past:

cardinals, bishops, priests and brothers. Then at last, by dint of gentle pressure applied by Robert Wright, they actually reached the back of the nave.

Throughout mass Isabel stood near Michelangelo's Pieta, her eyes on the Virgin's massive, spread knees which reminded her of St Omer cathedral and the little relief sculpture of Mary with the cat. Here in St Peter's hundreds of priests were trampling on Mary Ward's vision and Isabel recoiled from the sight of the Pope carried high in his litter of gilt and red velvet. I have smelt that man, she thought. He is no closer to God than I am, yet he stands in our way like a great lump of dead flesh.

Heresy, Isabel, she told herself severely, and was too weary to be shocked.

After the Pope had gone the crowds filtered out rapidly, bound no doubt for a night of feasting. Meanwhile the English Ladies would go home to rooms lit by the noxious flames of two tallow candles and the usual supper of bread and winter greens.

At least they could take advantage of the fast emptying basilica and spend some time peacefully among buried saints. In the huge nave the crowd had thinned into smaller groups of churchmen and dignitaries. A priest made a busy twirl sideways so that his chasuble floated out to reveal a sumptuous lining of gold silk. The fabric shimmered back into place as he met with a wealthy friend dressed in a striped doublet of delphinium blue and turquoise. The friend had a ready smile and threw back his head in sudden laughter. Isabel realized with a start that she was witnessing a meeting between Father Nicholas Turner and Edmund Thewing.

So, they were both in Rome but neither had come near the English Ladies. Turner was probably very reluctant to be seen with the notorious Mary Ward, but Thewing ought to visit. There he stood, strong-throated, vigorous and glossy-haired. His handsome eyes had the old trick of glancing often over his companion's shoulder for St Peter's was a place where deals could be struck and liaisons made.

Isabel began to wind her way across the nave. Thewing must be brought to account. His own sister was going hungry

324

in the Via di Monserrato while he lived it up elsewhere in the city. That doublet alone must be worth enough to pay a month's food and rent for the English Ladies.

Everyone else was heading for the great doors so she was going against the flow. She ducked to her left, dodged a pair of fat friars and was on course again but it was too late. Turner and Thewing, who had been standing to one side of the Chapel of the Presentation, had both now disappeared.

Two days later Mary Ward was at last granted an interview with the Jesuit father general, Vitelleschi.

The Jesuit College was next to the Gesù and in it were the hallowed rooms where the new saint, Ignatius, had spent the latter part of his life. Naturally women were not allowed access to this male enclave beyond the spartan public chambers and as usual had a lengthy wait before anyone came for them. Then there was a squeak of soft leather soles on the polished tiles and Father Carisbroke appeared.

Apart from in the Gesù, this was the first time Isabel had seen him since they parted company near Turin. He had not called once on his former friends. Mary greeted him kindly but in return he was very reserved and particularly avoided Isabel's eye.

He folded his hands neatly against his waistband and moved along the vaulted corridor with the same rapid stride that had become such a familiar feature of their long journey to Rome. Isabel had the sense of him disappearing until he was a tiny black pin-prick, though in fact he had simply turned through a plain, low door and brought them to Vitelleschi who was seated in the middle of three chairs. With him was Vives, looking very much at home and a little weary of all these outings on behalf of Mary Ward.

Vitelleschi was a slim Italian, perhaps sixty years old, clean-cut and plainly dressed but with the astute, wide-open eyes of a much younger man. Altogether he seemed a more promising churchman than any they had so far met in Rome. Carisbroke stood a little to his left and kept his eyes on the floor.

Isabel felt a pang of the old loving sympathy. In England Carisbroke had been vigorous, decisive and devious but now he was as dependent on Vitelleschi for what happened to him next as were the English Ladies. He did not belong in official meetings such as this, but to a world of clandestine appointments, coded letters and eleventh hour escapes.

I loved you when you were pitted against the English government, she thought. But I see you now as part of the Roman Catholic establishment and you are stunted and small.

Vitelleschi at once put the women at a disadvantage by speaking to them in Italian and barely waiting for Vives to interpret.

'So this is Mary Ward, of whom I've heard so much.'

Mary's smile, though very slow and rare, was extraordinary. First her eyes warmed, then her whole face was suffused with light. Neither the Pope nor Vives had been prepared to meet her gaze long enough to experience her power but Vitelleschi, who watched her all the time, suddenly gave a startled cough and refolded his hands. 'You have come a very long way to meet us,' he said. 'We are certainly honoured.'

Mary disliked time-wasting courtesies. 'Of course we also had to see the Pope.'

'And our friend Father Vives here tells me you have already had an audience with the Holy Father. You live up to your reputation, Mistress Ward, by never wasting a minute.'

'I wish others had the same priority. Whenever we ask for news from the Vatican we are told that the committee considering our case has not even met.'

Vitelleschi didn't answer but Isabel sensed that he was making a slight reassessment of Mary, whose faith in the speed of the Vatican machine he thought naive.

'As I'm sure you are aware, Father General, I am here to ask for your support. We have many opponents in Europe and your blessing would do much to silence them.'

Isabel had expected that like everyone else in Rome Vitelleschi would speak a few words of goodwill and send them away with a promise that all would be well in time. Instead they were gestured to a semi-circle of plain oak chairs opposite the men so that Vives, Vitelleschi and Carisbroke sat on one side, Winifred, Mary and Isabel on the other, as if they were before some kind of tribunal.

As the room overlooked an inner courtyard no sound penetrated from the street. A crucifix and a small portrait of Ignatius with eyes as usual turned heavenward were the only decorations. The atmosphere was scholastic and exclusive. Isabel again looked at Carisbroke. His hands were tucked into opposite sleeves and his large eyes were fixed on his superior.

Carisbroke. Help us, pleaded Isabel. She knew that he was so conscious of her that he registered each breath she took and remembered every word they had spoken to each other.

'The problem is, Mistress Ward,' began Vitelleschi, 'that wherever you go you seem to collect as many critics as you do admirers.'

'Because we are women, and many do not believe us capable of working for the church as men do.'

'With some justification, perhaps.'

In the long pause that followed Isabel understood that they had suddenly been plunged into very deep water. Then trip, trip came more and more words, issuing from Vitelleschi's mouth crisp as fresh print. 'Mistress Ward, I have had disturbing news from Liège only this morning. Five of your companions there are in prison for debt and I am told that the amounts owed to all kinds of tradesmen is a sum so great that you cannot hope to repay them in years.'

The women, who had received no letters for a month, were reeling. Isabel's thoughts flew to Edmund Thewing. He was at the root of many of their financial problems, but there he had stood in the nave of St Peter's, dressed from head to toe in costly silks.

Winifred said carefully: 'We perhaps made an unwise choice of friends. Money was borrowed on our behalf and we were promised time to pay it back. Instead we found ourselves directly responsible to unknown creditors. That is of course why we seek urgent confirmation of our Institute.

Only then will we receive proper subsidies from the church and dowries from English Catholics.'

'It's a shame that though the townspeople seem ready to make use of your schools they are reluctant to support you financially. Could it be, I wonder, that there is some lack of trust, a hint of scandal? You are often seen on the streets, I'm told, other than on your way to church. And I believe you've even encouraged young Jesuit seminarians to visit your house.'

Vitelleschi waited quietly with his knees pressed precisely together and his fingers entwined one with another. It was as if he watched the skin being peeled strip by strip from some anatomical specimen. 'And in England,' he said, 'one of your number was seen walking out alone to meet a man who I'm assured was certainly not a priest. And then some of your women dressed in immodest gowns and attended evening soirées where they mixed with very dubious members of the English court.'

Oh my dear God, Isabel thought, this is me. She saw herself crossing the wintry landscape to New River Head, entering Margaret Westward's tiny house and finding Bourne by the hearth. And then in the evening at Fitzroy House . . .

Who had done this terrible thing, twisted and misreported her movements to make them seem licentious and guilt-ridden?

'Mistress Ward, did you know of all this?' persisted Vitelleschi. 'Are you in close touch with what is happening to your women elsewhere in Europe?'

'My women are as carefully chosen and trained as your own priests. There is a good reason for everything they do.'

He did not like the comparison with the Jesuits. 'You are a very ambitious lady, Mistress Ward.'

'God asked me to do a certain job. I shan't give up.'

'If only,' said Vitelleschi sadly, 'there were not debts and scandals following always in your wake.'

At this Isabel could not help speaking out, though her intervention was not welcomed by anyone. 'Father General, we have many enemies because we are women. These people will defame us to prevent us winning your favour. Perhaps if you let us know the source of your information . . .'

He gave her a gentle, regretful smile.

'You see, there is good reason for everything we do. Have you asked Father Carisbroke's opinion? He knows us better than most.'

'Father Carisbroke has been most helpful. Incidentally, I asked him to be present today because he is travelling north shortly and I thought you may wish to give him messages for your friends in St Omer.'

There was a moment's silence as the women received this further blow. Carisbroke had proved himself to be ineffectual in Rome but at least he was a familiar, English face.

'So will you help us or not?' asked Winifred gently.

'My very dear lady. I am full of admiration for you all. And if we can only clear up these problems I would see no reason why your schools in St Omer and Liège shouldn't continue. In the meantime, anything, anything we can do to help, just say the word. And do let us know how you go on.'

To mark the end of the interview Vitelleschi turned to Vives and began a low-voiced conversation. Carisbroke got up and the women walked past him one by one. When they reached the street he said goodbye to each and at last looked directly at Isabel. His eyes, which had been the gateway to every significant choice she had ever made, were now blank.

Chapter 26

When spring gave way to summer the women were faced with a new enemy, heat. Their clothes were unsuitable for a Roman July and they wilted under the blanket of humidity that descended on them, even when they walked by the Tiber or climbed to one of the city heights. They made no concessions to the weather but continued their round of visits to anyone they thought might put in a good word for them. And to add to their labours, Mary insisted on starting a school to show the committee of cardinals what could be achieved. Every day twenty or more local girls crammed into a room on the second floor and were taught free of charge to read, write, make curtains, sew hems, pray and sing.

The archduchess's tiny pension arrived in fits and starts, brought by Vives' reluctant manservant, but it was barely enough to buy bread and paper let alone summer clothes or fans. News from Liège was worse than ever and one morning they learned that Dorothea Bourne had died in March, on the very day that Ignatius Loyola was canonized in St Peter's.

That afternoon Susannah and Isabel trailed up the Via del Corso to the Palazzina Borghese, a routine outing to remind the cardinal of their continued existence. Susannah, who was responsible for all the domestic arrangements in the Via di Monserrato, went out less than most and wore the extreme temperature like an extra skin, her cheeks streaming with sweat.

Isabel fixed her mind on the decades of the rosary and drove her body through the heat while Susannah puffed along at her shoulder, never saying a word. Heavy shutters were closed tight in every house and few emerged on to the streets at this time of day. Besides, anyone who could afford to had left the city. But it was possible that the cardinal, mellow in the breezy courtyard of his palace, might have a word of encouragement for them. At least there would be some movement of air in the gardens and the perfume of well-watered flowers.

Palazzina Borghese sat daintily among trees, gleaming white and scarcely a decade old. The women stood in a shaded porch while their message was carried away by a polite servant who returned later to say that though the cardinal was in a meeting and not able to speak with them just now they could rest assured that he was very grateful to them for calling.

Though this response was expected, Isabel suddenly felt so frustrated she couldn't keep quiet. Susannah's oppressive silence in the face of yet another disappointment and the prospect of a long walk home were too much to bear.

Though in full view of the palace she suddenly moved off the drive and dropped down in the inadequate shade of one of the cardinal's newly planted trees. The earth under her hand was crumbly and pulsed with warmth. 'I don't think I can stand this any longer. I keep thinking of Liège. I wish I'd been there to say goodbye to Dorothea. And at least if we were all together we could try and keep the school going. Something would be salvaged. At least we'd be cool. This heat will kill us all.'

Susannah looked back at the palace as if by gazing she might find herself in the courtyard among fountains and ferns.

'For God's sake, Susannah, will you please tell me what you're thinking. Please.'

A tear of sweat trickled from beneath Susannah's tight head-band but she said nothing.

'The lunatic idea of opening a school here,' added Isabel. 'We can't even speak Italian.'

When Susannah sat down a musky smell of perspiration wafted from her skirts. 'The school is popular.'

'We are providing free education for a few poor girls whose fathers are using us to keep them off the streets.'

'Then at least we are doing good. And the cardinals have allowed the school. That's something.'

'They want to keep us busy so we won't plague them any more. And meanwhile we'll go on waiting for ever.' She fell back on her elbows and looked through young, clenched leaves at a sky broiled yellow with sunlight. 'We are caged in here, right under their noses. And it's not just indifference but something more that gets in our way. There are too many people working against us. Vitelleschi knew every detail, all our movements in England and Liège. If our enemies were simply apathetic, we'd survive. But they're actively trying to stop us.'

Isabel had intended to provoke Susannah and had ended on a screech of hysteria. Yet when she went over what she'd said it all seemed true. 'And then I suppose if we ever do leave, if we ever scrape together enough money, we'll have to abandon the girls we've begun to teach. That's the trouble with starting the school. There's no kind or dignified way of leaving Rome later.'

'If we leave.'

'What do you mean?'

'Mary Ward wants a permanent house here.'

'We haven't either the women or the money to staff yet another house,' cried Isabel.

Susannah was in full sunlight which flooded over her black clothes and fuzzed them with yellow. She closed her eyes and sweat dribbled over the lids.

'Don't you feel it, Susannah? The pressure on us. Don't you long for home?'

Susannah's eyes clicked open and her fat tongue licked her dry upper lip. 'We may never leave,' she repeated, and got up with a clumsy drag forward to the knees, staggering when she was at last on her feet. All the way home she made no effort to keep in the shade like Isabel but plodded across the bleached cobbles.

Isabel was in a mood to tear and wound. The heat was hellish. She had lost all sense of what she was doing in Rome.

332

In the Via di Monserrato something was afoot. From the moment she swung back the heavy street door and entered the dark hallway Isabel sensed disturbance. Though the house was still hushed from siesta, families would soon burst out of rooms on the lower floors and take possession of the landings and street in the search for cooler air. Heat sat like a fat cushion at the top of the stairs but Mary Ward's parlour door was open and inside a shutter had been pushed back a crack so that a bar of scorching white light fell across the bare floor.

Mary Poyntz and Winifred hovered near the one good chair in which sat Edmund Thewing, holding tight to the arms as if he couldn't otherwise keep himself upright.

When he saw Isabel he tried to stand but reeled back with a gesture that was meant to convey a swagger of self-deprecation. He wore the same clothes that had made him so prominent in St Peter's but they had come horribly adrift. The peacock-shaded doublet was undone over a soiled shirt and the lace of his falling collar was soggy. His complexion, though tanned, had an underlying, greenish pallor.

He tried to produce a boyish grin but managed only the faintest shadow of a dimple. 'Ah, cousin Isabel, thought I'd call. Newly in Rome. Doing a bit of business. Wanted to see you and my sister. Is she here?'

Susannah, who climbed stairs more slowly than Isabel, had barely reached the last flight.

'Newly in Rome?' snapped Isabel. 'But I saw you in St Peter's during the canonization. I've been expecting you for months. Have you told Edmund what's happened in Liège?' she asked Winifred. 'Does he know about our debts?'

'He has expressed his sympathy.'

'Left it all in good order,' gasped Thewing. 'Didn't think it would all go downhill like that.'

'I think,' said Mary Poyntz, 'Mr Thewing is not well, Isabel. It was good of him to call under the circumstances.'

'Truth is, Nick . . . Father Turner told me where you were. Above all wanted to see my sister, thought she'd take care of me as I'm feeling so rough.' The whites of his eyes rolled under flickering lids.

'Where are you lodging?' asked Isabel. 'You should go home, Edmund.'

The other women looked at her in amazement. 'We can't let him leave in this state.'

'Nor can we nurse him here. If he managed to stagger this far he can get home again.'

Susannah now stood behind her. Thewing cast his sister a feeble, pleading look, dropped his head in his hands and seemed to be weeping. 'Truth is, rather frightened. Feel deathly. Wanted to see you in case . . . Very sorry.'

Poyntz made hushing noises but Isabel cut in: 'Sorry about what, Edmund?'

'One or two things, may not have been so helpful to you. I had to see a way forward. Everyone was offering me money. Now they're after me of course. Daren't show my face.'

It was as if he had been made of cheap plaster which was dissolving in the rivulets of his own tears. Even his expensive suit of clothes had been an illusion for the fabric was of such poor quality that it had gone limp and dull.

Susannah at last stepped in. 'He's my brother after all. I'll take care of him if we can get him back to his lodgings.'

'We need you here,' cried Isabel.

But Susannah had placed her large hand on her brother's forehead and didn't seem to be listening.

Edmund Thewing had smallpox, a disease rife in the city that summer. He was lodged somewhere near the river and Susannah's arrival with money to pay outstanding rent just prevented his eviction. His landlady was so terrified of contagion that she wouldn't even supply him with clean water or a fire to heat it. Each morning for a week Susannah set off to visit him, returning late at night. Once home she insisted on keeping away from everyone else. Normally she was impervious to sickness, but this time had no resistance. One night she shut herself in the smallest room and the next day was too ill to get up.

Isabel went to the door and watched her cousin.

334

Susannah's skin was blotchy, her open eyes already uncon-
scious with fever. Across her heavy breast was a tangle of
wet shift.

This must be put right. Susannah should not be ill. Isabel
marched down to the street and summoned Robert who
stepped out of some shady spot, ever on the alert. 'Please
take me to Edmund Thewing,' she said. 'My cousin is too ill
to go and I must at least reassure her that he is better.'

Rome, like London, had the ability to present a different
face every few yards. Within a stone's throw of each other
were an opulent palace and a pauper's hovel. Thewing's
rooms were near the Ponte Sisto and Robert guided Isabel
to a tiny courtyard edged with houses that seemed to have
shouldered each other into contortions of crooked roofs and
over-hanging balconies. Under a flight of stairs was a little
door, set back. Isabel told Robert to wait outside and lifted
the latch.

Edmund's room, sheltered by the projecting staircase
above, was cooler and quite dark. There was a smell of animal
flesh, as in a butcher's shop. Susannah's competent house-
keeping was evident from the clean floor and neat arrangement of furniture though flies had got in and knocked against
Isabel's face.

Thewing lay back on the pillows and didn't stir when Isabel
spoke his name curtly. Now that she had begun to understand how far he was to blame she could hardly bear talk to
him. 'Edmund. Are you awake?'

There was no reply though she could see he was propped
almost upright. Without looking away from the bed she
thrust aside the shutter to let in more light.

Edmund was watching her with wide open eyes. The
expression on his pock-marked face was one of outrage, as
well it might be for he had been stabbed neatly in the throat.
A fly clambered across a wound two inches wide and his
upper neck, chest and pillow were awash with blood. The
barley-twist hilt of his sword lay crookedly between his
fingers and on the floor by the bed, dropped from his dangling left hand, was an evil little dagger, the purpose of
which Isabel understood from Robin's fights in the garden

at Cuddington. It had a series of barbed, horizontal blades, like the teeth of a comb, and was used to trap the opponent's sword.

Isabel managed to call Robert. Though her voice seemed nightmarishly ineffectual he came at once, his long, silent figure stooped under the low ceiling.

After a considerable pause he said: 'I think what we'll do is call this death by smallpox.'

Isabel took in every detail of the little room, the swept floor, Susannah's laundered sheets so indelibly soaked with blood, the table on which were set out a cup and jug of wine, a towel and a bowl of water. Three or four flies collected on Thewing's throat, fed greedily, bounced away and bustled back for more.

She thought of Susannah working in this room, her gentle movements as she nursed her brother, and Edmund's flashing smile of thanks when he bothered to notice her.

Robert Wright had said: *Death by smallpox.*

Isabel examined her own steady hands and knew that this death would register as one of the smaller shocks of her life. Robert's innocent, hang-dog face loomed above her and his blue eyes held a glimmer of interest. He had been the best of servants, a true friend to Mary Ward, the extra strand of his loyalties only revealing itself once, she now remembered, in the Gesù when he had arranged for her to sit apart from the others, near the back.

'Robert. I wonder, do you know someone called Francis Bourne?'

His gaze became more focused. 'I do.'

'How long have you known him?'

'Ah. Now. Fifteen years or more.'

'And could you tell me where he is? I should very much like to talk to him.'

As he looked down into her face the deep, dismal lines beside his mouth were suddenly rearranged. He was smiling at last. 'Mistress Isabel, I suspect that Francis Bourne has left Rome all of a sudden.'

*

336

It was agreed that Isabel would walk back to the Via di Monserrato alone. Robert took her as far as the river and left her there with clear directions. She was distracted and quickly got lost, finding herself further along the Tiber, in an unknown district.

The water was low and choked with effluent. She suddenly longed for the frost and crispness of England in winter and saw herself moving against a backdrop of frozen trees at New River Head and raising her gloved hand to the latch of Margaret Westward's little cottage. The righteous, sure-footed Isabel who had confronted Francis Bourne that day and so easily believed him capable of treachery was now replaced by a bewildered creature who no longer had any idea of the way forward.

In Rome everything was blurred. Supposed friends had turned their backs on Mary Ward and pushed her into the wilderness. The English Ladies had blundered into a world where no one told the whole truth, secrets could be bought and everyone, even the most devout, was dispensable.

Francis Bourne had told Isabel all this in Margaret Westward's house. He'd spoken with considerable authority for he too was steeped in deception.

When she at last came to herself she was facing a high wall of extraordinary ugliness, scratched with obscenities, a blot on the Roman skyline. It was now the beginning of the working day and the path by the river was so crowded that she was nudged aside. Every man, woman and child who emerged from the gateway in the wall wore a yellow star. Their mouths were set, their eyes watchful and defensive. The morning air was noisy with abuse. In an upper window boys had gathered to hurl curses at the Jews. Isabel ducked as gobs of mucus flew across her shoulder.

A woman passed by, dressed in black like Isabel and clasping a small boy to her shoulder. She put her lips to the child's hair and a protective hand to the side of his face. Isabel gazed after them and saw the boy's plump hand clenched tight on the cloth of his mother's sleeve.

She felt a pang of envy so powerful that it left her breathless. These are Jews, she told herself. What are you thinking of? But she too wanted to be scurrying beneath the imprisoning walls of the ghetto with a little child hugged to her breast. To be brutally persecuted, to be crushed under an oppressive heel was so much simpler than to be among the persecutors, eternally engaged in a ruthless struggle for control.

The woman was soon swallowed up in the crowd but Isabel stood for many minutes feeling the emptiness of her own arms, her aching womb and crushing loss of faith.

Chapter 27

Death was commonplace in the Via di Monserrato that summer. Nearly every other day a priest might be seen scurrying away through shadows, mopping his brow and sneaking a glance behind, fearful of being pursued by the demon of infection. Afterwards a cart would clatter over the cobbles to remove the body for a hasty burial. Nothing kept in those temperatures.

It seemed to Isabel that Susannah gave in too easily. 'I can't understand her,' she protested. 'She's so tough. I've never seen her ill. Why now?'

'It's the heat perhaps,' murmured Susan. They were all afraid. The community could not support further loss and sickness was expensive as well as contagious.

After a week Susannah's skin had started to heal but she was fading fast. The women took turns sitting with her though Isabel was given longer than the rest. Even now she suffered the usual mix of emotion in her cousin's presence. Hadn't they enough troubles without the strongest among them falling sick?

She fanned Susannah's face and whispered: 'You must get well soon. I need you.'

Susannah's brown eyes gazed at her steadily, as once they had haunted all her days at Oakshott. 'You'll manage.'

'You're the only thing now that holds me to what is sensible. You are rock solid.'

Susannah gave a great, tired sigh. 'You say my brother Edmund is much better.'

'Better, yes.'

'Neither of us has been blessed with a kind brother.'

This statement made them more equal than they'd ever been and for several moments Isabel stayed where she was, crouched over the pallet with the edge of her veil brushing her cousin's cheek.

In October Mary Ward, with Isabel as interpreter, was summoned to meet Cardinal Ludovico in his town house, the Casino dell Aurora, which stood on the side of a hill in a steep, landscaped garden south of the Borghese estate. The cardinal appeared to have expanded since the winter and his tanned complexion and air of vibrant good health were evidence of a summer spent in the mountains.

Ten minutes were used up while he showed them his recent acquisitions. 'Do you know the work of Raphael, Mistress Ward? Can you see his influence in this tapestry? Before you go I must get someone to show you some other cartoons. Look at the dog and cat fighting over bones and the surprise on the disciples' faces at seeing our dear Lord. Exquisite colour and detail.'

Mary, who cared nothing for art, said: 'What a lot of work for some poor women.'

'Brussels. It was made in Brussels. Of course you're well acquainted with that city.'

Isabel was not fooled by this good-natured chat. Ludovico's self-assurance made him seem taller and broader than he actually was. He was cultured, glamorous, above all busy, and the fact that he gave them a shard of his attention emphasized the honour they were expected to feel.

'Has a decision been made yet?' asked Mary.

'A decision?'

'Regarding the confirmation of our Institute.'

'Oh, goodness me, you move so fast. No indeed, but I just wanted to have a word about one or two irregularities that have come to light. If only you'd accept enclosure, dear ladies, all this would be avoided. I think you must if you truly have the survival of your Institute at heart.'

340

'We never have any proof of so-called irregularities. It's all hearsay,' said Mary calmly.

The cardinal, who had been very reserved in the company of his uncle the Pope, now smiled far too much but his chill eyes stated quite plainly that the beginning, middle and end of the discussion had been determined before their arrival. 'No, indeed. No proof either way. Which is why I sent for you to clear up a little misunderstanding. A letter's been passed to me, in strictest confidence of course, which I believe was written by one of your women now in Rome. It's hardly the sort of missive we might have expected from a religious woman but there you go. I'm sure there's an explanation.'

The parchment he handed Mary was pulpy with age and written in a young, round hand:

Robin Stanhope,
If your sister gives you this you'll be surprised.
I pray for you all the time.
If my love for you is a sin I don't mind sinning.
I would take whatever you offered.
But perhaps you can't even remember who I am.
Susannah Thewing. Your cousin.

Mary folded the letter and handed it back to Ludovico who had been scraping the nail of one index finger clean with the other.

'The letter was delivered by me,' said Isabel, 'but many years ago. It was written by my cousin to my brother while he was in prison for alleged treason. Neither my cousin nor myself were then professed members of Mary Ward's Institute.'

'The cousin should be chastized for writing such an immodest letter.'

'As the cousin is dead of smallpox, she is neither able to speak for herself nor take punishment.'

'Possibly in the next life.' The cardinal smiled gently.

'Someone must hate us very much to have kept this document and passed it on to you.'

'No. I think it's that they fear the damage you women do.'

His emollient manner had not changed though he had come to the heart of what he had to say. 'Your antics in England are causing consternation among faithful Catholics. You and I both wish the English nation to return to the arms of the church of course but if you make its followers seem impure and eccentric, what hope have we?'

'Do your informers tell you how well our school is doing here in Rome?' Mary asked. 'Has that been noted?'

'Oh indeed. You are doing a grand job among our citizens.'

'We are only behaving here as we do elsewhere in Europe. Why not accept the proof of your own eyes?'

'I am trying to spell out to you that your present course leads you into all kinds of danger. You leave yourself wide open to criticism and therefore you must be enclosed, Mistress Ward. There is no point in arguing the matter further. The Council of Trent insisted on enclosure for women's orders precisely because scandal pursues them whenever they break out of their convents. You are walking proof of this.'

When they emerged from the Casino it had begun to rain but the servant did not offer them shelter. They hovered a moment, then stepped out on to the drive which wound downhill among a plantation of deciduous trees. Driving rain lashed into their faces and within moments formed trickles in their hat brims and drenched their shoulders and skirts.

Isabel stood stock still though rain fell from the end of her nose and into her mouth. 'I think now we must go back to Liège.'

Mary had never seemed so small. The rain which struck her smooth cheek and steady lips might well wash her away altogether. 'No, we have only just begun. We must simply find another way.'

'We won't recover from this. They don't want to confirm our Institute and they never will.'

'Then we must try something else. I have been sent invitations to go to Naples and Perugia and set up houses there. Everyone wants my schools.'

Isabel could have struck her. 'How will you staff them? How will they be funded?'

'I'll bring more women from St Omer or Liège. These Italian towns are begging me to educate their girls. The fees we charge the rich will subsidize the poor and enable us to pay off our debts.'

'We can't do it. It doesn't work. Already we've lost our funding from the archduchess.'

'Of course she wouldn't pay for us to educate Italian children. That's understandable.'

'Mary, you have come too far from your roots. Let's go back to England. Or at least to Liège where our friends need us so badly.'

'The loyal will stay loyal. The weak will leave. I never expected to have my Institute confirmed. From the very first I knew that the Jesuits would block it. Didn't my vision tell me so? But one day all will be well as long as we go on showing what women can do.'

'Die of plague and starvation. Languish in debtors' prisons is what women can do.' Rain had soaked through to Isabel's skin now and her wet skirt pressed against her legs but she wouldn't move on. It was easier just to stand in the rain and let it sink into her bones.

'Christ was not a great worldly success, Isabel. He ended up tortured, rejected and crucified. Nothing worth winning is ever easy. From where we stand we can see only our own tiny preoccupations. God has a greater plan.'

'We must help ourselves. We must think of the future for women who depend on us.'

'No. You take too much on yourself. It is not our job to consider the future.'

'If it was just our own welfare that was at stake I might agree with you. But there are hundreds who rely on us from the youngest pupil to people like Susannah who might have lived if we could have afforded to take her out of the city. We followed you to Rome, Mary. We trusted you with our lives.'

Mary's face through the streaming rain was very pale, her nose pinched. She gave Isabel a look of fierce disappointment. 'You promised your life to God, through me. You signed a contract. Have you lost your faith, Isabel? Has it suddenly got too difficult for you?'

'If the Pope himself tells us we are wrong, surely we must listen.'

'The Pope must be shown that we are right.'

'And in the meantime women die.'

'But not for nothing. Every saint who ever lives is a fool by the world's standards but I have never tried to live by those. One day people will see that we did right, and we'll be called prophets.'

Isabel spoke so softly that she was not sure Mary heard her properly through the rain. 'Or they will say what idiots, to be so misled by arrogance and ambition.'

For a moment nothing else was said. Mary's dark gaze was now unreadable as slate. 'Go to Liège then, Isabel, with my blessing. Do what you can for our companions there if that would give you peace of mind. I'll send Susan with you and she can bring back Barbara Babthorpe and one or two other women I need here.'

'And then what shall I do?'

'If you write to me from Liège, I will tell you where you should go next.'

'I may not write,' Isabel cried.

But Mary had turned away and was walking briskly towards the high gates that led on to the Via di Aurora. Rain water ran along gullies in the drive and her feet kicked spray into her petticoats. It would take a week for her clothes to dry out but for once Isabel was untroubled by such a thought.

She watched Mary quite dispassionately, a small, black-clothed figure whose sense of direction was so poor that at the gate she paused and looked to right and left, wondering which way to go. When Isabel caught up with her and guided her to the right she smiled with loving gratitude, as if no angry words had ever passed between them.

Chapter 28

Vives knew of a delegation of silk traders travelling home to the Netherlands after Christmas who would be prepared to include Isabel and Susan Rookwood in their party. As some half dozen servants and two priests were also of the group progress would be both measured and respectable. The chosen route across the Alps was through the infamous Valtelline Pass and for safety's sake it was advisable to journey well-armed and in large numbers.

Life in the Via di Monserrato was regulated by prayer and self-discipline so the parting was unemotional. The English Ladies came from their various work to gather at the door while Robert Wright shuffled into obscurity against the wall behind them, more than a foot taller than any of the women and with various bits of his clothing astray; the bottom of his breeches ungathered over his left calf, a line of stitching frayed on his shoulder so that the seam gaped. He bowed over Isabel's hand and murmured: 'Of course, as it's you I was to protect I ought really to come with you.'

'Loyalties change I think, Mr Wright.'

'Loyalties do.'

She kissed the others one after another and would have known blindfold who each was by the texture and smell of her cheek. Mary Ward was the last. She gave Isabel a wry, faint smile but it was as if she had said goodbye long ago and had already moved on. Isabel resented this coolness though Mary in fact was unchanged. It was Isabel who viewed her differently and through these new eyes found her unsympathetic.

They left the city as they had entered it, under the Porta

del Popolo. Isabel closed her eyes and folded her hands. The one reason for leaving Rome she had not anticipated when they arrived was a breaking away.

The coaches rumbled ponderously north to the heart of the war, their wheels sinking deep in ruts made by the wagons of papal troops who had been sent to occupy the Valtelline while the Spanish withdrew. At night landlords had no time for a pair of impoverished widows when there was healthy trade to be earned from businessmen and priests. Isabel mourned the buoyant progress Mary Ward's little group had made the previous year, spurred on by worship and high hopes. Now mornings were deadly as everyone waited for the laziest to have breakfast and the fact they were dependent on wheels proved an encumbrance rather than a luxury because the carts and carriages often sank in the mud or lurched so violently that passengers were thrown from the narrow seats. It grew colder.

The Valtelline Pass was a corridor for Catholic troops travelling from Spain and Lombardy to the Low Countries; to ensure a safe path Protestant landlords had been trapped and massacred by Habsburg forces three years earlier. Tiny village cemeteries were dotted with fresh white crosses and there was a military presence at every strategic bend in the road. In the early mornings when the skies were clear and Isabel saw unblemished peaks under a celestial blue sky she registered only frustration that this bloodied and complicated landscape should make their journey more tortuous.

But in the lowlands, as they came round the easterly end of Lake Konstanz, she was jolted wide awake.

The Spanish army was marching north. For an hour the ground vibrated with the ever more insistent beat of approaching footfall and suddenly the soldiers were upon them in such numbers that the civilian party fell back to the lake-side brandishing travel papers in case anyone should suddenly leave the ranks and demand to know what they were doing on the road. There must have been ten thousand men, most on foot, some with firearms, others with pikes or old-fashioned-spears. Catholic Europe had heaved itself upright and spat forth an unstoppable army.

When the last of the soldiers had gone Isabel stayed by the lake and tossed pebbles into the glass grey waters. In the distance the mountains merged with a flat, occluded sky while silence re-gathered like an old friend.

They reached Liège in May by which time more and more Spanish troops were filling the roads. Mary Ward must be just a pin-prick in the town's memory. She had spent a life-time seeking the right to fight heresy with persuasion and example but now the armies of the Catholic League showed a quicker, more effective method. Take ten thousand men and march them on a Protestant state. Once there, wipe out rival troops, lay siege to the towns and persecute the women and children. And behold, a new Catholic province of the Habsburg empire is created.

Isabel and Susan parted from their fellow travellers at the town walls and toiled up the long, steep hill of La Pierreuse to the house of the English Ladies. But the street door was locked and only after persistent knocking was it answered by a sulky servant with vacant blue eyes.

'Blanche Morton? Is she in?' asked Isabel, first in English, then French, and took a step forward as if to pass the girl on the threshold.

'There's no one here of that name.'

'Well perhaps you'd let the other English Ladies know we're here.'

'This house belongs to the Widow Gal.'

Susan whispered: 'Oh dear God.'

The house looked the same. Surely at any moment a boarder might glide swiftly across the hall or a girl's laugh resound in an upstairs room.

'Where are the English Ladies who used to live here?'

'I haven't the faintest idea.'

The women, each carrying an awkward bundle of pos-

347

sessions, walked back down the hill, beneath the impressive walls of the prince-bishop's palace and up the Mont St Martin. At least the door here was unlatched by a familiar hand, Margaret Horde, formerly Barbara Babthorpe's deputy in St Omer.

In the street the air had been cool and damp but the rooms inside, which at the best of times were dark and over-shadowed by other houses, were stone cold. No windows were open and no fires lit. There was a dull echo from empty upper floors. Margaret led the way to the old refectory fur-nished with just five chairs and a small, rough table.

Though the tiny community greeted the prodigals with great joy the news was very bad. They had been evicted from La Pierreuse and were staying on the Mont St Martin only because the local church hierarchy couldn't quite bring itself to throw English Ladies on to the streets. But the women owed so much money that they daren't go out in case they were attacked by creditors. Townspeople had turned against them because of the sums they owed and the Jesuits made it known that nobody could be a friend both of Mary Ward and themselves. The school was almost empty though a few poor girls still came occasionally, none of whom paid fees.

Of the other women who had once lived in the house many had returned to England or even married local men. Some, including Blanche Morton, had entered religious orders. Less robust members of the Institute like Dorothea Bourne had died of malnutrition or disease.

In Rome, the reported hardships of these women had woven their way into Isabel's dreams. The fact that it had all actually happened as she imagined made the memory of the past year even more intolerable. And yet the remaining few were stoical even when they realized that the travellers had brought neither money nor good news. 'You should see what Dorothea left us. Come and have a look.'

Upstairs in the little chapel were twenty or more canvases. Isabel, fresh from a city where most churches were hung with masterpieces by Caravaggio or Raphael, Bellini or Carracci, saw at once how crude the paintings were. In telling the story of Mary Ward's life Dorothea had depicted her as an ill-proportioned figure in a flat world. And yet there was magic to the pictures. In each Mary was the central figure, upright, demure and above all in the thick of things. She was shown resisting would-be suitors, tending the sick, converting the heretical and receiving messages from God. In the last picture she and her companions stepped into a ridiculously small boat, presumably to set sail from England. The one thing Dorothea had captured to the life was Mary Ward's most characteristic and infuriating trait: her unfaltering persistence.

The Teresian convent chosen by Blanche Morton was on the outskirts of town and Isabel reached it so late that she had to beg the nun at the gate to grant her an interview for a grudging five minutes.

The visitor's room was low and square, furnished with a bench, a table, a crucifix and two doors, one to the outside, the other to the convent. After nearly half an hour a shutter in this inner door slid back to reveal a small grille cut in the wood, and through it Blanche's dark, snapping eyes.

Isabel had sunk into an exhausted stupor but rose dizzily and pushed her hand through the bars. 'May we touch?'

'We may not.'

Blanche kept her distance like a wary animal and Isabel sensed they were not alone.

'What are you doing here, Blanche?'

'I am serving my time in the novitiate.'

'But why here?'

'I was called.'

'You might have waited for me.'

'We grew tired of waiting for you. We were starving. I saved who I could and then I came here. Dorothea was the last straw.'

'But, Blanche, this isn't what you wanted. Why didn't you go back to England instead?'

'Penance. I came here as a penance.' Behind the bars Blanche's face was a white, split triangle. Isabel had once known her as witty, energetic and resourceful; now, at bay, she was sour.

Here it is, thought Isabel, another unveiling. Why did I not see any of this before?

'Work it out, Isabel. After Mary Ward's so-called vision about becoming like the Jesuits there was a meeting. We saw no way of making Mary see sense so an alternative was suggested – a faction that would offer something more reasonable. We planted the seed and created the climate. Praxedes did the rest without consulting us but we were the trigger. Her death has been on my conscience ever since.'

'You say we. Who?'

'You know, Isabel.'

'Was Father Carisbroke at the meeting?'

'He was there, of course. He came to see me about a month ago, by the way, and reassured me I was in the right place. Mary Ward was lost in Rome, he said. He was on his way to St Omer and then America.'

Carisbroke had breezed through with his ambition all intact again while Blanche, another of his protégées, was left tight in her convent. Isabel rested her forehead against the grille. 'You take your penance very seriously. A life-time. Are you happier now?'

'How odd that you should speak of happiness, Isabel.'

In shadows behind Blanche was Isabel's own possible future, the enclosed convent she had dreamed of as a child. She imagined turning away, as Blanche must, and entering the cloister, her days slowly wheeling round and round until death came and her body was taken away to be buried within a few yards of this quiet house.

Blanche was fading. Isabel put her wet face to the bars one more time and called her back. 'What shall I do?'

'You signed a contract,' came the exact, low voice. 'I'm amazed you think you have a choice.'

The road to St Omer was empty. Any man fit enough to walk had been drafted north to fight the Protestant Count

350

Ernst Mansfeld. In peaceful hedgerows insects flitted and buzzed among head-high cow parsley. The sky above was breezily dotted with small white clouds. Isabel thought of Mary Ward faced with another gruelling summer under a heat-sodden Roman sky and felt only cold pity.

The English Ladies in St Omer, governed by Martha Canton, were now living in three sparse rooms but there was no sense of defeat. A school was still running and they were welcome everywhere in town. Their patron the arch-duchess provided a sporadic pension on the strict proviso that it should only be spent locally, though some was doubtless spirited away to Rome or Cologne on some pretext or another. The atmosphere in the house was as it had always been, busy, cheerful and reverent.

Isabel had written to Robin asking for the price of her journey to England and a bill of payment duly awaited her. In the Rue Grosse it was understood that she was going home out of compassion for her Aunt Teresa Thewing, now bereft of all three children and at the mercy of her nephew, Robin Stanhope, who had subsequently inherited the Oakshott estate.

Isabel feared Martha's judgement more than anyone else's so knelt out of reach in the chapel. She was pretending to pray but her mind was empty and she was horrified by her own indifference. Having cut away from the English Ladies she was watchful and critical of them, seeing flaws and petti-ness in their routine where none had been evident before. And she knew that this ferocious detachment was born of self-hatred. She, like all the professed women here, had signed a pledge to stay with Mary Ward. By stepping away she had loosened the bond and set a dangerous precedent.

In the evening she covered her face and made a farewell visit to the cathedral. The little stone Virgin with the cat was of course smaller and less lovely than she remembered and in any case her interpretation was now quite different. The vivacity of the Virgin was generated by the fullness of her days; the babe in her arms and the animals at her back. It was the domestic, not the religious life that was idealized by the sculptor.

Isabel sat through a Benediction for the last time, then took a different route back to the Rue Grosse, passing under the walls of the Jesuit college.

At the gates she paused. Across the courtyard was the print shed and the door was ajar. Inside a lantern burned and through the high, small window a man's head could be dimly seen, moving to and fro against the light. Isabel crossed the yard and pushed back the door. A priest stood at the far end behind the press, stooped over a table spread with pamphlets which he was counting into piles. There was no mistaking the rapid movement of his hand nor the girth of his slender waist.

When Isabel shut the door behind her Carisbroke turned and peered past the halo of the oil lamp. Through the thick panes of the window came the last of a cloudy St Omer dusk.

'So, Isabel.'

'I was told you had left for America.'

'The day after tomorrow I sail for Spain. After that America, yes.'

Isabel was silenced by the shock of finding him here so unexpectedly. But then she thought: Typical. One of his most powerful weapons has always been to catch me off guard.

At last he added: 'I obviously need to take some of our materials with me. We have been printing night and day to produce a series of pamphlets. It may not be possible to set up a press where I'm going.' She was expected to collude with the glamour of his self-image; cultured priest among the savages, the joke of expecting machinery in a wild country across the ocean.

So in the morning the press would leap into life, printing damp words on page after page. Trays of letters lay ready on the compositor's desk, bottles of ink were ranked on high shelves and there was a strong smell of new paper and linseed oil. Isabel thought of the words bursting from these silent machines brandished as symbols of superiority before the startled eyes of some hapless native. And behind the words the saviour of souls, the teller of truths and forgiver of sins, Father Carisbroke.

'You have finished with Europe then,' she said.

'We've spoken about this. England is thought too dangerous for me. It would be foolhardy to go back there. Sadly.'

It was the '*Sadly*' that whisked away Isabel's self-control. Sadly, intimated Carisbroke, England, which needs the ineffable blessing of my presence, is to be deprived. Let us all be sad, because England is to be without Father Carisbroke.

The old Isabel reared up, unruly and wild, fighting free of years of repression, self-denial and disappointment.

Carisbroke glanced warily at the closed door behind her. 'You should leave, Isabel. Shall I send for one of your companions? In truth, I really can't understand what you want. I thought you were in Rome.'

'Don't tell me your sources have let you down.'

'My sources?'

She picked up a pamphlet and read its title. '*A Mirror of Patience, a Life of Thomas More*. I don't expect this covers the art of betrayal. Except, of course, the betrayal of a faithful servant by his master.'

'Betrayal?'

'I'm glad I found you, Father Carisbroke, because there's one thing I always wanted to know.' She had drawn close to him and was flicking through piles of paper, a precious commodity that ought to be handled with care. He stood his ground. 'In the summer of the Powder Plot, when Father Garnet and my brother and Digby all went to Holywell with us, where were you?'

It took him time to reply. For a moment he had no idea what she meant. 'I believe I was here in St Omer with Catesby. We were trying to raise money and recruit support for a Catholic rising, should the plot succeed.'

'And when I first met you at Oakshott, that time the pursuivants came for you, did you know then that you would be abroad in the summer?'

'Of course.'

There. His reality had never been hers. His truths had never been as they seemed.

Her hand had fallen on to a forme of type and her fingertips were moistened with ink. He watched her uneasily. She was too close for comfort. They could see dust on each other's shoulders, pores in the skin, hair follicles, moles, a pulse in the neck.

Again he said. 'I thought you were in Rome.'

'I left. I decided it was hopeless.'

A small light flared in the back of his eye. So, she had learnt her lesson and come to her senses. She was here to be guided. His voice was throaty with the caress of the counsellor. 'And now, Isabel?'

'Mary thought honesty and example would win through. She has no idea how to operate in the real world.'

'I agree,' he said, though guardedly. 'She is out of her depth.'

She saw the act before it was performed. It flew into her mind and along her nerves. Her hands gripped the edge of the heavy table with all its neat piles of creamy pamphlets and over-turned it so that paper streamed with a watery rush to cover the floor and Carisbroke had to leap aside to avoid his feet being crushed. Next she swept her hand along the compositor's desk. Trays of letters sprayed in all directions. Hundreds of tiny cubes bounced under the press and into the corners of the room.

He closed his eyes for a moment, then stooped to heave the table upright.

The last she saw of him was his crouched, trim figure embarked patiently on picking up the letters, a task that would take at least all night.

Chapter 29

Lady Arabella Fitzroy, as always in the vanguard of fashion, wore an intricately tucked, lace-edged collar which spread across her shoulders but did not quite hide the undulation of her naked white bosom. Her right cheekbone was adorned by a tiny black patch and she wore no farthingale. Isabel was therefore at a distinct sartorial disadvantage for the women in St Omer had decked her out in a gown at least a decade old, complete with enormous padded sleeves and waist ruffle. After several years of living without the constraints of metal corsets she felt uneasily detached from her caged body. When she moved her arm the bulky sleeve interfered with the edge of her vision and her skirts, shortened by the farthingale, exposed broken shoes.

There was a new favourite in attendance, introduced as Lord Charles Falkner, a slender young man with a downy fluff of yellow curls and perfect calves. Clad in a doublet of aquamarine interlocked with lilac he added a dainty warmth to the newly decorated parlour of egg-shell blue.

'I intend to have the windows enlarged,' said Lady Arabella, 'and this wall knocked through. You, Mistress Stanhope, so recently returned from Italy, must find these rooms impossibly dark.'

Isabel, desolate and travel-stained, was unprepared for a conversation about interior decoration. 'Lady Fitzroy, I have left Mary Ward, and my brother is banishing me to Oakshott. I have broken my journey because . . .'

The sleepy rhythm of an exquisite fan stirred a stiff curl on Lady Fitzroy's forehead. 'Sometimes I think the only answer is to pull the whole house down and start from scratch. Did you go to Florence, Isabel, on your travels?'

'We did not.'

'You should have taken in Florence.' Lady Arabella's placid eyes trailed Isabel's ugly gown. 'And how was Mary Ward when you left her? Was she as thin as you are?'

'We are all thin.'

As if an invisible puppeteer had given a measured drag at her strings, Lady Arabella rose languidly to her feet. 'I have gone Spanish in my art. Come and see. Blue, in any case, is my colour at present so this painting seemed right. After El Greco. Have you heard of El Greco?'

Isabel would rather not have been faced with anything Spanish but followed obediently. Falkner detached himself from his alcove and the soles of his embroidered slippers padded behind.

'We are all agog,' murmured Lady Arabella, 'to hear the outcome of our dear prince's trip to Spain. Will he return triumphant with the Infanta on his arm?' She floated off again, her flame silk skirts, shot with gentian, caressing the marble of her long gallery. 'For myself, I never dabble in politics.'

Isabel was suddenly fixed with a remarkably shrewd gaze and she understood the warning. No blame. No recriminations. We have dealt with this.

Arabella continued: 'I asked Edmund Thewing, dear Edmund, to bring me a painting from Italy. He had a marvellous eye and collected for the Prince of Wales at one time. His death was a terrible blow. Smallpox is a scourge. But he sent me this just before he was taken ill. Perhaps you came across the artist in Rome. Artemisia Gentileschi, soon to visit London. A formidable young woman if her subject matter is anything to go by.'

The painting was of a bare-armed Judith sawing off the head of Holofernes. More horrifying than the gore of the half-severed head was the unfaltering dedication on the faces of Judith and her servant.

'I was wondering, Lady Fitzroy,' said Isabel, 'if you had seen anything of Francis Bourne. Have you any idea where I might find him?'

They stood side by side, facing the picture. When Lady Arabella stirred, her starched petticoats wafted a perfume of rosewater. The world-weary Charles Falkner had rearranged himself against a nearby column, legs crossed, arms folded. At the mention of Bourne there was perhaps a slight readjustment of the shoulders.

'Francis Bourne has so many occupations these days. I rarely see him. He now says he wants to enter Parliament of all things.' She turned to Isabel and her lashless eyes made a rapid blink, like those of a lizard clinging to a wall in a Roman courtyard. 'Lord Falkner will find him for you, however.'

'I'd like to go with him. I've been on the move for so long now I don't know how to be still.'

In the Strand the air was muggy and because of the low tide there was a stink of sewage from the mud banks of the Thames. Falkner picked his wary way through a succession of alleys between half-built shacks or teetering terraces. They were heading for Clerkenwell where the Bournes, said Falkner, had acquired a new town-house.

Isabel marched at the elbow of her fragrant companion and refused to think of the interview ahead. Falkner, who had a small, hesitant voice and was in any case distracted by the business of keeping himself clean, proved to be a restful and courteous companion so Isabel let her mind sleep. When last she had walked these streets it had been as a missionary alert to all human need; every sick child, crying baby and bare-foot woman had woven her way into Isabel's prayers. Now each was one sadness among millions. She and Falkner were simply passing by.

The Bournes' house was in the midst of a stylish colonnaded terrace, brand new and with a gracious white porch. Isabel announced herself as Francis's sister-in-law, parted from Falkner who bowed so low that his curls brushed the stone balustrade, and was shown up a gracious flight of stairs to a room with a large window overlooking the street. She watched Falkner wend his way to the corner and felt a pang of affection. He had seemed an uncomplicated creature, so cherished that he could have no cause to wish anyone harm.

After the bustle of London there was sudden hush, coolness, the creak of a board underfoot and the tranquil arrangement of many books.

The relief of being alone was extraordinary. Isabel fell against the window embrasure and covered her face while the earth swung round and stilled itself at last. When she looked up she saw through her tattered veil Bourne's private world and found it very peaceful and intimate. In her mind's eye he was always in the thick of a complicated interweaving of business and pleasure. She thought his life must be full of people and movement; long journeys, plans, meetings and performances. Never had she imagined him in such an oasis of calm.

The sun had dropped low in an overcast sky and a stormy orange light fell through the glass. In a nearby row of books she read familiar names: John Bodenham, Campion, Tasso.

By the window was a high-backed chair with a worn tapestry seat, a design of leaves and single flower heads. Shelves had been built on every wall but many were still empty. Others, containing more precious volumes, had glass doors.

She moved about, not touching anything. All these years that she had been hungry, cold and sleepless in the company of women there had been this other life that might have been hers. Not Lady Arabella's highly decorated world, but rooms of books, a measured existence, the chance possibly to do good from a distance.

John Donne. Sir Thomas North. Bacon.

The only other furniture was a small round table and two upright chairs. Above the mantel were hung sketches and prints; a fantastic figure, perhaps dressed for a masque, an architectural plan of the house, an engraving of some stern dignitary, possibly Cranfield. Isabel pushed back her veil so she could see clearly and breathe deeply. The room smelt beautiful, of leather and beeswax.

Copernicus. Machiavelli. Tacitus. Seneca.

A confident male footfall crossed the room above and came

358

rapidly down the stairs. There was a momentary hesitation on the landing then he was so suddenly in the room that she was startled.

He did not seem best pleased to see her. 'Mistress Stanhope.'

He was broader than in her memory, his hair fashionably near shoulder length but thinner and less lustrous, his beard trim and his blue doublet deep-pointed.

He came closer and peered into her face. 'I heard it mentioned that you'd deserted Mary Ward.'

'Robert Wright told you, I suppose.'

Their voices sounded unconvincing, as if the air between them was opaque and it would be hopeless to try and reach through it. His manner was distracted.

'I wanted to apologize,' she said. 'I thought it was you who betrayed us in Hoxton. And my cousin, the Jesuit Alan Thewing. I was wrong.'

'Past history. Think nothing of it.'

She pretended to herself that now the apology had been made she could go. But of course there was much more to be said. She had chosen Bourne to be her confessor. He, who at times had seemed omniscient, must show her what to do next.

Wine was brought, the position of the table adjusted, glasses filled. Meanwhile the room had darkened and the gold-tooled titles on the shelves faded.

They both sat down and sipped carefully. The wine warmed Isabel's throat and again she had a sense of what she had missed. But it was also dawning on her how little she knew him. She gazed earnestly at her glass but from the corner of her eye saw how he was clothed in experiences she would never share: the journeys, the encounters, the plays, the women. The young man who had tumbled Isabel Stanhope in the attic at Startsdon was buried deep.

'What about my cousin Edmund Thewing?' she asked abruptly.

He put his head on one side and studied her like a physician. She was conscious that her complexion was dull and her eyes sore. 'We all draw the line somewhere, Isabel. Most of us have a limit. Thewing had no scruples. He lost his way in a dangerous game. At first he was just under the wing of Lady Fitzroy, keeping an eye out for her, on the watch for unfriendly faces.'

'Such as yours.'

'Then he was recruited by a colleague of mine as a discoverer, an ear among Catholics. He was in an ideal position because Lady Fitzroy trusted him. She has a weakness for beautiful young men. Though I was able to warn you that we knew of your Hoxton community I had no idea Thewing would betray his own brother. And of course in Europe it was more difficult to keep track of him. He was in the arms trade, selling to the Dutch and Spanish. Not a good idea. He sold secrets to us, and to Rome about us. Smallpox was an ideal death, I'd say.'

She didn't know whether she was to thank him for these revelations. Instead she said nothing. He twirled the stem of his glass.

Grasping at a straw she said suddenly: 'Have you written a new play lately, Mr Bourne?'

He laughed and there was the old lopsided twist of the lips. 'My latest is called *The Italian Maid*. It's about a man who's out to avenge the duke who seduces and then murders his sister. Two poisonings, a knife in the back and a garotting. Bound to be a runaway success. It's being seriously considered by the management of the Rose.'

Isabel put down her empty glass. The wine had made her reckless. 'Anyway, you obviously have a talent for discernment. You were right about Mary Ward. I was a fool to believe in her.'

'I hope you didn't leave on account of anything I said. What I have learned is that there are very few in this world who are able to stick unswervingly to their principles. The only person who has done so through thick and thin is your Mary.'

'But we behave like innocent babes. Everyone in opposition to us wants something different and we are the least powerful of all. You worked for Cranfield and the English government. Thewing was selling us to our enemies both here and in the Vatican. The Jesuits hate us, even those we thought were friends. We don't stand a chance.'

'Isabel, one day I really will get a play performed. I must, because I share with Mary Ward the gift of obstinacy. There's not a theatre manager in London who doesn't shudder when my name is mentioned. Same method as Mary Ward. She doesn't choose to understand the obstacles because she's no time for them.'

'I thought you of all people would be pleased I'd left.'

'But if you're telling me truth, the reason why you abandoned her is unworthy of you. Your complaint is that she's a hopeless case in a church that we all know is up to its neck in international politics and questionable financial dealings. Now if Mary had fallen meekly in with the demands of such an institution I would have expected you to leave at once.'

'But women are starving. Dorothea died.'

'She died very happy. I saw her. She showed me the paintings she'd done and introduced me to the women she lived with. If she'd stayed with the family she'd have languished as an invalid on a couch at Startsdon for the rest of her life.'

Isabel turned aside her face. 'Then perhaps the real reason is that I no longer have faith in what we're doing.'

'Ah. Well.'

But even this wasn't the whole truth. She had qualified the statement with the words 'in what we're doing'. She might have ended simply, 'no longer have faith'.

She again had the impression that he wished her gone. His hips were pushed well forward and his head rested on the chair-back. He studied his highly polished boots.

'Did you pay Robert Wright all those years?' she asked.

'At first. He won't take my money now.'

'Why did you send him to us?'

'For Dorothea's sake. And to give you a measure of protection after what happened in London.'

The conversation faded again and she saw herself on the fringes of his life, a small intrusion that because of a vague, lingering affection he had tried to keep safe. More forlorn than ever she asked: 'So what are your plans for the future, Francis?'

'Politics. That's the future. I am with Bacon and Eliot. I see a greater role for parliament and I'm sure I could make things happen. We advised James to back the Swedish king and get a decent hold in Protestant Europe but no. He dithers. He squanders money and rides roughshod over his advisers. It's no way to run a country. And of course all the time I read. I wonder. Socrates, Galileo, Burton, Bacon. I'm with Mary Ward, Isabel. She and I both think we are here to make order out of chaos.'

'You didn't marry then,' she said boldly.

'Do you know, every time I thought of it, something more interesting turned up.'

Silence fell again. He had not refilled her glass so she stood, moving clumsily to clear her skirts from the table.

'Where will you go now?' he asked.

'Hoxton. Then my brother is sending me to Oakshott.'

He nodded. 'I shall arrange for you to be taken home.'

While he was out of the room she returned drearily to the window. The bank of cloud had deepened again and only a sliver of sunshine was left. She had never known anyone fill a room as emphatically as he did. Others seemed to slide in and out of space, apologetic, tentative or gentle. He thrust it aside.

When he came back he took the end of her veil and gave it a tug. 'I hate that veil. Veiled women. I hate seeing you like this, defeated. When you came to New River Head that time I was bowled over. I had never known such a woman. You were proud and definite and walked away so bravely through the frost. I heard that when your house was raided you held off the pursuivants and I could imagine exactly the spark in your eye and the tilt of your head. I knew what Dorothea had gained by joining you. You went on and on unfolding before me as I travelled through Europe, this Isabel who could talk to a Pope, teach little girls, above all be stalwart, be committed.'

'A flattering portrait,' murmured Isabel. 'Sadly a false one.'

'Of course, when you and I first met I had a different future mapped out for you. I'd install you at Startsdon or some other country retreat and watch you breed – seven or

362

eight little Bournes to be on the safe side. I thought mother-hood would knock Catholicism out of you once and for all. On rare occasions I'd bring you to court and show you off, escort you to the theatre. Though of course by now I would probably have taken several mistresses and forgotten all about you.'

He had thrown back his head and looked at her slyly down the slope of his cheek, smiling, mischievous, an expert at holding himself in reserve. Her nerves were jumping but she felt better. 'Mr Bourne, I had other plans. I was going to convert you and make you build me half a dozen priest holes. We were going to create a famous centre of Catholic teaching. You promised me.'

'I had no idea what I'd be taking on.'

'But now you do.'

He still held the end of her veil, clenching and unclenching his fist on the gauze. The fabric was crumpled and she with-drew it softly, inserting her fingers instead.

The servant was at the door. Isabel dropped a curtsey and moved away. 'I'm prepared to offer you one piece of advice,' he called after her, 'learnt by me after years of sweat and tears. First principles for a playwright. When the plot falls apart it's always best to go back to the beginning. Find out where you took a wrong turn.'

Chapter 30

R obin Stanhope had become a wealthy man. Deborah Bourne's marriage portion had included a small Norfolk estate and the right to farm taxes on sweet wine. Furthermore, since the unfortunate deaths of his Thewing cousins, Oakshott was also his. Because he had no better use for the house, he had given his Aunt Teresa Thewing permission to stay there during her life-time and when his sister returned to England in the summer of 1624, disgraced by years spent with the disreputable Mary Ward, the obvious place for her was Oakshott. Her presence would cut down on the requirement for paid staff and Yorkshire was sufficiently far away for everyone to forget about her.

Oakshott in fact had always made an excellent repository for unwanted females.

At first Isabel refused to take any part in the life of the house though she was welcomed with tears of joy by Oswald Fairbrother, formerly Anne Winshawe's steward. Rotund, white-bearded and given to muttered lamentations about the house's faded fortunes, he allocated her the same room on the second floor she had once shared with Susannah. She gazed out at the neglected lawns and thought that the tumultuous girlhood months spent here had all come to nothing.

But slowly the house entwined its austere arms about her and drew her in. The insistent rhythm of prayer and work was irresistible. Each morning she was woken at six by the thump of her aunt's great feet striding along the passageway and up the stairs to the attic floor where the chapel had now been reinstated. One day Isabel followed and hovered outside the door, stroking the wood with tentative fingers as if what lay beyond might injure her. The prayers, led fervently by Oswald, were such familiar incantations that they held her captive.

Once Isabel began to pray with her aunt she could not help eating, talking and working with her. Because Robin made such a small allowance the house was under-staffed so they had to cook and clean in order to keep loyal the few remaining servants. But the rigour of life at Oakshott was nothing to Isabel who had experienced much greater hardship in the Gatehouse Prison and the Via di Monserrato. Her contribution, however, was a drop in the ocean. Without the huge household maintained in the days of Anne Winshawe and Martha Canton the tapestries and linens fell into disrepair, the pantries emptied and the local poor went hungrier.

Teresa was a large woman with phenomenal energy. On some days she was so purposeful that she performed an extraordinary amount of work, brandishing buckets and scrubbing brushes as she cleaned the hearths and polished the lattices. At such times she rarely spoke but ate vast platefuls of food.

In another mood she might spend hours in the chapel, beating her forehead to the boards so violently that it bled and chanting decade after decade of the rosary. Then the deaths of her three children would be mourned and re-examined in harrowing detail. Alan, the Jesuit; hung. Susannah and Edmund, one a member of a revolutionary order of women, the other a selfless servant of the church with unspecified duties; both dead of smallpox but in the sacred city of Rome, thank God.

On her worst days the household would be woken in the small hours by her ranging about the house moaning the Pater Noster, turning innocent portraits to the wall for their godlessness and wagging her head from side to side in the knowledge that she had sinned and sinned so all the misfortunes that had befallen the Thewing family were her own fault.

Her relations with Isabel were equally spasmodic. Sometimes she called her Thomasina or Susannah, at others she

365

ignored her completely. Occasionally she burst into a room and watched her intently with fierce, speckly brown eyes.

One evening after chapel when all the servants had been dismissed, Isabel was waylaid by Teresa and Oswald. She must be shown the hidden side of Oakshott, they said, just in case. By candlelight Teresa's robust figure wavered to a monstrous shadow spread-eagled across the low ceilings. Isabel followed close behind and realized that she was being admitted to an inner circle. The thought was stifling.

She was taught to look beyond the steady-eyed portraits of female Winshawes in which each subject caressed with tapering fingers the jewelled family crucifix at her breast. One, of grandmother Anne Winshawe wearing a nunnish headdress and an expression of near hysterical fervency, hid a deep cupboard containing sacred books. Another, of an early sixteenth-century matriarch, was hung between Teresa's chamber and a lobby. It swung back on its panel to reveal a cavity deep enough to hide a visiting priest.

In the kitchen there was a little hutch, built into the ceiling behind a central beam and accessible only to the exceptionally nimble or desperate.

The third and final hideaway was reached from the schoolroom wing. By now the blood was pounding in Isabel's ears. Here was the room where she had spent a night in Carisbroke's bed and opposite was the uneven passageway leading to Nicholas Turner's chamber and the schoolroom. At the very end was a narrow staircase used mostly by servants and there, between floors, was a head-high linen cupboard. But beneath the bottom shelf was a false floor covering a layer of bricks to give an illusion of solidity. Beyond, a ladder led down to a secret room which in turn concealed a further priest hole. If the pursuivants actually found the first chamber they would give up, satisfied, and not look for another. Nicholas Owen, who had built this particular hiding place during a month's stay at Oakshott, had left nothing to chance.

'You try,' urged Teresa. 'One day you may have to show a priest. It's best to know.'

Isabel hitched up her skirts and climbed down until she

366

was inside the innermost chamber. The darkness and enclosure were horrifying, yet she closed the trap door on herself, abruptly obliterating sound and light. Even with her arms locked round her knees there was barely room to sit upright. Sawdust and soot irritated her throat.

She was wrapped in the young Jesuit, Carisbroke, who had spent a night here listening to the dull hammerings of pursuivants in rooms nearby. No doubt the delay had made him impatient. He had other houses to visit, funds to raise, horses to requisition.

The more cramped Isabel became, the more shrunken Carisbroke's image. She had imagined him leaping away on leaf-strewn paths to the open country while in fact he had lurked here until the danger was past and emerged the next day, stiff and dishevelled, to limp off in some new disguise. Far from being a free spirit he had been cooped up until Anne Winshawe thought it safe to release him.

Anne had orchestrated his movements from the first. She had welcomed him to the house, introduced him to her impressionable grandchildren and saved him from the pursuivants. It was not Father Carisbroke but Anne who had set Isabel on the path to Mary Ward. Since then she had been passed from one hand to another, Thomasina, Lady Fitzroy, Martha Canton. Carisbroke's allure had been his romantic arrival across Aunt Teresa's herb beds, his discretion, the secret meetings in hidden rooms, the suddenness of his comings and goings and the slipping of a little book into the pocket of her gown.

Isabel crawled out of the hiding place, clambered up the ladder and emerged into soft candlelight.

The tour was not over. Though it was November they must next go into the gardens which were pitch dark and blown about by a howling wind. Across the lawn was a steep slope and beyond it a series of rose-beds. The spiky bushes had been pruned to within an inch of their lives by Teresa and now looked like a series of clutching fists.

'In summer,' hissed Teresa, 'there's one yellow rose-bush, and beneath that on the side furthest from the house, is where we hid the chest. All the sacred vessels are there.'

Isabel looked back at the house. That black rectangle on the second floor was the window in which she and Susannah had stood to watch a mysterious nocturnal burial procession. She remembered her exact feelings of antagonism, privilege and fear.

Teresa thumped her heel to the wet earth. 'They ought not to be hidden away. What use are they here?'

'Perhaps it's safe now to dig them up and keep them in the house. You could use them in the chapel on feast days,' said Isabel soothingly. Oswald and Teresa stood on either side and she felt the pressure of their combined expectations. She was not giving them the response they wanted. 'You could wear the crucifix, Teresa. You should be next.'

The wind shook the skeletal rose-bushes and knocked Isabel back a step. 'Not for ornament,' hissed Teresa. 'They are for the glory of God. I told my mother not to bury them. I pleaded with her.'

So saying she stalked off back to the house. Isabel followed, fighting the wind and reflecting that an argument between Teresa and Anne must have been a memorable event.

In the spring of 1625 England crowned a new king who in turn had a new Catholic wife, not Spanish after all but French.

On 6 May, feast of St John before the Latin Gate, the women as usual had breakfast in the dining parlour. The unfortunate apostle John had been plunged by pagans into a cauldron of boiling oil and both women were affected by the story. Teresa anticipated similar torments for herself in the next life while Isabel dreamed of Rome.

When Oswald brought a letter and handed it to Teresa all three stared at it suspiciously. Nobody wrote except Martha Canton and her letters usually contained disturbing news. The recently-established house in Perugia, for instance, had been suppressed by the authorities and Mary Ward next intended to go to Bavaria. Isabel dreaded these letters and always delayed replying.

'Who's this from?' asked Teresa, turning her letter over and over.

'My brother Robin, I think.'

'Is it his seal?'

'Yes.'

'Why would he write to me?'

'Because you are the lady of the house.'

Teresa gave the stiff paper a jab with her muscular finger. 'He's never written before.'

'Would you like me to open it?'

'It's for me.' Teresa loved to enmesh Isabel in her knotty reasoning.

Isabel got up. 'I'll see you at dinner I expect. Until then I shall be working in the vegetable garden.'

'It's such a pretty seal that it seems a shame to break it. A fleury cross. Look.' The letter was at last unfolded. 'Can't make head nor tail of it. You read it, Isabel.'

Sir Robin, his wife, their three children and the priest Father Turner would be travelling north for the summer. There was plague in London and Robin wanted to bring his precious lambs as far from danger as possible. And what an excellent opportunity to visit his beloved aunt and sister.

Teresa was thrilled by this news and tore off to look out an ancient toy preserved from her own infancy. Isabel spent the morning savagely forking the cabbage beds.

Robin rode up on a splendid chestnut horse well in advance of the carriages bearing his family and underlings. He and Isabel had last met eight years ago and the present reunion was clouded with mutual suspicion. Isabel was greeted with the chill restraint due a sister who has been nothing but trouble all her life.

Teresa Thewing, by contrast, was treated to the full glare of his charm. He kissed her on both cheeks and complimented her on blooming health. In return she fixed him with her staring brown eyes as if amazed that such a specimen should exist.

So, thought Isabel, the mother is not as susceptible as the daughter once was.

Robin had filled out and become quite the country gentleman. His long unpadded breeches and pleated collar were rarities this far north and his hand swept fastidiously the seat of a chair before he deigned to sit on it. He then made a great show of shouting to the servants that the beds must be re-aired, the windows thrown open and the kitchens inspected by himself in readiness for the coming of Lady Stanhope.

Lady Deborah's arrival with her children and nursemaids was a relief to all.

Deborah, once a hoyden, was now crushed by a nervous deference to her husband and a slavish devotion to their unruly children. She had also inherited her mother's gift for untidiness and within an hour the house was filled with trunks half unpacked, baby clothes, napkins, ribbons and dolls. A carpenter was called in from the village to bar up the windows of the old schoolroom.

From the second carriage tumbled three more servants who filed up the back stairs and clamoured for rooms. Oakshott took a deep breath of amazement.

Last of all, dressed in the cape and boots of a coachman, came Father Nicholas Turner. He waited until the bustle of arrival had died away and the family was ranked expectantly on the steps before appearing in the doorway, framed by the black interior. The journey had made his complexion sallow, his belly was rounder than ever and he looked up at Oakshott with moist, sentimental eyes.

Isabel put as much distance as possible between herself and Turner. It seemed to her that he had not stepped alone from that coach, but with the entire Roman Catholic church buzzing at his shoulders. Surrounded by ghosts, he, the dark side of Rome, awoke in her the harsh pain of loss for the selflessness of community life, the intimacy of the English Ladies, their laughter and honesty. Turner, without any of these gifts, walked in a spiritual vacuum.

*

While Sir Robin rode about the estate, bullied the farmers and flirted with their sons and daughters, his wife worked tirelessly over her children. A special mush had to be prepared for the sickly baby, the sanitary arrangements scrutinized, her husband's clothes unpacked and her own gown changed for dinner. The Oakshott women were speechless onlookers to all this activity. They had no alternative gowns to wear.

Father Turner appeared at table, clutched Isabel's hand and gave thanks that she had finally seen sense and left Mary Ward. His trip to Rome, where he had been promised great things, had made him more sanctimonious than ever and he was now given to spontaneous prayers and sermons. The chapel was no longer a sanctuary for anyone else. He was always in it, poring over his correspondence and plotting.

Despite all this business, however, he had no intention of neglecting Isabel. Every couple of hours he would appear at her elbow, breathing heavily through his nose and with his hands folded piously across his groin. 'I am ready to hear your confession now, Mistress Stanhope.'

'Not today.'

'How can you hear mass if you've not been to confession?'

'I shan't come to mass.'

Fortunately Teresa was overjoyed to have a priest in the house again. She treated Turner as her spiritual slave and closeted herself away with him hour upon hour while she confided the disorderly secrets of her heart.

On Sunday morning Isabel threw on a straw hat and walked far from the house to avoid mass. The last time she had taken communion had been with Mary Ward in Rome.

That evening Robin ordered her to stay behind after dinner. His snowy collar was very impractical and now had a spot of gravy at its corner. Isabel thought wearily of the work involved in removing the stain; soak in salt water, scrub, boil, dry, pleat, starch, iron. Meanwhile she waited demurely in her plain little ruff and old blue gown.

'I can't understand you, Isabel. After all I've done for you. Why didn't you come to mass? I hope you're not getting weary of your faith. Father Turner says you've not confessed once. Why is that?'

She didn't answer.

'You would have been on the streets had it not been for me. I want my children to see their aunt at mass. You should set them a good example in that at least.'

'I owe you nothing, Robin. You keep us half-starved here. All my life I've been short of money. Worse, you tried to destroy our work in Rome. How did the Cardinal get hold of that letter from Susannah?'

He pretended ignorance at first, then said: 'I sent it to her brother. It was right he should see it.'

'You sent it via Turner, I presume.'

For once Robin looked uneasy. 'Father Turner had nothing to do with it and wouldn't approve of anything underhand. He had a blind spot where Thewing was concerned, I suppose because he was a former pupil, believed the best in him and thought him a model Catholic. But in any case, that's all in the past. My wife. My children. I think only of them now. I want our family to be first among the English Catholics.'

'I've spent hours with Deborah in the nursery and I've not seen you speak more than three words to her since you came. You see your children for ten minutes a day.'

But she was not enjoying this argument. Robin was nearly all the family she had left. Even now, at the back of her mind, glimmered the feeble spark of hope that he might love her.

She asked more gently: 'So why is Father Turner back in England?'

Robin's eyes were chips of blue stone. 'His name has been put forward to be our new archpriest. You should be less contemptuous of him, Isabel. He could prove to be a powerful friend. You should recognize the precariousness of your position and show some humility. There can be no question of marriage for you now. You're far too old and no self-respecting man would have you. You once said you might join an enclosed order. Is that still your wish?'

'My future can't be disposed of in a few sentences like this,' she cried. 'I'm not your possession.'

'I beg to differ. You're entirely dependent on me. You haven't a penny.'

Her impotence made her shake. 'No. I have no wish to join a convent.'

'Then you shall remain here, the recipient of my charity, I suppose, at least until Teresa's death. She will become more needy as years go by so you might be useful to her.'

The next morning Isabel approached Turner after breakfast and exchanged a few grudging words. Later she went to the attic floor. The passageway was dark and airless. It would be a very hot day and the sun was already baking the roof. She opened the door at the end, climbed the steps and entered the chapel.

Turner knelt near the little altar. Even though his back was turned she sensed his nervousness. She sat behind him near one of the open dormer windows overlooking the herb garden. There was a delicate perfume of warm wood and a hint of thyme.

'*In nomine Patris, et Filii, et Spiritus Sancti . . .*'

At the sound of her voice his shoulders quivered and his head sank lower.

'It's more than eighteen months since my last confession.

'I made a promise and broke it.

'I have doubted my faith.

'I have failed to love as I should.'

'Anything else?' he asked.

'Isn't that enough?'

There was a pause so long that in the end she said: 'What is my penance?'

He turned a fraction towards her and dropped his arm so that his plump fingers lay along the chair-back. 'I am flattered that you should seek my counsel at last. Your penance, my dear Mistress Stanhope, and it is a heavy one, is to follow the dictates of your own conscience.'

*

373

Later, Isabel and Teresa went into the rose garden together with spades and trowels.

Though Teresa had maintained her hedged herb beds meticulously this part of the garden was ragged. Ill-kept lawns merged with borders tangled with bindweed. It had not rained properly for some days and the soil was hard and stony but they dug patiently under the yellow rose bush, taking it in turns.

The air was loud with insects and birdsong. A white butterfly flitted close to Isabel's hand and rested a moment on the breast of her faded bodice. Beneath the surface the soil was damp and friable, its dark, peaty scent merging with perfumes of grass and roses. After more than an hour they found the chest, then had to ease it from its burial place inch by inch.

Oswald came with a barrow and wheeled it away under a huge pile of weeds. The women followed to the kitchen courtyard. At the far side was Oswald's parlour, a stark little room with a high ceiling and a crucifix on one white wall.

The floor was spread with a mildewy linen cloth and beneath it two other protective layers, one of canvas, the last of leather. In the centre rested the chest. The top was packed tight with lengths of crumpled velvet and in the careful arrangement of the contents Isabel saw Martha Canton's loving attention to detail.

From within the glossy folds emerged first the three-hundred-year-old chalice and ciborium, then the jewelled Winshawe crucifix, the paten, gold monstrance and lunette with its crystal disc for holding the Blessed Sacrament. All nestled within a shimmer of rainbow silk, a priest's striped chasuble.

The potency of these treasures was so intense that they seemed to fill the room with light and even sound. Surely everyone in the house must hear the explosion of brilliance. Isabel thought they should have covered the window in case some gleam of iridescence now shone out into the courtyard.

They worked fast. Oswald had supplied a leather bag which in the small hours Isabel had lined with a series of pockets. Each vessel was now stowed in its own little compartment.

Later she would sew them up and insert other layers of padding and hessian to keep them hidden. The plan was that she should travel by stage wagon from York to London and at Fitzroy House persuade Lady Arabella to have these precious things sold. Thus would Isabel be provided with a dowry.

Two days later at dawn Isabel saddled Robin's horse, exchanged a strenuous hug with her aunt, and rode ahead of Oswald on the road to York. It was high summer and the translucent sky was streaked with milky cloud. Robin's horse was very fine and Isabel sat high and happy, her hands light on the reins, her body tuned to the flow of muscles along its back. Beneath its pounding hooves the earth was a blur.

Tucked into her bodice was a letter to Mary Ward.